THE REPLACEMENT
CHRONICLES
PARTS ONE, TWO, AND THREE

Harper Swan

OTHER WORK BY HARPER SWAN

Raven's Choice
Part One: The Replacement Chronicles

Journeys of Choice
Parts Two and Three: The Replacement Chronicles

Gas Heat
(This story is offered free for those who join my mailing list.)
http://eepurl.com/b3MpEv

To readers everywhere of prehistoric fiction...

Raven's Choice

The Replacement Chronicles
Part 1

The present contains nothing more than the past,
And what is found in the effect was already in the cause.

—Henri Bergson

California, Early Twenty-First Century

MARK TROTS ACROSS THE PARKING lot to a low, unassuming building. Barely pausing, he jerks the glass door open and darts inside, the door almost smacking against the outside wall. From behind her computer screen, a receptionist's head snaps up, eyes wide.

"Conference Room Two—I'm Mark Hayek from the Parkinson's Institute," he says before she can open her mouth.

The receptionist pats her chest and takes a quick breath.

Mark blinks at her, chagrined. He hadn't meant to startle anyone.

She points across the room. "Go through that door into the hall. It's the last room on your right. Don't worry"—she shakes her head—"the fun and games haven't started yet."

"Thanks," he says, going toward the door. But now it's Mark's turn to be rattled. *Fun and games*—he doesn't like the way those words sound. Surely this blasted meeting hasn't been scheduled during the same time slot as something else. He groans inwardly and takes long, loping strides down the empty hall.

Genetics and Me, Inc. will provide important research used to further explore the genetics behind Parkinson's disease, and he fully comprehends that. But this meeting the company asked for means precious time is being taken away from his own worthy efforts.

Even filling the small, clear tube from a kit G&M sent over was time-consuming. He slipped inside a bathroom near the break area, taking the kit along, sure that he would only be in there a moment. But rapid-fire spitting into the tube was a bad strategy—his mouth soon went dry. He waited long minutes for more saliva to flow while several people tried the bathroom door, rattling it in vain before giving up.

The attached note said he could drop off the tube at their offices at Santa Clara. Instead, so he wouldn't have to leave work early, he mailed it in their provided prepaid packaging.

Mark's supervisor made it sound like an honor that she'd chosen him to be the lead collaborator with G&M. Mark now wishes she'd taken that honor for herself. Let *her* be at their beck and call.

A loud clattering behind the door of Conference Room Two makes him pause, hand on the door handle. He sighs. Apparently, they're just now setting up the meeting area. He checks his watch. If he is to be an errand boy, then he'll perform this task efficiently and get out of here as quickly as possible. *No longer than thirty minutes inside*, he promises himself. He doesn't bother to knock before going in.

A confusing beehive of activity greets him. People are pushing chairs to the corners of the plain, veneer-paneled conference room. A table is being set with food platters, wine, and beer. A man stirs a pot on a hot plate, steaming out a savory aroma. The smell is almost familiar—it reminds Mark of chili.

"Excuse me," he says to a woman in a lab coat as she rushes by. "I'm looking for Dr. Gregory Underwood."

She stops and searches the room. "Over there in the blue shirt. Right under the banner." She gives an explosive little laugh.

Mark stiffens and wonders what's so amusing but, remembering his manners, simply thanks her as he turns away. Tilting his head while he walks, he reads a banner hung from the ceiling. Oddly, it reads Proud to be Neanderthal.

He fingers his closely clipped beard. That's like saying you're proud to be extinct, and that doesn't make sense. Mark catches himself pulling at his beard and yanks his hand down. It's the latest habit he's been trying to break.

A somewhat stocky guy under the banner is fiddling with note cards on a podium, and Mark can't help but grin a little, although "Viking" would probably be a better description than "Neanderthal." Gregory Underwood's hair and eyebrows are as blond as Mark's are dark.

Mark reaches into his jacket pocket and brings out an envelope as he approaches the Viking. "Dr. Underwood, I'm Mark Hayek from the Parkinson's Institute, point man for our partnership. Here's my contact information." He places the envelope on the podium. "The institute sends its greetings and gratitude."

"Likewise from our side. Call me Greg, if you would." He grins at Mark. "We aren't too formal around here. Glad you could come for our party." Greg puts Mark's envelope under the note cards. "I'll show you around the place before we get started. Hey, Ben," he calls over Mark's head, "text me when things are ready."

Mark's head jerks back slightly. *Party?* No one had mentioned a party. What kind of loosely run organization had the institute paired him with? As Greg heads for the door, Mark bolts after him.

"Wait a minute. I'm sorry," Mark says. "As much as I'd like to, I really can't stay long right now. Maybe just for a quick tour. This is only a touch-base kind of visit."

Greg stops and turns so abruptly that Mark bumps into him. "You've *got* to stay. You're our guest of honor. Look on the back wall." Greg raises an arm, his fingers spread back toward the podium. "One of those is yours. We got your saliva sample in time to work it up, and man, do we have a surprise for you."

Mark knows he's frowning, but he can't stop. A surprise isn't necessarily a good thing. Earlier, he didn't notice the clothesline stretched along the wall behind the podium. He focuses on what is hanging there, and the sight is so offbeat that his brow loosens, and he barely notices his fingers once again going through his beard.

Colorful plastic clothespins hold T-shirts all along the line. Gracing the front of every shirt is a Neanderthal man or woman, redheaded and wearing animal skins.

WESTERN ASIA, LATE PLEISTOCENE

THERE HAD BEEN SIGNS—BRUISED GRASS here, a disturbed cluster of stones there. The men who'd come for Raven did not discuss such things with her. Their abrupt silences, whenever she approached to better hear them, made her isolation as the small group's sole woman almost complete. But while she was breaking off rosemary stalks growing against a rock, several large footprints nearby caught her attention. She straightened so briskly her dark braid flew back over her shoulder. She waved the stalks overhead and let out an owl hoot. Bear, her sister's mate and the journey leader, led them all over at a run, his wolverine hood flopping in agitation around his face.

Raven pointed out the prints. But instead of being grateful for an extra pair of eyes, Bear practically snarled at her.

"Stop wandering away over the steppe, woman, or you'll be taken by a lion," he said. The frown gave way to a sly smile, his lip curling over an eyetooth, white and sharp. "Or you could *accidentally* be left behind." His tall, fur-draped bulk blocked the sun, and the cool spring day suddenly seemed colder.

She did not snap at him—choking back the impulse with a small cough—that if left behind, she would simply follow the group's tracks until she caught up. Instead she said, "I need to replenish certain medicines before we reach the valley. Plants will be different there." The strong rosemary smell was suffocating, so she stuffed the bunch into her herbal pouch.

"Forget that for now. If you don't reach camp alive and well, I'll have to put up with your sister's sorrow. Understand me. I am fetching you only because she begged me to, so don't burden us."

His black eyes on her face, he motioned toward the other men, who, when she glanced at them, gawked back with curiosity from where they leaned on their spears. "Stay in our midst." His wolfish smile glistened. "Unless what you *actually* seek is to join your dead mate."

Although she kept her face calm and relaxed, his words made her taut inside, like sun-dried sinew. One full turn of the seasons had already passed since Reed had gone, yet her sorrow remained deep and wide. Her throat tightened, silencing her, and all she could do was lower her eyes to cut off his scrutiny. He turned away from her without saying anything more, and everyone followed him back to the trail.

But the freshness of those footprints could not be ignored, nor could the smell of smoke floating on the breeze. After huddling with the men, Bear halted their advance. He led them all, Raven included, up a large, wide outcropping of rock that sloped down toward a dry canyon on the other side.

They crouched on the ridge behind boulders while Leaf, the young scout, eased his way down a projecting ledge for a better look around a curve in the canyon walls. He froze suddenly with his head tilted forward.

Blue and clear though the sky was, Raven heard rumbling like the muttering of a distant storm. Suddenly, nearby rocks began to tremble. Birds flapped into the sky, and several rabbits bolted out of cover, running in confused circles on the canyon floor below as the rumbling became thunder.

The scout scurried back and leapt into the gap beside her. "Bison," he said.

A dark, shaggy flood poured down the old riverbed below them. Humps rose and fell behind bearded, horned heads as they stampeded through the rift, leaving—when they'd finally passed—a sudden, dusty silence pierced only by the distant howl of a wolf.

Everyone remained in place for so many heartbeats that Raven slipped her pouch strap over a shoulder, impatiently preparing to move down. She felt a light touch on her arm.

"There will be stragglers," the scout murmured. He'd no sooner said the words than a small group of bison rounded the bend in the canyon.

Another wolf howl ripped the morning air from close by, startling Raven, and she jerked her hand across a sharp rock. A narrow red streak welled across her fawn-colored skin. Before she could tend to it, several of the men grunted loudly, and she looked up.

What had howled apparently wasn't a wolf. Several burly figures, their bare chests and backs drenched in what appeared to be blood, waved spears and burning branches as they chased the bison, the beasts tossing their heads and kicking with their back legs. Raven drew a sharp breath and momentarily ducked lower before curiosity made her peer over the rocks and focus on the approaching runners.

An odd clicking started beside her ear, and the hair on her arms rose. She realized that the sound was young Leaf's teeth chattering. But before she could take a look at him, the gaps between boulders on the ravine's other side spewed three more brawny shapes onto the canyon floor.

Raven had difficulty understanding what her eyes were seeing. Stories she'd heard about the Longheads hadn't prepared her to expect that the forms below would look so much like actual men. Their bodies were broader, and something was odd about their arms and legs, a difference she couldn't quite grasp at the moment, but clearly they were men. Those last three weren't bloody, and the bloodied ones, nearing rapidly, confused her. She thought they might be injured before remembering how hunters sometimes covered themselves with blood from a boar or some other animal so the smell would panic large, hoofed game.

Two of the Longheads who'd just burst from the rocks darted out in front of a bison, isolating it. Confounded by suddenly facing two screaming figures waving spears, the bison's gait slowed considerably. This gave the third Longhead an opportunity to slip in closer from the side and bring his enormous wooden club down on the beast's back. Its hind legs bowed, and it stumbled, struggling to regain balance. The bloodied Longheads joined the others in jabbing their spears and screaming, but only one spear was dangling from a shoulder when the bison gave a loud bellow and began to fight back. With head lowered and horns hooking, it wheeled around so its back and flanks were protected by an indentation in the canyon wall.

The Longheads scattered, except for the one who'd swung the club. He dropped the wooden chunk and grasped the bison horn nearest him with both hands, attempting to wrestle the giant head to the side and down.

Raven's eyes widened at the Longhead's boldness.

Behind her, someone gave a hushed, breathy whistle.

"It's always been said that they are crazy." Bear's awed voice, low and husky, belied his disdainful words.

Leaf snorted. "*Crazy* doesn't say enough." His voice was filled with venom.

As for Raven, the fierce sights and sounds on the canyon floor had rendered her mute, her jaw tightly clamped. A shudder went through her, and she knew she would forever remember the brute struggle playing out below.

The Longhead's mantle of skins had fallen to the ground, revealing his enormous, straining muscles. He was making progress in pressing the bison's head downward, and the animal's foreleg on that side was bending ever closer to the ground. In an effort to loosen the Longhead's grip, the bison bucked its backside partway around. It managed to wrench the Longhead's hands from its horn but in doing so exposed its flanks again to ready spears. A moment later, the bison, with several spears now dangling from its sides, rammed its head into the cast-off Longhead. His body flew back against the canyon wall, crumpled to the ground, and lay still.

Even as the bison was brought down, blood streaming from nostrils and mouth, its tongue sliding out, Raven's glance kept sticking on the fallen Longhead like a moth alighting on oozing sap. Her hand patted her herb pouch, but she held back the urge to go see if he was still alive. With the other Longheads still there, that wasn't possible. Besides, he had likely died after hitting the wall with such force.

Reed would have said her concern was misplaced. He had believed the Longheads were beasts even if they did somewhat resemble men. She stilled her hand. If he was right, then two magnificent animals were dead. She would gladly feed from the one—she should not feel dismay over the other.

The Longheads straightened their fallen companion, stretching him on his back beside the canyon wall. But they stayed with him only a short while before butchering the bison, their arms slashing sharp stone through hide, gristle, and muscle. Chunks went flying onto several large skins nearby.

While they worked, they turned to each other occasionally and made noises in turn, mouths moving. Raven's shoulders hunched forward. Her ears strained to hear the indistinct sounds, and she looked at Leaf, crouching beside her, wondering if he heard them and if he thought those sounds were words. His mouth was a tight line, his eyes unblinking as he also listened.

All at once, four more laggard bison hurtled through the pass. The Longheads surrounded their kill, whooping and jumping with limbs spread-eagled, warding off the beasts. The four bison swerved and kept to the far wall as they passed. Using the roiling commotion below as cover, Bear signaled for their group to return to the other side of the ridge, and they rapidly crawled after him.

They stopped a short way down the other side. Bear shed his parka and threw it over a rock. He looked at the others, his eyes full of challenge. "There are only six of them, one dead. We are eight." He kept his voice low. "We'll reach the valley well before nightfall. The meat will still be fresh."

"If you will permit me to speak, great Bear," Leaf said in his somewhat high, cracking voice.

Leaf's manner surprised Raven. That was how one spoke to a respected tribal elder, not to someone leading a journey between camps. But then, Leaf was a much younger man, too young for Bear to send him out alone in all directions, his beard just downy black strands. He reminded Raven of her youngest brother when last she'd seen him—timid but at times brash.

"Speak," Bear said, frowning, "but keep your voice down."

"Each one of them has a lot more strength than any one of us."

"I do not believe it. Most of us are not so weak." Bear eyed the scout's lean frame with scorn. He made a fist of one hand and ground it into the palm of the other. Rippling muscles stood out on his neck, shoulders, and arms.

Instead of being reassured by this display, Raven felt a feather of fear float down her spine. Her future was tied to that man, who was, like his namesake, powerful and irritable and—her gaze fixed on his broad chest as she realized the strangeness of another thought—whose body build somewhat resembled that of a Longhead.

"They are worn from the hunt," Bear added. "Our spears and knives are better made. Haven't you said so yourself?" He stabbed a finger toward the scout. "You of all men should want to go down there."

The scout cowered, and though he was trying to control it, his teeth were chattering again. Raven looked back and forth between the two men. There was much to learn about her adoptive band.

"We ease ourselves halfway down, keeping behind boulders," Bear told them. "If more bison should come through, we go to the bottom while they're protecting their kill. If there are no more bison, we will depend on surprise. Wait for my signal."

He made eye contact, one by one, with each man. "I won't do it now—I'll wait until we safely reach the valley. But I will personally whip anyone who causes a rock slide, and if I am the cause, one of you shall crack the whip." The men averted their eyes and nodded their assent.

Raven was aghast at how no one protested that last, unyielding rule. And none of them, other than Leaf, had questioned Bear's plan for taking the kill. She had always assumed that, within the Fire Cloud tribe, every band behaved much the same. In Raven's old home band, decisions were reached with much more discussion and argument. She had to admit, however, that there was little time at present for arguing.

The men took off their parkas and lowered their leather bags and pouches from their shoulders to the ground, keeping only their spears.

Bear pointed his at Raven like an overly extended finger. "You stay here," he said.

She let her eyes slide away from him as if he were something slippery.

After they had gone over the crest, Raven clambered up to watch, defying Bear's order. The men were carefully working their way from boulder to boulder. When they were midway down, Bear raised a hand to halt them.

As everyone waited, a hawk flying overhead screeched its bothered cry, and crows flapped darkly from rock to rock, curious about the activity below. One of the Longheads who'd hidden in the boulders before the kill went again to his unfortunate ambush partner. After leaning in for a closer look, he returned to butchering. The wind picked up, whistling around the outcrop.

Raven adjusted her fur cape, worked her leggings farther up. She was being careful, but a few pebbles began to roll. She gasped. The small stones stopped moving almost as soon as they'd started, but her heart still pounded at the thought of being whipped by Bear. Her father had done enough of that, with braided leather strips, to last her a lifetime.

Yarrow was growing in a sandy place nearby, the leaves covered with white, longish hairs. Raven already had enough yarrow, but her hand closed unbidden around several stems. In her fist, the leaves felt like a bristling caterpillar as she crushed them until their weedy odor filled her nostrils. The stronger the plant smelled, the more intense its effects would be.

She had fought Reed's fever with the strongest yarrow she could find, mixed with elderberry—it didn't help. None of her desperate remedies worked. He'd been a stubborn man, and he battled his illness the same way, eating and drinking everything she gave him though he gagged. But his fever had proven more stubborn than the both of them.

Bear had made light of Reed's death, and Raven still stung from that. There was no way to avoid him when she was going to live at his hearth. She should put aside her sorrow, seek another mate, and make her own hearth again. She quietly dusted the crushed leaves off her hands.

Raven had just decided that no more bison would push through the canyon when a noisy blend of grunting and snorting drifted over the wind. A group of cows with several large calves trotted around the curve, seeking the main herd. They sped up, determined to pass. Again, the Longheads shunted the animals away, and as the last group had, the bison hugged the wall opposite the kill and lunged through in single file. The last one gave a bleating bellow upon smelling the bloody meat and bucked its way down the canyon.

The Longheads turned to watch the bucking bison, and Bear's group used that distraction to surge down the outcrop and dart from the lower ledge. His spear jerking forward, Bear headed the charge across the gap.

Caught unaware, the Longheads ran, spears abandoned along with the butchered kill, but after scrambling a short distance down the riverbed, they rallied. The largest one picked up a big rock and threw it. It hit the ground, tumbling to a stop in front of Leaf—who immediately flew into a rage.

The scout writhed and ranted. Shrill, singsong words poured from him, strange and without meaning, while his arms and hands contorted oddly. At this spectacle, the Longheads started like spooked stags and dashed away, not stopping that time. Raven realized with amazement that they'd been unnerved by hearing their own words pour out of the twitching scout, who sounded like some dying bird. Leaf's noisy deluge trailed off. She stared at him, pressing her tongue distractedly against the back of her front teeth. The young man intrigued her. She would like to know him better and hear his story.

The group finished what the Longheads had started, bundling the meat into skins before binding leather straps around the packets in preparation for back-hauling and were almost done when Raven took advantage of the others' preoccupation and sidled over to the lifeless Longhead. The men had already taken a look at him during the time she was bringing their skins, pouches, and other things from the outcrop. After she'd come down from one of her trips, she found Leaf urinating on the prone body's stomach. When he spotted her, he reddened and quickly adjusted his loincloth before rejoining the other men.

She stopped a few steps away, repulsed but fascinated by the elongated skull top of the dead Longhead and the hue of his deeply muscled chest, which was as pale as birch except for the irritated skin where the bison had hit him. He was young. Bright, reddish-brown hair covered his head and chin, and his skin was clear and unwrinkled.

Her nostrils twitching from the distinct smell of Leaf's urine, she bent over to get a better look at the upturned face, with its huge, projecting nose and taut cheekbones angling almost to the mouth. His eyes were widely spaced and open, and the thing that surprised her most was that the irises gleaming under the heavy brows were as green as new-growth grass.

She tried to gather the bits and parts of him into an overall impression but was unsuccessful because the eyes kept snaring her attention, disturbing her. It did not seem possible that eyes could be that color. Raven lowered her head even more, looking into the large, sunlit orbs as if trying to find her reflection in a mossy pool. She suddenly felt as if he were looking at her just as she was at him—and then he blinked.

In one swift movement, she leapt up and back. "He is alive!" she shrieked.

The Longhead sat up, and then, with his back flattened against the canyon wall, he pushed himself upright so that he was standing. He felt his right shoulder, left hand probing, grimacing as he bent his elbow out slightly and attempted to raise the arm. He quickly lowered it again, giving a low moan.

Their spears aimed at the Longhead, the men made a semi-circle around him as Raven slipped back, out of their way. The Longhead ignored them. His chest heaved, his breathing ragged. He shook his head as if to clear it, then he grasped his upper arm again and worked it back and forth.

Mesmerized, Raven couldn't look away. He was massive and imposing, even if he was shorter than most of the surrounding men and not much taller than Raven. His legs and arms were a little shorter than a normal man's, but his core was longer and much larger than any man's she'd ever seen—except for Bear.

"Here's your chance, Leaf," Bear said. "Will you finish him off, or shall I?"

Raven's head snapped around. Bear, his wolfish smile playing around his mouth, was watching Leaf. Surely he wasn't going to make the scout kill the Longhead on the spot. For that matter, why kill him at all? He was obviously injured and not a threat. There was no reason for it—other than cruelty. Raven glanced at the unsuspecting Longhead, still working his arm around. Her mouth was as dry as steppe grass in winter, and her heart pounded.

Leaf looked around at the others. He swallowed several times and cleared his throat. His eyes blinking rapidly, he slowly raised his spear over his shoulder.

Raven couldn't help herself. A small anguished cry, part gasp and part moan, slipped out.

Upon hearing her, the Longhead's frozen senses thawed, and he returned from wherever he had been. His eyes focused on the men surrounding him, on the threatening spear. For the first time, he seemed to realize his predicament. He pressed back into the rock wall and tried to raise both arms but ended up clutching one arm with the other.

Bear glanced back at Raven, his eyes cold, and she knew he'd heard her also. "Lower your spear, Leaf," he said. "I was only making certain of your bravery—and having a little fun with you."

Leaf let the spear roll out of his hand onto the ground. He was breathing heavily, his jaw clenched. Several of the men laughed nervously, and Bear raised a hand, silencing them. "Why risk breaking a spear at this point? We'll decide what to do with the Longhead later, but right now, I want Leaf to question him. Longheads haven't been seen around here for some time. Leaf, ask him where they came from and why they're hunting here."

Bear was having fun with them all, Raven understood. He obviously had little respect for anyone. Her musing was interrupted by those strange noises falling once again from the scout's tongue.

Calmer and not as shrill, Leaf sounded like a squabbling crow instead of a wounded one. His hands and arms moved and waved in slower patterns. The men's spears lowered. They gaped at Leaf, and then all eyes went to the Longhead when he replied in the same fluid, flapping way, using only one arm, his injured arm kept still, his voice more often a deep warble than a hoarse caw.

If the Longhead found it strange that Leaf knew his manner of speech, he didn't show it by trying to flee the way the others had. Twice, he paused his gesturing and talking in order to rub his right arm, wincing briefly.

Leaf turned to Bear. "They are from over the mountains, several days' journey from here. He says the hunting is better on this side of the mountains. Their tribe is hungry, and they need meat. They intended to return after they made a kill."

Raven didn't know what caused her to look down the canyon. "They're back!" she shouted.

All the men except Leaf—who snatched up his spear and pointed it toward the captive—spun around to face the five Longheads standing not much farther than a spear-throw away.

Every Longhead carried rocks, and their heavy-browed glares were so menacing that Raven wondered if she should perhaps run away down the riverbed.

One of the bloodied ones called out something. Leaf spoke without turning, his eyes never leaving the captive. "He says to take the kill. But when we are gone, they want to take their brother."

Bear grunted and ran his hand over his face. "They'll have to do something first before they get their brother. Tell them to go back over the mountains. They should hunt there and never return to this side. When our trackers see they've crossed over, we'll send their brother to them." He waved at the butchered carcass. "They can scavenge the kill after we leave. But tell them to back off for now."

Raven was annoyed by Bear's false largesse. He wasn't really being generous. His group would carry away the best parts, leaving very little.

With slow and deliberate movements, Leaf laid his spear down, turned, and walked a few steps forward. Several men hurriedly took his place guarding the captive. The largest Longhead's hands opened, and his rocks tumbled onto the ground. He stepped over them and took several steps toward Leaf.

The odd speech and flapping went back and forth for some time. Then the Longheads suddenly turned and left, walking rapidly. Slow fright crossed the captive's face—his brow tightened, and his mouth opened and closed. His feet shuffled in the dirt as if to follow his departing brothers.

The hawk screamed again; its cry echoed up Raven's tensed spine, making her shiver. She watched the Longhead, her fingers helplessly kneading her cape. If he bolted, the men would spear him, and the other Longheads would surely react. She was standing within the captive's line of sight, so she opened her eyes as wide as she could and shook her head. The movement caught his attention, making him focus on her. Fear emptied from his face, and his brows winged up in surprise before collapsing into wariness, eyes narrowing. His feet stilled.

Raven turned away before someone noticed their converging, intertwined stares. Her thoughts fogged with glee—he had understood her!

Woven leather ropes were pulled from bags for binding the Longhead, but when several men grabbed his arms, he yelped shrilly.

"Stop," Raven cried and pushed through them. "I am a healer," she said loudly—as if they hadn't understood the reason behind her earlier plant-gathering and hadn't yet noticed the dots of red ochre on forehead and chin. "I will determine what is wrong with him."

She walked up beside the captive and looked at the way his arm dangled crookedly from the shoulder. "His arm was wrenched out of place by the bison," she said. "He hasn't been able to reset it."

"Then there's no need to tie that one," Bear said. "We'll make a leash by tying the good arm behind him with the rope going up his back and around his neck." He pointed at two men. "Guard him on either side after you bind him."

He called out to Leaf, who was vigorously breaking the Longheads' spears by bashing them against the canyon wall. "Leaf, you walk behind him and hold the trailing rope good and tight. If he tries to escape, choke him. Let one of the guards carry your spear and pouch. The rest of us will haul meat, with the guards taking the smallest loads."

Raven sputtered. "Surely, we should fix his arm. He must be in great pain."

"And make it easier for him to cause trouble? I think not. Would you heal a cave lion? Get away from him, or he'll snatch you with his good paw." He looked around at the other men—

they grinned and snickered. Raven turned away and went over to where the meat sat packed, ready for carrying. So her hair wouldn't get in the way, she quickly redid her fraying braid before bending and taking hold of a bison-filled pouch.

"We won't stop often," Bear told the group after all the meat was loaded onto backs. "Only at the springs to fill water bladders. And we'll go at a rapid pace. Predators will soon notice the smell. We need to be in the valley before dark."

What he'd just said was reasonable, but Raven was again discomfited by the way everyone put up with him and his needless, lashing words.

The canyon's river had long ago taken another route. Only grass, woven through with flowering plants, poured from the mouth by which they returned to the steppe, a flat high plain dotted here and there with random low juniper trees. Horse, bison, and mammoth herds could occasionally be seen moving in the distance. Overhead, the sun was a large, heated pebble moving slowly across the vast blueness. Raven paused and adjusted her load in order to open the front of her cape, glancing back at the roped captive while doing so.

He must have been dauntless, walking with a steady, slightly rolling gait as if not much disturbed by his plight, his awkwardly hanging arm of little consequence. At first, everyone walked behind him, the better to watch him. But eventually they tired of staring at his back. Thereafter, the only ones not in front of him were the two guards and Leaf.

Raven let herself drift back past the uneasy stares of the guards to walk beside Leaf. "Tell me, scout," she said. "How is it that you know the Longheads' words?" She thought he might not answer. His face clouded, and he blew out his cheeks several times, loud puffs bursting forth like stormy gusts.

Finally, with a strained voice, he told her how he'd been captured his eleventh summer. He was fishing in a stream when a group of Longheads came upon him during one of their hunting forages. He'd lived with his captors for two turns of the seasons.

"Surely it was difficult to learn their words," Raven said.

His face twisted in a grimace, and he shook his head. "Not really. A whole turn of the seasons has passed since I escaped, but still I think sometimes in their gabble—and I still can't eat red deer." At her puzzled look, the young man gave a bitter laugh. "Let me show you something."

Leaf passed the leash back and forth between his hands and teeth so he could peel off his fur parka, leaving it hanging by its hood from his head. Black spear tattoos, often worn by those who scouted, pointed down his biceps. He held out both arms. Although his left arm was a normal size, his right arm was huge and layered with muscle. It was a limb that belonged to a more mature man. His right hand was also out of proportion, overly large, as through it were swollen.

"Their words are few enough. Learning them wasn't hard," he said. "But they made me work and polish hides with red-deer ribs from dawn to dusk every time there was a kill—with little help. That was hard. Just seeing a red deer makes my stomach ache."

He spat toward the Longhead's heels, barely missing them. "And seeing this one makes my head hurt. Bear has no right ordering me to walk behind him as if I'm tending him. He should have let me kill him." Leaf snatched the rope.

Raven felt a large bubble form in her throat when the captive's neck and head jerked awkwardly. His shoulders stiffened, but he didn't try to look back at them.

"I keep wanting to choke him," Leaf said. The guards glanced over with unfriendly eyes. "Not Bear," Leaf added hastily, nodding his head at the captive. "That one. He's from the same tribe that took me. I know because they always hunt large prey using blood."

Raven composed her face, swallowing the bubble. "I'm sure Bear only asked for your help because you alone know the Longhead's words and ways."

She moved closer to his side. With a quick and light touch, she ran her fingers over his hand holding the leash. "I wish they hadn't taken you, but we're fortunate you escaped and are here with us now." Her fingers again flickered over his hand, back and forth. "And I wish your other hand had not been so lazy and had helped this one more," she teased gently.

Leaf looked fixedly at her hand covering his, and she thought he had calmed down. But then his brown eyes flared at her like a wounded wolverine's, pained and vicious. "They eat their own people. Did you know that, healer?"

His grin was cruel, and she drew away. At her abrupt movement, his face fell.

"But only if someone happens to die when the hunting is bad and everyone is starving," he said hastily as if apologizing for shocking her. He looked into the distance, and pain lingered in his eyes.

A piercing whistle silenced them. Raven knew it was Bear before she saw his bearded face glaring back at her. She noted with a start that their small group around the captive had fallen back a short distance from the rest—the guards had been caught up in Leaf's story just as she had.

"Better go," Leaf said softly. "Don't want to make him mad."

When she reached Bear, he plunged his hand through her cape's arm slit to grasp her upper arm. He pulled with such roughness that her feet skittered as he snatched her around to walk in front of him. Several nearby grouse, wriggling and flapping in a dirt bath, took fright and lifted off in a whir of dust.

"You're slowing us down," he said.

She couldn't help throwing a scathing look over her shoulder. After her father, he was the most dominating man she'd known. His large shadow followed her closely, and the stony weight of his eyes upon her every movement was every bit as uncomfortable as the heavy load of meat.

The sun had floated a good way toward the horizon before they passed from low hills into the valley where their journey would end. After the expansive steppe, the foliage seemed close and lush. A large lake surrounded by trees sparkled in the distance, and soon they could see the low bluff where the camp's dwellings perched. This band's spring camp was much larger than the camp Raven had come from.

She suddenly felt timid. Even though Bear left her before they reached camp, she maintained a rapid pace. Her legs were tired to the point of collapsing, but she refused to let herself trail the others. It would not do to seem weak in the eyes of her new band.

She was almost totally ignored, however, as news spread about the other, unexpected newcomer. Someone blew a long note on an aurochs horn, and excited shouts echoed around the lakeside. The recently returned travelers piled the meat to one side. When the gathering crowd began pressing too closely, the weary men formed a fence with their spears around Leaf and the Longhead. Bear soon climbed onto a nearby stump and began narrating their journey. Everyone became quiet, hanging on his words.

Raven stood at one edge of the massed group and, from time to time, looked unsuccessfully through the crowd for her sister. Disconcerted by seeing so many unfamiliar people in one place, her glance fled from face to face. From the riled looks forming on some of them and a background muttering near the end of Bear's tale, not everyone was in agreement with giving the Longhead his freedom.

A loud voice suddenly croaked throughout the clearing, "If you know where to find a pool, then you know where to catch fish."

The crowd parted as an elder hobbled to the front, pushing everyone aside with his walking stick. He stopped in front of Bear and waved the stick at him. "How will we know?" he asked in his rasping voice.

With a disgusted frown, Bear crossed his arms and stopped talking.

"How will we know that he won't come back with the others and raid us, now that he's seen our camp?"

Bear opened his mouth, but before he could speak, the older man began laughing. Bear was forced to wait while the elder struggled to control his wild cackles.

"Before your time, we threw them in lakes and rivers when we caught one." The elder wiped his eyes. "Have you ever seen their bones? No? Well, I have. They're thick and heavy. Longheads drown if you don't let them back on land soon. Ask your father. He knows all about this." He jabbed his stick at Bear. "You need to seek his counsel."

Raven looked sharply at the Longhead. He stood there, watching everything calmly, his hand spread over an enormous bruise coloring his chest and abdomen. She had to remind herself that he couldn't understand.

Bear jutted out his chin. "I take it upon myself to make decisions," he shouted, "because I've just been told that although my father yet breathes, he is scarcely with us. I can no longer receive his counsel. The only elder left now is you, and you've just given me yours." His smile was a dismissive sneer.

A murmur went through the crowd, and Raven began to understand why the men had deferred to Bear throughout the journey. The elder's voice still echoed in her ears. It was as if she heard him say the words that tripped through her mind: *When the old bull falters, the young one takes the herd.*

But the band wasn't a herd of animals—Bear risked making enemies if he released the Longhead without bringing everyone around to his side. With annoyance, Raven realized that in this situation, she *did* side with Bear. The Longhead should be allowed to leave.

Bear grabbed one of the meat-filled skins and held it up. He looked at them all through eyes like dark slits. "The Longheads wouldn't fight over food, but I believe they would have fought us to the death if we had killed this one," he said. "And I know from my father"—he glared at the old man—"that they don't want anything to do with us. But they called this Longhead 'brother.' He is of some importance to them."

He lowered the skin. "I'll need help from some of the men to build a pen for our captive and to split up the meat. It is best that the rest of you leave." His face became hard. "Every hearth will get its share…but only if someone is there to receive it. If not, that hearth will be passed over."

The elder mumbled something about whelps with eyes still closed and turned away.

When the crowd began dispersing, Raven felt a hand on her hair and turned her head. "Willow!" Relief surged through her.

Her sister's face bloomed in a big smile, the slight gap between her front teeth—which she shared with Raven and had also been their mother's—reassuringly displayed. Willow's five children stood behind her. They watched shyly as their mother slipped her hands under Raven's cape and around her, holding her close.

"Little sister, I thank the Earth Mother you are here," Willow said. "I feared you would be lost to me forever. When I heard you would be sent far away, I pleaded with Bear to fetch you," she murmured in Raven's ear. "And I had our healer, Old Cloud, talk with Bear about you helping out with her tasks."

Her eyes blurring, Raven touched her tongue against the back of her front teeth, lightly dabbing the small opening. She had always been close to her sister, but Willow's manner and appearance were so similar to their dead mother's that Raven, for a disoriented but sweet moment, felt as if her mother held her.

"I miss you," she said, and realized that sounded odd. "I've missed you. Thank you for accepting me at your hearth."

Willow's hands rubbed up and down Raven's back, and she gave a little laugh. "How could I not have fought to get you here? I always stood up for you when no one else would." Her fingers tapped Raven's spine. "My bad little sister, who forever made life interesting."

Raven stiffened at that, but she managed a smile when she slid out of her sister's embrace. It was true she had always been getting into trouble as a child, and she supposed Willow was also thinking about the matter of the baby.

When Raven had reached fifteen summers, she began spending time with her aunt, their mother's sister and band healer. She trailed along whenever her aunt attended illnesses or injuries. Raven began assisting her in every way, even during birthings.

Fern, the youngest mate of an elder, after bearing two perfect children, gave birth to a boy whose cheek was marked with a large purple splotch. Fern was appalled—that kind of mark was always a bad omen. The child would be weak and sickly, she had said. She told Raven's aunt to expose the baby out on the steppe. Raven tracked her aunt, following the baby's cries, and rescued the small bundle before a predator could find him.

Upon her return with the baby, there had been a big uproar in the camp. Her father demanded she give him up. When she refused to do so, he wrenched the screaming infant from her arms. She retaliated by attacking with teeth and nails while he held the baby out of her reach. After he kicked her off, her mother and brothers held her tightly on the ground.

"There must have been brambles in the bedding when you were birthed!" her father yelled. "You're too full of thorns, always scratching and pricking." He left with the baby, and on returning, he used the flat of his hand on her face and body for a good, long time before finishing with his whip. Raven had never been told where he'd taken the child, and she'd never asked.

Then there was the question of Fern's sickness several years later when, after being treated by Raven for a minor stomach problem, she became dangerously ill. No one ever accused Raven of not tending Fern properly. She continued working with her aunt as always.

But when Reed died, Fern pointed out to anyone who would listen that no man in their band needed another mate—every family who wanted another woman at their hearth already had one. Besides, it was almost unheard of for a grown woman to remain in her home band unless she was a healer, and they already had a healer. And Raven was childless. No great loss would occur if she were given to some other band within the Fire Cloud tribe. If no other band wanted her, then that was too bad, but she could be swapped as a slave to another tribe.

By that time, Raven's parents were also dead, her brothers and sister living with other bands. Although her aunt thought it best that Raven stop helping for a while, she let Raven know that she still supported her. But everyone else, who'd once welcomed her approach with a smile or a nod, began letting their eyes glide over her, past her, through her. Shunned, she had become like mist.

Reunited, Raven grasped her sister's hand and kissed it before turning to meet her two nephews and three nieces. She hugged each one and picked up the smallest, a boy barely old enough to walk.

"The girls look like you and the boys like their father," she said to Willow, smiling at the tallest girl, just beginning to blossom. When her sister didn't reply, Raven followed Willow's eyes across the clearing to where Bear was slicing bison meat. He looked up and waved a bloody hand but didn't move to come over.

"He's busy now," Willow said. "We might as well go on to the hearth."

As Raven followed her sister, she glanced back at Bear. He was watching them leave with a face as frozen and blank as snow.

Using hardened wooden tongs, Raven quickly placed hot stones from the fire into the nearby hollowed-rock basin they'd filled with water, seared bison, and roots. She breathed in deeply as the stew began to steam, becoming more than food, the smell speaking of survival itself.

The children, losing their shyness in the excitement of having a new kinswoman, buzzed about the hearth. But when Bear arrived, the children became subdued. Even the toddling boy stayed out of his father's way.

"Bear, you've safely returned to us—it lightens my heart." Willow arose from the fireside. He went to her and caressed her cheek.

Willow smiled up at him, and when he embraced her, Raven felt a softening toward her sister's mate. There was, perhaps, a whole other side to Bear.

After several infusions of hot stones, the bubbling stew was ready. Willow served them all, using gourds to ladle it into wooden bowls. They settled around the fire in the dusk. Raven held the first sip of hot broth in her mouth and savored its rich, meaty flavor while she watched the oldest boy help the youngest drink from his small bowl. She swallowed only when Willow asked of news about their old home band.

Bear said very little during the meal. While they'd finished cooking, he sat among a pile of rock flakes and chips off to one side, striking a flint core with a hammerstone. Raven was made uneasy by how his eyes, cold and probing, turned her way every time he knocked off a flake. She would hear the clink of stone hitting stone, and then the thick neck would twist toward her. She tried to ignore him, but his scrutiny dampened her happiness at seeing Willow again. His animosity was apparent. He obviously didn't want her at his hearth.

The day was all but gone by the time they'd finished their meal and cleaned the gourds and cooking area. Bear had already gone into the tent when the children pulled Raven inside, begging to be the ones chosen to sleep on either side of her.

Willow, who followed close behind, laughed at the uproar. "I suggest you take turns sleeping beside your aunt, starting with the youngest two for tonight," she said.

"She'll sleep in the lean-to," Bear said abruptly. "There's no room for her here."

The children's faces fell, and they were quiet. The look her sister gave Bear seemed keen and searching, but when she turned to Raven, her face was serene. "Maybe we can work out something later," Willow said, shrugging.

"Well, come on before it's full dark." Bear held open the flap. "There's no moon tonight."

He walked her the short distance to a lean-to built against a large rock face. Skins covered long sapling poles embedded in a knee-high stone base. The top of the skin-covered area was sealed against the rock face with smaller stones. The lean-to seemed secure enough, yet Raven couldn't help feeling offended. An entry space opened into one of the sides, and Bear stood beside the flap, waiting for her to go in. When she didn't move right away, he tapped his fist against his chin several times.

"Move things if you need to," he said and left.

She watched him enter the family's double tent, the spiked poles of both tops leaking wisps of smoke blending into the dusk. She could understand that he might not particularly want her to sleep in the tent he shared with Willow, but a covered crawlspace closed off by a hung skin led to the children's tent. He would have neither seen nor heard her there.

In the dimness, Raven pulled out skins and hides from the stack filling much of the lean-to. The next day, she would gather grass straw for the bottom layer, but until then, deer hide covered with bear pelts would do. She picked a spot on the dirt floor closest to the rock side and away from a corner woodpile, which could be full of spiders. After the bed was made to her liking, she undid her braid and stripped off cape, tunic, leggings, and boots before slipping between the thick furs, her shell necklace clicking as she settled.

Although Raven resented being put apart that way, the lean-to was cozy. In the distance, an owl hooted, and she began to drift off with the day's events shifting dreamlike behind her closed eyes. The Longhead's face floated by. She wondered if he'd gotten any bison and whether his painful arm would keep him from sleeping. An injury like that needed to be repaired immediately, before too much damage set in.

A sudden brightness against her eyelids made her eyes open, and she struggled out of her heavy covering.

Bear was coming from under the entry flap, a stone lamp in his hand. An acrid smell of burning bear fat filled the lean-to. Alarmed, she gasped and pulled several pelts over her nakedness. "What is it?" she asked.

"No need to be frightened." He put the lamp on an upended log before he moved over and knelt at the end of her pallet. "I simply want you to hear my decision. You've been too long without a mate. You should be bearing children. After much thought,

I've decided the best mate for you would be"—he thumped his chest, making a hollow sound—"me."

The lean-to suddenly seemed like a trap. Raven's fingers dug into the fur, tugging the pelts closer.

Bear's eyebrows lifted. "Don't you want a child? Your mate didn't start a bud growing in you—in what, four turns of the seasons? Every time your sister weans one, she has another to suckle. If I can't aid the Earth Mother in swelling your belly, then no man can."

He pulled the pelts from her hands, dropped them beside the pallet, and looked at her through the flickering shadows for a long moment before fumbling at his leather loincloth. Then he pushed her down onto the furs and clambered on top. Because of his height, his enormous chest covered her face, and all she could do was lie flat like a stone on a lake bottom until he finished. She gasped for breath when he rolled off.

He sat up and lifted her right hand. "You should be more careful, plant woman," he said, tracing a slow finger over the crusted scratch made earlier when they'd hidden in the rocks. Then he grasped her arms and pulled her so she was also sitting. His fingers skimmed her hair. "Black and shiny as your namesake's feathers." He thrust his fingertips into its thickness.

Her scalp tingled at his touch. There was no mistaking these intimacies—he was wooing her. But Raven was wary. Earlier, he'd made it clear how he felt. He disliked her, and most likely it was only the mating that put him in a better mood—if so, that goodwill would soon fade.

She made herself smile. "I am fortunate to be at your hearth." She drew one of the displaced furs up against the chill and looked him in the face, holding his eyes. "The Earth Mother favors you."

His brows rose. "And what does that mean?"

"You have courage and strength. Because of your decision to take the meat, the settlement will sleep deeply tonight, their stomachs full. And the bargain you made with the Longheads showed much wisdom." She found it easy to say those things because they were true.

The corners of his mouth turned up slightly—only a hint of sharp eyeteeth. Black eyes glittered in the lamplight, and again his fingers smoothed her hair.

Emboldened, she continued, "I'll put the captive's arm back in place tomorrow. That will help him survive the trip so he can rejoin his people—"

"*People*—why do you call them people?" He frowned and pulled his hand away. "You saw them. We were with that wretched beast all afternoon. Surely you understand that he isn't like us."

"It's just that—"

He slashed a hand through the air in front of her face, cutting her off. "And they frighten away game, so when we go out on the steppe, we find nothing, and then the band sleeps hungry—not like tonight. The elder was right. I should throw him in the lake. That's what a truly wise man would do."

"Very well, beasts then—animals. It's just that animals capable of planning a hunt with fire and blood can surely plan revenge."

Raven ran a hand under the fur covering and along her ribs. They felt tender, as if mildly bruised. "Your decision to bring him here instead of killing him was a good one. But a one-armed ma—beast won't survive on the steppe or in the mountains, and his whole tribe might come if he doesn't show up."

He tilted his head to look at the poles supporting the top of the lean-to and seemed to be considering her words.

"I have reset many out-of-joint shoulders," she said. In reality, she'd only helped with a few.

She let the covering slide to her lap, despising herself but not knowing how else to sway him. His eyes strayed down, turning smoky.

She lowered her voice, making it warm, breathy. "I can do so again. I know how to."

His tongue licked his top lip as if savoring honey, and then the covering was completely off her.

At some point during the night, Raven dreamed she was a real raven, a bird. She sat upon a limb and groomed her glossy plumage. The pinions slid cleanly through her bill with a satisfying swish.

A rustle of feathers came winging through the air, and a young raven, a fledgling, landed clumsily beside her. It pleaded for food. The fledgling's beak hung open, flashing the bright-pink interior of its gullet. It made the loud bawling sounds that young—and sometimes not so young—ravens used while begging.

Moved to action by this display, Raven began working her throat to bring up food, and she put her beak into the fledgling's open pinkness. But then she realized her throat pouch was empty. There was no feeling of fullness, no rounded swelling— only empty flatness. She pulled her beak away from the young bird and flew away, searching for food.

Raven awoke early and found herself alone in the lean-to, the camp quiet. She turned over, and a gust of her body's scent marked with Bear's muskiness wafted past her face, the odor overpowering the fur smell. At some time during the day, a bath in the lake would be necessary.

After slipping on her clothes, making her braid, and dabbing ochre on her forehead and chin, she peeked around the lean-to's flap at the main tent. Her stomach fluttered with the prospect of facing Willow. She didn't know how her sister would react to the night's unexpected happenings.

No one was about, and she couldn't hide all day, so Raven went out to the smoldering hearth and started grinding herbs with the small mortar and pestle she always carried in her pouch. She ground willow bark for pain and swelling. On reflection, she also ground valerian root for sleep, to be used later in the day. The Longhead should move his arm and shoulder right after the joint was reset, but he would soon need deep, healing sleep. She scooped water from a nearby water vat into a small gourd. Her hand funneled a handful of ground willow bark into the gourd. Using a twig, she stirred the potion.

Raven was searching the hearth's embers for a small stone to heat the mixture when she heard Bear's voice behind her—gruff and terse, nothing like the night before. She straightened and faced him.

"I want to make something clear," he was saying. "Neither I nor anyone else will hold you in high regard because, out of pity, I joined you in those pelts. You are likely barren, and nothing will come of it." His eyes were pointed icicles. "I have a question for you. And I want the truth. Are you a spirit seeker as well as a healer? Many of you are both."

"I do my best to heal people. That's what I do. Isn't that what Willow told you?"

Bear looked at her strangely. "I want you to remember this, healer. If you cause any problems, I will cast you out onto the steppe or—" He kicked her pouch lying on the ground. "Or I'll feed you all your medicines."

Raven considered his sullen face, wondering if he somehow knew about Fern. Regardless, he was an overly volatile man. Her fingers shook as she stirred the willow brew. Leaf was right—it was best not to make him mad.

"As for the Longhead, I'll put his arm bone back into his shoulder," Bear said. "It isn't fitting that you do it."

"Fine," she replied, weary of his crossness. "But I need to give him this brew. It will deaden some of the pain."

He paused, frowning and doubtful.

She hurriedly added, "It will help make him more docile. More like a—a newborn aurochs, like a calf."

To her surprise, his mouth twitched into a slanted grin. The idea of the Longhead behaving like a calf must have pleased him. He waved at the gourd. "Finish with your medicine. Let's get this over with before we end night fast."

Leaf was already at the pen when they arrived. Raven wondered how long he'd been staring at the skin-covered form on the ground. The skins were completely still and didn't move even when Raven cleared her throat. The captive, it seemed, was dead. But when Leaf shouted, he stirred and arose, throwing off the skins. Air rushed out of Raven's lungs—she'd been holding her breath.

The night before, they'd encircled him with posts set into the ground and tethered him to them using long, braided leather ropes tied around his neck. The ropes going to the posts had enough slack that he could stand or lie down in the center. To define the pen's boundaries, the enclosure had been secured with more ropes, wound from post to post around the circle.

Several sturdy guards stood nearby. Bear told them to unwind the ropes going around the pen but to leave the ones attached to the Longhead's neck.

Raven turned to Leaf. "Tell him we're going to set his arm and that he should drink this." She showed Leaf the gourd. "But first, I will need to examine him." Leaf translated, and the Longhead looked over at her. She searched his face to see how he felt about what he'd heard, but his expression gave nothing away.

When the ropes were gone from around the pen, Raven entered the surrounding posts, fully expecting Bear to stop her. He didn't, so she put the gourd down carefully on the ground, all the while aware of the Longhead's eyes following her. To reach him, she went between two of the tethers. She paused a moment and then gently moved her hands around on his shoulder and arm. His skin was hot, feverish.

"What in the great Mother's earth are you doing?" Bear shouted, starting toward her.

"I have to determine whether the bone has come out the front or the back," she said. "Let's hope that it's the front, or relocating it will be difficult."

Bear glowered but stepped back out of the circle, and Raven continued her examination. The Longhead stood still while her fingers probed. She took a quick look at his face and experienced that odd swirling of impressions she'd had on first seeing him up close. He looked strange, which was not to say ugly. It just took a few more heartbeats to make sense of the striking eyes gleaming under those heavy, menacing brows and the well-shaped mouth under such a large, protruding nose.

Luckily, the arm was out of joint in the front, but the whole limb was tight and swollen. Too much time had passed. The bone wouldn't go back in easily, maybe not at all. She brought the gourd over and mimicked drinking from it before pressing the handle into the hand of his good arm.

He looked so intently into her face that Raven felt he was trying to see into her mind and hear her thoughts. With eyes still on hers, he raised the gourd and drank. His trust warmed her, and she wanted to smile at him but dared not.

"Well, which is it?" Bear asked when she emerged from the circle.

Raven looked at him hesitantly. She doubted he understood that medicines needed time to work. If Bear straightened the arm at that point, her potion would only ease the soreness after the arm was fixed, doing nothing until then. When the more immediate pain sank its fangs into the Longhead, he possibly wouldn't be mild like a newborn calf but more like a raging bull.

"It's out the front," she said. "We should wait until the potion takes better effect."

"There isn't time. There are other things to be done this morning," he said. But still he stood there, his fingers pulling and working the bottom of his parka. Seeing how they were all watching him expectantly, he huffed out his chest and moved inside the circle of posts.

The captive's brow tightened when Bear stopped in front of him. For a moment, the two bulky forms faced each other as if about to wrestle. Then Bear lifted the bad arm and began to slowly pull. A growl rumbled from the Longhead's throat. Bear dropped the arm, turned, and tromped out of the circle.

"Since you boasted you could, you do it, healer," he hissed, rubbing dampness from his face.

Raven walked into the pen area again, and something resembling relief crossed the captive's face. Her stomach roiled like a pool of eels as she began taking the looped rope ends from around the post tops, so the ropes fell without tension from his neck. Although no one told her to stop, Raven sensed the men grasped their spears tighter. They eyed her silently, faces full of interest and something more that made her overly conscious of every move. She took a quick glance at Bear, and he was watching her as closely as the rest.

Though it would give the men even more to stare at, Raven shed her fur cape in order to free her movements. Clad only in leather tunic and leggings, she felt as vulnerable as she imagined the Longhead must have felt.

She asked Leaf to tell the captive to stand with his back against a post. Leaf said a few words, and the Longhead complied by going over and facing a post, ropes trailing. Exasperation flashed through her. Either Leaf hadn't said the correct words, or the Longhead hadn't understood them.

Raven wanted him firmly in position before she did anything. Instead of asking Leaf to try again, she decided to take
matters into her own hands.

At first worried that Bear would interfere once more, Raven
quickly forgot him in her efforts to situate the captive. She
pushed and prodded so that he moved with her in a shuffling
dance, the dangling ropes writhing like whip snakes. To the
touch, his flesh was more like fire-hardened wood than skin
and muscle. Places on his back and chest that had been exposed
during the journey were sunburned. But where his lower skins
had slipped some from his middle, the skin was shockingly white
under her darker hands.

When he was in place, Raven took his injured arm, which
his good arm was cradling possessively, and carefully moved it so
that it hung down. She took a big swallow. That had gone well,
but things would soon get difficult. It would help if he stopped
looking at her. His eyes distracted her. If only he would look
away…

She stood so the arm was centered directly in front of her
and grasped his wrist with one hand. With her other hand, she
moved the dangling ropes aside and pressed her palm against
his bad shoulder, pushing him firmly against the post. The head
of the dislocated bone made a lump against her lower palm as
if it wanted to come through his skin—she fought an urge to
shudder. Next was the hard part, possibly the dangerous part.

Ever so slowly, pulling from the wrist and rotating the whole
arm, Raven raised his arm up and out to the side, away from
his body. Nothing happened. The bonehead still poked into her
palm. She lowered her thumb and pressed it into the lump.

Although the morning was cold, Raven felt a flush of heat as
she again realized that, although the Longhead's arm was hugely
muscled, it was shorter than those of most men. She wondered

if she was indeed doing the right thing for his kind of arm as she desperately slid more fingers onto the lump and pressed harder.

The Longhead's face turned a stinging red, and his shoulders heaved with labored breathing. When Raven thought she could not possibly keep pressing any longer, she heard a *pop*. Although muted, the sound seemed to fill the quiet morning air.

Instead of screaming, he howled, jerking his face toward the sky, neck tendons straining. The ear-numbing wolf sound wailed into the day, full of pain yet saturated with relief. She dropped his arm and stumbled backward.

Raven had once been facing a tree just as lightning struck it. His howl did the same thing to her that the lightning had done to the shuddering, leaf-shaking trunk. She quivered from head to toe and felt she might split in half.

Upon hearing the sound, some of the men had run a short distance. Others were still stabbing their spears about with rabbity jerks as the howl trailed off. A few, including Bear, were laughing weakly—he was bent over, his arms crossing his middle as if trying to hold in the laughter.

Raven took up her cape as well as the gourd and walked shakily past them all. She found her way back to the hearth. No one was around when she arrived, not even the children. Willow was avoiding her. She felt a desperate thirst and scooped water from the bottom of the almost-empty vat. It felt gritty in her mouth, but she swallowed anyway and then spat out bits of rock, making sounds like a frightened lion cub.

Maybe the family had gone to haul more water from the lake. Raven followed a trail to the water's edge while chewing dried meat from her dwindling supply. The hard, slightly salty strips were mildly rancid. Her thirst came raging back, so she knelt on the lakeshore and lowered her head to the water.

Willow and the children were nowhere to be seen—nor was anyone else, for that matter—so she stripped for a quick, cold dip. Afterward, she lingered near the forest edge and gathered herbs. A gentle breeze blew, whispering soothingly through the new spring leaves. Calmness settled over her, so she was caught off guard when her eyes momentarily overflowed like springs, dripping onto her cheeks.

When Raven returned to the pen a short while later, the posts had been rewound with ropes, and gawkers surrounded it on all sides. The men were sizing him up, she thought, just as male animals did, seeing which one had the largest antlers or tusks. The women stood in small clusters, taking care not to stand too close to the pen. Perhaps, to them, he was only a curiosity like a white hyena. Raven herself wasn't clear about how she viewed him. All the stories she'd heard as a girl and then from Reed still filled her head.

Children ran in and out of the crowd, and several boys jabbed long sticks through the wound ropes. The captive grasped a stick poking him in his ribs and broke it in half, to their whooping delight.

"Stop your torment," Raven yelled at them. "The Longhead needs rest before he leaves. If he doesn't get back soon enough, his brothers may come looking for him and find you instead." The threat was a variation of what exasperated parents said to their children. *I'll leave you out on the steppe, and the Longheads will get you.*

The grownups and some of the children gave her hostile looks, but most of them left, as if her words or maybe her presence made them uncomfortable. "Unwind the ropes," she told the guards. "I need to treat him."

His grassy eyes focused on her hands while she stirred the water and ground valerian. When she handed him the gourd, he gulped the mixture down, not wincing at the bitter taste, and then noisily sucked out the last drops. She passed him the last of her dried meat. He devoured it, barely pausing to chew.

Raven realized, from the smell coming from a small dirt mound nearby, that he'd dug a hole with his hands to cover his wastes. With his lack of mobility, the area would soon become fouled. She couldn't clean this up herself. The jokes made about that would last for many seasons—she would never gain any esteem with the band, and she had a feeling that Bear would be furious if she did such a thing.

"His enclosure needs to be cleaned," she said, filling her voice with authority. She turned to one of the guards. "Go fetch a slave—and he needs something more to eat and drink." The guard pulled a sour face but left to do her bidding.

A voice beside her said, "That is what they made me. A slave."

Raven hadn't realized that one of the loiterers was Leaf. He stood with his head on his chest, his stance very unlike his usual scout's alertness.

"And you are no longer a slave," she said gently. "It should never have happened to you, but there is no slavery in your blood."

His head swiveled, birdlike, and he gave her a long look from the corner of an eye. His lips parted, and she thought he would say something, but he smiled wanly and turned away.

"What is their word for *eat?*" she called after him.

"*Aulehleh,*" she thought she heard him reply, the beginning sound lilting up slightly more than the rest.

Sounds of children playing came from behind the double tent, and Willow was moving around the clearing when Raven checked to see if anyone had returned. Her sister had the appearance of a wilted flower. Her shoulders slumped, and her long hair fell forward around her bowed head, unbraided and messy. Clearly, she hadn't slept well due to Bear callously spending his first night back not with her but out in the lean-to. A pang went through Raven. Willow was suffering because she'd cared enough for her younger sister to want her close by.

She remembered with shame how, after the first onslaught, she'd all but invited him to continue. They'd coupled as thoughtlessly as rabbits several times during the night.

Willow began stoking the fire, bending over the hearth. She didn't look up or respond when Raven entered the clearing and warmly greeted her. Neither did she make any comment when Raven began telling her about straightening the Longhead's arm. She finally finished with the fire and squatted before the hearth opposite Raven, her face a frozen frown. Raven stopped talking.

Light clouds crossed overhead, their shadows webbing the clearing while Raven's heart went cold, like an icy stone, as she understood that her sister regretted sending for her. Willow might even have said certain things about Raven so that Bear would cast her out as he'd threatened.

Excited laughter burst from where her nieces and nephews played. Raven looked at the neat clearing, the well-built double tent and lean-to, and the warm, cozy hearth from which she might soon be banished. She wondered how she could have been so stupid as to not listen when her father talked about the importance of tribe. Raven grasped now that without the tribe, she would be nothing, an animal dead on the steppe.

She pressed her tongue against the back of her teeth, probing the gap, and anger sparked through her. Surely Willow had suspected that could happen. With so many men dying, not only from disease but also hunting wounds, it was common enough for a bereft woman to be taken in by her sister's mate, sometimes as his additional mate or most often only temporarily.

Raven flung her words across the fire: "I am like a newly crafted spear, a just–knapped quartz blade, a fresh kill. One day soon, I will be as a worn spear, a chipped blade, an old kill. The freshness will be gone. I assure you that things will soon become more like they were before I arrived."

Willow's eyes flipped up. For a long beat, she looked through the smoke at Raven, her face astonished. Then she sighed. "You always were full of words. Sometimes they worked for you, and sometimes they didn't," she said sharply, but her face relaxed.

Willow had thawed, and she remained so, even when Bear returned to the lean-to, night after night.

For four days, Raven visited the enclosure, making sure it was cleaned regularly and the captive was being given food and water. On the fifth day, she went by later than usual. She'd been collecting plants daily and taking them to the camp healer, Old Cloud, a timeworn woman who welcomed her help. The day before, Raven had interrupted her gathering to set traps near the burrows of steppe hamsters that had moved into the valley.

According to Bear, the trackers who'd followed the Longheads would probably return soon, and then the captive would be released. She didn't say anything to Bear—he would make some jab about feeding lions—but she'd decided the Longhead should have fresh meat for his journey. The string traps were set to catch the hamsters at dusk when they left their burrows, so she went to check them first thing upon awakening the next morning. Willow could always use any trapped hamsters for a meal if the trackers hadn't returned by late day.

She hurried, hoping that predators hadn't found the traps during the night, but she needn't have worried. She found four large adult hamsters with their legs noosed. Raven picked up a nearby hand–sized rock. "In this manner, the Earth Mother feeds her children," she murmured, touching the rock to forehead and chest. She ended the hamsters' struggles with quick blows and took out a small quartz blade to clean them.

But before she could begin, a strong feeling came over her that she should go immediately to the pen and check on the captive. She could clean the hamsters later or, if he was released sometime during the day, he could clean them himself after he left. She decided to gift him with the blade. He would at least have something ready-made to take with him.

Yet she lingered at the burrows, kneeling in the grass, rubbing small ripples on one side of the knife, left from its crafting. She rarely used the blade for anything. It had been her father's.

The reddish color was unusual for quartz. It looked as if it had been dyed with red ochre or as if blood had soaked into the stone. He'd handed it to her from his death pallet, saying, "You were born with well-sharpened edges, but no matter how much I struck you, I was never able to shape your core. You're made up of something that's too hard in some ways and too soft in others."

She placed the blade in her smallest bag and attached it to the bound hamsters using the bag's drawstring. The captive would know what to do with her gift.

When Raven got to the pen, the hamsters hidden in her herbal pouch, the guards were dismantling it. "When did he leave?" she asked, trying not to sound frantic.

"Right after the trackers arrived," one of the guards said. He grasped a post and with a groan pulled it out of the ground.

"And when was that?"

"The sun had only just topped the lake trees," he said.

Raven stepped back as the post thudded onto the ground.

"We followed him until he passed the boulders, then we came back."

She looked at the sun, barely over the trees. He hadn't been gone long, and she remembered an area with large boulders from when she'd first come down the valley. If she hurried, she could catch up and give him the hamsters.

Raven nodded her head. "Very well, I'll leave you to your work." She swatted lazily at a beetle trying to land on her tumble of hair, which she hadn't taken time to braid that morning, and then she sauntered away as if what he'd said was of little importance.

At the camp's edge, her fingers quickly secured the pouch's leather straps so it rested tightly on her back. She began running and soon spotted the large boulders a short way up the valley.

His large footprints, with their splayed toes, were easily found. She tracked them, running when she could, all her senses focused on her surroundings. The spring day was clear. The morning hummed with bees enticed down powdery throats of newly opened flowers, and butterflies flitted about as she sprinted along.

In the distance, buzzards flew. Raven could barely keep her eyes on the ground for watching them. Ever since her failed attempt to rescue the baby, their arrival filled her with foreboding. She momentarily slowed her pace and shaded her eyes, looking upward. They had probably scented an old animal carcass, or... they had spotted something freshly dead.

But she quickly realized the buzzards were only searching, their spiraling dance across the sky moving toward her, the innermost buzzard becoming briefly the outermost as they glided closer. She forced herself to stop watching them and continued on.

The trees and foliage became thinner. Raven was some distance from the camp and felt anxious. She looked up from tracking often, eyes darting everywhere. Large predators and their prey mostly stayed away from camps, avoiding the frequent food searches and constantly burning fires. The tribe depended heavily on fire for safety, hence the Fire Cloud tribal name. Clouds of smoke could be seen hovering over a Fire Cloud camp from far away. However, Raven had come a good ways from the camp's smoky protection. All she saw, though, was a fox ambling along.

Raven followed the footprints up a path that parted heavy grass. It looked like the path she'd returned on while carrying Fern's baby. She'd held the infant close under her parka to warm the small limbs, and its lips had moved like a minnow's mouth against her leather tunic as it made dry, mewling gasps.

Wetness dimmed her eyes, and she almost missed the Longhead's tracks veering off the trail. Alongside a plummeting stream, deeply sunken footprints wound up to where rocks dammed the stream's downward flow, the water forming a pool before noisily spilling out on its way to the lake. She saw signs of him all about the pool edges, including a leather skin he'd covered himself with while in the pen. Partly eaten bulrush tubers lay scattered about.

A twig cracked, and he walked out from behind a tree as if he had hidden there until he'd recognized her. Even at a distance, the red marks and chafing left from the ropes stood out. Seeing his neck raw like that made her own neck prickle.

But now the ropes were gone, and he had safely started his journey—in large part because of her and the things she'd done. She lowered the weighted pouch onto the ground, lightness filling her chest along with her limbs, and grasped the hamsters by their bound legs, eager to reveal her cache.

She held them toward him. "Aulehleh," she sang, the sounds lolling cheerfully in her mouth before going out over the pool. She hoped that she had formed the word correctly enough for him to understand her.

He must have taken some sort of meaning, because he came directly toward her. Not slowing or picking his way, he walked across stones and briars alike with his odd gait, as if his feet were hardened leather. Although he had on his filthy lower skins again, he had bathed. His damp hair and beard were a mass of reddish-brown waves. Even his eyebrows had curled from the water, she noted as he got closer.

He reached out, but instead of taking the dangling hamsters, he grasped her forearm. Raven looked down, perplexed by his broad hand clutching her.

Now the hand of his injured arm was reaching up slowly for the hamsters, and she thought that if she yanked that arm sharply with her free one, the pain might distract him enough for her to pull out of his grip. But she didn't make a move.

Instead, she lifted her eyes to his face, disturbingly near hers, and became lost in his features. She wanted to use her fingers to rework things, to press that huge brow down and to reshape the nose to be smaller. Her observation was cut short when he tossed the hamsters aside and pulled her down with him onto some new-growth plants thickly covering the ground.

Over the days of his captivity, Raven had become used to entering the space around him. But she became undone when he was the one to close the gap between them in such a sudden and complete manner. Her mind flailed, trying to figure how best to escape, but her limbs betrayed her by freezing stiffly, and the small sounds quivering in the air, she realized, were her own whimpers.

She could only guess what his expression meant as he looked down at her. His hands went to her neck, and she began to tremble, thinking of how he'd forced the bison's head almost to the ground. But he was only reaching for her necklace.

He fingered the shells for a few moments, turning them over. It reassured her, his curious touching, until she became unnerved once more upon observing his large fingers, broadened at the tips, good for grasping—or choking. He eased his hand down her tunic top, placing his palm on her chest, and she knew he could feel her heart's violent beating.

He was saying something. His vibrating, rumbling voice was low, almost whispering, as though he were soothing a fretting infant. His face was not unkind, and Raven's thumping chest calmed a little.

Then he was moving quickly, as if he realized too much time was passing. He pulled off his lower skins and pushed up her tunic.

Her breath quickened, and a surge of wildness pushed through her, not entirely caused by fright, when his weight and surprising warmth pressed her into the plants.

He lay beside her, panting for a little while afterward, one heavy thigh over her legs, pinning her. Raven twisted herself onto one elbow and slowly reached toward his face. No longer feeling a need to change and rework everything, she simply focused on whatever was beneath her hand, letting her fingertips roam from top to bottom. Under his lips, which were defined like notched stone, although soft, his bearded chin slanted back sharply. Perfectly made for close suckling. She tried to imagine what he had looked like as a baby with that chin tucked into his mother's breast.

He took her fingers away and smelled them, and suddenly she was on her back again. And perhaps she was wrong to do so, Earth Mother help her, but she yelled without restraint into the blue sky over them, having lost all caution along with fear, and she thought he had somehow made her into his kind and kindred.

He lay still on her for a long while, his broadness covering her. Raven felt strangely tranquil, almost paralyzed, and she drifted off, dreaming again of ravens. The fledgling raven landed beside her raven self as in her other dream. But that time when the young one cajoled and begged, Raven's throat pouch was so full and swollen she thought she might burst if she couldn't feed it. She had dipped her beak down to its open, pink-lined one when she awoke.

He was gathering things. He tied the hamsters onto the waist of his furs before putting them on. He widened a hole in the skin taken from the enclosure and stuck his head through it so his chest and shoulders were covered. Then he walked over to a limb that seemed to have been formed into something like a spear.

Raven noticed, as she straightened her tunic, that their time in the plants had made a kind of nest and that much of the nest was made of fox flower, the very thing she'd put in Fern's medicine—enough to sicken her but not nearly enough to kill her. She pulled up a scant handful and rolled over languidly to reach her pouch, tucking the plants inside. She yawned and stretched before kneeling to put the pouch straps over her shoulders. As she was about to get up, her shadow disappeared.

For a large man, he moved silently. Raven hadn't seen him approach, but he loomed over her. Not giving her time to rise, his good arm and hand swooped down and pulled her up by the wrist. There had been no way for her to know that she was one of the things he would gather before going on his way.

He walked rapidly up the valley toward the hills leading to the steppe, pulling her with him. She didn't resist and wondered at the lethargy sunk throughout her body and mind, her thoughts oozing, slow and sticky.

But he wasn't mired along with her in that honey-filled trance. The bone-jolting rapidity with which he hauled her along began rousing her, and she thought about their ultimate destination. Raven had no idea what living with Longheads would be like, or even if she could manage to stay alive in their camp.

Leaf had told her they ate their dead when they were starving. She wondered if they would eat her if she died when times were bad and whether she could eat one of them if hungry enough. Perhaps after what had happened that day, there was no act too strange or base for her. But she didn't want to find out.

"No, no," Raven said loudly over and over, so he would understand the word. "No!" She scrabbled at his fingers in an effort to peel them from around her wrist and tried to pull her arm out of his grasp.

He paused and looked back at her with brows lowered, clearly irritated, and then continued dragging her along.

After they'd gone on for a while, she gave up trying to get loose. She began crying in a quiet, hopeless way.

He stopped suddenly, dropped his spear, and turned to face her. Her wrist fell free. Before she could react, a hand clapped down on each of her shoulders. Her reflection in his eyes was surrounded by green, and it seemed to her that he smiled right before his hands lifted up and off.

Raven flew down the valley like a swallow released from someone's fist, leaping rocks and streams, feet barely touching the ground. Once she'd covered some distance, she paused to adjust her pouch. She looked up the valley, hoping for a last glimpse, but he had already gone out of sight.

California, Early Twenty-First Century

DESPITE HIS EARLIER MISGIVINGS ABOUT the seriousness of Genetics and Me, Mark is impressed with what he sees on his tour. The company has obviously committed to providing a reasonably priced product so the general public can pursue their individual genomes.

"Really wish you would stay a while," Greg says, back at the conference room door, behind which erupt gusts of laughter and animated chatter. "You're what—only ten minutes away at the Sunnyvale facility?" He raises his hands up, palms out. "Promise you won't regret it."

Mark feels like a complete jerk—Greg has done his utmost to be a gracious host since they first met. Perhaps he should stay. After all, he *is* there to forge a goodwill connection. "Okay," he says. "For a little while."

"Great." Greg opens the door. "Come with me up front. I'll introduce you to everybody." They wind through the crowd, and Mark sees a lot of curious looks glancing his way. He stops at one side of the podium, trying not to fidget.

"Listen up, folks." Greg taps the microphone. "I've got just a few things to go over before we dig into that wonderful-smelling bison chili and other goodies. First, I want to let everyone know that we have a distinguished visitor with us today. More distinguished than even he realizes," Greg says with a chuckle, looking at Mark.

Mark wonders what Greg is talking about. He wants to look away from the blue eyes boring into his but concentrates on maintaining eye contact.

"This is Mark Hayek from the Parkinson's Institute, one of our new research partners. But that isn't what impresses me most about him," Greg says. "Mark, when Genetics and Me heard about recent research showing that Neanderthal ancestry can be found in the genomes of many people living today, we used that research to work up the percentage amounts each of our customers carries. And of course, we also did it for ourselves, and that's what today's party is all about."

Greg turns his eyes from Mark to the group. "Everyone here will receive a T-shirt with his or her Neanderthal ancestry amount printed on front. The piece of tape with your name on it covers the percentage—I didn't want anybody spoiling the surprise factor by seeing the amount early. These shirts are a new product at our online store, so get the word out, people."

He turns and pulls a T-shirt from the clothesline. "DNA amounts go from zero to two percent—or that's what we thought until a few days ago. The winner of this genetic lottery," Greg says dramatically, "is standing right here beside me."

Mark takes the T-shirt from Greg and pulls off the tape beside the redheaded Neanderthal man pictured on the front. The shirt reads *3% Neanderthal DNA*.

"Show us!" someone in the crowd yells, and Mark turns the shirt around and holds it up.

"Wow, look at that," the woman standing closest to Mark says into the brief silence. "We didn't totally replace them after all." Clapping and whistling reverberate throughout the room. Mark gives a small bow before heading for the podium as Greg steps aside.

A familiar discomfort makes him swallow when he gazes around the group. His stomach growls, the sound fortunately low enough so that he feels a gurgle rather than hearing it. The rich bison chili smell saturates the air, and Mark realizes that in spite of his nervousness, he's hungry—a try-anything kind of hungry.

Mark thanks them for inviting him. He promises to mix with the group and get to know everyone better while they eat, keeping his remarks short before turning the podium back over to Greg.

While Greg works through his notecards, Mark contemplates the Neanderthal on his T-shirt, and his surroundings fade. He wonders what his Neanderthal and Early Modern Human ancestors would have thought if they'd known that one day, in the distant future, some of their descendants would throw a party for the sole purpose of celebrating their commingling.

Journeys of Choice

The Replacement Chronicles
Part 2

CHAPTER 1

Western Asia, Late Pleistocene

RAVEN OPENED THE LEAN-TO'S CLOSURE flap to see what the day revealed. Early-morning fog filled the camp with damp mist, and a detectable odor of decay wafted from the camp's edge, where the remnants of an aurochs carcass lay in a swampy bottomland used for general debris, cracked bones, and skeletons. Whoever had dragged the remains there after the band's feast several days earlier hadn't submerged them well enough. The odor was irritating, but that wasn't the only reason for her concern. Moisture-laden breezes would carry the stench across the valley and attract notice from far away. Large predators didn't often come near the smoky camp, but with the enticing smell and an empty belly, one or more might decide to risk a visit.

She stepped out of the lean-to and glanced toward the double tents, listening intently, but all was silent. Bear and Willow still slept. She had the moment to herself, or almost to herself—another woman was tending her hearth in a clearing farther down the bluff. Raven raised her hand in a friendly wave. After a longer-than-polite wait, the woman lifted her arm limply in return. Raven turned her back and went over to her sister's hearth, stifling the urge to shrug. That had been the way of things for two passing moons.

Raven threw more branches onto the smoldering embers. She planned to get the fire going before relieving her bladder.

While she was stoking the coals, the smell from the aurochs again caught at her, this time affecting her as if she'd stumbled upon a rotted kill being ravaged by vultures. Raven retched over the ashes, nausea uncoiling in her stomach. She looked up at the tents, stiffening. Sounds were coming from the children's side, then the youngest started wailing, wanting his early-morning feeding. Bear might come outside any moment; he often did when a child began crying. If he saw her being ill, he might guess the reason.

She straightened, cupping a hand over her mouth, and strode out of the clearing. In case the woman down the way was watching, she coughed into her hand, as if she had a scratchy throat. Doing so, she risked her stomach's complete revolt and also increased pressure on her full bladder. She hurried along, following, out of habit, the path that led downward, even though it would take her closer to the smell's source.

The area where people generally went to relieve themselves bordered a different side of the dank marsh than where the carcass lay. A self-contained depression, the marsh drained into itself, away from the lake, usually absorbing all unpleasant miasmas. If not for the nature of its use, the spot would have been pleasant. Hazel trees surrounding the edges had put on fresh green leaves. Over to one side, purple-headed swamp thistle grew, tall and strident. Slippery white calla covered the banks, and bulrushes thrust up from the mire.

Normally, Raven would have plucked leaves from a few choice plants to add to her medicine pouch. But that morning, she was blind to the foliage and beauty of the place. Her head was reeling, and her belly was quivering from the smell as she pushed aside the vines and reached the muck. Instead of being an invigorating background to a new day, the clamor of birds marking sunrise worsened her discomfort. As quietly as possible, she threw up bitter bile, her stomach heaving in its efforts. She straightened and pulled leaves from a nearby vine, wiping her mouth before stumbling behind a bush.

The surface of the pool steamed with vapor as the rising sun began striking the water. As she prepared to leave, a movement on the far bank near the carcass caught her eye; a small shadow slinked through the haze into a thicket. The quiet, sinuous way it disappeared led her to believe the animal was some kind of small cat. Raven's brow wrinkled. Even a small animal could be dangerous if a curious child approached it too closely. She sighed. Conversation with Bear was something better avoided, but she needed to mention that danger as well as other risks the smelly leftovers might bring. If he thought her a nagging woman, so be it.

Sunlight, dimmed by the white blur of lifting fog, flickered through the trees as Raven hurried back up the path. She felt much better but already dreaded when the next bout of nausea would arrive. They were becoming frequent and more difficult to hide. Blue jays called out harshly and burst from a tree as a man lurched into view, coming downward. Raven was glad that she'd woken early enough to have already finished at the pool.

She recognized him as the man called the Wanderer, his height and loping walk unmistakable. Like a stork's, his stomach was a bulging pouch over legs too long for his body. He traversed the land between camps, tagging along with traveling groups, staying short periods of time with various bands. He swapped things that he carried in several bags—fine pieces of quartz and flint, skins, wooden bowls, and other items—for whatever objects anyone had that struck his eye. Bear complained that the Wanderer always came out of a swap with more than he took in, but he tolerated the man, who was presently staying with the band in a guest tent.

The Wanderer leered as he passed by, his long nose a beak probing in her direction. Raven turned her head without speaking, dislike rippling through her. She hoped he would be leaving soon.

Most of the camp had come out of their tents during her short absence, and everyone had gathered around hearths against the morning chill to break night-fast. Again, their rudeness disturbed her. Those that she cheerfully greeted replied with the barest show of warmth. She was still the strange woman in their midst, the healer who'd tended their departed captive a bit too eagerly before he'd gone.

Upon overhearing several of the camp's women whisper that she'd been overly solicitous of the Longhead, Raven had felt a small thrill of shocked titillation, as if she were gossiping along with them and the person they'd mentioned had been some other newly arrived healer. And whenever she remembered how she'd tracked him up the valley's slopes, hiding her movements from the camp, her mind would blur and refuse to complete the memory. That the captive Longhead leave the band in a timely manner had been crucial. Yet the day after he'd gone, her feet had traveled several times to where he'd been held, her eyes searching the area as if the dismantled pen would suddenly reappear. The small clearing was empty, of course, beaten-down grass and postholes the only surviving evidence of his captivity.

When Raven arrived back at the hearth, she encountered all of her sister's children starting down the path. Dawn, the oldest, carried Flint, the youngest, tightly in her arms. Upon seeing Raven, he squirmed until Dawn put him down, then he toddled over to throw himself into her arms. She spun him high in the air to his squealing delight before lowering him. "Take care," she said to Dawn. "I glimpsed something that had been gnawing the aurochs bones down there." She waved a hand at Flint. "Nothing big, but watch out for this one."

Dawn nodded. "I'll carry him the whole way." She swept up the protesting Flint, and they continued on.

Raven glanced over at the racks near the tents, where dangling strips of aurochs meat hung. The thin slices needed to air-dry for another day before they reached the level of dryness necessary for crumbling the meat into small pouches. The charcoal pit underneath was still smoking, keeping blowflies away, but she saw that several of the strips were slipping from the looped strings holding them. She hurried over to tighten the loops. Even before she reached the racks, arguing voices came from within the main tent.

Willow's voice was firm. "It is your duty if she's to live here. The ceremony will only take part of one day."

Raven gave a little gasp and pressed several fingers against her mouth for a moment. *No. Please, Earth Mother, no.* She quickly began pulling the loops tighter around the loosened strips. One of the strings was wearing through; a fresh length would soon be needed.

"My sister is not so selfish with her days. Surely you've noticed that she's a big help when she's not gathering plants for Old Cloud."

"I don't see the need for a ceremony. It won't make her work any harder. Her living at our hearth doesn't make it necessary for me to be bound to her for a whole afternoon."

A silence passed, and Raven hoped that Willow had given up. Her chore finished, she began to move away, but her sister's shrill words froze her feet after only a few steps.

"I want her out of that lean-to. If it pains you to mate her with me present, I'll stay with the children on certain nights. Or I'll stay in the lean-to. But I'll not watch my own blood treated like a slave." Raven heard furs flapping wildly as if Willow were straightening bed coverings.

"I found her childless. I have sought to relieve that sad absence."

"Then what if she *does* bear your child? Will they both live out there through the cold winter? The baby would sicken and die." Willow gave an exasperated cry. "Use common sense, Bear. Better that you help her leave our hearth before her belly grows than make her remain out there. A baby has to be given consideration."

"Willow, so far there is no baby to consider."

"I know that."

Another silence followed. Then a popping sound began, and Raven saw him in her mind's eye, cracking his knuckles the way he did when faced with a decision. "I will think about this. Don't hurry me."

Raven breathed out a soft rush of air. She put a hand on her abdomen, pressing gently. His reluctance gave her time for carrying out her plan, the thing she must do before she searched for another hearth that would take her in.

"Hasn't there been any sign that she's carrying a child?"

Willow made a disgusted sound. "Of course not. You must have found during your recent visits to the lean-to that Raven was… that she… well, I still don't understand why you want to wait."

Bear's voice, low and ominous, came quickly. "Be silent, woman. I won't discuss it further."

Raven had heard enough. She slipped back to the fire pit, wondering why he hadn't immediately gone along with Willow's suggestion that Raven leave their hearth. Her very presence seemed to irritate him.

She sat before the fire while making more string by peeling fibers from stems of hemp bane and twisting them in different directions. When Raven became aware that her moon blood was late once more, she'd had the foresight to ask her sister if she had an extra thong and any spare moss. If Willow knew the truth, she would tell Bear immediately, pestering him with a stronger argument, then he might go through with the ceremony.

Raven quickly finished the string and put it aside for the moment. She went over to slide a flat stone off a storage pit lined with a skin and leaves. After skewering pieces of moose left from the previous night's meal, she propped the filled sticks over the flames. The meat's juices were already sizzling when the children returned. The day before, Raven had found early blueberries growing against the sheltered corner of a rock outcrop. She sent Dawn to fetch them from the lean-to where they were stored beside her pallet.

Just as Bear came out of the tent, his daughter returned carrying not blueberries, but a smooth, tan-colored material. "Auntie, look what I found. I stumbled over this in the entry." She held out a good-sized animal hide.

Raven took it from her. The deerskin had been worked and polished until it felt as soft and pliable as a baby's skin. Indeed, a hide softened to such an extent would usually be used to wrap and swaddle an infant. At that thought, blood rushed to Raven's face.

"There's only one person I know in this camp who can work a hide that finely," Bear said. He looked at Raven sharply. "That young wolf pup hasn't come sniffing around you, has he?"

"I don't know who you're talking about."

"Oh, don't you?" The children were watching their exchange with keen interest. Bear waved a hand at them. "Why aren't all of you leaving to fetch water?"

"They haven't broken night-fast yet, Bear. The water can wait awhile," Willow said, walking up behind them. She smoothed the hide with a hand. "It's a lovely piece." Lifting a section, she rubbed it against her cheek. "This is simply Leaf's way of returning kindness."

Bear grunted, shrugging, then went to the fire. He bent down and plucked up a skewer.

"Did you find the berries, Dawn?" Raven asked, her voice chilly.

Her niece looked over guiltily, her pretty face full of surprised hurt.

Raven gave her a quick smile. "It's all right, sweet one. Take the skin back with you, and leave it on my sleeping pallet."

A noisy chattering of squirrels erupted from one side of the clearing. Raven noted their fussy warning out of habit. Perhaps crows were close to their nest, or some kind of small ground predator lurked below. It could be that a badger had lingered outside its burrow after sunrise. She searched for Flint and saw him safely standing in front of the tents. Badgers were known for not loosening their grips after biting. Her concern made Raven remember her earlier decision to tell Bear about the rotting carcass in the swampland. The squirrels' chattering intensified, and she looked over at the large trees where they skittered about. A shadowy form, much too large, for a badger, darted among the trunks.

Her forehead tightened as she strained to see into the shaded glade. Whatever had frightened the squirrels was gone, but she decided to mention that she'd seen something there as well as the cat she'd seen earlier. That would strengthen her argument about the smelly carcass being a menace to the band.

She took a quick glance at Bear, who was hunkered over, gnawing clean a small bone he'd come across, his black hair falling into his face, and found she was reluctant to bring up either of those matters. He would stomp around under the trees, making a show of searching, before he declared that she was imagining things. Then he would accuse her of implying that he wasn't tending the camp's affairs correctly.

Bear threw down the bone, took up a skewer, and slid off another piece of moose. Tilting his head back to get his thick hair out of the way, he dropped the whole chunk into his mouth. He chewed hard to manage the piece, and nausea walloped Raven again. *Just like a bull bison with a large piece of cud.* She fought to quell the bile rising once more to her throat.

His appetite for food was as outsized as all of his appetites, and Raven discovered that she couldn't abide the thought of him entering the lean-to ever again. She still resented how he'd forced himself on her the first time he'd come in, rudely awakening her. He'd used the same argument Raven heard him use with Willow earlier—that she should be bearing children. But she also remembered, with disgust, how after the first time, she'd encouraged him in order to take his mind off killing the Longhead, even allowing herself during the following nights to be greedy along with him after her long drought. And now her sister wanted Raven bound to him by ceremony, even though he often went from her tent to the lean-to in the same night.

Perhaps she should give up on keeping the truth from him. If told she was with child and ill because of it, he might leave her be. After all, he would have accomplished his goal of impregnating her. But she was afraid he would continue his abusive ways, and so she put aside those thoughts. The child within her was going to perish as soon as she could collect the proper plants.

A heavy feeling settled over Raven, and she wanted nothing more than to crawl onto her pallet in the lean-to, but she made herself sit down to eat a small amount of meat and a handful of blueberries so no one would notice that she didn't have an appetite. Surprisingly, she felt better afterward.

She stood up from the hearth. "I want to straighten the lean-to," she said. "It's becoming crowded in there as we store the spring gifts provided by the Earth Mother. I barely have room for stretching out." Willow gave Bear a meaningful look, and as she hurried across the clearing, Raven wished she'd said things differently.

The first thing her eyes lit upon was the beautifully worked skin folded neatly on her sleeping pallet. She took it up and pressed its softness into her face. While breathing in the leathery smell, Raven realized that the shadowy form she'd glimpsed earlier hadn't been an animal. Leaf, the scout, had been hiding in the trees, watching to find out whether she'd found his gift. He must have put it in the lean-to when she'd gone to the swamp area. She felt a rush of affection for him. Underneath his defiant stances, she'd long understood the younger man's need for friendship and his desire for the occasional kind word. The Longheads had snatched him from his family at a tender age and forced him to live with them for several years. No one knew where his people had gone, so he hadn't rejoined his tribe. Some said his particular band had journeyed to a land far away.

Willow's voice came from outside the lean-to. "Don't forget to fetch water when you're finished at the hearth. And I want all of you to go. Make sure you take enough bladders for filling." Willow's neatly braided head appeared from around the flap. "Raven, come with me. I have something to tell you."

Raven felt tempted to say, *Why don't you come in and see where I dwell?* Willow had not once entered the lean-to since Bear had led Raven to the crude entrance several moons before. She always sent the children for whatever she needed. But then, Raven's banishment from the main tent had never been Willow's idea. To pretend that it was and show spite toward her only kinswoman in the valley would have been foolish as well as unfair. Without saying a word, Raven followed her sister.

The children were at the lake, and Bear had left, so they had the warm tent completely to themselves. Willow sat on furs covering the bed pallet and patted a place beside her. Settling onto the thick coverings piled before a small rock-rimmed hearth, Raven looked around. She'd hardly been inside the tents since Bear had made it clear he didn't want her in them. How spacious the area seemed—the large skin-covered poles swept high to converge at the top, providing adequate room for smoke to waft upward so that everyone didn't constantly inhale smutty air. Fire was such a comfort, one that Raven could pursue only by going outside to the cooking hearth, because the lean-to was too full of storage items for her to safely start even a small blaze.

Raven knew she should have been grateful that she was living with kinsmen, and she realized that she was being overly petulant that morning because of her uneasy decision. As a healer, she'd struggled to preserve the lives around her. It pained her that, for the first time, she'd decided to use her knowledge differently. She was going to destroy the life closest to her, the tender bud growing within, and she would also be inflicting a harsh and risky remedy upon herself. The medicines wouldn't be as gentle as the ones she'd given Fern, which had caused only a mild illness to teach her about the nature of suffering. Her eyes unfocused as it struck her that she was no better than her old nemesis, who'd also wanted to rid herself of an unwanted child. *Stop it,* she told herself. Fern's situation was completely different. Fern had a mate, an esteemed elder who doted on her—yet she'd left her newborn baby to die on the steppes. Feeling faint, she took up a fur flap and fanned herself.

Willow looked at her curiously.

"I'm not used to the heat," Raven said.

"Perhaps you will soon have reason to become used to it," Willow replied and took a deep breath. "I've talked with Bear about you becoming his second mate. That is, I mean he would strengthen his... his bond with you, and as his mate, you would move in with us."

Raven stared at her flustered sister. "Isn't this coming a little late? Why didn't you think to discuss that with Bear before he brought me here? You know well that I have already been mated by him, and often."

"I'm talking about the binding ceremony, Raven." Nettled-red splotches covered Willow's face. "You're right. We should have talked about what would happen when you arrived. It's just that at the time, the most important thing was getting you here." Moisture swept her sister's eyes, and her mouth opened slightly in a grimace that revealed the small gap between her front teeth that was identical to Raven's. "I thought that eventually we would find another mate for you."

Raven's heart softened. Willow had been trying to save her when she'd persuaded Bear to fetch her younger sister from their old band. If not for Willow, she would have been cast out, an unwanted woman given as a slave to a distant, unknown tribe.

"How does Bear feel about the prospect of being tied to me for all of an afternoon until the sun sets?"

"He will agree to it shortly. First, he wants to know what your feelings are on the matter."

That lie troubled Raven. Her sister was willing to stoop in order to settle the situation.

"He shouldn't be pushed," Raven said hastily, her voice rising. "Give him another moon to consider, and I won't be offended if he decides that I should have the ceremony with someone else. Isn't there any man here who doesn't have a mate or perhaps has a family that would accept a second mate at their hearth?"

"Soon after you arrived, I made discreet inquiries. So far, none have indicated that they… that they desired… really, sister, the only man without any mate at all is Leaf."

She understood. None of them wanted her. If only the band would make an effort to meet her halfway, they would change their minds about her, she was sure. She didn't believe she was entirely without charm.

"Leaf will find a young girl," Raven said. "There's no rush for him; the boy is barely out of childhood. Doesn't he remind you of our youngest brother? And as for me, some man will eventually need a woman to tend his children when his mate dies from illness or childbirth. Not that I wish those things on any woman," Raven said hastily. "The Earth Mother isn't always kind, though."

But Willow didn't seem to be listening. Her face was turned toward the hearth fire. "He'll pass another summer shortly."

"Who?" Raven asked impatiently. "Who will pass another summer?"

"Leaf—who else are we talking about?" Willow moved restlessly on the furs, angling herself so that she faced Raven. "You're four or perhaps five summers older than he is, but you don't look it. You've had no children to age you. You're as fresh as a young girl."

Raven sputtered. "But I think of him as a brother."

"He doesn't see you as a sister," Willow said softly. "The whole camp has noticed the way he follows you about, gazing at you as though you're both the sun and moon. He's becoming quite the man, you know. He'll be expected to seek a mate before long—from another Fire Cloud band. And you are from another band."

Raven looked away. It was true that whenever Leaf wasn't scouting or hunting, he always seemed to be close by. Very often, she would encounter him when gathering plants or while going down a path. Other than Willow's family and Old Cloud, he was the only one who had anything to do with her. If Willow was right, then his pursuit had been there in front of her, and she'd been blind to it, thinking of him only as a lonely boy she talked with from time to time. This lack of astuteness worried Raven. She'd always prided herself on being keenly aware of whatever was going on around her.

She wasn't entirely convinced, though. Willow could be mis-understanding the reasons the boy sought Raven out, or perhaps she simply wanted a quick and ready solution for what to do with her sister.

Raven wished that she already had some other place to go. She loved her sister and her nieces and nephews, but she was tiring of the uncertainty and turmoil. Her suspicions about Willow's motives were confirmed by her sister's next words.

"It won't be long before the band will move out onto the steppes for summer. Everyone will be too busy then to make time for a binding ceremony."

Raven's head ached, and her stomach made a slow roll. She stood up rapidly. "The day is going by, and I've promised Old Cloud that I will find plants to treat stomach upsets this morning. Some of the children have been complaining."

Willow's mouth pursed as if she'd bitten into a green plum.

"I'll think about everything we've discussed while I'm gathering," Raven said. She slipped out of the tent before her sister could protest.

Near the lake, the first herb Raven found was barberry. Its leaves and flowers were good for the stomach. Her healer aunt had taught her well, and in spite of their healing powers, many plants were harmful during pregnancy, including barberry. But Raven wanted to find tansy, a stronger plant that her aunt had whispered about. It was usually used only if a healer thought that a woman's life would be put in danger if she bore a child. *Usually*, she'd whispered several times in emphasis.

Raven grasped the barberry, pulled the flowers and leaves from the stems, and slipped them into her pouch. If she didn't succeed in finding tansy that day, she could at least relieve her queasiness in the meantime.

She found herself dallying, snipping first one plant and then another with her fingers, her mind not focusing on the task at hand. Irritated by her reluctance, she attempted to quell her self-doubt by asking herself if she could accept having Bear's child even if she were living in the best of circumstances. She believed that Bear had embedded the sprouting bud inside her because the Longhead captive, although he looked like a man and had behaved like a man, was probably too different to impregnate her kind.

Bear had taken full advantage of her vulnerability without considering her feelings or Willow's. Ridding herself of his child would be sweet revenge since the only reason he'd given for his behavior was that he wanted to produce a baby. Raven's discomfort about what she was doing abated a little.

But perhaps she was wrong, and the child belonged to the Longhead. Raven had refused to think about that possibility in any detail. However, if Bear deserved scorn for his behavior, then in all fairness, she would need to confront her memories of what had happened on the valley slopes and determine if the captive's use of her had been any different than Bear's.

She'd minded the Longhead during his captivity, quite tenderly at times, massaging the arm and shoulder she'd repaired, working his arm gently about to help increase the range of movement. Although he hadn't returned her smiles, something in his face had told her he hadn't minded her ministrations. She'd stopped doing all those things when one day, she'd noticed that the skin he wore wound about his lower body was stretched out of shape. The guards also saw the skewed piece of fur, she knew, by the smirks on their faces.

He was at the mercy of the band, without anyone but her to look out for him. Perhaps she'd been too caring. Even so, understanding what had passed when she'd given him the hamsters she'd trapped wasn't an easy task. It wouldn't have been difficult to ladle blame onto that single word of his language she'd learned and used that day—a word Leaf had told her meant "eat." When she'd uttered that word in the best way that she could, the Longhead's reactions had been immediate, as though she'd offered him not only food, but herself, as well.

She had no idea what a Longhead's child would be like, especially if it were a girl. Those heavy brows and the heavily muscled build made an unattractive combination when she struggled to imagine a female infant. But then she remembered how she'd envisioned the Longhead as a baby, his chin tucked into his mother's breast, and she felt an unexpected yearning to hold that imagined child. Raven touched her chest, and her breasts felt swollen. They'd become exceedingly sore over the last few days.

Raven realized that she had completely stopped searching for tansy and was standing under a dead tree that shadowed a high bank beside the lake. She needed to stop her musing and get on with her task. Going through with her plan was the only way she could change her plight. Unless she found a mate other than Bear, she would never be happy, and finding someone else wouldn't happen if she were pregnant.

Bright-yellow clumps grew on a plant only a short distance from where she stood. The small, circular flowers were tansy blooms. The plants had been around her all along, she suspected, but she'd failed to recognize them. She gathered a large amount of flowers, leaves, and stems before returning to camp.

Finding privacy for making a potion proved impossible with the children always in and out of the lean-to, then Willow suggested everyone go out and search for new-growth tubers. Raven decided to put off her undertaking until the next morning.

They dug for parsnips and other edible roots using sturdy pointed sticks. While Dawn helped her mother and aunt pull them out of the ground, the younger children cleaned off the dirt and put them into a leather bag.

Willow turned to Raven when they were finished. "Bear won't be at camp when we return, so we'll wait before preparing a meal. Red deer were spotted on the far side of the lake this morning, and he left with some of the men to try their luck."

"Perhaps he'll have to sleep in the forest tonight," Raven said, and the words came out a bit too cheerfully. "Maybe we should at least cook some parsnips now."

Willow's eyes cut over, and she frowned. "They're not going so far as that."

Bear and the other hunters did return before nightfall, bringing several deer they'd killed. Those were soon processed, cooked, and eaten by the families of the men involved in the hunt. After helping with cleanup, Raven sat with her nieces and nephews around the fire, relating animal legends she'd learned as a child. When the others left for their tent, she went inside the lean-to.

She twisted and turned on her pallet, dreading the rustling sounds of the flap being lifted and Bear's footsteps coming toward her. She tried to think of something that would make him leave again. She'd faked her moon-blood days some days before, so she couldn't use that excuse. That hadn't stopped him more than a few nights anyway, and his lust had kept him from noticing that she'd been lying. If she said she had a fever, he would feel her forehead and tell her she was fine. She couldn't say she was nauseated. That was all too true and might cause suspicion.

After a long while passed, Raven realized he wasn't coming. All the earlier talk with Willow about the binding ceremony had cooled his desire. At that agreeable thought, she fell asleep but awoke later when a pair of owls began hooting back and forth. When they suddenly quieted, Raven snuggled into the furs. The night felt late, and she wanted to sleep a while longer before daylight.

She dreamt she was soaring above the camp. After flying over the lake, she turned toward the hills at the valley's edge. When she reached the dammed stream where she'd caught up with the Longhead while he rested, she swooped downward, flying low. She had only the moonlight to see by, but it seemed to Raven that the grass where they'd lain was still flattened into the shape of a large nest, even after two moons had gone by. She flew on, going high once again.

Upon leaving the hills, she flew over vast, moonlit steppe-lands. Below, a cave lion pulled its kill through thick grass toward a cave. After going farther, she went directly over a group of bison bunched around their calves and shaking their horns at a pack of hyenas. When she'd gone a good way, the land below suddenly narrowed, an enormous amount of water spreading out on either side. She flew down the center, returning to the steppes. Mountains loomed in the distance. Raven flew higher, but spying a pass, she swooped back down to follow the course of a river through a narrow valley.

Eventually, the land widened out into a larger valley, and she circled around, reveling in the open area beyond the pass. The mountain peaks were beginning to stand out against the first light of morning, and as she spiraled, Raven spotted the dark outline of the mouth of a cave. Movement on the ledge caught her eye, and she flew over. When she got closer, Raven made out the muscular form of a Longhead sitting beside the mouth.

She glided toward him, slowing her flight. He was looking intently at something he held, and Raven saw that he was making a tool from a long piece of bone. The expression on his face said his efforts weren't going well.

Her throat caught. That Longhead wasn't just any Longhead. His heavy brow and thick reddish-brown hair were familiar. The captive had survived his journey.

She landed a short distance down the ledge and flapped several times to get his attention. When he didn't look up right away, she *quorked* then made excited rapping sounds, *rap-rap-rap*, ending with a bill snap.

He lifted his eyes from his task—a flash of green—irritated that his work had been interrupted. When he bent over and picked up a rock, the feathers on her head rose, and she shook her head back and forth, alarmed by his gesture. He paused, fingering the rock as he watched her. Raven shook her head again, over and over, back and forth, hoping that the movement would somehow remind him of the first time he'd noticed her. She'd warned him not to run from his captors, by shaking her head repeatedly. Even if the movement did jog his memory, he wasn't certain to associate her present bird form with her human one.

Squinting, he blinked slowly several times and lowered his hand holding the rock. Raven stretched both wings out behind her and turned in a quick circle. His large eyes opened wide, and his jaw tightened. She remembered the feel of that jaw, lying not on feathers, but along the bare skin of her neck, and an ache kindled deep within her raven's body.

She suddenly convulsed, the feathers all puffing out at once, then a large egg lay upon the rocky ledge in the morning light. It was beautiful. The egg's shell was the color of a clear sky and splotched with the same green as the Longhead's eyes. Small speckles of bluish-purple the color of ripe, dark plums gleamed on the smooth surface. Astonished, she nudged it with her beak. When she looked at him again, he sat frozen, his stare fixed on the egg. She croaked at him, a deep gurgling sound.

Raven sat straight up on her sleeping pallet, her eyes flitting open. The image of the egg faded away. She carried the Longhead's child. That dream left no opening for any other interpretation. All Bear's efforts to impregnate her had been for naught after she'd caught up with the Longhead at the pool. Raven was glad that the baby wasn't Bear's. All the delight her dream self had felt at seeing the Longhead still warmed her, and she almost laughed aloud.

But the reality of her situation quickly returned. Nothing had changed. As soon as her pregnancy was found out, everyone would assume Bear was the father. Willow, and perhaps the whole band, would pressure him to have the ceremony with Raven, ending her chances of finding anyone more pleasing.

She also had to consider the child's appearance. A big, burly boy would probably be accepted as Bear's, even if he looked a little strange, but if the child was a girl... in truth, her options had lessened. She had no choice but to poison the baby until it left her body.

Daybreak had arrived while she dreamed, and final doubts cast aside, Raven dressed in a rush so she could prepare the tansy before any of the others awoke. She hurried into the clearing and filled the largest wooden cup she could find with water. After crushing leaves and flowers and mixing them in, she poured the mixture into a bladder. In order to ingest everything, including the potent leaves and flowers, she would have to stir it well before she drank. Heating the potion would make it go down better and hasten the effects, but there wasn't time for that. She darted back inside the lean-to for the thong and moss Willow had given her when she'd faked her moon days. She would be ready whenever the bleeding started.

Raven didn't dare go far from camp for fear that if she became extremely ill, she would find it impossible to struggle back. She walked rapidly toward the lake, planning to hide in the forest near the water while waiting to see how difficult the process became. When she reached the trees bordering the shore, Raven untied the bladder opening and stirred the mixture with a small stick. She threw the stick away and placed the whole top of the bladder into her mouth, tilted her head back, and gulped. Although she'd stirred well, when the liquid was gone, she could feel that the bladder still contained lumps of crushed leaves and flowers. Her fingers became clumsy as she fumbled through her pouch, searching for her small stone knife. Finally finding it, she slashed open the side of the bladder, dropped the blade, then scooped and swallowed until she'd ingested all of the bitter, sodden mass.

Between the lichen-covered roots of an elm, Raven settled down to wait, her back against the sun-warmed trunk. After cleaning her hands of the tansy, she undid her braids, combing out a few snarls with her fingers. A beam of sunlight stretched through the branches, lighting up the strands. Raven's fingers stopped moving. Taking in a sharp little breath, she held up a length to see it better. There were glints in her hair the color of dark plums, the same shade of speckling as the egg in her dream.

CHAPTER 2

California, Present Day

MARK BRAKES HARD SO HE won't go through a traffic light. His body lurches forward then back again as the car skids to a stop in a pedestrian crossing. In his rearview mirror, the woman driving the car behind shakes her finger at him. He jerks his eyes away. *Ignore her,* he commands himself. *Do not look at her again.*

He sits, fingers tapping the wheel, and checks the various stores around him, searching for one that sells flowers. Whole Foods is a short distance down El Camino Real in the next block. They have flower displays just beyond the foyer. He won't have to waste time walking up and down aisles.

The light stays red forever. In spite of himself, he glances in the rearview mirror, but the woman has lost her fury and is only sitting there. Finally, the light changes, and he drives on.

Mark turns into the Whole Foods parking lot. After a few minutes, he realizes that finding a parking space near the entrance will take too long. He pulls into the next empty spot he sees. As Mark starts toward the store, a man pushing a grocery cart his way eyes him. The man's close scrutiny is disconcerting, but Mark understands that his T- shirt is the only thing that's drawing the man's eye.

A group of girls wearing tight-fitting tops over shorts comes out of the Whole Foods foyer as he enters. They stare at him, too.

"How cool," a blue-eyed blonde says.

But their stares aren't staying on the shirt; their eyes rove upward, meeting his. "Awesome indeed," a slender Asian girl adds. They all laugh at their cleverness, a tinkling chorus of sound.

Mark glimpses his reflection in the glass of the main door before it slides open. His dark hair and olive complexion make a startling contrast with the red hair and light-colored skin of the Neanderthal pictured on the shirt. An eye-catching combination, he supposes.

This isn't the first time that feminine attention has centered on Mark because of his shirt. He met Sandy, his current girlfriend, the weekend after receiving it. While he was walking from his condominium complex to the nearby deli, she stopped him to ask about its meaning. It soon became obvious that she was curious about Mark, as well, and he asked her along with him to eat at the deli café. Afterward, they returned to his condominium.

Sandy's interest lately hasn't been as keen, and he isn't sure how to tighten their loosening bond before it slips toward yet another dead-end relationship—but the flowers he intends to buy today aren't for Sandy.

His mother e-mailed, asking him to come by this afternoon, and the flowers are a peace offering. Her message was full of sarcasm about her doting son who visits so often. He can't put her off this time, she wrote, and she needs adequate time to discuss something important with him. None of his quick in-and-outs, please.

He doubts the importance; she's merely jabbing a hook into him so that he'll leave work before nine o'clock. But she has managed to make him feel guilty. He decided to go along with her game and responded saying he would come early.

Mark rests his chin on his chest for a moment, looking down at the Neanderthal. His mother won't keep quiet once she sees his shirt. He should change it before going over, but he doesn't want to. Wearing the shirt feels... right, although he can't think why.

He's worn it almost every day for six weeks, since it was given to him during the party at Genetics and Me headquarters. He even puts up with teasing at work every time it's spotted under his lab coat. "You *are* Neanderthal," one of his colleagues at the Institute said, "putting on the same shirt every morning."

At his weekly collaborative meetings with Genetics and Me, they are much more tolerant. Mark appreciates their uncritical acceptance, just like he's grateful for the tireless way Greg and his cohorts provide information from their genetic data for use in Mark's Parkinson's research. In spite of Mark's first take on the man, he has to admit that Greg's work ethic approaches his own selfless slogging. Neither Mark nor the genetics team is working harder because they'll make more money. Although research grants are being showered on both The Parkinson's Institute and Genetics and Me, none of the scientists are receiving pay raises to match their increased workloads.

After six weeks of daily washings, the shirt is fading. The percentage near the shirt's neckline declaring the amount of Mark's Neanderthal ancestry is now a light gray instead of black. At his last meeting with the Genetics and Me staff, Mark found himself interrupting Greg's praise for the quality of his research to ask how he could get another T-shirt. Usually, he would have basked in that kind of acknowledgement from someone he respects. The problem is that every time Mark checks the company's online store, he finds they don't have a shirt available with his three percent Neanderthal ancestry.

"Sorry, but there aren't any more with three percent. We had that one T-shirt made especially for you, at extra cost," Greg told him, smiling an apology. "With that much Neanderthal ancestry, you are rare—a genuine outlier."

Mark realized how petty he was being, but he felt so let down that he barely participated in the meeting until after he hit upon a solution. He could buy a shirt with two percent on it and use a marker or decal to change the number into a three.

Holding the mixed bouquet, he waits on the stoop of the small house his mother rents with his help in San Carlos. As usual, she takes a long time answering the doorbell, even though she's expecting him. He pictures her pressing tendrils back into her bun and quickly putting on lipstick, primping for her son.

He holds the flowers out to the side when she opens the door so she can give him the habitual hug. She smells of sweet gardenia perfume.

"How nice to have real ones," she says, taking the neatly wrapped cone. "Their cost is outrageous now." Her eyes go immediately to his shirt. "Mark, is that what you wore to—did you come straight from work?"

"I went by the condominium to change clothes first," he lies. Pushing past her into the house, he enters the living room.

After closing the door, she walks through on her way to the kitchen. "I'll put these in water. It will only take a minute."

Mark sits in an overstuffed chair and looks around. The place is filled with even more artificial flowers than he remembers from his last visit. There are paper flowers and expensive silk ones, but the majority are of a cheaper plastic. Several sturdy bunches are made of clay, and a few are delicate swirls of porcelain. Every shade imaginable assaults his vision, although reds and yellows are dominant, and the clusters represent a variety of types, ranging in size from small bell-shaped flowers to large sunflowers.

Where does she get all these fake flowers? He imagines her slipping into cemeteries by night and flitting from grave to grave, gathering blooms that catch her fancy, her white-streaked black hair flowing behind her.

"Mark, my brother has died, in Turkey," she says abruptly after she's sat down and is facing him over a coffee table laden with blue roses. "He had a heart condition."

"I'm sorry to hear that. What was he doing in Turkey? I thought he lived in Israel."

"Sami did live in Israel, but some of his businesses were in Turkey. It's so sad. He never had the chance to retire to our old village in Lebanon like he wanted." Her voice quavers. "I was to visit him if he ever moved there. Now I'll never know exactly where your father was buried." She pulls a tissue from her pocket and dabs the corners of her eyes.

Both Mark's uncle and father fought for the Southern Lebanon Army, and they fled for Israel when Hezbollah defeated the disintegrating SLA. Sami arrived safely in Israel, but Mark's father was wounded and died during the escape.

He searches his memory for other family details. Early on in the struggle, Mark's father sent him and his mother to California. He was supposed to join them there but chose to stay and fight. Mark's mother divorced his father several years after the move, so Mark is suspicious of her show of grief.

He was only four when they left Lebanon, so Mark barely remembers his father—his uncle, not at all. His mother seldom discusses her past, and although Mark has always known he has Lebanese ancestry and that his name was originally spelled Marc, he never dwells on it. In his mind, he's a Californian.

His mother is still working the tissue around her eyes. She doesn't even look Lebanese. Mark has the olive skin and typical dark eyes, but his mother is very fair, with hazel eyes. Only her hair is like his, black and full. For the first time, Mark wonders if she's his real mother. The thought shocks him. He doesn't know if she would tell him the truth if he asked. Then it occurs to him that he already knows how to find out if he's her son. His fingers tap his chin. All he needs is a saliva sample.

Looking at his shirt again, she begins spelling out loud. "N-e-a-n... Mark, how do you say that word?"

"Neanderthal," he replies, giving his chin a final emphatic tap.

"What is a Neanderthal?"

Mark wishes again that he had changed into a different shirt. He knows what's coming. He shifts in the chair. "The Neanderthals were a type of hominin. They were an ancient people that used to live on the planet—in Europe and Asia."

"Is this another one of your obsessions, like your fascination with Star Wars when you were barely out of diapers? Or the stray cats later on?" She clicks her tongue several times, tutting. "You kept me running to the humane society. And that first year in middle school when you began quoting historical dates for anybody who would—"

"I've heard all this before, and I'm not obsessed. I just find Neanderthals interesting."

"What about your girlfriend? Does she find them interesting?"

Mark turns and gazes out the window at his car, parked on the curb—such a short distance away. The curtains are parted, and the window is raised slightly. A bee flies through the narrow ribbon of empty air and lands on the ledge momentarily before taking off into the room. It wanders futilely from flower to flower until, with an angry buzz, it lands on the plastic bougainvillea cascading pinkly down one side of a hutch.

His mother hasn't noticed the bee; she's busy making more observations about his life. "A woman will put up with a job-obsessed man even if she does prefer to be the center of his attention. But Neanderthals?" She bends forward, looking at his shirt, her eyes locking onto the redheaded man dressed in skins. "What a brute!"

A loud buzz fills Mark's left ear as the bee zooms by.

His mother laughs, drowning out the bee's sound. "My goodness, what must their women have looked like?"

The bee alights upon the blue roses nearest him on the coffee table and crawls quietly over them. Mark imagines the black and yellow stripes smeared over the blue petals. His fingers twitch, and he thinks about taking off a shoe. Instead, he takes a deep breath and clears his throat. "Mother, you said you wanted to discuss something important?"

He regrets his harshness as soon as the words are out.

She raises her eyes from the shirt, giving him a wounded look, and sits back. "Sami has left me half of his estate. Some of the paperwork came this week. He also named me as the person taking care of everything, his… oh, what is that word?"

"Executor." This is an unexpected turn of events. "You'll need to see a lawyer. Where does the other half go?"

"To his son, your cousin, Antun. I've already called a lawyer, Andrew McNeal. He took care of things when your father died. Andrew contacted the lawyers in both Israel and Turkey. He says they're insisting that I go to Turkey and take possession of Sami's ashes and that I have to sign documents over there."

Mark gets an inkling of where this is going. "Why can't they send the ashes and paperwork here?"

"It's complicated, it seems. I wish I could do everything without involving you, but with all my problems, I can't see myself traveling halfway across the world. Andrew says you can represent me if I sign a few papers."

Mark's breathing speeds up. "For God's sake, mother. You're talking about a trip that will last a week or more. You know I can't leave work for that long."

"Don't curse at me, son. I don't have the money for traveling over there. Surely, you must realize how hard it's been for me to pay my bills since my job vanished." She sighs. "I've been thinking I should move in with you."

"I'll pay for your tickets," he says, but she's not listening.

"And I don't feel well. I have no energy, and I constantly ache all over. Dr. Wu says all I have is mild osteoarthritis. I think he's wrong. There's more to it than that."

His mother has always had similar complaints. Mark usually ignores her when she carries on about aches and pains that never turn out to be anything serious, but now he focuses on her.

"You may be predisposed to develop certain diseases. A DNA test will let us know. All we need to do is collect some of your saliva in a small tube for analysis, and I'll do the rest. I'll bring a kit over within the next few days and get that started."

At last, she's quiet for a moment, but now a wet sheen covers her eyes. Mark squirms on the seat cushion.

"My intelligent son. You would do that for me? I know so little about such things."

"I'll take care of it." He runs a hand over the chair's plush arm. "Now about this inheritance. I seem to remember that Uncle Sami's wife died some time back."

"Yes, several years ago."

"If Antun is the only one left, I don't understand why he didn't make him the executor. He's not a child anymore, is he? He should take care of this."

"Antun is about your age, I think."

"Then why did Uncle Sami leave it to you to collect his ashes? The two of you weren't that close, were you? Surely his only child should have them."

"We did e-mail each other from time to time, but no, we weren't that close. He didn't like it when I divorced your father." She pauses for a moment, rubbing her forehead. "You know, I remember Sami wrote about Antun in his last e-mail, something he was upset about. I can't remember if I deleted the message."

They both sit silently for a moment, then she moves onto the sofa, sliding over to touch his knee, her eyes pleading. "Mark, I need this inheritance. Will you at least go see Mr. McNeal?"

The noose is tightening. "Surely the lawyers in Turkey and Israel can mail the paperwork here for you to sign. Or it could be sent electronically."

"I don't think so. It seems that…"

The doorbell rings. Both their heads jerk toward the small foyer.

His mother shrugs at him as she rises. "Now, who can this be?"

Someone begins pounding on the door—a little too enthusiastically.

The air pressure changes in the room when the door opens. The bee takes off and zooms straight through the window as if it knew the way out all along.

"Pastor Betros," Mark hears. "What a nice surprise."

"Nadia, *you* are looking well. I was down this way and thought to drop by."

"Please come in. I want you to meet my son."

Mark leaps up from the chair and goes into the foyer. He encounters a lanky man hovering over his mother. "Mark, this is Pastor Betros from Our Lady of Lebanon."

"So this is Mark," the man says, all bright smiles. "I've heard so much about you."

Mark shakes the man's hand. "Nice to meet you," he mumbles. Pastor Betros looks nothing like the Maronite Christian pastors of Mark's childhood. His shirt is unbuttoned partway down, revealing a small cross tattooed on his collarbone.

"I have to go now." Mark avoids his mother's eyes and steps through the open door onto the stoop.

"Oh, that's too bad," Pastor Betros says.

"I'll call you in a little while, Mark," his mother says. The door closes behind him.

Mark drives to the Stanford open-air mall, something he never does, but if he's not home, he can't answer the phone. She'll call after the pastor leaves—whenever that might be. He turns off his cell, although his mother seldom calls him on it and doesn't message. After wandering aimlessly for a bit, he finally buys a Starbucks coffee and sits with it in a courtyard, ignoring the mob of passersby, his chair turned toward an enormous, plant-filled pot.

They'll have to talk more about Sami's will, but communicating with his mother again so soon is more than he can abide. Besides, he doesn't know how to convince her that he definitely won't travel to Israel and Turkey. The lawyers will have to figure it out on their own.

Buying airline tickets, packing, and dealing with the logistics of travel wastes a lot of valuable time. But slippery details are only a small part of a trip like that. The worst of it will be the types he'll have to interact with—all their agendas opposing Mark's need to get things over with as efficiently and quickly as possible—and all of it thrown at him in different languages. Mark has never met Antun. He vaguely recalls seeing a picture of a smiling, dark-haired boy sitting in a boat. *Does Antun even speak English?*

A strong breeze swirls leaves and flower petals onto his table from the nearby plant. Mark covers his coffee cup with his hand, even though it has a lid. He can't afford to support his mother where she lives, but he doesn't want her moving into his condominium, either. A timely inheritance *would* be helpful—if she can get it. If the lawyers in Turkey and Israel are incompetent or turn out to be thieves, though, then his mother will end up with nothing. He drums his fingers on the metal table. Although he no longer feels close to her, the thought of his mother being victimized by slimy lawyers rankles him.

He remembers when they first arrived in California, just the two of them, as poor as church mice, trying to make their way in a strange land. She'd been his sole companion, a loving and supportive presence, until he began school. He'd been so proud to be at her side as they explored San Jose together. The stylish floral scarves she wore around her shoulders accented her somewhat-exotic looks, and she attracted notice no matter what they were doing—searching for a seat at a Maronite church or strolling through a grocery store. Men took sideways glances at her as they walked by, and eventually, that particular kind of attention began to make him ill at ease.

Mark suddenly recollects that Sandy is coming over at eight. He stands, gulping the last of the coffee, and tosses the cup in a waste bin. Sandy can answer the phone when his mother calls, then he'll get on the line to tell her that they were just going out the door. Always hinting that it's time he was married, his mother is happy he has a girlfriend. She would leave him alone for the rest of the evening after speaking to Sandy.

He doesn't bother with checking the phone upon entering his condominium. He knows there's a red light blinking insistently. Sandy won't come for another hour, so he'll ignore any more calls until she arrives. It'll only take a few minutes to brush his teeth and comb his hair. He has ample time to check a few things on the computer first.

Greg has told him he should set a password at the Genetics and Me site. This way, Mark can access health and ancestry information pertaining to his genome. He's been meaning to look into it but has been working a seven-day workweek lately, arriving home so late every night that he mainly sleeps when he's there. The only time he gets home early is when Sandy is coming over.

He thinks up a password, logs in, and goes directly to the section on ancestry composition. A map comes up, along with percentages. He's seventy-five percent Middle Eastern and North African. No surprise there. But he's also twenty-five percent Northern European, more specifically British and Irish.

He pushes back from the computer, the chair wheels grinding over a plastic mat. Had his mother—if she is his mother—taken a British lover while still in Lebanon? Was that man Mark's father? But no, he's thinking about the wrong generation. His mother is the fair one, not Mark. He's seen pictures of his long-deceased grandparents from her side, and they both look Lebanese: olive skin, with dark eyes and hair. Yet their daughter looks different. How did that happen?

The phone rings in the living room, and as always, the sound jangles through him. It's not just that he's trying to avoid talking to his mother tonight; he detests the telephone—the noise it makes and those awkward silences that have to be filled. Now he has two of the despicable things. He should get the landline taken out, at least, and only have the cell. After a few rings, his mother's voice leaves a message. "Mark, check your inbox," she says and hangs up.

He scoots the chair forward again to the computer and goes into his mail. Although she's still hounding him, e-mail is definitely better than the phone. When he opens her message, he encounters a list of URLs from various websites. *Maybe I shouldn't have taught her how to do that.* He clicks on one of them at random. An essay fills the screen: *Famous Neanderthal Caves in Israel.*

"Ha," he says into the quietness. His mother is clever in her own way. She knows him well.

He skims through the piece and finds himself becoming intrigued. Israel was the home of Neanderthals, and Early Modern Humans as well, tens of thousands of years ago.

He goes to another site; this article is about Turkey. *The Neanderthal Caves of Anatolia*, the title reads. Mark stares at the cave pictured halfway down. He envisions himself standing there in the mouth where Neanderthals once stood while they scanned the valley below for game. A reluctant dollop of wanderlust plops into his mind, boosting his curiosity. *Perhaps I should take some time off and go see these places...*

But he's in the middle of the collaboration with Genetics and Me. And then there's Sandy. Their relationship seems so fragile. Her great hobby is mountain climbing. He goes with her whenever he can, but she always grumbles that he doesn't make enough time for it. All he wants to do is work. And when they *are* finally together, he only wants to travel as far as the bedroom, she always adds with an accusing frown.

"But in spite of all the sex, you are one cold dude, you know that?" she said the last time they were together. "Deep down, you don't really care for me. You never touch me unless we're in bed." She placed both hands over her heart. "Nary a hug nor kiss do I receive," she said, her voice full of drama.

These complaints confuse him, because he has a lot of feeling for her.

"You're a fake," she said. "Seriously, you are. Those soulful brown eyes and kissable-looking lips of yours are false advertising."

No, he doesn't think their relationship can withstand a couple of weeks' absence. He turns off the computer and goes to the bathroom. While he combs his hair, the Neanderthal on his shirt watches him in the bathroom mirror.

"What are you staring at?" he snaps. "I don't want to travel around the globe to see your bones."

He shakes his head. He's losing it—talking to a T-shirt, for Christ's sake. After he brushes his teeth, he changes into a solid-blue shirt with no picture on it.

Eight o'clock comes and goes. He texts Sandy to find out what's holding her up, but she doesn't reply. Half an hour later, he decides he'll have to call her. He paces through rooms, holding the cell against his ear. When he passes the phone in the living room, he sees there are two messages. He clicks off the cell.

"Mark, check your inbox," his mother says again, then to his surprise, Sandy's voice comes on. She never calls on his landline, always his cell. She must have called early, a lot earlier—at a time when he wouldn't usually be home.

"Hi, Mark, I'm not coming tonight. I think you know why. Us—together—just isn't working out. I hope we can still be friends."

He punches the erase button. She could at least have been more imaginative. They all say the same thing, and he's never remained friends with a single one of them. But the damning heart of the matter was what she hadn't said, only hinted at: *You can't give me what I need.*

He runs his fingers through his hair and looks around the room. Climbing gear is piled in a corner. Books about Neanderthals and Parkinson's lie jumbled together on the furniture and floor. He supposes that Sandy's replacement will complain that all he wants to do is talk about Neanderthals—if there is a replacement. Mark wonders how many times he'll go through this before he tires of playing the game or becomes too old to have any appeal.

He's uncomfortable approaching women, always waiting for the bolder ones to come to him. But a day will arrive when he'll walk by a group of ladies, and they'll all turn their heads away. He could eventually become one of those solitary men who, after their youth has fled, rely on prostitutes for their physical needs. And that idea bothers him.

A major reason for not traveling to Israel and Turkey is gone. He still needs to consider his job, but after Sandy's rejection, the PI's hold on him has somehow weakened. Maybe he will be a good son after all and go to Israel and Turkey on his mother's behalf. His reward for doing so will be the opportunity to study real Neanderthal skeletons in museums instead of poring over photographs in books with a magnifying glass or enlarging images on the computer. Mark looks down at the phone. *I'll call her before it gets too late,* he promises himself.

CHAPTER 3

Western Asia, Late Pleistocene

COOL WINDS WERE BLOWING ACROSS the lake as Raven reclined between the elm's embracing roots. She gulped the
sharp, fresh air far inside her lungs and held it there for a long
moment before exhaling slowly, the calm release deepening her
relief over having finally taken action. She'd started down her
chosen path—however physically trying the way.

Ripples flowed across the lake's surface, making the water
shimmer and twinkle with more stars than were ever visible at
night. A steady stream of light swirled over Raven's face. Fixated
on the glare, her eyes widened, and she fell into a trance.

A vision arrived upon the breeze: she saw herself standing
with an arm clasped around a small child who was riding upon
her hip. With her other arm, Raven was pointing toward the
sparkling lake. She looked down to see the little one's reaction to
noticing the wondrous light, but before she could focus on the
child's face, the vision ended.

The winds made her shiver, drying a sticky sweatiness that
followed the trance. Her fingers tightened around the roots that
cradled her against the tree. That eye-opening view of a possible
future was surely from the Earth Mother. Those kinds of visions
rarely came to Raven. She didn't easily fall into a trance, even
though her aunt had instructed her in such things, having her
gaze for long periods into a fire after ingesting morning glory

seeds. Raven was always reluctant to participate in that sort of learning. She felt uncomfortable seeking the future, even though her aunt had always stressed that trance-induced visions revealed only possibility, not certainty.

Raven forced her fingers open. She wasn't tied to that futile glimpse that had arrived too late in the run of things. She had made her choice. It couldn't be undone. But her earlier tranquility leaked away rapidly, and Raven's eyes swept up and down the lake's edges in agitation.

Movement brought her attention to a small form prowling the shoreline. Dark-gray stripes crossed over its back, slashing through a lighter gray. It was another one of those small cats, or most likely, it was the same one she'd seen at the bottomland. The animal limped badly, one foot not even touching the ground. As the cat came closer, low- hanging teats became noticeable beneath the thick fur, and Raven understood why it had been scavenging the aurochs bones for any remaining scraps, however putrid. It had kittens hidden somewhere. The bad leg limited its hunting, and the cat was desperate for nourishment to keep producing milk for its babies.

When the cat was opposite her, it stopped suddenly, eyes darting up the bank. Raven knew she hadn't moved, but somehow, the small feline sensed her presence. Perhaps it smelled her.

The cat's eyes found hers, enlarging in alarm. It froze, but the connection held for only an instant, then the cat began running, stumbling on its lame leg several times, as its striped fur dipped in and out of view through foliage.

Sadness filled Raven over the injured creature's plight. Here was a mother struggling mightily to keep its young ones alive. She pressed her fingers into her brow, her fingernails digging in painfully. Meanwhile, Raven was trying to destroy her young so that she wouldn't be bothered with any kind of struggle.

Strings were being yanked tightly around Raven's heart. Perhaps, for some women, the course she'd decided upon was the right one. It made no sense, though, that she'd once tried to save a baby marked for death because its splotched face was thought too different, only to later end a baby's life, partly for the same reason—its difference and the problems it would cause.

The infant's face probably wouldn't be marked, but it would still be a very different kind of baby, its traits hidden and unknowable until after birth. In her brief vision, she'd felt but not seen the child's body pressed into her own, those small legs clasped around her, those tender hands clinging, but that was enough to provoke dreamy speculation, a belated curiosity.

If it were Bear's, what she was doing would carry some justification, although she wasn't even sure about that anymore. But the Longhead was a different situation. Being somewhat shunned by everyone around her just as he was, Raven had sought him out. She could have asked Old Cloud to help her heal and tend him, delegating many of the tasks. Instead, Raven had jealously shielded him from the band's hostility. And although Raven had glimpsed his desire for her, she'd recklessly chased after him the day he'd left when she could have been well rid of him. She was suddenly able to lay blame for her present situation everywhere—except on the baby.

With apprehension, she noted a quiver in her leg muscles. The poison was beginning to take hold. A dismayed cry escaped her, swept away by the breeze.

Only after she'd gulped another deep breath did Raven realize that the trembling wasn't an effect of poisoning. Only a short while had passed since she'd swallowed the tansy. But then her whole body started shaking. She crossed her arms and held her shoulders, trying to sit still. Her whole being seemed in revolt. She leapt up, urgency clutching her.

Raven thrust several fingers down her throat, over and over, but although she gagged, very little came up. After days of trying not to vomit, she found it impossible to do so. She slid down the bank, knelt, and began frantically palming water into her mouth. Using her fingers once more, she choked on the lake water as it rushed back out without bringing up even the smallest bit of tansy.

She started back up the bank, running wildly from plant to plant. Bright-red elderberries stood out against the greenery higher on the sloping bank. Raven struggled up and snatched the whole plant out by its roots. But she remembered that the reason elderberries caused vomiting was because they were poisonous unless cooked. The elderberries along with the tansy would kill her as well as the baby. Loosing a small scream of frustration, she slung the plant away, tripping over a hidden tree stump.

Trying to catch herself before falling, Raven lunged down the steep side, stopping abruptly at the water's edge. She stood there, panting and squinting, fighting to collect herself. Up close, the shimmering waves were painful to behold. A dead fish floating in the shallows was a further affront, and although it did cause a welcome nauseous feeling, nothing happened. Raven leaned over and desperately scrutinized the bobbing fish. The aurochs skeleton had made her fight being ill every time she got a whiff of it. She didn't understand why the fish didn't have the same effect. Perhaps because the aurochs was larger, she thought, and felt a twinge of hope.

She straightened—but not before she saw broad paw prints near her in the mud. The hair on the back of her neck stood up as she recognized the flat four-digit tracks of hyenas. Hopefully, the beasts had moved on. Raven grabbed several rocks and, after taking a quick look around, ran along the shore. She turned down the path toward the camp, feet pounding the ground. When she reached the swampy pond, she saw with dismay that a woman and several children were on the opposite side. Although the aurochs's odor already made her queasy, she needed to get in closer. She crouched behind a bush to wait, but luck was with her. The family left almost immediately.

Raven snatched off her moccasins and splashed through the shallow water without stopping to take off her leggings. If anyone else turned up at the bottom and saw her, they would think she'd lost her mind.

She stood over the reeking bones, clutching her moccasins against her chest, staring at the swarming maggots. Unhatched eggs lay in heavy rows along the animal's ribs. Her stomach clenched with painful spasms, and she finally rid herself of the tansy.

But then she couldn't stop throwing up. She staggered out of the steaming muck and clung to the nearest tree, trying not to retch loudly. She managed to get her moccasins back on before sinking to her knees, heaving, tears streaming from her eyes. The sound of voices came from the direction of the path leading back to camp. Raven moaned and struggled to get onto her feet.

Suddenly, she was being lifted from behind so that she stood again. She let out a startled yelp, but before she could twist around and see who had grasped her, she was pulled backward into thick foliage, her heels dragging. The moccasins came off again. She struggled weakly to get free, her stomach convulsing all the while.

"Shh, Raven, be quiet," a low voice said in her ear. "Let me help you."

She was pulled onto matted leaves. The voice sounded familiar, and through blurry eyes, she saw Leaf kneeling in front of her. He grasped her shoulders, looking into her face as she retched loudly again.

"I'm sorry," he whispered. "But I have to do this." He slid behind her, wrapping one arm and hand tightly around her chest. The other hand, he clamped firmly over her mouth. "You have to be quiet."

"Who left this exposed?" Bear's angry voice boomed through the trees. "I'll lash the laziness out of them."

Raven gagged quietly against Leaf's hand as someone answered, the words not loud enough to understand.

"Whipping is too good for that pair," Bear bellowed. "They didn't even bother to crack the bones for marrow. We should stake them out. They'd get *their* bones properly cracked by the hyenas seen roaming the valley yesterday."

The sound of sloshing water reached Raven's ears, and several men began cursing. Then came a large splash, and after a short while, more sloshing.

"Where's Leaf?" a different voice asked. "He was to let us know where the hyenas are. We need to wash this filth off, but I don't want to be surprised by a large pack at the lake."

"I should flog him along with the others. He's never where you need him anymore."

Leaf's arm stiffened around Raven.

Stamping feet came toward the brush where Leaf and Raven were hiding. "You men sound like a herd of horses," Bear said.

"This evil muck sticks like pine sap. It won't come off."

"You'll be in the lake soon enough."

Leaf's chest pressed over Raven's back, pushing her down so that they were both huddled close to the ground. The musty smell of rotted leaves filled her nostrils. Leaf's chin pressed into the nape of her neck, and his breath blew through her unbraided hair as they listened to the men passing nearby.

After a while, when she hadn't gagged for some time, Leaf stood up, pulling her with him. She leaned back against him, steadying herself. He lowered one of his encircling arms to her cape opening.

"Were you so desperate to be rid of this that you were willing to harm yourself?" he asked, his fingers a gentle pressure spread over her tunic front. "I don't know much about a healer's plants, but you swallowed a large amount. It took me a while to figure out what you were doing until I remembered that when one of my mother's babies stopped moving inside her, she drank medicines out of a bladder just like you did."

Raven's heart almost leapt from her chest, and she muffled a gasp.

His hand rested firmly on her abdomen. "I've watched you being sick for half a moon cycle now, and I know what that means."

Raven's nostrils flared. She pulled away to turn and face him. Her eyes, she knew, were as wild as those of a cornered deer. "Who gave you leave to trail me everywhere?"

Leaf flinched, but his gaze held steady, not blinking under her anger. "I would carry your secret even into death," he said, lifting his hand hesitantly toward her cheek.

Raven moved her head back slightly, startled and surprised by the strength of his declaration.

His face flushing, he lowered his hand. "But you won't be able to hide the swelling for long."

They stood silently; cranes migrating overhead called out loud whoops on their way to the lake. "All too true," she finally murmured.

"Join with me," he said hoarsely. "Stand bound with me in ceremony, Raven. We'll say the child is ours."

She was about to respond to his touching offer, when his hand darted out to lay a finger across her lips.

Doubt washed over his features. "No, don't say anything now. You've just been ill. Wait until your mind is clear."

Raven grasped his fingers, unfurling them before he could lower his hand. "You move upon the world like an unseen spirit—a helpful spirit, for me this morning." In an impulsive gesture of gratitude, she briefly pressed her lips against his palm, closing her eyes. His hand trembled, and she heard his breath rasp in shallowly, as if dipped from an almost-empty vat.

She opened her eyes, and he seemed in shock, his eyes glazed like those of a blind man. Then he focused on her, and his pleading face held a question. But she had no ready answer for him, only an abundance of tender feelings. In all probability, no one had touched him with affection since before the Longheads had stolen and enslaved him.

"We'll talk of your kind offer again soon," she said.

His face fell, and his eyes hardened in doubt.

"I promise you." She placed a hand over her heart. "Earth Mother hear my promise."

But the idea of joining with Leaf made her uncomfortable, not only because of his youth. He assumed the baby was Bear's. What if he took one look at the newborn, and something about the child seemed different but all too familiar? While living among the Longheads, he'd probably seen many of their babies. Her duplicity would strike him like lightning, destroying any feelings he had for her—but then again, the child might not look very different from Bear.

Raven put aside her thoughts. She had other, more immediate concerns, such as the condition of her clothes. Her cape was smeared with dirt and vomit, and her leggings were clumped with mud. "I need to bathe and to wash my clothing in the lake, but the men who moved the carcass are probably still there," she said, retrieving her shoes from the leaves.

"I know a place where you won't be seen. The hyenas may still be in the valley, so I'll return to camp with you afterward. No one should be out wandering alone today." While watching to see how she would respond, he retied the string binding his long dark hair at his nape.

Her instincts about predators being attracted to the smell had turned out to be correct. "I would be grateful," Raven said. She didn't point out that if he hadn't been following her like a shadow, *he* would have been alone.

Leaf found his spear where he'd dropped it earlier then led her farther around the lake where the water bulged from the shoreline, forming a hidden basin. Raven was entranced by the sheltered pool surrounded by willow trees. The lake was so large that much of it was still unfamiliar. She began unwinding the crisscrossed cord from around one of her leggings, eager to clean away the stench. When she pulled off the legging, she paused to look at Leaf, wondering if he meant to stand there while she washed. An awkward moment passed, and she thought about asking him to turn his back.

He cleared his throat. "I'll scout the area for the hyenas," he said before slipping away through the woods.

Raven rinsed out her mouth and drank a small amount of water before she shed her other legging and put both into the shallows. They wouldn't dry quickly; she would have to tie them around her waist after washing them. Once back in camp, she would grease them well with bear fat to counteract any water damage. Rather than completely immersing her cape, she took handfuls of water and rinsed the matted areas. The bottom of the tunic was also a mess, so she stripped that off and dipped the hem repeatedly in the water.

After draping everything on bushes to drain, she slipped into the clear lake, which was dead calm. Closer to camp, the lake had not been so freezing cold. Although her feet quickly became like iced fish, the water freshened her, and she felt more like herself again. She didn't stay in long, wanting to be dressed when Leaf returned.

She'd no sooner finished than he walked out of the woods. He wouldn't look at her directly. His eyes slid over her in quick glances while she braided her hair, not settling on her face. When she asked if he'd seen any signs of the hyenas, he shook his head, still not meeting her eyes. Raven suspected that he'd been watching for at least part of the time she'd been cleaning her clothes and bathing.

His behavior troubled her, not only because it displayed a devious side, but also because he didn't seem capable of performing his scouting duties whenever she was around. That was becoming noticeable to everyone, including Bear.

"Do you think the baby was hurt by the plants you swallowed?" he suddenly asked, as they began walking back around the lake.

"No, I didn't absorb enough to do any harm before I threw them up. A small amount of tansy is actually beneficial."

He appeared satisfied with her answer, his mouth turning up a little at the corners.

Raven smiled in return, happy that he didn't think badly of her. She looked at him closely. A growth spurt over the last couple of moons had rendered him taller and broader. He wasn't a thin switch of a boy anymore. "I haven't thanked you for the skin you left me. It's one of the nicest things anyone has ever given me."

A fleeting ripple of pleasure went over his features. "It's for the baby—but you can use it for yourself besides."

"I'll save it for when—"

He grasped her arm, stopping her. "Don't move."

She followed his eyes and saw five large hyenas along the shoreline, rounding a curve in the lake ahead. They loped along in single file. Although they rarely prowled around forests, their shaggy, spotted fur and ungainly gait made them immediately identifiable.

Raven tensed to flee, but Leaf tightened his grip on her. "They haven't seen us," he whispered. "They're going in the opposite direction."

She barely heard his last words, because at that moment, several large woodpeckers in the tree behind them began running up and down the trunk, screeching loudly. Looking up into the limbs, Raven picked out their nest.

One of the hyenas glanced back and, upon seeing them, slowed its trot. It let out a loud whoop that echoed across the water. Goose bumps trailed down Raven's spine. She looked about desperately, hoping to find a place that could be defended against the frightful possibilities that would face them, but she saw nothing to give her hope.

CHAPTER 4

The Levant, Present Day

EXHAUSTED FROM HIS TWENTY-FOUR-HOUR TRAVEL ordeal, Mark stands in the Ben-Gurion airport near a sign that says Meeting Point, located conveniently a short distance after customs. Several days before leaving home, he e-mailed a picture of himself so that Antun will recognize him at this agreed-upon spot, but his cousin failed to send a picture in return. Now Mark waits impatiently for someone to approach. He hopes that Antun hasn't given up on him. After disembarking from the plane, Mark encountered an unexpected delay upon entering customs.

He found himself having an overly long chat with an official from airport security who wanted to discuss Mark's purpose for visiting Israel. Mark explained about Sami's death and how he was charged with bringing his uncle's remains from Turkey to Israel. He told the man of his appointment with an Israeli solicitor who will give him directions on how to accomplish the task.

They somehow wound up talking about Mark's Lebanese ancestry. Mark had realized by then that the more he protested being detained, saying he had to meet his cousin, the longer the official was determined to probe, so he related his childhood history in as few words as possible. His inquisitive interviewer appeared to soften when Mark told him that his father had died while fighting Hezbollah. The questions stopped, and he dispatched Mark to the welcome hall with a perfunctory, "Welcome to Israel, Mr. Hayek."

The intercom system calls out flights in several languages, and Mark, still waiting for Antun, twiddles his used boarding pass between his fingers. He wonders how their first meeting will go. Antun must surely resent having someone involved in the probate who, although related, is a complete stranger. Mark has been up front in his e-mails, telling Antun that he's representing his mother only because she requested his help, mentioning her sorrowful and surprised gratitude that Sami remembered her in his will. In case Antun *was* upset with the situation, Mark also wrote that he would stay at a hotel, but Antun insisted that Mark stay with him, saying he would be insulted if Mark didn't.

A man who seems strangely familiar approaches the area. He doesn't have any luggage, so Mark doubts he was on the flight. He's a local, but Mark doesn't recall ever meeting anyone from Israel.

Perplexed, he studies the man's dark eyes, the beard-stubble shadow, and the slightly spiked black hair. In spite of the extra weight the guy is carrying, Mark suddenly feels as if he's looking in a mirror—the resemblance is that strong. With a start, he realizes that this is Antun.

The big smile on Antun's face erupts into roaring laughter at seeing Mark's puzzlement. He stops a short distance away, clutching his stomach as if trying to contain his mirth. After a moment, he slaps his knees and straightens. "I'm sorry," he says, "but you look like you've seen a phantom."

"It's just that…"

"I know, I know. I didn't send a picture because I wanted to surprise you. We look like brothers." Antun clasps his fists to his chest. "And that is what I will be for you during your visit—your brother." He comes so close that when he stops, all Mark can see are his intense dark-brown eyes, filled with sincerity.

"My condolences for your loss," Mark says, edging back a step.

Tears fill Antun's eyes. "Thank you, my brother."

Mark attempts to avoid what he guesses is coming next. He sticks out his hand to shake Antun's, but his cousin pulls him into a typical Lebanese greeting. Mark hears sounds of choked-back amusement as he clumsily swings his head to and fro, from one side of Antun's face to the other, receiving and giving kisses, his nose at one point swiping his cousin's face.

Antun doesn't let go immediately after the last peck is done with. He grasps Mark's shoulders, pushing him to arm's length, and studies his face as he talks. "It's okay," he says, "that you and your mother are involved. This is what my father wanted, and so that's what I want. Family comes before everything."

Some of Mark's tension dissipates. "I'm glad you feel that way."

This close, Mark sees that Antun's features aren't entirely like those of a clone. His eyes are closer together than Mark's, his nose is larger, and his stockiness gives him a jowly appearance. The overall likeness *is* amazing, but there are good reasons for their resemblance. Antun is Lebanese, after all, besides being a cousin.

The strangeness of it strikes Mark. Besides his mother, this man is the only relative that Mark has seen since they left Lebanon when he was four. They are kin, and their common ancestors go back far in time. He pictures the three of them—his mother, Antun, and himself—standing at the end of a line filled with people-shaped dominoes all collapsed onto each other, the last ones pressing upon the three survivors who have not yet toppled.

When his cousin suddenly lets go and reaches down for one of the suitcases, Mark resists shuddering in relief at having his personal space back.

As Antun drives them to the neighborhood where he lives, Mark's ears ring from listening to his cousin's non-stop gabbing. He supposes that this is better, though, than being stuck with someone sullen and taciturn, the week-long visit spent in strained silence, or even worse—being in the constant company of someone who doesn't speak English.

"You speak English well," he interjects in order to contribute something.

Antun's old BMW swerves alarmingly as he pounds several times on the dash, letting out a short bark of laughter. "Seriously, cousin, you sound just like an American. Let's see: Arabic, Turkish, Hebrew, Italian, Spanish, French, and," he adds, with a flourish of his hand, "English. The Lebanese are like the Swiss with the number of languages we speak." He glances at Mark. "What? You only speak English?"

Mark bristles a little at the accusatory tone. "I know some Spanish. That's the only other language you really need in California." Mark doesn't mention that his mother has been trying to teach him French for years. Although he doesn't believe her, she says that he spoke excellent French when they arrived from Lebanon and did so until he began school.

"It's not important. I will be your brother *and* your translator while you're here. Does that suit you?"

"Fine," Mark says as they stop in front of a Parkomat garage. Once they get out and the car is secured, they walk the short distance to a newly renovated building and go up to Antun's place on the third floor. After showing Mark to a bedroom, Antun says, "*Mi casa es tu casa.*"

Mark puts down his suitcase. "*Gracias.*" His cousin is an agreeable sort. They will get along well enough.

Later, after he's unpacked and freshened up, Mark finds Antun in the living room. "This is a nice apartment," he says, glancing around. High ceilings give the place a spacious feeling.

The room is decorated in an expensive, modern style but with an abundance of ancient-looking vases, bowls, and other objects displayed. "Or is it your condominium?"

"I own the apartment, or you could call it a condominium— same thing." Antun's tone has become uncharacteristically cool. "I moved here several years ago, after my divorce."

Mark looks at him. "You were married?"

"For five years."

The curt reply alerts Mark that he's rubbed against something raw. "Sorry, I guess I'm being nosy, but I know so little about you. I don't even know what you do for a living." Again, he's sent all kinds of details about himself in his e-mails but hasn't received any back.

"No, no, you have every right to be curious. I have nothing to hide from you, my brother." Antun claps a hand on his chest, a gesture Mark decides is his customary manner of projecting sincerity. "I'm a simple antiquities dealer, here and in Turkey— that's why my home is full of these beautiful things from the past," he says, opening his arms expansively.

Mark's ears perk up. "The very-distant past is an interest of mine. I suppose you've seen the archaeological sites near here? The caves?"

Antun nods with enthusiasm. "Not in many years, but they are interesting—many different layers of occupation from thousands of years. We'll go see the ones at Mount Carmel—but not tomorrow. We're meeting with my father's solicitor. But the next day for sure." He reaches over and pats Mark's shoulder. "How does that sound, my brother?"

"I would like that," Mark says.

After a meal thrown together from Antun's refrigerator, Mark excuses himself, telling his cousin that he's worn out from his travels and needs sleep. Upon reaching the bedroom where they deposited his luggage, Mark takes out his laptop. Genetics and

Me should have his mother's genome posted by now. He's been dying to see it ever since the night he saw his own.

Mark also wants to find out if she's forwarded his uncle's e-mail that mentioned his cousin. Antun seems reliable enough, and he's affable, but Mark is curious about what was said in the message now that he's met him. He's sure there was only some sort of a typical father-son spat between them that his uncle brought up simply as an aside. He wonders if Antun knows he won't be getting his father's ashes.

When Mark can't open his browser, he realizes he doesn't have Antun's access password. Irritated, he shuts down the laptop, his eyes blurring from weariness as the screen goes blank. Across the room, the platform bed, with its clean lines and green coverlet, looks like a cool oasis. He stumbles across the room. The password can wait.

It becomes obvious the next morning how much Antun went out of his way to make himself look more like Mark for their first encounter. The man who greets him in the kitchen is clean-shaven, has slicked-down hair parted on one side, and is even dressed differently than the day before. His jeans and shirt are most likely designer-label brands. Antun exudes a strong fragrance of expensive cologne that easily overpowers the smell of fresh-brewed coffee. Mark is the dowdier version, looking as though he has perhaps been homeless for a while, living on the streets, unable to get a decent shave or nice clothes.

"Good morning, Mark. I hope you slept well, my brother."

Antun seems to be watching him closely, gauging his reaction to the change. Mark keeps his expression neutral. "Like the dead, thank you," he says and immediately wishes he'd chosen a different way to express himself, considering the reason he's with Antun. "And I need some of that great-smelling coffee in order to come back to life," he quickly adds. "Where do you keep your mugs?"

Mark looks toward the cabinets. He sees Antun as well as himself reflected in the glass-covered fronts. A distortion in the glass makes Antun's face appear to be smirking, filled with a devilish look. When Mark jerks his head around to face him, Antun is wearing an indulgent smile.

"No, no—you are my guest." Bowing like a waiter, he indicates a table against one wall. "Please sit down. How do you like your coffee?"

"Black," Mark says, feeling vaguely disconcerted. His own reflection hadn't been distorted in the glass. From across the room, he watches Antun pour the coffee. *Perhaps he is a chameleon.*

The attorney takes off her glasses and lightly taps a corner of the thick black frames on the conference table. She is somewhat attractive without them.

"The unsealed part of your father's revised will is very clear on this point. The probate cannot move forward, and the will cannot be read in its entirety until the deceased's ashes are collected from Turkey by his sister or, in this case, by Mr. Hayek here, whose paperwork I have, naming him legal representative." She speaks with an accent, but Mark doesn't have a problem understanding her.

Antun is the one having difficulty with comprehension. "Mrs. Aaron, I'm not disputing that this is what the will says. But it's ridiculous—and rather shocking. I've never heard of anyone Lebanese being cremated, or for that matter, anyone Israeli. And I don't think it's possible." He then says something that Mark thinks is in Hebrew.

"Let's stay with English please, shall we?" Mrs. Aaron motions at Mark with her glasses. "For Mr. Hayek's sake."

Mark looks at her gratefully.

Antun turns to Mark. "I was telling Mrs. Aaron that as far as I know, there isn't a crematorium in the entire country of Turkey. What are we to do? Ship his body elsewhere?"

"Ah, but there is one now," she says, and they both look at her. "On the Mediterranean coast. The city of Antalya tried for years to get one approved because of their crowded graveyards—and as a convenience to expatriates. It was completed two months ago, shortly before Mr. Lahoud—Sami—had his will redone. His remains were sent to the crematorium by his Turkish solicitor." She looks in apology at Mark. "He always asked that I called him by his first name."

"Has he already been cremated, then?" Antun asks.

"Yes, he has."

His eyes shoot animosity in her direction. "For the record, I resent not having had the opportunity to see his body beforehand, and I want to know the details of the original will." His voice is gruff and demanding.

Mark shifts in his chair, concerned by this change in his cousin's demeanor. He watches the solicitor for her reaction.

Mrs. Aaron frowns and puts her glasses back on. "Everything is being done exactly as Sami wished. He insisted that we delete the previous testament from our computers. Sami himself shredded every hard copy of the old will."

"Well, can't you at least give us the gist of the new one?"

She sighs. "I risk repeating myself, but my hands are tied until the urn containing his ashes is brought to this office. The entire document will then be perused, and everyone will know the details." Her lips close in a tight line.

Mark believes that Antun will respond heatedly, but he only gives a small smile and shrugs. "I suppose I'll have to be patient."

Mrs. Aaron taps her forefinger on the table. "I will tell you, though, that Sami wanted his final resting place to be in Lebanon, near where his brother-in-law died—your father." Her nod at Mark is full of respect, almost deferential. "He thought his sister could more easily do this if he were cremated. It may be some time before it's safe enough for her to go there with his ashes—I hope that she will someday." Mrs. Aaron pauses and looks pointedly at Mark. "Until such time, the urn will remain in California."

She spreads a palm over the file in front of her. "Gentlemen, if there are no more questions, I have clients waiting."

A question immediately pops into Marks mind, but he's not about to ask it. His mother told him that she was inheriting half of Sami's estate. *From what source did she get her information if the will's details haven't been released yet?* Attorney McNeal hadn't mentioned that detail during Mark's short meeting with him. Perhaps she was mistaken and the only things she'll receive from the estate are the ashes and a few token items.

"I don't have any," Mark says. "Thank you for your time." He looks at Antun, expecting him to protest not being the one to take possession of the urn, but his cousin only shakes his head without looking up.

"May you have a safe trip to Turkey, then," Mrs. Aaron says, and the three of them stand up. She shakes their hands before they leave.

During the drive back to the apartment, Mark mulls over everything he's heard. He feels bad that Antun wasn't given an opportunity to see his father's body before he was cremated. "I'm sorry that Uncle Sami did things this way. He certainly never mentioned any of this to my mother."

Antun shrugs. "It's not a problem. We should respect the final wishes of our loved ones. Right?"

"Yes," Mark says, hoping Antun will change the subject.

But Antun doesn't say anything at all; he's glumly staring out over the steering wheel. The sound of traffic through the open windows fills the void. Mark glances from time to time at his cousin's morose face. Only a short while has passed since Sami's death. Despite all of his earlier animated good cheer, Antun must still be in mourning for his father. Mark respects his cousin's silence, not making comments or asking questions about what he sees along the streets.

At the Parkomat, Antun still appears downcast, watching distractedly as the car is automatically lifted and shunted into place. He sighs deeply, but then without warning, he claps his hands together loudly.

Mark starts at the sound.

"I have a treat for you!" Antun says brightly. He turns his smile on Mark like a spotlight.

"We'll pick up falafel for lunch a few blocks from here. They have the best in the city." He starts walking away. "Come on, it's just around the corner."

"I haven't eaten falafel in a long time," Mark says. "I've forgotten what it tastes like."

"I know. Don't tell me. You eat American hamburgers."

"Cheeseburgers, usually."

"I knew it."

Mark munches on pita bread filled with crunchy green balls of falafel as they return the short distance to the apartment. He has to admit that it's very good.

"All the legal talk has made us gloomy," Antun remarks. "My father enjoyed life. He would want me to show you a nice time, so we'll go out later. Out on the town. Isn't that what Americans say?"

"Yes—out on the town. Thank you, that sounds good," Mark says. He's relieved at the mood change. Silent Antun is harder to take than long-winded Antun.

At the apartment, Antun excuses himself, saying he's going to his study. He needs to answer client e-mail and get paperwork done. He suggests that Mark rest up before the night's activities. The mention of e-mail reminds Mark that he needs Antun's Wi-Fi password.

He's at a loss when Antun hesitates, a shadow crossing his face.

"I didn't have time to look into a rate plan for my cell, so I didn't bring it. I told my mother I'd e-mail her," Mark says. *Surely he doesn't think I'm a security risk.*

"Of course, of course. Here, I'll write it down." Antun writes on a notepad, rips off the page, and passes it over. "You can use my mobile phone if you'd like to." He takes his phone out of a pocket. "The password for it is the same as the last four digits of the Wi-Fi one."

"No, no, I prefer e-mail." Sensing Antun's puzzlement at his refusal of the phone, he adds, "E-mail is fine."

Antun gets up to leave the room. "I hope I won't have to, but I may leave to meet with a client this afternoon. Help yourself to anything you need while I'm gone. I'll see you later."

"Thank you. I will."

Settling at the small desk in the guest room, Mark gets out his laptop and enters the password, but he stops before tapping the key to join the network. His cousin's reticence at providing the password is weighing on him. He wonders if security problems are even more common in Israel than in the US, then he has another disturbing thought. What if Antun somehow gets access to Mark's e-mails and sees the one that Sami sent his mother? Perhaps his cousin is a technology wizard and can do those kinds of things.

Stumped for a moment, he puts his hands in his lap. Then he thinks of a solution. If Antun does go out, Mark can slip down to one of the many coffee shops he's seen and find Wi-Fi. But coffee shop link-ups carry risks also—and that's just playing to paranoia.

Uncertain about what action to take, Mark decides he won't do anything for a while. Making a frustrated sound, he shuts down his computer and moves over to the bed. He does need a nap before they go out, but first, he will try and work out why he feels this ridiculous lack of trust toward everyone he encounters. *Am I really an "antisocial geek-monkey," like Sandy said?* However, when he lies down, his residual jet lag drags him into sleep before a single coherent thought crosses his mind.

CHAPTER 5

Western Asia, Late Pleistocene

AS THEY STOOD WATCHING, THE other hyenas, alerted by the one that had spotted them, turned in Raven and Leaf's direction. Their eyes, noses, and rounded ears were dark smudges. They began circling around each other with their tails carried high, cackling wildly, as if discussing their next move.

Leaf calmly let go of Raven's arm. "Follow me," he said. His pouch bouncing lightly on his back, he began to run toward the hyenas. Raven paused for only a heartbeat before leaping after him. The hyenas were coming directly at them, even though the beasts were still at some distance, and it took all of Raven's will not to turn and dash in the opposite direction.

After a short distance, Leaf veered into the woods before again turning to circle the lake. Raven followed, her heart going even faster than her feet. He was heading for the path leading toward camp, but she didn't understand why he thought they could out-run the hyenas. Their excited giggles sounded ever closer.

Leaf stopped abruptly under a tree. He slid his spear up to rest across several branches then pulled himself onto a wide limb. Balancing there, he helped Raven up as she reached the trunk. They moved higher, their progress slowed by Leaf having to maneuver his spear through the branches. He stopped mid-tree and sat on a forked limb. Looking down at Raven, he patted a branch near him, and she climbed onto it.

A few moments later, the hyenas were under the tree, searching for them. The beasts didn't think to look up at first and scrambled about, urinating and sniffing the soil for tracks, all the while grunt-laughing. One came closer and began nosing around the trunk. It squatted, resting its front paws on the bark. As it straightened in order to smell higher, it looked upward, right into Raven's face.

For a few heartbeats, the hyena observed her, head tilting to one side in curiosity, its dark eyes oddly hypnotic. The wet nose rooted the air to smell her. Then its large maw opened, revealing rows of sharp white teeth. A triumphant cackle erupted from its long throat, and its front paws scrabbled against the tree trunk. Raven started and almost lost her balance. She grasped an overhead limb to keep from falling, while the hyenas climbed over each other's backs, snarling, trying to see up into the tree.

Leaf jabbed his spear downward. Whooping, the hyenas scattered, their short hind legs bent close to the ground, tails straight out behind them. They were gone for only a few moments before returning.

"Go away, you miserable beasts," Raven shouted at them.

"Hold this for me." Leaf passed his spear over to Raven, pulled his pouch around in front, and took out a ram's horn. Blowing through a hole in the pointed end, he gave three long blasts. At the noise, the hyenas fled once more.

Leaf looked at Raven. "That will bring help—if we're not too far away to be heard. Hopefully, Bear's group hasn't reached camp yet. I spotted them on the way there while you were bathing." He blew three more blasts before putting away the horn. "Keep this for me, too," he said, holding out the pouch. "I need to be as nimble as possible."

She took it from him, looking at him askance. "But what are you doing?"

"I don't like them any more than you do, but I want to make sure they stay until Bear can get here."

He began slowly climbing downward. At first, the hyenas didn't notice him. They were busy rubbing their hindquarters on nearby bushes, secreting white paste all over the leaves. The strong rancid-grease odor assaulted Raven, and she once again struggled with nausea.

When Leaf was on the bottom branches again, the hyenas came bounding back. He rapidly climbed up a short distance, just out of reach of their jaws. Yapping in their faces, he began taunting them. They became frenzied, leaping upward as he dangled a foot. Whenever they calmed, he would rattle branches and pretend to climb down, rousing them again.

Suddenly, their wild cackles changed to squeals of fear and pain. Three of them stumbled away from the tree, spears hanging from their ribs. Bear and his men followed the wounded ones closely, wielding clubs and spears. The other two beasts darted toward the lake, hind legs bent low, tails tucked under their bellies. A handful of men chased them, spears held at the ready.

Unable to flee, the dying hyenas snarled and bit at the air as the men surrounded them. Through the foliage, Raven saw several clubs rising and falling. It was over quickly.

By the time Leaf recovered his spear and pouch from her and climbed down, the hyenas were dead. His disappointment was obvious as he trotted from one animal to the next. Raven was about to follow but changed her mind when she heard Bear's voice—better to wait until they'd all left, even if she stayed in the tree for the rest of the day.

Bear approached Leaf who stopped inspecting one of the beasts to face him. "It bothers me how near camp they were. You found them here?"

"No, I was coming from down the lake, heading for camp, when I saw them."

"They were also coming this way?"

Leaf hesitated. "No, they were going around the other side of the lake."

Bear frowned. "Help me understand," he said, his feet scuffing the ground. "They were on the other side—going away from you—but now they are closer to camp than when you first spied them. Why is that? Do I have to remind you about what happened only a few seasons ago? The baby snatched from under his mother's nose? That was hyena."

Leaf scowled. "I wasn't leading them to camp. I kept them here, didn't I? I had to get close enough for you to hear the horn." He tilted his chin up and looked directly at Bear. "Besides, I wasn't alone."

"Well, who was with you?" Bear asked. He waved his hand at the surrounding trees. "I don't see anyone."

Leaf glanced up to where Raven sat. She knew when his eyes met hers that he realized his mistake. He quickly averted his gaze, but to no avail. All of the men followed his glance, turning their faces upward, just as the hyenas had earlier.

Raven sighed, losing all hope that she might remain hidden. For all his scouting talent, Leaf wasn't crafty enough to deal with Bear. She climbed down, overly conscious of her bare legs, and dropped to the ground with a thump.

Bear stalked over, glowering. "You left this morning before anyone could warn you about the danger. What are you doing out this far? Surely enough plants grow near camp to satisfy any healer."

Raven didn't answer. If she defended herself in front of the others, it would only exacerbate his fury.

Bear turned to Leaf, his expression suspicious. "And you were sent to scout for hyena, not for this woman."

One of the men made a choking sound. He backed away under a tree, coughing loudly into his hands, his shoulders shaking.

Raven saw flames in Bear's eyes as his temper caught fire. He whirled toward her. A loud cracking noise went through the forest when the flat of his hand caught the side of her face. The blow spun her off balance, and she fell to her knees. Crouching, she clutched where she'd been hit, the skin stinging beneath her fingers.

An enraged cry came from Leaf, then the sounds of a struggle swept over her. "Let go of me!" he shouted.

"After I break your foolhardy head!" one of the men yelled. "Help me, somebody. He's slippery as a fish."

Raven heard quick footsteps and more tussling. After a short while, the clearing went quiet except for labored breathing and a few muttered oaths.

Bear's disdainful laugh filled the stillness. "Do you really want them to let you go, boy?"

"She was cleaning her leggings in the lake when I found her. I couldn't just leave her to the hyenas."

"You should have! After sating themselves with her tender flesh, they would have left for their caves to vomit her up so their pups could get a taste. We would have been rid of the beasts—and her, as well." A foot toed her bent form, and Bear chuckled as though he'd made a joke.

"I find their meat barely edible, but a lot of you enjoy it." His feet shifted beside her, taking turns nudging her ribs while he talked. "We'll butcher them here. I want the remains buried deeply, so that something else doesn't come into the valley."

The feet finally moved away. Raven stayed on the ground, her head bowed, paralyzed by humiliation and nausea.

The men who'd chased the other two hyenas returned, hooting about how they'd cornered and killed both beasts. Bear sent them back to butcher those, too.

After a short while, she heard his heavy footsteps approach again then saw his moccasins in front of her. He lifted her by an arm while she watched him warily through hair loosened from one of her braids.

"How can I make you understand?" he said in a low voice. "Willow was beside herself, not knowing where you were. You can't just wander away whenever you please." He breathed heavily several times, an impatient sound. "I had to punish you so that you will learn; you made me do that."

His blameless tone incensed her. Before he'd hit her, the desire to hurt had contorted his face into something ugly and unleashed. She glared at him in disgust the same way she would a large, poisonous spider.

He stared back, as if he were trying to drown her in the black pools of his eyes. The sounds of butchering became muted, and the wind picked up, sighing through leaves. Raven felt her will throw up a barrier. A strange elation filled her. He would never completely dominate her, and one day, she would somehow be rid of him.

Bear snorted and broke eye contact. "I don't believe you've learned anything. Go to the lean-to and stay there." He looked at the two closest men who'd stopped working to listen. "You might as well get up since you're not doing anything. I have a chore for you." The two abashed men stood immediately. "Walk this woman back to camp, and return afterwards," he told them.

All of the camp's residents were away from their hearths that afternoon, but Raven remained in the lean-to. The two men who'd failed to adequately dispose of the aurochs remains were to be flogged in the central clearing. Everyone had been summoned to witness the thrashing and to hear Bear explain his reasons for doing so.

Willow woke Raven from a short slumber. Bear had sent her to let Raven know that she need not attend the gathering. Willow sat on the pallet and stared at Raven's swollen cheek as she gnawed the side of a thumb. "He's never once been rough with me. This isn't like him. He's changed."

Raven made a dry sound. "I irritate him. Bears don't like ravens. I've seen them swat at ravens while feeding." She placed a hand on Willow's arm. "The sad truth is that the situation will worsen if I live in the tents. We must convince Bear that I should make a hearth with Leaf."

"So you've decided that Leaf could be more than a brother. Or is this only desperation?"

"No, you were right. He's very near grown." She looked aslant at her sister from her watery, injured eye. "It will be a pleasure to watch him become a mature man."

"I almost envy you."

Her wistful voice was surprising. Willow had been entirely content when Raven first arrived. Raven's unhappiness was spreading in the way that an illness hopped from one person to another. The children couldn't help but be affected, as well. Surely Bear was capable of realizing that it would be better for everyone if Raven left his hearth.

"It's partly that Bear is overly wrought-up right now," Willow said. "His father's illness is no better. He's torn about whether he should leave him here or try and take him along when we leave for the steppes."

"I've not seen Old Wolf even once. Old Cloud hasn't asked for my help with him. All I do is gather plants. I'm pleased that I can help her that way," Raven added, not wanting to seem ungrateful.

But Willow was preoccupied with her own thoughts. "We'll have to approach Bear before long, though. An advance group leaves tomorrow for the caves. He won't take time to hear us out once the whole band begins moving." She paused for a moment.

"Don't look so worried. He's always been sensible." She pulled Raven into a quick embrace. "I have to go now, or he'll wonder why I'm not there."

Alone again, Raven sat on her pallet. She thought about going out by the hearth fire. There would be time to scoot back inside when everyone began returning from the thrashing. She got up but hesitated in front of the opening. The air was clear and still, and noises such as cracking whips and screams would carry well.

Bear wouldn't lash the men severely enough to make them useless for long. He was too practical for that. But Raven didn't want to hear their agony. She rearranged the pallet so she could crawl in and cover her ears and was about to slip inside the cocoon of skins and furs when she sensed a presence.

Looking up, Raven saw Leaf just inside the flap. She leapt up. "Are you trying to get us whipped also?"

He shook his head. "No one saw me leave, certainly not Bear. He was too caught up with putting forth the legend of himself as sole protector of the band." He held out a stone knife blade. "I came to return this. You dropped it when you were drinking the poison."

Raven cringed at those words. He'd witnessed her that morning at her worst, during one of the lowest points of her life.

Taking the knife from Leaf's hand, she remembered the one she'd given to the Longhead. Her father's red quartz blade was much nicer than the one Leaf had returned. Knives were difficult to retain, for some reason.

She stood there, tapping a finger on the blade, wishing to ask him a question but not wanting him to think her odd. She decided that it didn't matter. "Did you see a small cat limping beside the lake while I was sitting there? This may sound strange, but I'm beholden to that cat." She patted her stomach. "Because of it, this child still lives."

He nodded. "I've seen it. It's recently had kittens." He paused and nodded again, looking thoughtful. "It's a mother."

From the way he spoke, Raven knew he had some idea of why she'd changed her mind about the baby. "It can't hunt with an injured leg. I want to leave her food—if I can find the den."

"I'll locate it."

Smiling at his willingness, she bent to put the knife in her pouch.

When she straightened, he was right beside her. The way he moved without being heard was uncanny. In his hand, he held a small piece of highly worked, wrinkled leather that he was dampening with water from a small bladder. "Allow me," he said. "The ochre is smeared almost into your eye from where Bear—" He inhaled sharply.

His face was stony as he gently wiped her swollen cheek. "Forgive me for giving away your hiding place."

All remnants of her earlier irritation with him vanished. "You are forgiven."

He shook his head vigorously. "I have no excuse for it but my own stupidity."

"Truly, I've already forgotten it."

"I tried to hit him."

"I know."

He dabbed lightly around her eye. "Does it hurt?"

"Not very much."

His hand slowed, and she focused on his face, so near hers. He was eyeing her mouth so intently that she found her own eyes going down to *his* lips. They were pressed together in such a strained line that she took pity on him and leaned forward to kiss him.

He moved toward her like a dammed stream when barriers are removed. Raven found herself responding to his eagerness, and heated joy coursed through her. She could find happiness with this younger man. Of that, she was suddenly and breath-lessly certain. Any reservations she'd had earlier were forgotten.

Raven broke the kiss, gasping. "This is rash."

He groaned, sliding his mouth down over the hollow of her throat.

"I've talked to Willow," Raven said. "She'll speak with Bear about me moving to your hearth. You've said my secret is safe with you. But I must stress that Bear cannot find out I'm carry-ing his child, or he won't consent."

He pulled away abruptly and looked at her, his head slowly turning to the side so that he gazed at her out of the corner of his eye. She'd seen that bird stare of his before, and the cold accusation it contained chilled her. She didn't understand why her pregnancy might bother him at that moment, when it hadn't that morning. Possibly he believed that she wouldn't leave Bear's hearth.

"I swear that I will try my best, with Willow's help, to per-suade him," Raven said.

He turned his head to face her, his eyes shining again. "I believe you."

Although his fervent answer was reassuring, her unease lingered as she mulled over that earlier stare, so knowing and hostile. Leaf brushed her lips with his before going to the flap. After looking out for a moment, he left as quietly as he had entered.

Although the nausea had abated for a while, Raven suddenly felt very tired. It was the baby, she realized as she crawled under the furs. The child wanted her to be still. She obliged by sleep-ing for the rest of that day and on through the night. If the men being whipped cried out their agony, she didn't hear them.

When she left the lean-to early the next morning, she found a slave woman waiting outside. The woman accompanied her to the bottom area and back, ignoring all Raven's demands that she explain why she was following Raven like a shadow.

When she returned to the lean-to, Raven heard Bear come out of his tent, speaking with another man about hunting. She peeked around the flap. After talking for a bit longer, they left. Thinking she would go outside in Bear's absence, she put on her cape. But when she opened the flap, the same woman sat beside the hearth fire, and Raven realized that she'd been made a prisoner. The slave woman was her guard.

When the woman saw her and started over, Raven snatched the flap closed, but then she decided to pretend she needed to relieve her bladder again so she could at least get out for a short while. She stepped outside.

Willow was at the hearth fire when they returned, her face drawn. She deliberately ignored the guard as she went about preparing food. "I'll talk with you later, Raven," she called out.

Her sister didn't come right away, but the children slipped in from time to time throughout the morning, bringing her water and tidbits of food along with skins and tunics for mending.

Around midday, Raven heard Willow's raised voice. "I *will* take food to my own sister—Raven, open the flap."

Raven jumped up and held the skin aside as Willow brought in a large bowl of steaming stew. Raven swept the mending from a half-log to make a place for the bowl.

Willow's forehead puckered as she looked around the lean-to. "This is ridiculous. I won't stand for it." She picked up the bowl she had just put down. "Come with me. We'll eat in the tent."

"Are you sure? Seeing me there will harden Bear against us. He won't listen to anything we say."

"I do not care. He'll have to listen whether he wants to or not. I'm so unsettled that I can barely attend the children. I snap at them whenever they come near, and they are hurt by it. This can't go on."

Raven rose reluctantly and followed Willow outside.

"Go to the slave hut," Willow said to the slave woman as they crossed the clearing. "You aren't needed here."

The woman gave her an angry look but turned quickly on her heel and trudged away. Raven hoped that Bear wouldn't be too harsh on the woman for having left her post.

Willow sent the children to look for frogs and turtles at a nearby stream while she and Raven mended skins. Willow held the pieces of rent leather firmly on a smooth stone slab while Raven punched small holes around the torn areas and through the patches underneath, using a small bone awl. They would stitch the parts together later with a bird bone needle and sinew.

Every time she glanced at her sister's determined face, Raven felt hope mixed with trepidation. A tremor went through her shoulders when she thought about Bear arriving and seeing her in his tent instead of in the lean-to.

Late in the afternoon, they heard men talking and laughing out at the hearth. Bear's voice, full of good humor, drowned out the others. "We'll grow fat on all the game we've taken today. No leftover hyena for tonight's meal!"

Raven looked up at Willow, and they stared at each other.

"This is a good time," Willow whispered.

The others nosily took their leave, and Bear opened the flap. He stopped short just inside. "What are you—?"

"I asked her to help me mend skins." Willow smiled sweetly. "We heard you talking about the hunt. Sit and tell us what you've brought back. Here, I'll make room for you." She put aside the mending and moved over. "But first—" She paused and nodded at Raven. "We also have good news."

He raised his brows, not moving to sit.

Willow glanced up. "Bear, please sit down."

Instead of sitting where Willow had made a place for him at her side opposite Raven, he sat down heavily between them.

There was something aggressive and off-putting about the way his large male body suddenly separated them. "Now that I'm seated, please tell me. What is this news?"

"Leaf has let it be known that he's searching for a mate. Raven has agreed to join with him, although he hasn't been told yet." Willow's laughter was as soft as a summer breeze, and she waggled a finger. "We can be certain that he won't have any objections." She stood and stepped over Bear's legs. Taking Raven's hands, she pulled her up and kissed her on both cheeks. "My dear sister will finally have her own hearth again."

They both turned to smile down at Bear, showing him faces of sisterly accord. After a moment, the corners of Raven's mouth began quivering from the effort.

Bear stared up at Raven. "Don't you want a child before you're an old woman?"

Willow laughed softly again. "I'm sure Leaf will be happy to help the Earth Mother provide her with one."

"How do you think that barely fledged boy can succeed where her dead mate couldn't and I—" He snorted, and although he looked at Willow, his finger pointed at Raven. "The Earth Mother made that woman's spirit overly stubborn. Only a man at the peak of his strength will overcome that defect—if she isn't barren." He shook his head, his expression full of disbelief. "You women, hatching that idea. That boy is still a sapling!"

"He's a rapidly growing sapling that has lately taken on heft," Willow said.

A cicada began rasping nosily near the tent, interrupting the growing silence within. Willow began again, her voice rising over the cicada. "Why don't we find—"

"Shh, be quiet." Bear inclined his head toward the flap. They listened as the insect's rasping developed into a full drone before finally fading away.

"You hear that?" he asked. "Summer is almost upon us, and we haven't yet moved out of the valley." He ran his hand across his chin. "I have enough to deal with without this nonsense. I'll find her a mate from another band or tribe as soon as possible. She's nothing but a problem. It's best that she goes elsewhere."

Discussing her as if she weren't there was typical of him. Leaving Willow's side, Raven walked to the flap. "Whenever someone agreeable is found, I'll go with him," she said and left the tent.

With smarting eyes, Raven strode from the clearing. She remembered Leaf's happiness when she'd promised to try to join with him, and she dreaded seeing him again. He would think she'd failed him.

She went down a path, searching for a quiet place where she could gather her thoughts. Hearing twigs crackling underfoot, she glanced back and saw that Bear was following. She turned down another path and walked faster, but leaves rustled behind. She glanced back again. He was even closer—a snake slithering after her. Her brow tightened, and her head began to hurt.

"Just wait, woman!" he called out. "I have something to tell you."

She went a few more steps before stopping to face him. She could probably outrun him, but that would achieve little.

He smiled as he approached, but she knew that smile all too well—his full wolf smile, the eyeteeth on glimmering display.

"I don't know where you think you're going," he said when he reached her.

She looked at him, expecting to be ordered back to the lean-to.

He caught her look. "It's all right. You don't have to stay in the lean-to anymore. Not ever again."

She watched him doubtfully.

"I wasn't thinking clearly. There's no need to search elsewhere." He shook with barely contained mirth. "I have just the mate for you. Conveniently, he's here in camp—at least until tomorrow. I'm sure you've seen him walking about."

At first, she didn't understand whom he was talking about, but then she remembered the stork-legged, big-bellied man she'd seen several mornings before—the Wanderer.

"He's even from our tribe," Bear said. "Since you've shown such a desire to leave my hearth, you can begin by staying with him in the guest tent tonight. That way, when he leaves, you'll be there, ready for traveling. A group is heading for the caves tomorrow. The pair of you can go along with them."

His smile went from ear to ear. "I'm sure he'll agree to it. He used to travel with a woman, but I haven't seen her in a while. She used to help him haul goods for swapping, and I'm sure he misses a woman's warmth at night."

Her eyes were blinking rapidly, and although she knew he saw her distress, she couldn't compose herself.

"What? I was expecting your gratitude. Well, if you decide that he isn't to your liking, there is another choice. You can leave for the steppes tomorrow morning—by yourself. I'm not worrying about you any longer."

His face took on that tense, predatory look he always wore when he slipped inside the lean-to, and his hand reached for her shoulder. "But I want to try one last time for that baby," he said, pushing her against the tree behind her.

He pressed against her, and she could feel his excitement against her abdomen—where the child grew. Raven's growing panic went beyond her revulsion at remembering the Wanderer's greasy hair and leering mouth. A baby wouldn't thrive being constantly dragged from band to band. And what if the Wanderer resented a small child's needs slowing his travels?

He would swap her baby away.

She cried out like a wounded bird. "Willow will hate you for this, and the child I carry will die with me on the steppes."

Bear backed away. "What did you say?"

"I had very little moon blood." She spat her words at him. "I bear your child."

His mouth dropped before snapping shut. "Sly vixen—why were you lying? Does Willow know?"

She shook her head. "No."

"Why didn't you tell us? Surely not because of Willow's foolishness about Leaf?"

She didn't reply.

His mouth curled in a smirk. "Never mind. But you're not the only one who lies well. I wasn't really going to turn you over to the Wanderer."

They stood staring at each other. Raven's tongue clung dryly to the roof of her mouth. She was suddenly very thirsty.

"Work harder at getting along with me, Raven," he said, his voice a warning. "Willow can raise the child just as well as you—have no doubts." He paused. "I won't undo your lie. I have no desire to live with two quarreling sisters. Tell Willow that you're with child whenever you like." He turned toward the path, stomping back the way he'd come.

Raven didn't try to untangle her thoughts as she returned to camp. She emptied her mind and kept her eyes dry, focusing on her surroundings. In spite of the many birds flitting from tree to tree, the air they crossed seemed vast and empty. Her only consolation was that Bear hadn't insisted on walking with her.

CHAPTER 6

The Levant, Present Day

Antun's driving en route to the Mount Carmel Caves is making Mark's hangover worse. He tells his cousin that he's still feeling the night before and that he'll nod off for a while. Mark doesn't really believe he can sleep; he just hopes the nausea will lessen once he closes his eyes and the scenery stops racing by. And feigning sleep will also quiet Antun; every glib word from his cousin is a small hammer tapping Mark's skull.

"I thought you Americans were big drinkers," Antun says.

"Not this American." Mark is dehydrated, having limited his water intake to very small sips to keep down the nausea, and the hot air blowing through the windows is making his mouth even drier. "I wonder if we could let up some of the windows."

"Sorry, but the air conditioner isn't working." Antun chuckles. "Believe me, we need the windows open."

His cheerfulness is aggravating. Antun doesn't seem to be suffering any ill effects from the excesses of the night before. Mark lets his head fall back on the headrest, quickly closing his eyes as the BMW swerves across the centerline to pass the car in front. But his hangover and Antun's driving aren't the only reasons Mark is less than chipper.

They began the evening at an outdoor café on Shenkin, a narrow street near Antun's apartment, filled with shops and restaurants. Even before the food had been served, two women showed up at the table. Antun promptly stood, asking the women to join them. Mark stood, too, as Antun introduced him.

"This is my cousin, Mark—a very prominent and famous scientist from California in the States. Mark, my friend Leah."

Blond and Slavic, Leah probably possessed Russian ancestry. She reached over and shook his hand.

"And this is Yasmin," Antun said, indicating the second woman, who moved forward.

Mark was caught off guard when she ignored his proffered hand, swooping around to brush her lips against his cheek. He returned her greeting with a quick peck. She looked to be somewhere in her twenties.

"Scientist, yes, but I don't know about—"

"Don't be so modest, cousin," Antun said. As Leah and Yasmin's glances took him in, their smiles appraising him favorably, he had actually winked at Mark. "He's renowned all over the world."

A little later, when the women went to seek out the restroom, he tried to set Antun straight. "Why did you tell them that crap about me being prominent and famous? It's not true—it's not necessary that you flatter me."

"But that's what they want to believe. Israeli women love brilliant scientists. Lighten up—enjoy the night, my brother." When Mark frowned, he said, "There's no harm done. Here, have more wine. I ordered the best."

Mark did have more—and then even more. In spite of his earlier irritation with Antun, he soon found that he was enjoying the evening. The excellent wine, along with a certain kind of coaxing from Yasmin, created a building sense of elation, keeping him pleasantly rooted in the immediate present.

Her English wasn't that good, but everything he said seemed to fascinate her. She leaned in, long black hair falling forward, her dark eyes drifting from his eyes to his mouth every time he spoke, concentrating on understanding him. She was quite beautiful—Sephardic ancestry, he was sure. Her ancestors must have migrated from Spain five hundred years before, spreading across the world during all that time.

Antun and Leah withdrew into their own conversation, and Yasmin scooted her chair a little closer to Mark, enveloping him in the scent of her sweet-smelling perfume. Every time she responded to something he said, he felt the fingers of a well-manicured hand upon his leg nurturing their conversation, emphasizing her words with a light tapping over his knee or a scraping of red fingernails along his lower thigh.

After a short while of this focused attention, he realized that he was getting an erection, and he wondered if she was aware of the effect she was having on him. To lessen the intensity, he looked away, lifting his glass to his mouth. As he took a sip, he caught Antun staring across the table at them, his eyebrows raised. Out of the corner of his eye, Mark thought he saw Yasmin nod.

His erection started fading, and the night suddenly took on an unearthly clarity. He became overly aware of his surroundings: the lights and noise from the street and the other three at the table, their closeness almost suffocating, their mouths constantly moving, their eyes flashing like little knives. He shook himself mentally, and the world settled somewhat, becoming coherent again.

Mark managed to carry on as before. He held up his end of the conversation with them, smiling or laughing when he knew it was expected. Even after Antun paid the bill and they returned with the women to the apartment, he kept up appearances. When a drunk Antun began swearing his ballyhoo about how Mark was more like a brother than a cousin, Mark enthusiastically swore that he felt the same way about Antun.

But after Antun disappeared down the hall with Leah, Mark became weary of the effort. He sat on the couch, where Yasmin joined him. She turned his head toward her and began kissing him. Mark tried to respond, but he kept picturing Antun's face with his eyebrows flying up.

When she started fondling him, he moved her hand. "I've had too much to drink. It won't be any good." He went over to a window and, after standing there a moment, opened it to gaze down over the quiet, leafy street.

"How do you know it won't be good if you won't try?" she asked, coming up behind him. She began again with her fingers, running them around his ribs and down to his pants. "What do you like?"

"Stop it," he said, louder than he'd intended. A man walking down the street looked up at him.

Yasmin stiffened. "What is the problem?" When he didn't answer, she took her hands away and went back to the couch.

He glanced over his shoulder. Yasmin's face looked clouded as she reclined there, her dress riding high on her thighs. Mark was sorry that she was offended. The way the evening had turned out wasn't her fault. He sat in the chair across from her.

"Talk," he said mildly. "I would like you to do just that—tell me your life story. I will be *indebted* to you for doing so," he said in a measured way.

She sat up, straightening her shoulders, her breasts pushing enthusiastically against her low-cut top.

Any lingering doubts as to the nature of their short acquaintance were immediately clarified by how she perked up at the word "indebted." Mark felt like a fool for thinking her attentions had reflected sincere interest.

He soon found that she'd misunderstood his request. By asking Yasmin about her life story, he'd meant her actual history from birth—details about her parents, where she'd lived, and so forth. Instead, she began telling him about her sexual adventures in graphic detail, beginning with her early teenage years.

Giggles escaped her as she searched for the exact words to describe her girlish escapades. "You know what I mean." She tossed her hair back, tittering about an episode with a professor after she'd entered university. "He bent me over his desk."

He began to feel aroused again in spite of himself and was considering joining her on the couch when Antun and Leah came back into the room. Their sudden appearance vexed him. He'd meant to slip Yasmin some money after she'd talked for a while, but he felt awkward about doing that with the others there.

Antun's curious prying eyes took in Yasmin before turning on Mark. "Alas, these busy ladies are going on to other places tonight. Regrettably, we must now say our farewells."

With an effort, Mark pushed himself up from the chair, but Antun held out a hand, forefinger wagging. "Don't get up. I'll show them out. Just relax. I'll be back in a minute."

Before he could sit again, Yasmin crossed over and gave him a clinging hug. She was perhaps still hoping for at least a tip, but Mark had grown numb. His fingers barely clasped her during the time she pressed against him. She broke away suddenly, and he saw her sulky face slip away behind Antun.

Mark wanted nothing more than to retreat to his bedroom, but upon hearing voices coming from below the window he'd earlier opened, he couldn't stop himself from going over and looking out. The evening was not quite finished with him yet.

Antun and Yasmin were on the steps outside the building's entry. Leah waited a small distance down the street, glancing back impatiently as she lit a cigarette. Hebrew, harsh and guttural, drifted upward, the two voices interrupting and tumbling over each other. The only words Mark understood were a loud string of sarcastic "okays" from Antun as he counted money into Yasmin's open palm.

Without bothering to close the window, Mark staggered down the hall until he found the right room, and entered. His fumbling fingers locked the door. Stripping as he went, he was unclothed by the time he reached the shower. With the water running over his head, he forced himself to put the night's events out of his mind by thinking about the upcoming trip to the caves. He would be on the same part of the Earth where Neanderthals had once lived. But try as he might to forget her, Yasmin's disappointed face kept floating through his thoughts.

Mark hears a voice as if it's coming from a great distance. "Wake up, cousin." Someone is shaking him. "We're at the caves."

His lids feel gritty when they open, and he struggles to orient himself. When he sees Antun, everything that's occurred since he left home trots through his brain.

Now that the car has slowed, the air no longer cools him. He's sticky all over. Mark rubs his eyes and steals another look at his cousin. He's grateful that Antun is being more reserved than usual. Antun has barely mentioned the night before, acting almost as if it never happened. The car pulls into a parking lot. Mark reaches into the backseat for his camera and backpack, and they get out. Bleary-eyed, he trudges along the path leading to the entry.

"I see you're dressed for the occasion," Antun says with a laugh, indicating Mark's T-shirt. Earlier, while they were waiting for the car at the Parkomat, Mark saw him eyeing the faded shirt disdainfully, but he didn't make any comment at the time.

Mark now relates the sequence of events that led to him receiving the shirt. He tells Antun how all peoples with European and Asian ancestry carry Neanderthal genes. Mock horror fills Antun's voice as he looks at the image on the front. "What? He's no relative of mine."

"Don't be so sure." Mark taps the top of the shirt. "It says here that I have three percent ancestry, and you and I are related."

"That may be so, but I do not claim him."

A flare of indignation heats Mark, but he douses it quickly. Antun isn't exactly insulting a close relative.

But then with a dry voice, Antun says, "Must come from your father's side."

Mark's brow crinkles, and the pain that has been ebbing revives with a small stab to his right temple.

"What a face! I'm only jesting," Antun says.

"I know, I know. It's not you. I'll take an aspirin in a few minutes and get rid of my headache. I'll be fine."

Mount Carmel looms over them. In spite of his malaise, Mark is excited when he picks out the three main cave entrances on the pocked, rocky face. To think that Neanderthals once went up the same trails that he'll be climbing in a few moments is mind-boggling. His day can only get better.

Chapter 7

Western Asia, Late Pleistocene

R AVEN GLANCED AT THE SKY, once more checking the sun's progress. The bright orb had shifted very little since the last time she'd looked. Bear flexed his body, signaling his discomfort, the movement only seeming to tighten the ropes around them. Their binding ceremony had been going on all afternoon, and the binders, snickering and making earthy comments, had been overly enthusiastic when winding the ropes the last time. Raven and Bear had already been bound twice by then, the first time while standing side-by-side and the second time while standing back-to-back.

For the final binding, they faced each other. Her mounded stomach pressed against him, and Raven could barely breathe. She turned her face sideways, so as to not have her nose continuously poking into his chest. Flowers woven throughout the braided ropes gave off an odor so strong that she had to resist sneezing, yet she could still detect Bear's robust and all-too-familiar smell. She had dreaded the day, but his dour docility was a relief after her nightmare during the night before. In that terrifying dream, the band had tied her to a real bear, a moaning creature that she thought would tear her apart at any moment.

All the band was gathered, drinking honey water and feasting from the hearth in front of the largest cave—all except those who were too ill to attend—and Leaf, who had not yet put in an appearance. Raven didn't think he would come, even though he risked facing Bear's wrath because of his lack of respect. She scanned the wide outcrop above them anyway, her eyes lingering at each of the two cave mouths in turn to see if she could catch a glimpse of him somewhere.

Trilling ululations came from behind Raven, and she stopped searching as the sound surged over them. The women, single file, led by a beaming Willow, came in and out of Raven's vision as they danced with small steps, circling the couple. Their high-pitched calls gave way to chanting, and several men playing vulture-bone flutes joined the women. Momentarily forgetting her discomfort, Raven smiled, enjoying the distraction. She caught Willow's eye the next time she passed, and their shared hopefulness saturated the air between them. Her sister had been overjoyed when Raven finally told her that she was with child, never suspecting that she'd been pregnant all along.

Eventually, Willow and the other chanters left after crying out one last time, their exuberance pouring across the steppe. Alone again with Bear, Raven tried not to fidget as his heavy silence wore at her. She sensed his mood becoming darker, and she felt the same strong awareness of danger she had during her dream the night before. Finally, the sun slipped below the land, and they were unbound. Raven shook out her tense hands and arms in relief.

She followed him the short distance up to the nearest cave as the group below yelled their encouragement, calling for the Earth Mother to aid them in their endeavors. They would be given a short period of privacy that evening, a rarity at the crowded caves, the idea being to provide them with a good opportunity for beginning a family. But of course, with Raven already carrying a child, that was merely custom.

Since the band had moved into the two caves half a moon cycle before, Bear had seldom approached Raven. When he did seek her out, his exertions were over quickly, and they were subdued compared to his previous energetic lustiness. After the seclusion of the lean-to, he had difficulty adjusting to the open lifestyle of the caves, where nothing was ever completely hidden. A limited privacy could be afforded by draping skins and fur blankets over poles held by forked branches set into the cave floor. But the caves were often chaotic, and when a toddler ran into a pole and began screaming under the fallen blankets, Bear had jumped up, straightening his clothes and cursing as he fled outside.

He began searching for her away from the caves. Several times, he came upon Raven at the nearby river and pulled her with him into the trees that grew there, displaying his old vigor. She began gathering plants elsewhere to avoid him. He was, at least, showing Willow more attentiveness than he had in the valley, sleeping at her side every evening. Raven noticed that his irritation with blankets hung over poles lessened late at night when he thought most people, including Raven, were sleeping.

Once they entered the cave and the well-wishers' shouts faded, Raven fully expected Bear to take advantage of their solitude, but he surprised her.

"I need sleep," he said. "There are too many crying babies every night. I stayed outside with the sleepless old ones most of last night, listening to their tales and feeding the hearth fire."

Delighted that he was leaving her alone, she made sympathetic clucking sounds. Raven occasionally went out if she awoke for a while during a particular night, although she wasn't fond of doing so. Tending the fires throughout the night was an important chore in keeping the camp safe, but she didn't look forward to the day when, because of age, she would sleep less and be expected to join the fire-tenders.

"The band has become overly large," he said. "I'll split it in two before we return to the valley next fall if a group doesn't leave voluntarily during the summer."

Her ears perked up at that information. If Old Cloud left with the separating group, then Raven could become band healer. A pang of guilt cut short that line of thought. Old Cloud had shown her nothing but kindness, and Raven shouldn't have been wishing her away.

Bear sprawled out on some furs and was soon snoring. He often seemed uneasy when she was around, but that didn't stop him from sleeping. Raven attributed his discomfort to the fact that she was a healer. Many people believed that those women who understood medicines were somehow unnaturally close to the Earth spirits found within every living and non-living thing. Raven had never felt, though, that she had any type of mystical connection to those spirits. Her dreams often seemed out of the ordinary, but everyone considered their dreams to be strange.

Raven sat down quietly a short distance from Bear. From watching him sleep, it wasn't obvious that he was a man who insisted on dominating his world. Relieved from all concern, his face was smooth and benign. Since she and Bear were bound through traditional ritual, Raven dared to hope that they would learn to tolerate each other, for Willow's sake as well as her own—and for the sake of the unborn baby.

Regret filled her, though, whenever she thought of Leaf, and she wondered where he'd gone. He no longer constantly followed on her heels, and she missed him badly. Several times while gathering plants, she was sure she'd spotted him near the river, but it always turned out to be someone else.

The growing desire to see him became a painful tightness in her chest, usually at night, when she was no longer occupied by the day's work. She often thought about their last time together, what they'd both said and done, and she always wondered if he'd ever found the mother cat.

Her anguish continued until Leaf finally did turn up, a good half-moon after the joining ceremony, but although Raven had glimpsed him at the edges of several hearths, she'd not yet been near enough to look into his eyes and see if he hated her. He walked away each time she tried to get close. Raven couldn't follow, because everyone would see her chasing after him. She heard from Willow that he was staying by himself at night in a small overhang cave he'd found nearby. Raven tried not to worry about him. He'd always scouted by himself and knew how to be careful when alone. He always took care to leave the cave area well before sundown so that darkness wouldn't catch him crossing the steppe.

Although she couldn't blame Leaf for ignoring her, his aloofness hurt, and she searched for a means to let him know that she regretted how things had turned out. Still, she had to be cautious. Gossip was always present in the overcrowded caves. She was especially careful to not even look Leaf's way whenever Bear was nearby.

One evening, a party of hunters that included Leaf returned at dusk with an already-butchered aurochs as well as several deer. Raven expected Leaf to leave immediately, but he joined the group working on the venison. She felt a tingle of excitement as twilight approached, making it less likely he would leave for his overhang that night.

By the time they were finished, not only was it full dark under a moonless sky, but the band had not yet eaten the portions set aside for a meal. Raven was among the women cooking those choice parts, continuously turning a skewer over a fire made larger and hotter than usual so the meat would brown quickly. Everyone was gathered close by in anticipation. Almost a week had passed since the band had eaten from a major kill, and their daily meals had consisted of watered-down stews of rabbits and other small animals mixed with roots and greens.

Children began straying closer to the fire as the tantalizing smells honed their hunger. The small daughter of the woman cooking beside Raven was pulling on her mother's tunic, whining to be fed. The mother loosened the clinging hands. "You'll eat soon enough. Now let me be." She shoved the child away, who stomped a short distance from the fire and fell on the ground in a tantrum, screaming and kicking up dust.

"I'll find one of the older girls to watch the young ones if you'll keep an eye on my skewer," Raven said.

The mother nodded, and Raven went in search of Dawn. The child must have thought Raven was coming to fetch her, because she jumped up and ran from the group, her little legs churning at top speed. Even when she reached the edge of the light thrown from the blazing hearth, she showed no signs of slowing.

Raven darted after her into the night. As she entered darkness, a tall, shadowy form passed in front of her.

"I've got you—hush now," Leaf's firm voice said.

The little girl's cries became whimpers.

Raven moved toward them, barely able to discern their forms, although she knew that Leaf could see her silhouetted clearly in the glare from the hearth. She reached out to touch his arm. "I'll take her, Leaf."

Her hand found only air, and then she saw him outlined against the firelight, gliding back to the group.

"I'm sorry," she called after him, her voice breaking, but he showed no sign of having heard.

Hidden from the others by darkness, she stood for a moment, biting her lip and watching the bustling life around the hearth. After composing her face, she reentered the light and began searching for Dawn.

By the time the band had been at the caves for a full moon, routines had become fully established, based around the never-ending quest for food and its preparation. Scouts searched for animal herds daily, and when they were found, hunting parties quickly formed. Many women also hunted, catching small game with traps and using slingshots and throwing sticks to bring down their prey. They even joined hunts with the men whenever called upon to do so. Only those who were pregnant or had young children stayed behind on those rare occasions. Nothing was wasted, whether the kill was big or small. Almost every part of the animals taken had a use, particularly the skins, used for clothing and coverings.

Everyone fished with nets in the nearby river, and the older men and women often tried their luck with baited bone hooks dangling from woven string. To supplement their meals, women and children went out almost daily to collect edible roots and plants.

In many ways, Raven's life on the steppes was similar to her life in the valley. She helped Old Cloud maintain a fresh supply of medicinal herbs and joined the others in searching for and preparing food. But at the steppe caves, she slept with her nieces and nephews at night. Helping them prepare for sleep was a new occupation, which she greatly enjoyed. Soon, however, another activity helped fill her days.

Although she'd lived with the tribe on the steppes off and on for her entire life, Raven had never paid much attention to the stony outcrops that dotted the grassy plains, not even when gathering plants at their base. Raven rarely made stone tools herself, but she enjoyed watching them being struck from the rock cores, especially when a usable blade came flying off. As a young child, she'd often watched her father, a master toolmaker. He'd been amused by her clapping delight, and those sessions among the mounded rock chips were the only times she'd felt any closeness with him.

Raven discovered there at the caves that she had a knack for finding quality stone. She easily spotted the minor color variations in the chalky covering that indicated a fine-grained flint. When she returned one day with a few choice nodules that had caught her attention, several of the men asked her if they could have them. Before long, those men began asking her to keep an eye out whenever they saw her leaving the cave. Once, she even led them to an outcrop streaked with a rare type of flint so they could get as much as they wanted.

She saw their requests as a sign that the band was finally starting to accept her—even if most of the women were still overly reserved. She wished that Bear wouldn't give the men such cold stares whenever she talked with them about her finds. They would stop requesting her help if he kept that up. A long time passed, however, before he mentioned her stone gathering.

Always prone to moodiness, Bear had fallen into a prickly melancholy. Willow worried about him, and she agreed with Raven that his low spirits had something to do with his father, who had been left in the valley to die.

Before the camp had moved, the old man had been hanging on to life, even though he could barely walk and his speech no longer made sense to anyone but himself. Bear had resisted making a decision about his father's fate for so long that, in the end, his options were limited. They'd made a travois for Old Wolf to see if they could take him with them, but the old man had thrashed about so much that he'd fallen off. Even tied down, he'd fought the ropes until they came loose, and the group had finally given up. By that time, their departure was too close for them to starve Old Wolf, which would at least have allowed him a proper death ceremony.

Only a few days before the band left, Bear decided that he would smother his father on the morning of the journey. He was going to ask some of the men to hold him down while he pressed a piece of fur over the old man's face. Then they would bury him with a quick ceremony right before leaving. But when the time came, Bear announced that Old Wolf would be left in the valley still alive. Several women offered to stay with him until his end, but Bear wouldn't agree to it. A retrieval journey would have to be planned for them, and there wasn't any way of knowing when to fetch them because no one knew how long Old Wolf would linger.

Only after a successful hunt was Bear in good spirits, and his children, sensing that, approached him for attention at those times. But after a short while, he would become surly again, snapping at everyone like a river turtle. Not even Willow was exempt from his biting words whenever she tried to reason with him.

He also seemed to have forgotten how to moderate his vast strength. Whenever he tousled Flint's hair, the little boy would struggle not to cry. The last time Bear had chanced upon Raven by herself at the river, he'd been overly rough. She had several bruises and scratches from his grasping hands, and the way he slammed his body against hers made her fear that he might damage the baby. Even though she missed her occasional solitary rambles, Raven started collecting plants only when she was helping the other women gather food.

Scouts returned one evening with reports that bison were nearby, grazing on a large plateau that ended in a ledge with an abrupt drop-off. Bear immediately came up with a hunting plan based on an account he'd once heard of another band driving bison off a cliff. The panicked beasts had lost all caution and charged over the edge. Such a take would provide enough meat to last even into winter if dried and stored in the cool backs of the caves.

Eager to try that strategy, Bear began organizing a hunt, calling for quick action. Blood, provided by a boar that had wandered too close to the caves that morning, and fire would be used to cause the stampede. Except for small children and their mothers, pregnant women, the slow-moving elderly, and the ill, everyone would join in the actual hunt. Anyone who was able would prepare storage and help dry the meat as it was brought back.

Raven was mildly disappointed at being left behind, but she and Willow went with several other women to clean rocky debris from deep within their cave so that a storage pit could be dug. After setting up bear-fat lamps and torches to provide light, they began filling baskets with broken stone.

Bear suddenly appeared at Raven's side. "You'll come with us," he said. "We need everyone possible to help with the stampede. That should please you, considering your fondness for assisting men."

He smirked while he spoke, and Raven was angry that he would say such a thing in front of Willow and the other women. She knew he was talking about her searches for stone, but the others might have taken a different meaning.

Willow's face was a frown in the flickering light. "You know Raven shouldn't go."

"If she can climb up rock faces, then she can yell and wave her arms."

"What if she's charged and can't move quickly enough to keep from being trampled?"

"She'll be in the hind ranks along with the young people, but she can still run, can't she? I'm not trying to get her killed, Willow, even though death does seem to follow on her heels."

Willow adjusted her hold on the basket of stone she held. "Raven had nothing to do with Old Wolf's poor health. He was dying before she arrived, and we don't even know if he's dead yet."

Bear looked at them with vacant eyes. Then, wordlessly, he reached out and grasped Raven's wrist. Pulling her along with him, he moved past Willow. His free hand swept her aside, and

Willow, her arms still wrapped around the basket full of rubble, slammed into a large stone icicle hanging from the cave roof.

A short while later, Raven decided that Bear hadn't hurt Willow intentionally. He'd only been careless about his strength, as usual. As the scene replayed in her mind, she finished smearing boar blood on her bare forearms and passed the bloody wooden bowl to the next woman.

But even if his actions were only the result of his haste to finalize the details of the hunt, Raven couldn't forgive how he'd left without even turning his head to check on Willow. He'd simply taken up a torch and continued on his way, still grasping Raven's arm. Raven had cast a look back and seen Willow sprawled on the cave floor, covered by the basket's contents. Before she could discern if Willow was badly hurt, the other women, rushing to her sister's side, had blocked her view.

Raven belatedly became more cognizant of the frantic activity going on around her, resembling a disturbed ant bed. She waved her arms, drying the blood on them so that drips wouldn't ruin her good leather tunic. Most of the women had stripped off their tunics and tied old skins around their waists to cover hips and legs, leaving their chests bare. Raven's mind was so fogged with the details of what had happened back in the cave, she hadn't noticed their unusual attire until too late. Her stomach knotted, though not from the smell; her nauseous response to odors during her early pregnancy had passed. She felt sick that she hadn't pulled away from Bear and gone to her sister. She'd been cowardly, afraid he would slap her down as he had the day of the hyena kill.

Her thoughts were interrupted by a sharp horn blast. Everyone began gathering in front of the largest cave. Bear climbed partway up the incline so everyone could see him as he spoke. He quickly laid out his plan for the hunt. Most of the group would form a narrow corridor through which the bison would be forced to stampede. Raven tried to focus on what he was telling them, putting aside the image of Willow covered with stones.

To keep the noise down, they departed in small groups. The people in Raven's group went last because they would be in the back row, away from the central action. As they got closer to where the bison were and began creeping, almost crawling, across the plateau, the earlier arrivals were so well hidden by tall grass and shrubs that Raven had difficulty spotting them. Although she couldn't see the bison, she heard them snorting and milling about uneasily as the smell of blood drifted their way. By the time she was in place on one side of the corridor, smoke was twirling skyward. She remained hidden when she heard several hawk cries signaling the men, bloodied and wearing only loin-cloths, to charge the bison with burning branches. The ground vibrated as the bison surged forward. Double crow-caws came from the grass in several places, and Raven jumped up and began screaming and waving her arms.

Raven was well away from the charging men but fairly close to the drop-off, so she saw the lone figure leap up and begin running in front of the stampeding animals, their massive, shaggy heads rising and falling. He was clad in a bison skin and wearing their horns on his head. Although he ran at top speed, the first bison were only steps behind. Bison were often lured into pit traps this way. So strong was their herding instinct, they would follow any perceived bison in front of them.

Just before the man went over the cliff, something about the way he moved made Raven realize that the runner was Leaf. Her dutiful screams became urgently shrill as several bison followed him over. The edge looked so sheer that she didn't see how he could have possibly hidden away from the animal's hooves without tumbling over the side.

Only a few bison broke ranks, causing anyone in their way to scrabble for safety. The rest of the small herd fell to their deaths.

By the time the last one went over, Raven's throat was as raw as her nerves. There was no sign of Leaf.

The others in Raven's group began to return to the caves to fetch skins for packing the meat once it was butchered. They yelled back at her impatiently. She barely heard them. The smell of bruised grass tickled her nose while she stared at the place where Leaf had disappeared. Suddenly, a bison skin flew up onto the ledge, then he was climbing over. When he was on his feet, he looked in her direction. For a moment, they stared across dusty air at each other. When he bent over abruptly to collect the skin, she ran to join the others.

Willow was stuffing things into several leather bags when Raven found her in the corner area where she slept with Bear.

"I thank the Earth Mother you are all right," Raven said, hurrying over.

She stopped in her tracks when Willow turned around. A large lump surrounded by a bruise covered one side of her forehead, and her cheek had already ripened into a plum color. Her eye on that side was swollen completely shut.

Willow with a bruised face was beyond belief as well as disturbing. It was Raven's turn to be consoling. She went over and stretched her fingers toward her sister's cheek but, thinking better of it, let her hand drop. "I know that's terribly painful and tender," she said. Raven wished Bear had pushed her instead. The swollen stain signaled that something had changed, and not for the better.

"It's not so bad. I had a nasty headache, but it's almost faded away."

"I can give you something for the headache, and I'll make poultices—but what are you doing?" she asked as Willow reached down and packed a child's tunic into one of the bags.

"The hunt was so successful that Bear wants to share the meat—with our old home band. Messengers are starting out immediately. The band isn't so far away, but we'll travel too quickly for me to take Flint and Berry. I know I can ask you to take care of my little ones while I'm gone." She looked at Raven with her one good eye. "I'm staying with our aunt for a while."

"Bear is sending you as a messenger?"

"Of course not. While we were cleaning this"—Willow fluttered her fingers beside her bruises—"one of the messengers came from the hunt to tell his mate that he was leaving. Bear doesn't know I'm going. He's still at the cliffs."

Willow's calm demeanor only fanned Raven's distress at how the day was unraveling. "But must you go? I don't think he realized what he did."

"I can't believe that you, of all people, are defending him." Willow gave her a sharp look. "He's gone too far—ignoring everybody's counsel, hurting anyone who gets in his way. Hopefully my absence will shock him into changing. Now about Flint and Berry. Will you tend them?" She sighed, a quiver of chin and mouth. "I'll miss them terribly."

"You know that I will. I'll keep them under my wing, but I can never replace their mother. How long will you stay?"

"At least until the bruises have faded."

A staggering sense of loss sliced through Raven, and her eyes brimmed with tears. She collapsed against Willow, holding on to her. "I love you the same as I did our dead mother. Please don't leave."

"My sister, so near to my heart." Willow gently pushed Raven away. "Don't make me weep—it hurts my eye. Someone has to try and save him from himself. Go now and find my three oldest for me. The messengers await us."

Reluctantly, Raven left her side. She hoped she wouldn't be able to find the two girls and their brother before the messengers tired of the delay and left. She was not so lucky. The children were in the clearing in front of the cave.

CHAPTER 8

The Levant, Present Day

MARK WISHES HE COULD HAVE come by himself. He's being childish, he knows, but he wants to grab hold of the past during his coming explorations by pretending he lives in one of the caves. This game of make-believe that he likes to play, whenever he visits ancient and historical places, gives him a feeling for what life would have been like at an earlier time. He's been able to achieve that satisfying depth of insight at other ancient, historical sites, but Antun's presence is so distracting that he doesn't even want to try losing himself in the past.

They go inside the visitors' center first. Some of the information found in the center's pamphlets, he already knows from his research during the long trip over, but they have good diagrams of the caves.

Antun flirts with a woman working the information desk as Mark studies a display about a female Neanderthal skeleton that was discovered at the site. It's one of the most ancient found in Israel, about 120,000 years old. Mark is so engrossed that he barely hears a cell phone ringing, and then Antun is beside him.

"I have to call someone, and the information I need is in the car," he says. "Go on without me. I'll catch up. I hope you don't mind."

"No, no, don't worry about me," Mark says as Antun leaves. His lethargy fades at the prospect of being able to explore with-

out Antun's company, after all. Before setting off, he remembers
to get an aspirin and his sunglasses out of his backpack.

The caves are up a steep flight of stairs, and the rocky, semi-
arid surroundings remind him a little of the American West,
although with a few more trees. Right outside Tanur Cave, a
superb observation point overlooks the whole area. Mark takes
in the view then goes inside. He scrutinizes the cave's crannies
but leaves shortly after a tour group enters.

From Tanur Cave, the route continues to Gamal Cave. A display occupies the cave, and barriers keep anyone from actually
going inside. Static figures reminiscent of store mannequins,
men and women dressed in skins, sit within. He's disappointed.
They look nothing like Neanderthals. Of more interest is the
cave ceiling. It's blackened in patches with soot from hearth fires
made over thousands of years.

He takes off his sunglasses and faces out from the cave
mouth, imagining the lusher landscape of the past, picturing
it filled with extinct Pleistocene animals. Although he has to
block out banana fields in the distance, he manages to envision
a prehistoric scene in his mind's eye, but then Antun's booming
laugh echoes against the mountain wall, coming from somewhere
below. He tries again, but nothing happens. The plains in the
distance remain stubbornly filled with their present-day fields.
Mark puts the sunglasses back on. Being a tourist is all he can
hope for. He goes on to the last and largest cave, Nahal, where
an audiovisual presentation illustrates prehistoric life.

Leaving the last cavern, he spots a sign that indicates a
steeper side-trail leads back to the parking lot. As he makes his
way down the path through tall boulders, he hears voices, one
of them Antun's. They seem to come from a cluster of trees and
bushes a short distance from where the car is parked. The grove
is like a shady island within the sunny landscape. He's only gone
in a short distance when he glimpses Antun through the foliage.

He's sitting on a large rock along with three other men. One of them passes his cousin a small metal tray, a pile of white powder in the center. Mark stops abruptly before they see him. He watches as Antun lowers his head, his forefinger holding one side of his nose closed.

Not knowing how they will take him crashing their party, he edges away slowly, until he's outside the trees again. Mark isn't a complete stranger to recreational drug use, having dabbled during his teens and early twenties. That had stopped, though, when he'd figured out that he was sacrificing the pristine configuration of his brain neurons for the sole purpose of persuading certain people to enjoy his company. He'd concluded that he didn't care whether those people liked him or not. It wasn't worth it. If Antun wants to ruin his brain, fine, but Mark wonders how high he is and whether that will affect his driving.

The men might see him walking past the grove and guess that Mark has seen them. He hurries back up and around, passing the caves again, so that he can approach the parking lot from the other direction. When he's in front of Tanur Cave, he sees Antun coming up the steps. He waves at him and goes down.

Antun's face is flushed, his eyes glittering with drug-induced excitement. "I have a wonderful surprise for you. Don't ask any questions, or you'll ruin it. We're going to see another cave right now, and the surprise of it is where the cave is located. Come on," he says when Mark hesitates. "We're going to Haifa."

On the road, Mark fears he will never see Haifa. Anton's high spirits make his driving even more aggressive than earlier. He refuses to yield to other drivers, impatiently darting out in front whenever another driver shows hesitation. He sees Mark holding on to the side door.

"Aha," Antun says. "You were so lost in your dreams earlier, you didn't notice how people drive in Israel. We all drive this way." He begins passing the car in front of him but starts cursing in French when a car approaches from over a hill. He brakes and barely squeezes the car back into their lane before the air blast from the passing car buffets Mark's eardrums. He's relieved by the respite when Antun stops at a McDonald's.

"A McDonald's lunch, so you will feel at home by eating a cheeseburger. Some places in Israel, they're awful, but they make excellent ones here," Antun says. "Good milkshakes, as well."

Mark orders a cheeseburger and a strawberry milkshake.

The cashier gives him a withering look. "I'm sorry, sir," he says in English. "We don't serve those things together here."

"Excuse me?" Mark thinks he hasn't heard correctly.

Antun laughs. "No milk, no milk. I didn't notice the kosher sign—they don't serve milk products along with meat at this McDonald's."

Suspicion thumps through Mark's mind like an agitated rabbit's foot. It's ridiculous to think that Antun would do something so petty, but Mark believes he's been set up. Antun's chortling is entirely too self-satisfied. Mark orders a plain hamburger and a coke.

Mark is relieved that the drive to Haifa has been a short one; their actual time on the road was little more than half an hour. He looks around distractedly when the car stops at a small marina. A man farther down the dock jumps from a boat and waves to get their attention.

"Are we going for a boat ride?"

"Yes, a boat is the best transportation for where we're going," Antun says, his voice giving away his smug glee at seeing Mark's puzzlement.

Antun is waiting for him to ask exactly where that might be, but after the McDonald's episode, Mark refuses to play along. His lips are pressed together as though they've been glued.

Mark isn't entirely sure, but the man who's waving them over looks like one of the men he saw with Antun in the tree grove—the one holding the tray. As it turns out, he's the boat's pilot. He nods when Mark boards but doesn't say anything, motioning with an offhand gesture toward the cabin below deck. Mark shakes his head, and the pilot shrugs. The man doesn't seem high, but he would rather not be cooped up if the worst were to happen.

His headache is gone, the sky is clear blue, and the water has only a light chop. As they go farther out into the Mediterranean, Mark, seated on a cushioned bench, tries to enjoy the ride. Before long, they're far enough from the coast that land is no longer visible. A short distance later, the boat turns north. The vessel skims the water while Antun talks to the pilot, the pair ignoring Mark. Eventually, the boat turns again, going toward the coast. From off in the distance, a gleaming speck approaches rapidly. It turns out to be another vessel, larger than the craft they're in.

The pilot swears loudly and cuts the engine. Mark stares at the lettering on the vessel as it pulls alongside. The markings are impossible to decipher, but they're a type of writing he's seen somewhere before. Several naval men wearing blue uniforms and caps scrutinize them with stern faces. The men don't appear to be Israelis.

During a rapid-fire exchange between the pilot and the uniformed men on the other boat, Mark hears the word "American." He wonders how long they'll be detained. The air is still and oppressive over the calm sea. He begins to sweat.

Antun crosses over. "They only want to see your passport. It's all right," he says when Mark gives him a questioning look. "We know them."

Mark opens his camera bag, gets out his passport, and hands it to Antun, who returns to the other side. He stumbles on a rope by the railing, and for a heart-wrenching second, Mark is sure that his passport will go into the sea. But Antun catches himself and passes it over to one of the sailors. The man glances from the picture to Mark several times before handing back the passport.

Words are exchanged, and one of the men reaches over the side as if to shake Antun's hand. After a quick clasp, he straightens, and Mark glimpses a wallet-sized packet sliding into his uniform pocket.

As soon as they pull away, Antun returns the passport. Mark has figured out why the words on the other boat were familiar, and he's fuming. "Is this legal? Why didn't you tell me we were going to Lebanon?"

Antun looks at him, eyes turned down at the corners. "Don't be upset. I thought you might like to see the land of your ancestors again—where your roots are."

Mark throws up his hands. "The Lions of the Levant is in Lebanon now—that terrorist group is all over the news. I don't want my American head cut off," he hisses.

Antun appears to be genuinely taken aback by this outburst, as if he hasn't realized until now that Mark is capable of anger. "The country is safe as long as we stay in the south. You like caves, and now you're going to see a very interesting one. Don't be melodramatic." He shakes his head, saying something in French.

The pilot calls out, pointing toward the coast. His eyes narrowed against the sunlight, Antun takes a quick look in the indicated direction before getting up to join him at the helm.

His mother's insistence on teaching Mark French was successful after all. He understood Antun's last words perfectly. "You are acting more Lebanese than your blood allows you," he said. Mark doesn't know what he meant by those words, but

Antun obviously knows information about the Hayek family that he isn't sharing.

During the climb up a steep coastal path, Antun tells him that although skeletons were found there during the 1940s—one Neanderthal and several ancient modern humans—the cave they're going to is privately owned now and has been neglected for years.

Mark looks at him askance.

"Not to worry," Antun says hastily. "I know the owner." Mark is beginning to believe that his cousin knows just about everyone in this part of the world.

Antun stops at the highly arched cave mouth and gives Mark a flashlight, saying he's going to meet up with some friends nearby who are waiting for him, and that he'll be back shortly. "You can't get lost in there. It's shallow. But don't wander too far from the cave."

"I'll be fine." He just wants Antun gone.

Mark forgets his irritation when he enters. He puts the flashlight in the bag and gets out a camera. The flash goes off like lightning as he eases his way into the gloom. Several disturbed areas show where the excavations Antun mentioned had taken place, but most of the cave seems undisturbed.

He's still getting some light from the cave entry when he spies a ledge high up the wall and decides he wants to take a few pictures from that vantage point. On examining the wall, Mark sees there are a lot of indented places that will make good handholds and footholds, almost as if they'd been made intentionally for climbing. They're not that noticeable, but he has a practiced eye from the weekends he spent climbing in the Santa Cruz Mountains with Sandy.

Mark carefully makes his way up and pulls himself onto the ledge. He takes out the flashlight and shines it around the flat slab. The ledge is empty except for pebbles and dust. He turns and arcs the light over the wall beside where he's sitting. The surface there is almost smooth, marred only by a round hole up higher that punches into the rock. Mark lowers the flashlight and places it inside a small depression on the ledge so it won't roll off. He takes up the camera and points it toward the entry for a long shot.

As he takes the picture, the image of that rounded hollow space above him goes through his mind again. He'll have to check it out before going back down. Mark crawls farther along the slab, to shoot from a different angle.

But now he can't stop thinking about exploring the hole and finds it hard to concentrate on the camera. He doesn't understand how a small, insignificant indentation can suddenly transfix him so completely. Mark is sure that other people don't constantly go off track the way he does.

He puts the camera in his bag and snatches up the flashlight as he stands. The opening is too high for his eyes even when on tiptoe; he stretches so he can slip a hand inside. When Mark gropes around, several fingers rub against something that pricks. He snatches his hand back, thinking he's been stung. A scorpion comes to mind, but the flashlight shows only a scratch on one finger. Mark reaches gingerly back inside. His fingers touch the sharpness again; it seems to be nothing more than a rock. He digs around it to loosen it. After a moment, his fingers get a good hold, and he pries the lump out. Kneeling, Mark places it on the slab.

When the light falls over his discovery, he holds his breath for a long moment before the air rushes out in an incoherent exclamation that shatters the cave's silence.

Too slender for a spear point, yet longer than an arrowhead, the finely worked piece has a naturally notched tongue on one end perfect for hafting if anyone wanted to add a handle. Even dusty, the stone's reddish color sparkles. He rubs both sides briskly on his jeans then polishes it with his shirt.

Holding the bladed stone in one hand, he turns the flashlight on it again. The bloodred quartz gleams. Ripples along the surface, left over from its crafting, seem to move in the light like small waves. A shiver goes down Mark's spine as he realizes that he's the first person to hold this beautifully worked stone since its owner left it in the cave thousands of years before.

CHAPTER 9

Western Asia, Late Pleistocene

HALF A MOON CYCLE PASSED before Willow's youngest children stopped crying for their mother. They still asked when she was coming back. Raven always answered, "I don't know, but you'll awaken one morning, and she'll be here, sitting beside your pallet."

Bear had asked only once about Willow's return.

The day Willow left, Raven decided not to be the one to tell him that she'd gone. When he returned late from the bison kill and shook Raven awake, asking for Willow, it became obvious that no one else had dared do so, either.

Raven had informed him, whispering fiercely, that after he'd pushed her, Willow had left to seek her aunt's care. He raised his eyebrows and cupped his ear forward with a hand as if he hadn't heard her hissing words correctly.

"Truly, her head was bursting from the pain, and the side of her face that hit the stone was so swollen, she couldn't see out of one eye." Raven kept her voice down, struggling not to rant. There would be enough gossip as things were. "I was willing to treat her here, and I know Old Cloud would have also, but our aunt has more experience with head injuries."

The confusion that covered his face was replaced by an indifferent stare. "Well, did she say when she was coming back?"

"She'll return when her head has healed and she can once again think clearly."

Raven was afraid that her tone might provoke him, but his arrogance left him as he thought about what she'd said. After a moment, he got up and went to lie down on the pallet he'd shared with Willow.

During the following days, Bear's melancholy deepened, and for once, he became more subdued than irritable. But soon, like the children, he adjusted somewhat to Willow's absence. After sleeping alone for many nights, he finally told Raven that as his mate, she should be sleeping under his blankets. She went reluctantly, but that was when she discovered that he dreamed about Willow, muttering her name over and over.

They took up their routines, and Raven was disconcerted to realize that she was getting along better with Bear, the person she disliked most in the world, since Willow, the person she liked most, had left. Although Bear didn't make her happy and Raven well knew he wasn't happy with her, they had developed a tolerance for each other's company. Raven thought at length about the reason for that unexpected development when Bear slept one night with his hand resting on her belly, his touch for the first time giving comfort. She decided that their shared loneliness was the only thing bringing them closer, a sad and bitter truth.

When a moon had gone by, Bear decided that if Willow didn't return in a few more days, he would go fetch her himself. Raven was smiles for the rest of that day as she anticipated seeing Willow again, although she did wonder if Bear would start treating her badly once more upon her sister's return.

The morning he was to make the trip, Raven sat in the cave mouth, making a new tunic for her expanding middle while also minding a group of children playing games with river-rock pebbles. When a horn blew, she looked out over the steppe and saw a small traveling party in the distance. She threw the partially completed tunic over a nearby stone.

"It's your mother come back. Now your father won't have to go for her. Let's run to meet her," she called to her niece and nephew as she leapt up. "Put down your pretty rocks," she said, prying open Flint's clenched fists. She took their hands and as quickly as possible went down the incline.

A cluster of people, including Bear, stood a short distance from the hearth, watching the approaching travelers. Raven was about to sweep past them with the children when his arm blocked her way.

"Wait here. Let them come to us," he said.

She stopped, looking at him in irritation. As eagerly as he wanted his first mate's return, he couldn't resist punishing Willow a bit by making it seem as though she wasn't unduly missed.

They waited without talking, the cicadas filling in their silence with long, whining trills. Raven recognized people from her old home band among the travelers, but the one person she most wanted to see was somehow hidden from view. No matter how many times her eyes roamed over the group, Raven couldn't pick out Willow's familiar form. Her sister had always moved as nimbly as a young deer, but the people approaching her were dragging themselves along like wounded game. *Where are Willow and the three children?*

Raven's gaze became stuck upon a shockingly familiar face, and she realized with dismay that it was Fern she was staring at—the elder's mate whose doomed baby she'd tried to rescue.

A shrill lament suddenly tore the air, competing with the cicadas. The sound struck Raven to the bone. She shuddered, watching Fern and the only other female in the group, a young woman, as they wailed and pulled at their hair. The travelers stopped, and a man, whom Raven remembered as being overly talkative, stepped forward.

"Oh Great Bear, I beg your permission to speak freely," the man said. "But before I do speak, and I ask your pardon for this delay, I must have your promise that I will not be harmed for bringing bad tidings."

Bear stared at him with an ashen face, his jaw working silently for a heartbeat before the words broke from him. "You have my promise." He turned toward the wailing women. "Stop that!" he thundered, and they became silent, as did the chirring cicadas.

His face wary, the man spoke into complete silence. "A cave collapsed. It was as if a mountain fell in on itself. We labored for a day trying to remove the debris." He held out his hands. "My fingers are swollen from the gashes—"

Bear grasped him by his tunic and pulled him close. "Tell me, man, or I swear I'll forget my word."

Squirming to keep his feet on the ground, the bringer of bad tidings looked Bear in the eye. "They were in the collapsed cave. Willow and the children." Bear thrust the man away with such force that he stumbled and fell.

"No!" Bear wailed at the sky. Covering his face with his hands, he staggered away from the group, moaning loudly.

Raven was frozen to the spot as the two women took up their lament once more. She felt hollow, as empty as an old tortoise shell. A world without Willow wasn't conceivable.

Flint, always unsettled by his father's unbounded displays, pulled on her hand. "Pretty rocks," he said, pointing back up the path leading to the cave. He raised his arms toward her, expecting to be picked up.

Berry was old enough to know that something had gone terribly wrong. "Where's my mother?" she asked, looking up at Raven, her little face crumpling into tears.

Feeling as if she were speaking to them from a distance, Raven picked up Flint. "She's joined with the Earth Mother now.

Come, we'll go find the pretty rocks." Those words expressed her last coherent thought of the day. Her knees began to buckle, and someone snatched Flint from her grasp.

"Go get Old Cloud," a voice yelled as everything started spinning dizzily around her.

Her memories of what happened after she fainted were so confusing that Raven later believed her mind had temporarily broken like a rock shattered by a misplaced blow. Someone must have taken the children from her, because the next thing she vaguely recalled was crying uncontrollably into her sleeping skins.

Shadowy forms of women came and went as they tried to console her. They all seemed like strangers, but when Old Cloud hobbled over, Raven recognized her. She propped Raven up and urged her to drink from a cup she held. After drinking, Raven started apologizing for not bringing her a certain kind of plant. Her words poured out in a frantic, garbled torrent. The elderly woman shushed her, gently pushing her back down. The potion she'd given Raven rapidly pulled her into a deep sleep.

She fell into something like a dream, imagining that the captive had entered the cave and that, in her surprise, she'd leaped up from the pallet. But when Raven smiled at him in greeting, his heavy face and form suddenly changed, and he became someone she'd never seen before, a man dressed strangely, his hair overly short. The features of his somewhat fair-skinned face were exceedingly fine and pleasing, however, and she felt a twinge of disappointment when they became misty and faded away.

A little later, she heard someone breathing out, a sighing exhalation, and she opened her eyes. Leaf was leaning over her. She reached up to touch his cheek, but he proved as elusive as ever, vanishing before her hand found him. At some point, Bear slipped onto the pallet. She awoke pressed against his back and heard him weeping along with her as she fell again down a dark hole.

She came awake the next morning with Flint's fingers running over her eyes and nose. She remembered his three dead brothers and sisters and closed her lids again. But he didn't give up. "Hungry, Auntie," he said, tugging on her shell necklace. Raven's mother had given her the necklace when she'd joined with Reed, just a few short moons before her death.

Raven gently took Flint's hand down and closed her fingers around the shells, hoping to take strength from this last remaining link to her past. She tried to rise, but a large, invisible weight was holding her down. She knew without looking that Bear had gone, or the child wouldn't have approached her. Everything blacked out again for a few heartbeats.

"Come, little one," a woman said. "I'll feed you."

Raven turned her head and saw a blurry image looming over her.

Flint made a surprised sound as he was lifted.

"I'll take care of him," Fern's voice said. "You go back to sleep, Raven."

Something in Fern's voice grated so harshly across Raven's awakening consciousness that even though she tried, Raven couldn't escape into sleep once more. She forced herself off the pallet and out of the cave. After pausing for a moment on the ledge, she went down to the hearth on unsteady legs, ignoring everyone's stares as she wobbled along.

She sat down heavily on a log to gather her wits. She didn't know how long she'd been there when Fern approached with Flint in tow.

"Here, I brought you water," Fern said.

Hesitantly, Raven reached for the proffered cup and took a sip, her thirst overcoming her dislike for the woman.

"My mate and youngest child perished in that cave, you know. Thank the Earth Mother, my eldest was with my sister's band." Fern squinted at Raven disapprovingly, her braids dangling as she leaned forward. "Take hold of yourself. You're a healer. You know that death is always with us."

Fern's eyes seemed to merge, becoming a single piercing point, but Raven didn't look away.

"*You* understand that truth more than others—don't you, Raven?"

Raven straightened her shoulders and shifted back. The woman only leaned in closer like an aggressive serpent, her mouth parted, the tip of her tongue showing. "Willow was strong. She wouldn't have lost her head the way you have if it had been you who was crushed in—"

"Go away," Raven snapped at her.

"I am only trying to help you," Fern said, more loudly than necessary. "Your aunt also died, in case no one told you." Fern swept her braids back over her shoulder and sauntered away, pulling Flint along. He looked back at her over his shoulder, and a fresh sorrow surged through Raven. She hadn't thought to inquire after her aunt, so shocked was she by Willow's death.

Raven lifted the cup to take another swallow but stopped herself. What if Fern had put something in the water to avenge the time Raven had given her an improperly mixed medicine? She looked down into the cup at the clear liquid and decided it was fine. There hadn't been any underlying herbal taste. Fern wouldn't risk doing anything so soon after arriving.

She sipped once more as she watched Fern approach Bear to ask if he would like for her to bring him food. That was a scene she would observe over and over during the following days.

The children's abandonment, she could understand. Now that their aunt had become so somber, always talking about their dead mother, they were drawn to Fern's cheerful playfulness. The thing she couldn't tolerate was Bear's dismissal of their mutual sorrow. It sickened her to see how easily Fern seduced him into forgetting his grief for Willow.

Whenever Bear was at the caves, Fern buzzed about him continuously, as though she'd found a full honeycomb. Even when not waiting on him like a slave, she lingered by his side. She would bring the children over to see him for a moment or find something nearby that needed to be done. Raven was outraged by how he encouraged her, his eyes following appreciatively whenever she pranced past him, hips moving under her tunic.

Raven was hastening his defection, but she couldn't hide her displeasure. For several nights after that awful day, Raven would awaken and realize they'd been clinging to each other as they slept. That had ended when her thoughts were no longer clouded and she remembered why Willow had left Bear in the first place. From then on, she slept on the edge of the pallet, vigilantly keeping her distance. On some level, he seemed to grasp the reason for her anger and as a result usually left her alone.

Only a short while passed before the newcomers asked if they could stay permanently with the band. Raven had expected that would happen. So few had survived the cave's collapse that Raven's old band had effectively dissolved. Remembering Bear's complaints that his band had become too large, Raven hoped that he would ask them to find another group, but he didn't. She suspected that Fern's presence was the reason he tolerated the packed caves. His mood had lightened considerably, and she bitterly admitted that Fern had accomplished that feat whereas Willow and the children had been unable to do so.

Besides wriggling her way into Bear's favor, Fern also ingratiated herself with the women. Although some had tried for a time to comfort Raven through her sorrow, they once more began distancing themselves, Old Cloud being the only exception.

Fern relit the fires of their previous disquiet concerning Raven by openly displaying her scorn and encouraging their gossip.

Whenever Raven joined in daily foraging, she caught the others throwing glances her way as they talked. They averted their eyes when they saw she was on to them, but Fern's poisonous regard wasn't as subtle. Her dark, unblinking sparrow eyes always watched Raven as if she were a worm that should be pecked.

"How fortunate that Lily came with me," Fern said one day, referring to the girl who'd arrived with her from the collapsed cave. "I understand that Leaf was having difficulty finding a suitable mate. Anyone available here was far too old! But our sweet Lily is even younger than Leaf. They'll have beautiful children with the Earth Mother's help."

Raven ignored the jab, trying to signal that she didn't want a fight, but that didn't stop Fern from constantly fashioning her voice into a spear. When several days had passed without any of her remarks provoking a response, Fern took to making comments about Longheads.

"This is overcooked again, almost burned," she would say about anything Raven had prepared at the hearth. "Even a Longhead wouldn't eat this!"

If Raven protested mildly that the food was good and not burned, Fern would make yet another reference to Longheads. She displayed a limitless curiosity about the band's former captive, lobbing questions at Raven that became increasingly improper. She got the eager attention of a large group gathered at the hearth when, after commenting on the soft skin of a baby she was holding, Fern cut her eyes over at Raven. "How does a Longhead's skin feel, Raven?"

"Like anyone else's skin," she mumbled.

"I was just wondering. You're the only woman I know who has actually touched one of those beasts." She rubbed her hand over the baby's backside. "Well, was it as soft as this baby's bottom?"

Fern's comment finally managed to prick the numb detachment that had lingered since her sister's death. "Of course not!" Raven said loudly over the laughs and sniggers.

Raven avoided Fern as much as possible. Because of her continuing grief, she had little will to engage her attacker, and she had no one she could turn to for help. She couldn't confide in Old Cloud about how she was being treated. The older woman had her own problems. Even with Raven's aid, walking between the two caves took her a long time. She didn't need to be burdened.

Leaf continued avoiding Raven. He no longer followed her like a shadow—or at least, Raven couldn't discern that he did. Although she had yet to see the two of them together, he would soon join with Lily in ceremony. That was what Fern had told her, and if it were true, then that was final proof that he wasn't concerned about Raven anymore.

Fern's tart tongue often drove Raven from the hearth before she'd eaten, but bringing Fern's comments to Bear's attention would only lead him down the path toward Raven's secret. That was to be avoided no matter how hungry she felt. She became overly aware of her ribs underneath her tunic. Realizing that things had gone too far, Raven began hunting with throwing sticks and snares in order to acquire enough fat for herself and the growing baby. She stopped foraging with the women, searching alone again for medicinal plants, seeking the solitude needed for cooking her catches away from curious eyes and awkward questions.

So far, Fern hadn't made her attacks in front of Bear. This baffled Raven, until she realized that with her restraint, Fern was nurturing her growing relationship with him. By ridiculing Raven, she would insinuate that he'd shown poor judgment in choosing her as a mate. Fern understood Bear well enough to know that he didn't like criticism, especially from women. Then there was Raven's pregnancy. Fern knew that after his loss, Bear would want to build up his family again. A large kinship web was desirable for building alliances, and the best way to accomplish that was through children who would eventually find mates within other tribal bands. He would never discard Raven entirely—unless he realized the baby wasn't his.

Raven felt secure enough of her position that she didn't feel overly upset when Bear told her that he would take Fern as a second mate. She had already accepted the inevitable.

"You'll share my pallet until the ceremony," he said. "Then you'll sleep with the children. It's just as well—the way you crawl away from me every night."

The light from a torch's flame revealed a hint of distress around his eyes. Raven was astonished to find that her behavior had affected him. "It's my sorrow," she said. "It won't leave me in peace."

"If you think I don't miss her and the children, you're wrong." He propped himself on his elbow and looked down at her on the pallet. "But your grief isn't good for the baby you carry—or anyone else."

Raven realized that he was right. She'd been so consumed by her pain that she hadn't been focusing enough on the baby. She resolved that from then on, her every action would aim for the preservation of the only thing she had left: her child.

So when he lay back on the pallet, she waited until she thought most of the children in the cave were asleep. Then, putting aside her aversion, she rolled over on top of him, and he let her stay there instead of immediately twisting her over on her back. He was more subdued that way, less like an impatient, noisy stallion, but Raven knew that Fern was somewhere close by, her ears pricked like a fox to catch every rustle and gasp.

The next morning, as Raven left the thicket of bushes where the women relieved themselves, Fern also stepped out, blocking her way.

"Ah, Raven, I hoped I would find you here. We need to talk."

Raven moved to pass her. "There is nothing I want to discuss with you."

"Not even your first mate and how he died?"

Raven stopped, mystified by what she meant.

Fern smiled. "I assume that Bear let you know we'll soon be joined."

"He told me. What does that have to do with Reed?"

She pouted. "I didn't really expect to be congratulated by someone so crude. But never mind."

"Get out of my path." Raven started around her.

"Wait—you'll sorely regret not listening."

Raven paused again.

"It will be my duty as Bear's loyal mate to protect him. I'll have to let him know how you poisoned Reed."

Raven stared at her. "What are you talking about?"

"You weren't successful in killing me, but poor Reed wasn't so lucky." Her eyes went to Raven's middle. "Was it because he couldn't get you with child?"

"That's not true. I would never have harmed Reed."

"Well, either you poisoned him, or you're unfit to be a healer. I'm surprised Old Cloud hasn't caught on."

"No one will believe the lies of someone who wanted their own baby dead simply because of a splotch on his face."

"I only did what any good mother would do. I spared him a lifetime of suffering and kept him from burdening us all. You were too stupid to understand that."

Raven wanted to slap Fern; instead she lunged past the vile woman. She might hit back, then anyone who came along would see them fighting and tell Bear. He would surely want to know the reason.

"You'd best stop and listen, Raven. I think Bear *will* believe me when I tell him how you nestled up to the Longhead—fondled him even."

Raven turned slowly.

"I've talked with the men who guarded him. They spoke freely about what everyone else whispers in my ear. They told me you couldn't stay away from him. That every day he was captive, you entered his holding pen and put your hands all over him. They said that he responded like all male animals do around a female in heat. It's an unnatural thing, playing with a beast like that. It's disgusting." Fern spat on the ground at Raven's feet. "You're disgusting, Earth Mother help you."

A more highly esteemed woman with a large family and friends could perhaps have weathered that kind of gossip when it'd first started, but Raven had not been in any position to do so when she'd arrived. Nor was she at that moment. She shuddered inside to think what would happen if Fern knew the whole truth.

Her relentless gaze bore into Raven. "All of this pains me, but the things you've done in the past are creating problems now," Fern said. "For the sake of Bear's unborn child, I've asked the Earth Mother to help me decide what should be done."

Raven was indignant at the way Fern was implying that her scheming was the Earth Mother's will, but didn't want to confront her about it at the moment. Raven shifted uneasily. "What is it that you want?"

"Bear has to uphold his reputation if he's to remain respected as head elder. He'll shed you if he realizes how the band feels about you. I can enlighten him now, or things can go on as they are—with only a small change. You will begin living in the other cave."

"I can't just leave his pallet all of a sudden. He won't stand for it."

"Come up with a reason." Fern shrugged. "Tell him you're ill. You're devious enough to think of something." Her expression was like a wolverine's, merciless and determined, as she brushed past Raven. "I won't wait long."

Raven made her way to the river, seeking the solace of water. She sat on a large rock, her head brimming with bitter, bruising possibilities. It was all too easy to imagine what would occur if the baby was born favoring the Longhead in appearance. Fern would be the first to point that out, and Raven knew what the entire band would conclude. At best, she and her child would be cast out, but Raven could conceive of a much worse outcome. Bear, with Fern fanning his fitful tempers into a rage, could kill her and the baby. Raven spread her hands over the front of the tunic pulled tight over her belly. *That must not happen.*

When thunder grumbled in the distance, she looked up and saw an unusually large raven land on the opposite bank. It pounced, catching a creature small and tender enough for the bird to devour. The bird made shrill calls over its lucky catch and began feeding. Raven watched as its beak dipped up and down, gulping, filling its food pouch, reminding her of the many times she'd dreamed about ravens.

It stopped feeding and nodded at her over the rushing water, making friendly knocking sounds, as if trying to tell her something. With a loud flap, the raven took up the remnants of its kill and flew over the river and across the steppes. Her eyes followed the enormous bird as it slowly melted into the horizon. Raven's body suddenly felt swept with frost, and her thinking took on a chilling clarity. For many moons, her greatest fear had been that she would be cast onto the steppes, deserted and alone, but the raven had pointed the way. Her only remaining hope *was* in traveling across that grassy plain.

She should have gone with the captive when he'd tried to drag her along with him on his way back to his tribe. That would have saved her the trouble of finding him. Locating him would be difficult, but Raven had a good idea where his band dwelled. The trackers, who'd followed the Longhead brothers, had described their journey when they'd returned. She also had vivid memories of the dream in which she'd flown over the steppes and seen the Longhead outside his cave. Those memories would guide her, especially when she entered the mountains. Because she was presently living on the steppes, her trip would be shorter than if the band were still in the valley.

A plan began bubbling as she watched a blanket of rain in the distance, sweeping across the plains, coming in her direction. When thunder cracked closer by, she left the rock and ran toward camp.

That night, Raven pretended her abdomen was cramping. When Bear asked her what could be the cause, she said she wasn't sure and that she would go the following day to consult Old Cloud, who was more experienced in childbirth matters.

The next morning, she packed things into several pouches whenever she could do so without causing notice. The largest pouch, she stuffed with as many dried meat strips and fat balls from the bison hunt as she could carry. The band had a great amount of food stored; no one would notice what she took. She packed the smaller pouch with stone blades and other things she might need, including the skin Leaf had given her for the baby.

Several days before, Raven had noticed a spear with a cracked handle near one of the paths leading to the river. It had been almost completely covered with leaves, and when she went looking for it, she found it still there. Almost immediately after that find, she discovered a way that she could vanish without prompting a search. The spear shaft was splintered near the top. Raven used a sharp stone to finish sawing it off, making it the perfect length for her to carry easily. She couldn't be seen bringing a spear inside the cave—that would be too unusual—so she hid it in a rock outcrop directly opposite the caves. From time to time, she gathered dandelions that grew along the base there, and no one looked at her late that afternoon when she meandered over.

She got quite a fright when she went around the back. Fresh leopard prints were sunk everywhere in the sand, which was still soft from the deluge of the day before. Raven held the spear tightly as she looked about, but the beast was gone, its trail vanishing over a stony area that led away from the outcrop. If the leopard hadn't already left, it would have caught her when she came around the side.

Her heart pounded as she hid the spear among the rocks. The prints were a harsh reminder of how difficult crossing the steppes alone would be. "Earth Mother, lead me," she whispered, and it occurred to her with the very next breath that if the band thought a leopard had taken her, no one would waste time forming a search party. She didn't have a family driven by mourning to seek out her remaining shreds slung over a tree branch, saved by the big cat for a future meal.

Encouraged by the way things were falling in place, she left the outcrop and started toward the farther cave, seeking Old Cloud.

That evening, she told Bear she'd been in pain throughout the day. "I'm frightened for the baby," she said. "Old Cloud wants me to stay several days with her. She'll make a fresh potion for me to drink whenever the pangs come on." She picked up her bags, hoping he wouldn't notice how full they were. "I'll come back as soon as she says everything is fine."

He frowned, but after a moment, he nodded.

As Raven went out beneath the blankets hanging around their sleeping area, she saw Fern a short way down, tucking Flint and Berry into the pallet where they slept. When she straightened, Raven was ready with a defiant glare. As their stares battled, she hoped never again to see Fern's smug face with its round bird eyes.

Her steps were light but sure as she went down the beaten path to the other cave. That night, she would take a pinch of valerian to help with sleep. She wanted to be alert the next morning, and a very small amount wouldn't hurt the baby. For the first time since Willow's death, Raven felt strong and focused. The desire to protect her child was like a guiding flame.

CHAPTER 10

The Levant, Present Day

THE COOL STONE BLADE IN his hand feels as though it belongs there. Standing in the cave's mouth, Mark raises it to the light and studies every detail. Once hafted, it would make a beautiful knife. In the sunlight, the color is even more brilliant, practically shooting off reddish sparks. The crafting is delicate, yet he knows with certainty that the worked edges can be deadly.

Mark's breathing slows, in sync with the long waves washing up on the coast below, as he senses those people who held this blade before him. Vague images flit in and out of his mind.

He can't take his eyes away. Now he understands why so many people collect objects made in the past. This sort of compelling relic forges a link connecting those who went before to those who are here now, providing a satisfying feeling of continuity. He's never wanted any particular object this strongly—not even his Neanderthal shirt. Taking the blade will be akin to robbing a historical site, but he's in Lebanon without a visa. He'll surely be detained if he tries to turn the blade over to anyone with the proper authority to deal with it. The right thing would be to leave it where he found it—but he's not sure he can bring himself to do that.

Mark digs around in his bag, rearranging the water bottle, camera, and other things he's brought along as well as the items he's collected during the last few days. He makes room in a corner for this latest addition and turns back into the cave. He'll explore a little more—that will give him time for deciding whether or not to return the blade to its ancient hiding place.

As he shines the flashlight around the cave, he remembers how he was irresistibly drawn to search the hollow. Mark isn't superstitious, but it's as if he was intended to find the blade. "It was meant to be" is one of his mother's favorite expressions. He rebels inwardly against her casual fatalism whenever he hears her say those words, although he's never pointed out the faulty assumptions behind them.

Mark doesn't find anything more and turns around when he reaches the back wall. He passes the ledge on the way to the mouth without so much as a glance upward.

"It was meant to be," he says once he's standing in front of the cave again. A startled seagull squawks and leaps, soaring from the cliff. His mocking voice imitates his mother, but the irony that drenches his words is meant solely for him. He suspects that when he finally gets a chance to compare their genomes, he'll find that the woman named Nadia Hayek is indeed his mother.

When he makes his way down to the beach, Antun and the pilot are wading to the anchored boat, carrying a cooler between them. They wrestle it aboard, then Antun starts back to shore. As his feet splash out of the surf, he looks up and sees Mark. "I was just coming to find you." He's shouting to be heard above the sea breeze. "How did you like the cave?"

"It was fantastic!" Mark yells back enthusiastically. He almost apologizes for his earlier outburst, but an apology won't change the fact that he's in Lebanon illegally because of Antun.

Long, sturdy rods lie on the deck when Mark climbs over the side. He dries off with a nearby towel, waiting to see if Antun will explain their presence, but he's busy moving the cooler. Mark rolls the bottom of his pants back down then slips his shoes on. "Have you been fishing?"

"*We* have been fishing, and the catch has been good, all caught while the three of us were far out at sea—you understand?" Antun's smile is patronizing, as if he's explaining something to a child.

Mark doesn't smile back. He's weary of the puzzles Antun tosses his way. He kicks at an empty bait bucket, not applying enough force to knock it over. "And what's this?" The breeze whips his words around them. "I suppose I'm the one who swallowed all the bait."

Antun gives him a quick look. His laugh is a snort. "That you did."

They go back out into the Mediterranean, reversing the course taken earlier from Haifa. When they turn in toward Israel, the pilot gets on the radio at intervals, speaking in Hebrew. Mark isn't surprised this time when an Israeli patrol boat approaches them.

When they come up alongside, Antun tells Mark that he'll need to get out both his tourist visa and passport. A net is proffered from the Israeli boat. Mark, as well as Antun and the pilot, put their papers in. When everything has been checked, the net is passed back over. Everyone says "*Shalom*," and the patrol boat revs several times before leaving.

Soon, they're making their way into port. Nothing looks familiar. "Why are we at a different dock?" Mark asks.

"Security has to check for weapons and other contraband." Antun's eyes are indecipherable. "They already know we aren't suspected terrorists, but they'll want to know what we bring with us."

Mark's stomach trembles, small aftershocks of the hangover. He rubs a finger over his lips, which are parched from the sun and wind. Perhaps the security officials will only look through the boat and not in his bag.

"You understand that Israel has to be very careful," Antun says with a hint of sarcasm.

"I wasn't complaining. Do they know you at this port, as well?" Mark asks.

If Antun noticed the tit for tat, he ignores it. The corners of his mouth flip up. "They know me very well. With any luck, they'll only spend a few minutes on us."

Mark's stomach settles somewhat.

As soon as they pull into a slip, security officials leap on board. They are polite and courteous, but they are very thorough, swarming everywhere over the deck. After a minute, several go down into the cabin. Mark glances at Antun. He's being quiet, not attempting to engage them. Either he was lying about knowing them, or this particular crew isn't friendly.

The cooler is near where Mark sits. The official who approaches it looks to be the youngest of the group. He nods at Mark before undoing the catch. When the lid is lifted, Mark sees eight or nine fresh sea bass.

As the official straightens, he looks at Mark, speaking Hebrew.

"Sorry, I only speak English," Mark says, trying to exude relaxed friendliness.

"Ah yes, the American." The man's dark eyes roam over him curiously and light upon Mark's shoulder where the strap lies. "Will you pass me your bag, sir?"

When Mark grasps the shoulder strap, an unnatural calmness fills him now that it's almost certain the blade will be found. With surprising speed, he thinks up a story. He'll say that he found it among the rocks near the caves at Mount Carmel. He's pretty sure that the knife-shaped stone is just a replica that someone recently lost—perhaps bought from the gift shop. He'd forgotten about it while they were fishing, but of course—in the unlikely event that the piece turns out to be something of archaeological value—he'll donate it to a museum in Tel Aviv. He hands over the bag.

Out come the brochures from Mount Carmel. "Did you enjoy visiting the caves, sir?"

"Very much so." Mark stands up, gesturing at his shirt. "As you can see, I'm interested in Neanderthals."

The younger man squints at the T-shirt. "What is the meaning of the number?"

Just as Mark had earlier with Antun, he explains how he came to have the T-shirt and what it represents. "You have some limited Neanderthal ancestry yourself," he says at the end of his drawn-out account. He's discovered a latent talent for chatter as glib as any Antun can produce.

The official's face is doubtful. "*I* do?" he asks, poking his own chest with the hand holding the brochures. The sudden movement causes the slick paper to slide through his fingers and flutter onto the boat's deck.

Laughter erupts from the dock. The inquisitor's head jerks around. All of his companions are already off the boat. One of the older officials calls out sharply in Hebrew. His face red, the young man scoops up the pamphlets and stuffs them back in the bag before giving it back to Mark.

"*Shalom,*" he says curtly and leaves to join the others.

All of Mark's muscles relax at the same time, leaving him limp. He slings the bag over his shoulder and sits down heavily upon the bench.

The boat slowly makes its way around to where their car is parked. "They're being extra careful today," Antun says. "There must be a heightened alert."

"What did the older guy say to the one that checked my bag?"

Antun laughs. "He told him that he *was* a Neanderthal—said he needed more training in how to deal with tourists so that he won't rudely take up so much of their time."

Mark again feels oddly defensive about this recently discovered branch of his family tree. "Their brains were larger than ours," he says to no one in particular as they prepare to disembark.

Mark attributes Antun's slower driving on the return to Tel Aviv as well as his big yawns to the diminishing effects of whatever he inhaled earlier. When they're back at the apartment and Antun says he needs to work in his study for a few hours, Mark suspects he may want to be alone for another reason.

"I'm going for a walk," Mark says. "I usually walk or run every day before work, and I miss it."

"You don't mind going out alone? Won't you get lost?"

"Not at all. I'll be fine," Mark says with confidence. He hates to be lost and has developed a knack over time for finding his way around in strange places.

"Just punch in the door code when you return." Antun rattles off the number. "Do you need me to write it down?"

"No need to." Mark repeats the number. "I'll remember it."

"Don't be too long. I'm cooking fish later." Antun walks away abruptly, the leather-soled slippers he's changed into slapping the tiles.

Late-afternoon shadows from trees and buildings line the avenues as Mark strolls along. He heads for Shenkin Street. As soon as he locates it, he's fighting crowds. It seems that in Tel Aviv, everyone comes out early on Friday nights.

While waiting for a group of teenagers to pass, Mark presses close to a kiosk. An English-language newspaper catches his eye, and he scans the headlines on the front page. An article near the bottom is about Manot Cave, near the Israeli border with Lebanon. He buys the paper, tucks it into his shoulder bag, and turns off on a less-trafficked side street, where he finds a café that has free Wi-Fi. His mother will be wondering what's happened to him. He's decided that he'll have to take the risk of going online in a public place.

After ordering coffee, Mark pulls out his laptop. Debating as to whether he should check out his mother's genome first or begin with reading her e-mails, he decides to quickly pull up the Genetics and Me website. Responding to her messages will take a while, so he'll save that for last. He's bemused by how badly he misses her now that she's thousands of miles away and can't aggravate him with a summons. He wants to write something with more pith than a quick reassurance.

He logs onto the site and goes to ancestry composition first. Scanning the information, he sees that she's fifty percent Middle Eastern and fifty percent English and Irish. He presses a forefinger against his lips for a moment, clueless as to how she's ended up with this particular genetic mix. He clicks on the tab for ancestry comparisons and then types Nadia Hayek and Mark Hayek into the boxes. After a second, all of the chromosomes come up in rows of nice straight horizontal lines. Mark is automatically assigned blue, his mother red. A lot of purple crosses the screen for every chromosome.

He swallows, his breath catching. Nadia Hayek is truly his mother. Several relieved sighs escape him. A woman at the ridiculously close café table alongside his turns her head his way.

He blinks to stop his eyes from stinging as he glances over. Large dark eyes gaze at him almost tenderly. Embarrassed, he looks away. She reminds him of Yasmin.

Antun's remark about Mark acting more Lebanese than his blood allowed makes more sense now in light of the genetics. But Mark would like to know exactly what he was implying. Antun seemed to be insinuating that their kinship wasn't very deep.

Mark sips coffee, thinking about what he's just learned. He knows now that his fair-skinned mother didn't adopt him, but perhaps she herself was adopted. He remembers again the pictures he's seen of her parents and their lack of resemblance to their supposed daughter. Mark might not be related to Antun, even if they do look a lot alike. He finds this thought doesn't upset him at all.

He's stumped until Uncle Sami's ashes come to mind. They are to be his soon. Surely cremated remains contain enough bone fragments for DNA extraction. He feels ghoulish. Not long ago, his uncle was a living, breathing being.

Mark puts down the cup. He clicks on Mail and sees that his mother has sent a dozen e-mails during the three days he's been gone. He's sure that at least half of those accuse him of uncommunicative callousness.

Her first e-mail has an attachment. He opens it immediately and finds his uncle's message to his mother pasted in a document. It's in French, and his mother has included a translation underneath. He reads it in French then in English. The message states clearly that Antun has fallen in with a bad lot and has broken his father's heart. "Very often, children will disappoint you," his uncle wrote.

Sami went on to explain that he was sure Antun was consuming drugs daily. He suspected cocaine, as he'd seen no needle marks. But he also believed that Antun was illegally trafficking in antiquities stolen from museums throughout the Middle East. The group Antun was dealing with was not only evil, but so technologically savvy that Sami dared not even mention their name in his e-mail for fear they would somehow intercept his words and hunt him down to kill him.

Mark runs several fingers over his chin, his beard making a rasping sound. The drug use, he already knows about, but surely his uncle wasn't correct about the last accusation. The whole world has become aware of how terrorist groups are selling off valuable antiquities that have been plundered from Iraq, Syria, Turkey, and elsewhere, but it's highly unlikely than Antun would risk his business reputation by dealing with such a notorious bunch.

After being around his cousin for only a few days, Mark knows that Antun isn't beyond breaking the law when it suits him, and this may have offended his father, but Sami's message seems full of paranoia. *Perhaps his mind was failing along with his heart...*

Although Antun's thoughtless bad-boy behavior is irritating, Mark has a hard time picturing him in the role of international criminal. He clicks out of the document.

As he guessed, his mother's messages are missives designed to make him feel guilty about not getting in touch, and she wants to know if any diseases were found in the test tube of her saliva he had tested. She's also upset that he has to associate with "that bad seed," as she calls Antun. She begs him to be careful and to come home as soon as possible. He has to write her daily, she says, or she'll become sick with worry.

Mark has forgotten that she agreed to genetic testing because he told her she could obtain health information. He goes back into the Genetics and Me website. The results show that she doesn't have any serious inherited conditions and only a slightly elevated risk of developing diabetes and psoriasis. He mentions the latter in his message, careful to reassure her that her health is fine.

To address her worries about Antun, he writes that he's positive Uncle Sami was wrong about Antun. Mark hasn't seen anything to be overly alarmed about. Perhaps Antun uses drugs socially, but Mark, of course, doesn't join him in that activity.

He pauses, his fingers over the keys. *How to explain that I'll be communicating erratically?* After saying that nothing is wrong, Mark can't very well mention that he's afraid to use Antun's Wi-Fi, particularly since his suspicions are based solely upon a vague uneasiness.

Time is moving by. Mark needs to write something, so he says that because he's traveling to Turkey the next day, he won't have time to e-mail until he gets settled there. He describes Tel Aviv and tells her how much he and Antun look like each other. Before sending the message, he ends by saying that he doesn't mean to cause her worry. He loves her and misses her. Mark reads the last sentence again, puzzled by how words of affection appear trite and clichéd when written down.

He quickly responds to the few messages from the staff at The Parkinson's Institute. They all write that he's greatly missed but shouldn't worry. His projects will be waiting for him when he returns. Rather than reassuring him, well-meaning words like these will normally cause a spike of anxiety, alleviated only when he arrives back at work. But right now, California and the Institute seem like part of another world, a mythical, faraway place.

When he puts away his laptop and gets up, the Yasmin look-alike catches his eye again. He gives her a smile and says, "*Shalom.*" She can't help that she looks like someone he'll struggle to forget for some time.

Chapter 11

Western Asia, Late Pleistocene

THE LEOPARD TRACKS STILL LOOKED fresh. No wind had blown nor rain fallen since the day before to blur the prints. Raven pulled up purple-flowered mallow growing between the low, flat rocks that led away from the outcrop. Instead of saving the plants as usual, she tossed them on the ground, marking the spot of her supposed demise. Then she threw one of her gathering bags full of dried herbs beside the mallow.

She lay onto the mallow and bag, rolling over them while thrashing her arms and legs to show that she'd struggled. She thought about cutting herself and dripping blood around the area but decided that wasn't necessary. A leopard kill was not always bloody. If a large cat had actually leapt on her and cut off her breath by clamping its jaws over her throat, very little blood would have been spilled before it dragged her away.

Too many footprints in the area would seem unnatural to the band's top trackers. She saw Leaf in her mind, bending over the outlines of her moccasins, trying to determine what had happened, so she took great care in returning to the outcrop, walking on top of stones and grass. Several times, she stooped to gently brush away a misstep with her hand.

Once there, she climbed up and squatted for a moment on the mounded top. She rested, silently observant, listening to the sounds of the awakening camp, seeing the swallows fly to and from the ledges, taking it all in one last time: the smell of roasting meat on the air, the sunrise brightening the rocky walls, the timeless maws of the caves. An ache filled her so completely that her eyes closed tightly for a heartbeat.

Without looking again at the camp, she climbed down and collected her bags and the spear. Stepping in her earlier footprints, she made her way to the rock-covered ground winding off into the distance.

As she crept through the landscape that morning, she often reminded herself to be patient, to not plunge ahead. Time after time, she scrupulously scanned her surroundings for dangerous animals, from the highest perch possible, often only a small hill or rock pile. Only rarely did she come upon a tree tall enough for climbing, because the steppes were mostly grassland dotted with low junipers. She sometimes caught a tantalizing glimpse of trees near the distant river, but she resisted the temptation to walk along the bank there. Except for an occasional spring, that meandering strip held the only water available for prey and predator alike. If she didn't stumble upon a spring before her water bladder was empty, she would risk walking over, but she wouldn't linger.

A cool, dry wind blew persistently during early afternoon, pressing the grass in the direction that Raven traveled. The breeze pushed her along as she flitted from one shadowy hiding place to another. She felt like a feather caught up in a draft, never knowing where she would land before day's end.

That feeling of aimless floating became unbearable before long, and although the sun was still high, she began searching for a place to pass the night. Several times, she was held up for long stretches before moving on, once when she spied a wolf pack crossing in the distance and again when a group of wooly rhinoceroses paused to graze in her path. She became increasingly concerned as the sun trailed downward. The constant vigilance had worn her out, but she hadn't yet found suitable shelter. A small rock overhang a short distance back looked promising, but a split in the river had brought that waterway temporarily too close by, so she'd gone on. In retrospect, she realized that firewood and brush would be easier to find there. If she kept a strong fire going throughout the night, animals on their way to the river would go out of their way to avoid her camp. The fact that her water was almost gone helped make the decision to backtrack.

Upon reaching the overhang, she secured her bags and walked over to the river, taking only her spear and several water bladders. While she was filling the bladders, a large brown bear loped down the opposite bank. Raven froze, barely breathing, hoping it wouldn't notice her, but the wind was blowing in the animal's direction.

Probing the air with its snout, it searched the area until it found her. Under its hostile gaze, she slowly tied off the tops of the bladders and hung them over her shoulder. Then she raised her spear, showing the animal that she would put up a fight if need be, all the while talking calmly, telling the bear that she only wanted water, just as it did. She lowered her spear, careful not to jab the point in the bear's direction. With pounding heart, she slowly backed away from the bank until she was hidden in the trees.

Raven gathered an armful of fallen limbs on her way back to the shelter, struggling to carry the spear until she laid it over her arms along with the branches. Seeing the bear had unnerved her, so before collecting more wood, she used a spindle stick and dried grass to start a fire in front of the overhang. The much-colder air of approaching night had replaced the earlier cool breeze, and the fire's heat felt good against her cheeks.

She went out again and continued collecting until she had a large woodpile, including a knot of resinous fatwood that would rapidly raise the blaze higher and hotter if needed. But her best find was a long log that had been part of a tree trunk. Once she broke the rotted branches off, she easily rolled it to the overhang. It stretched along the front like a barrier. When ignited, it would burn for a long while.

After eating from her provisions, she raked embers around the log, using a branch. Once that was done, she rested on her side against the rocky wall of the overhang, gazing into the flames. She felt as if she were still moving across the grassy plains. Then she was falling into the unresisting grass—falling, falling, falling.

When she awoke, night had fully arrived, and into the dark, Raven was calling for her sister, howling, "Willooow!" Breathing hard, she sat up, dismayed. Now any beast near the river knew where to find her.

The log still glowed, but the other limbs had almost burnt completely into ash. Remembering the woodpile at the end of the overhang, she was about to crawl over, when movement on the other side of the log stopped her. A man stood in the blackness, and her heart sank as she thought she recognized Bear. How easily he'd found her. The taste in her mouth was worse than a swallow of thistle tea. He would drag her back to camp and imprison her there the way he'd tried to in the valley. Now that Willow was gone, no one would intercede.

The upright form made a snuffling sound, and Raven realized she was looking at the bear she'd seen earlier. It stood on its hind legs, white teeth glistening as it moaned. An icy spasm sped through her. She leaned over, snatched up a partially burned limb, and threw it at the beast. The smoldering wood trailed sparks as it hit the bear's flank. The animal dropped to all fours, snorting in alarm, and shuffled away. Raven quickly found the fatwood knot and threw it on the coals. When it began crackling, she added more branches, and the flames flared upward.

She wanted to sleep while the fire burned brightly, but her heart raced at even the most harmless noises, and her eyes, straining to see through the flames, wouldn't close. Finally, she rolled over onto her side and pressed against the shelter wall. "What have I done?" she murmured over and over against the rocky face until she finally slept.

The next couple days were repeats of the first day: halting to carefully observe her surroundings, gathering courage before crossing over to the next stop, hoping that she hadn't missed a well-hidden animal that would suddenly leap on her. The elders claimed that the tribes were the Earth Mother's favored children, but everyone well knew that she provided food for all her offspring. Raven's greatest fear was that a pack of hyenas or wolves would suddenly appear. They covered ground rapidly, and even if they didn't notice her in their path right away, it would be difficult to hide before they were upon her.

On the fourth morning, Raven decided to increase her chances of survival by appealing to the Earth Mother for guidance and protection. Twice she chanted her plea while tossing pinches of ochre into the air, first while facing the rising sun then again facing the direction where the sun would set.

When she next stopped, Raven made out the almost imperceptible ears of a hidden lion poking up through grass in the distance. Instead of fear, she felt relief. Raven remembered how the Earth Mother had interceded for the baby's life by sending a vision. How rapidly she'd located danger was yet another sign that her child was meant to thrive. They were favored to prevail in the rivalry between life and death.

Hoverflies droned in the grass while Raven waited patiently for the lion to move on. She crouched within a crack at the top of a large boulder, where the gap was barely large enough for her and the pouches. Behind her lay another large pocked boulder that she'd used as her previous stopping point, and when she quickly scanned the whole area, an odd striped pattern on that boulder's surface caught her eye. When the striped area moved, she identified a small cat climbing along the top. It must have been hidden when she'd made her plea to the Earth Mother while paused there earlier. A twinge of despondency wound through her thoughts. She'd never had the chance to ask Leaf if he'd found the mother cat she'd seen at the lake. That one on the boulder was only partially grown, a largish kitten.

The cat suddenly turned, ran across the surface, its tail in the air, and jumped downward as if playing, pouncing perhaps on one of its siblings. Raven frowned—how unobservant she'd been not to have heard or seen a den of cats.

She wanted to return and find them, but she needed to remain focused on the lion. Raven glanced out across the plain at the pointed ear tips. That beast was obviously not going any-where for a while; she would only be at the boulder for a few moments. Leaving her bags in the split, she slipped down to the ground with her spear. Crouching low, she ran over.

Edging slowly around the boulder, Raven searched for a hollow or crack where kittens might be hiding. A couple of crows on the opposite side began cawing excitedly, and she paused. A shiver of fear went down her back. Perhaps the crows were only anticipating her appearance or cawing at the cats—but it could be that something was lurking behind the boulder. The hair rose on the back of her neck, and she changed her mind about find-ing the kittens. Grasping the spear tightly, she turned to flee.

"It's me, Raven," a familiar voice said. She stopped in her tracks as Leaf came around the boulder. He blocked her way, a frown on his face. "Where in the world are you going?"

The happiness that had flooded her at seeing him faded. "Have you been sent by Bear to drag me back, then?"

He winced at the hostility in her voice. "Not me. I was the one who told Bear that a leopard had taken you and that later, hyenas had snatched you from the leopard. I showed him bone fragments from an old antelope kill and told him that those bits were all that was left once they'd finished."

Raven cringed at the thought of being obliterated by hyenas, her splintered bones scattered about.

"You hid your tracks well, but I found where the leopard left the stones—it wasn't dragging anything. Then, after searching farther, I found your trail. Once I knew that you were out here alone, I couldn't sleep." Looking down, he scuffed the ground with a foot. "The truth is—I can't abide not ever seeing you again." His raised his head and drew in a sharp breath. "So here I am."

With a small cry, Raven dropped her spear and leaned forward to embrace him. When he abruptly moved back a step, a frustrated sound slipped from her. Blinking in confusion, she lowered her arms and looked away.

He reached across the gap separating them. Placing his hand on her cheek, he trailed his fingers down to her chin, pinching it slightly to turn her face toward him. "She'll be hard to get back if she runs away," he said.

"What do you mean?" Surely he didn't think she was going to run away from him like some startled deer.

"I have a kitten in my pack. It was the only one I was able to keep alive when the mother disappeared. I don't want to take it out right here. I'll let you see it later."

Her eyes widened at those words. How was it possible that he could persuade a wild animal to travel with him?

"But you haven't answered my question," he said. "Where are you going?"

Raven's curiosity about the cat vanished, and her throat tightened. He would leave her once he heard her intended destination. She twisted her face away from his hand. "I'm searching for the Longheads. I helped the Longhead captive not long ago.

Maybe his band will return the favor now by allowing me to live with them. I know it's possible," she said defiantly. "After all, you lived with a group for several turns of the seasons."

His mouth dropped, and she believed that he was lost to her, but his shocked expression quickly faded. "I'll help you find them."

Raven looked at him sharply. She hadn't been expecting that response. "And then where will you go?"

"Perhaps I'll stay with them also—for a while," he said in such a matter-of-fact manner that Raven wondered if she'd heard him clearly.

"But we must keep moving, without so much talking," he said. "Voices carry out here. We'll talk about this again when we stop for the night."

"A lion is in my path." She stooped and picked up her spear. "I've been waiting for it to leave. I'll show you."

The lion was weaving its way through the grass when they climbed up on the boulder where her bags were. It was at a good distance, moving away from them, so they collected the bags and set out. They were still within Leaf's accustomed scouting range, and he had a sure foot as he led them at a quicker pace than Raven had been taking. She realized that his vision was better than hers when, from a hillock, he pointed over the steppes. She tried to pick out what had caught his attention, but all she saw was vague, shimmying movement in the distance.

"What is it?" she said under her breath.

"A herd of horses being followed by wolves."

"You have the eyes of a hawk!" she exclaimed, forgetting to keep quiet.

He put a finger across her lips to quiet her but smiled while doing so, letting his finger linger longer than necessary. She returned his smile, realizing how much she'd missed him—his expressions, his manner of talking, and the way he looked at her.

Relieved from the strain of solitary vigilance, Raven became calm. Fear lifted from her thoughts, and for the first time, she realized that the vast, grassy steppes woven through with flowering plants had a beauty of their own. But her pleasure in the day was somewhat ruined by the little thorns of dread that kept pricking her. She'd decided to tell Leaf the truth about the baby when they stopped for the night; in all probability, he would figure it out anyway once he saw the child. And he deserved to know. She wasn't going to hide her secret from him any longer, even if it separated them forever.

Leaf knew of a cave near a spring where he'd stayed in the past, and he found it in the late afternoon. They lowered their bags gratefully onto the cave floor and sat, resting a while. Leaf reached into his bag and pulled out the kitten. When it saw Raven, it hissed and darted away, hiding under Leaf's leg.

"I don't think it likes me," she said.

"She just needs to be around you for a time."

"The mother died?"

He shrugged. "Most likely. Her den was in a large tree with a hollow trunk. I left her food, but she soon stopped returning for it. The four kittens had become used to me—I'd crawled in and picked them up when the mother wasn't around. So when I realized they were starving, I began chewing meat into a pulp so I could feed them. Only this one survived, though. She was the largest."

Leaf pulled out a small braided rope. He reached under his knee for the cat and attached the rope to a leather band encircling the small animal's neck.

His manner of controlling the cat reminded her of the way the Longhead had been restrained. "It's a captive," she said.

He gave her a keen look, grasping her allusion. "I can't risk her roaming off while we gather kindling. She's not large enough to hunt for herself."

Raven nodded hastily and looked down. Talking with him about Longheads wasn't going to be easy.

He weighted down the rope with a heavy rock, and they went out to gather fallen branches and brush along with some dried dung they found around the small water hole bordering the spring. After making a fire in the cave mouth, they ate. Leaf had also packed dried meat from the bison hunt. Raven watched in fascination as the kitten came out of hiding and mewled to be fed. She sat still so the small creature wouldn't take fright again at her presence. They talked very little, watching the cat eat, until all the small pieces that Leaf bit off for it were gone and the animal had slipped into the bag once more. A soft rain began, stray drops sizzling in the fire's outer edge.

From time to time, Leaf glanced at her with an air of expectation, and Raven knew he was waiting on her to begin; she cleared her throat. "I know how you despise Longheads. I can't believe that you would live with them again." She hesitated a heartbeat. "I saw you relieve your bladder onto the captive when everyone thought he was dead."

He reddened slightly. "That was nasty of me. I wouldn't do that now. Not after knowing you."

Her eyebrows rose.

"Do you not realize that you're the one who gentled me—took the sting out of me?"

Not knowing how to respond, she looked into the flames.

"When I lived at their camp, I was always focused on trying to please them. It was only after I escaped that I understood more clearly how they'd deprived me of family and tribe. I hated them then for some time—until you came and your words soothed me." He glanced at her while he poked at the fire with a stick. "But they cared for me in their own way. They freely shared their food, and when I was ill, they gave me medicines just as you would and worried over me." He threw the stick into the fire and looked over, his brow puckered. "But I won't be their slave again. If it came to that, I would go, even if it meant leaving you with them."

She watched him silently, unsettled by those last words.

"We may have another choice besides living with the Longheads, though," he said.

"It isn't possible for us to survive a winter alone." An edge of shrillness crept in. "The baby will come during winter."

He gave her a chiding glance. "I know very well how long you've been with child. I would never endanger you or the baby. What I'm trying to tell you is that I want to join my birth tribe. They will accept me—and you as my mate because of these." He threw off his parka and pulled his tunic over his head.

Raven contemplated the swirling tattoos crossing his chest.

He placed his hand over them, a reverent gesture. "The Wind tribe lived in the lands where warm breezes are born. The tattoos show the wind."

"Ah," she said, moving her hands and arms around, stirring the air, struggling with the idea. "The tattoos show the wind and how it moves, touching everyone when it blows. Are the tribe's bands still living in those lands? Where are they now?"

"I was with several bands that left together. I was only a child, and I don't remember why we were leaving. After traveling a long distance, we came out of mountains and crossed a spit of land with water on both sides. I remember it well—all that water stretching for as far as you could see. Then we traveled on and began living at the edges of Fire Cloud lands." He paused, lost in thought.

Raven had a flash of memory. In her flying dream, she'd crossed that land strip bordered by water that he'd mentioned.

"So those bands that left are nearby?"

"I don't know," he said. "I've heard they went back across the mountains. If that's true, I'll have to search farther, and we would have to winter somewhere." He looked at her sideways. "Maybe longer—the baby needs to grow before we undertake such a journey."

Raven felt her lips moving, the words trotting out before she was ready, and she barely recognized her voice, it was so fainthearted. "I must tell you something."

Leaf watched her while the fire crackled in the silence, glancing down at her rigid fingers held tightly over her belly before looking again at her face. Taking a quick breath, she plunged ahead all at once, like someone entering icy water. "This baby isn't Bear's."

He didn't even blink. "I know whose it is—that's why the Longheads would take us in, but given a choice, I'd rather stay elsewhere. Even if my tribe is gone, a few more bands of your tribe dwell this side of the mountains. We could stay with one of those."

Raven was too stunned to respond. All this time, she'd been guarding her secret when he already knew. Sticky moisture gathered on her skin as she stared at him. She didn't want to ask how he'd come about his knowledge.

He watched her from the corner of his eye. "I figured that you wanted rid of the baby because you were somehow sure it wasn't Bear's."

Mortified, she covered her face with her hands. He was only partly right. She'd decided to rid herself of the baby no matter who the father, and that was even worse.

"It's all right, Raven," he said softly. "What happened between you and the captive. Several of their women whose mates had died were curious about me, even if I was still something of a child, and under the pretext of sharing warmth on cold nights, those women took me under their sleeping furs. They considered our mating as a mutual kindness."

Before she'd known the captive, she would have been shocked by what he'd told her. That night, though, she felt only relief. "Then you'll stay with me?"

He was quickly by her side, pulling her hands down, making her look at him. "The day we fetched you from your home band, I understood that you were my only hope for happiness. I would follow you to the edges of the world."

The weight of his words frightened Raven a little. Mostly, they mystified her. She was simply a woman who'd struggled her entire life to find her footing. She wished she could see herself through his eyes and discover what he saw in her.

He took one of his finely worked skins and laid it on the cave floor beside the fire, and it was very natural to join him there. His exuberance made her forget, for a time, her lingering anxieties. For someone so young, he seemed very experienced as he explored her limb by limb, and under his touch, Raven couldn't help but sense those other, very different women. She knew her past was also on his mind when afterward, he ran his hand over her belly. "You're not all that big yet."

She laughed. "Wait a few more moons. Then you'll see."

His eager face wore flickering shadows from the fire as he leaned on an elbow. "The next baby the Earth Mother gives you will be my doing."

Even though she smiled at his cockiness, doubts nagged her. What would happen if they did live with the Longheads and their old captive still showed an interest in her? She quickly pulled him closer, tamping down her misgivings.

Traveling with another person was much better than trekking alone. Raven no longer felt lonely with Leaf always there—and there was the cat. The kitten lost all fear of her when she began feeding it. Her ability to feel such fondness for a wild creature surprised Raven. The small animal slept most of the day in Leaf's pack, but in the evenings, it delighted her by playing with the straw and small sticks she trailed around their camps.

And looking out for dangerous animals was much easier when there was another pair of eyes. Raven and Leaf stopped often and stood back to back, especially when they found a high spot, him scanning in one direction while she searched the opposite way.

Raven had watched binding ceremonies all her life, but now she understood, for the first time, the significance of tying a couple so they faced in opposite directions. The side-by-side binding had always been clear: the couple faced the world together.

The meaning of the last constraint, the frontal binding, was also obvious. Although Raven and Leaf hadn't been united through ceremony, she felt as if they had been, and the fulfillment of the activities—promised by that intimate, final part of the ritual—was presently overwhelming her.

Just as Raven had once worried that Leaf was too distracted by her to perform his scouting duties, she worried that he was endangering their lives for the same reason. A hunter's story kept going through her head about how he'd observed horses so intent on mating that they hadn't noticed lions in the surrounding brush. The stallion escaped, badly clawed, but the mare had been killed.

The days after her binding ceremony with Reed had been intense, but she didn't remember them as having been frenzied. Leaf behaved like someone dying of thirst, so great was his need. Even when not pulling her toward a shelter of some kind, his hands were all over her. Whenever they scouted back to back, he ruined the effectiveness of that stance by turning around and taking down her bag so he could mold his body against hers.

"I wonder why the binding ceremony doesn't include this position," she said pointedly when he pressed from behind her yet again.

"It should," he murmured, nuzzling her neck.

Their progress across the landscape slowed to a crawl. Although Raven enjoyed his spontaneity, she was beginning to feel the same sense of impending peril she'd had while tied to Bear during the joining ceremony. Leaf's reckless fervor seemed dangerous.

But that unease didn't make her stop him when at midday following their third morning together, he grasped her hand and looked at her with eyes so liquid, she thought they would overflow. He gave her a long kiss before leading her into a ring of tall boulders. They caressed standing for a while, and he kissed her again, his tongue exploring the small gap between her front teeth.

"I love this small mistake that the Earth Mother made while forming you," he said. He lifted her to sit on a small ledge, her back pressed against smooth rock, her tunic pushed up. He was about to remove his loincloth when a loud, rasping voice coming from outside the circle of stones interrupted them.

"I could use your help," a man was saying loudly. "You should know that already. You crossed my blood trail only a few steps back."

Raven froze, staring across at Leaf. She knew that his face, alarmed and startled, reflected her own. The man's voice was one she'd heard before, but before she could place it, Leaf reached for her.

CHAPTER 12

The Levant, Present Day

AN ENTICING ODOR OF FRYING onions fills the air as Antun moves about the kitchen. His pupils are large, lit up in a way that's becoming all too familiar, and his spirits are in fine fettle. He's singing a lilting Bollywood song that he says is popular across the Middle East.

Mark watches from where he perches on a stool, amused even though he shouldn't be.

Antun breaks off singing. "You are going to love this!" he says, spreading apart his red, spice-stained fingertips like a blooming rose in front of Mark's face.

For a moment, all Mark can see is Antun's big hand with its opened fingers. He resists the urge to swat the hand aside.

"I swear it," Antun says. "Have you ever eaten Lebanese fish with rice?"

"Yes, but not for many years."

"Then you haven't been truly living all that time. I will raise you from the tomb, like Jesus." He chortles at the irreverence. "With that short beard, you look like a Jesus murai I've seen at a Lebanese church in Galilee."

"Then so do you—look like Jesus. At least you did when I first met you," Mark says, his voice starched. "Until you shaved off the stubble." His words are accusatory, but he can't take them back. If his cousin takes offense, that's too bad.

But it will take more than Mark's outing to puncture Antun's mood. He tilts his head back and roars his laughter at the ceiling. "Touché! My brother does have wit, after all." Still shaking with laughter, he lays out several fish and whacks off their heads with strong blows of a cleaver.

Mark jumps, and one of his eyelids begins to twitch. The twitching increases when Antun, humming, pinches more spices into a steaming pan and throws in one of the fish heads. After putting on the lid, Antun wipes his hands on a kitchen towel and turns to face Mark.

"There," he says, leaning against the counter. "It needs to simmer for a few minutes, for the flavor."

Mark blinks to stop the small spasms and casts about for something to say to take his mind off the fish eyes boiling in the pan.

But before he can think of anything, Antun waves his hand at a nearby shelf. "Those are my sons."

There are photographs of two small boys in metal frames set in front of several cookbooks. Mark has seen pictures of these boys throughout the apartment. The only room he hasn't been in is Antun's bedroom, but he's sure the furniture and walls there are also filled with their photos. He's been reluctant to ask about them, not knowing the circumstances of Antun's divorce.

"Elie and Sarkis. They're your cousins, too, you know."

"Yes, I know," Mark says, although he isn't completely sure that they are. "Do you see them often?"

Antun folds his arms, subdued now. "Not nearly enough. I'll use part of my inheritance to take their mother to court once more. I didn't have the means to fight her wealthy family during the divorce. Israeli fathers pay the highest child support in the world—not that I'm protesting that," he adds. "I want to support them, but on my own terms." His eyes hold Mark's. "Isn't that a reasonable request for the court?"

All Mark can say is, "Yes, of course."

"I'm happy you agree." Antun unfolds his arms. "But our meal awaits my attention." Before pouring rice into the steaming broth, he takes out the head, to Mark's relief, and throws it in the garbage. He filets the fish then sautés them in a separate pan, crooning a French tune as they sizzle.

The meal, fresh fish and savory rice set off by a salad of bitter greens, is delicious. Afterward, they watch television before Mark excuses himself for the evening.

He showers and, although he's sleepy, pulls out the newspaper he bought earlier on Shenkin Street. The article that grabbed his attention is about a fifty-five-thousand-year-old cranium found in Israel's Manot Cave. Some of the skull's details overlap with known Neanderthal features. This particular individual lived during the period after a wave of modern humans came out of Africa into the Levant. Geneticists believe that interbreeding events between Neanderthals and early humans occurred during that time.

Mark stops reading to glance again at the pictured skull. The article hints that the cranium could be from a Neanderthal-human hybrid. He studies the map included with the article. The cave in Lebanon where he'd found the quartz blade was close to the Israeli border and probably only a few miles from Manot Cave. Mark rereads several sections, then he takes out the blade. He doesn't know enough about Paleolithic tools to determine how old the piece is or which ancient group might have made it, Neanderthal or Early Modern Human.

After securing the knife, Mark goes to bed and dreams of those who lived in the nearby caves so long ago. One of the skin-clad women holds a sturdy baby, and the child's features mark it as a hybrid—the infant has enormous eyes, and its little chin recedes slightly. The mother's face is identical to Yasmin's, except that her skin is darker.

Mark gets up early to pack, but since their Istanbul flight isn't until midafternoon, Antun decides they'll kill time by going to his antiquities shop. The streets are almost empty when they arrive in front of an elaborate metal-grillwork door, and Mark comments on how few people are about.

"Today is Saturday," Antun says, shaking his head at Mark's ignorance. "The Jewish Sabbath. Even if it weren't, the store would still be closed. I won't reopen until my father's estate is settled." After unlocking the grill door and the wooden one behind, he inclines his head at Mark. "Closed, that is, except for an esteemed guest whom I wish to entertain."

"I appreciate that," Mark says, wondering why Antun's words often leave him feeling not only annoyed, but obligated, as well.

They enter a modern, tastefully designed store, long and narrow. The walls are taken up by well-lit shelves of expensive wood. Most of the displayed objects are everyday items of ancient life: glass and pottery vessels, clay oil lamps, and bronze and silver coins. Ancient jewelry, as well as small sculptures and figurines, fill some of the shelves.

As they wander through the store, Antun relates the histories of the various pieces. Mark pauses in front of a weapons display. The smaller daggers remind him of the quartz blade.

"I have something here from every major Levantine civilization," Antun says proudly.

"You're very knowledgeable."

"I love my business." Antun gestures at the shelves. "I am honored to be the temporary custodian of these bits and pieces from ancient lives."

Mark gnaws his bottom lip. Antun's reverence sounds sincere, although it's probably part of his sales pitch to everyone who enters the shop. "Is there ever a problem when a buyer tries to carry their purchases through airport security?" he asks.

"Rarely. As a licensed dealer, I provide a certificate identifying the object. If they have the certificate, then there isn't a problem. Why? Does one of the displays catch your eye?"

"Everything here is fantastic, but I found something at the cave yesterday that I would like to take home with me if possible."

"At the Mount Carmel caves?"

"No, the one in Lebanon."

When Mark takes out the blade, Antun's eyes pop.

"Do you know what kind of trouble we would have had if Israeli security found that?" Antun's voice is edgy as he holds out his hand. "Let me see it."

Mark hands it over.

"Where exactly in the cave did you find this?"

"On a ledge high up the cave wall. Can you give me a certificate for it?"

"Yes, I can give you one that will probably get you through airport security. It depends on how knowledgeable the attending officials are—this is very old." Antun turns the blade back and forth in his hand, hesitating. "I don't know." He shakes his head. "If I certify it, they could possibly want to know how I obtained it."

He looks at Mark. "I know you want this, but why take the risk? I'll buy it from you."

"It's not for sale."

"Give it some thought. Will you at least let me put a handle on it? As a gift. I have a few scrap handles that were found without blades."

Mark hesitates; it would be interesting to see the knife with a handle.

"Come in here," Antun says. He opens the door to a small workroom and begins opening and closing drawers. Mark gazes around at things that are waiting for cleaning and appraisal before being displayed.

"Aha! Let's try this," Antun says, holding up a handle that resembles antler. "It's stag horn from India—also very old!"

The smell of the glue is so strong that Antun has on a mask, and he wears gloves throughout the process. He pulls off the mask before he begins wrapping twine around the top of the haft near the blade. "There," he says, the handle attached to his satisfaction. "Luckily, this particular brand dries quickly, and the smell soon lessens. I suggest we leave it here while we search for a restaurant that might be open today. That way, the glue can dry adequately." He looks at Mark. "But really, I'll give you a good price."

Mark's forehead tightens. *How long ago did people begin quibbling over things left behind by the dead?* "I appreciate you putting on the handle, but I'd rather take it with me. Do you have a box and something I can use to prop it up while it dries?"

For a moment, Mark thinks Antun will refuse, but he rummages around in a bin until he finds a small box and a piece of Styrofoam. While his cousin watches disapprovingly, Mark takes them and arranges the knife so that the glued part isn't touching anything within the box.

"Don't bring it with you to Turkey," Antun says later in the car. "You won't enjoy being in a Turkish prison for however long it would take me to get you out. Leave it at the apartment until we return."

Antun's advice makes sense, even though Mark doesn't like his tone. Mark is reluctant to leave the knife, but he shouldn't risk taking it along. "I'll do that," he says.

Mark hopes that will make Antun drop the matter—at least until they return from Turkey and he has to get a certificate out of him. But after they eat lunch and pick up their suitcases, Antun mentions the knife again on the way to the airport.

"What did you do with your nice piece of stone?"

"I left it in the apartment."

Antun brakes for a traffic light. The car stops, and pedestrians begin crossing the street. "Where in the apartment?"

"In the bedside table," Mark says casually. He watches people pass in front of the hood, wondering if Antun will send someone to search for the knife. He sighs and looks over, speaking loudly to be heard over the traffic revving across the intersection. "How can I explain? There are things you just somehow understand that are meant to be yours." The words are lame, even corny, but he doesn't know how to convey the knife's strong grip on him without sounding loony.

The change in Antun is startling. "Bah!" The exclamation explodes out of him, and his brows undulate like storm clouds. "I suppose that also sums up your feelings toward my father's property. Well, let *me* explain to you—I'm the one who helped him build his businesses." He pounds his chest with a fist. "*I* took care of things during his depression after my mother's death. *I* took over when his steps slowed. Now will *you* please explain—why is your rich American mother to be given a slice of it?"

Mark's mouth hangs open for a moment while he stares at Antun. His jaw snaps shut as the traffic light changes and the car lurches forward. He sputters. "She's not rich. My mother—" A groan halts his response.

Antun slaps the palm of his free hand hard against his own forehead. The fleshy sound makes Mark wince. "A thousand pardons, cousin! I don't know what possesses me. I just feel I'm being treated unfairly. Can you understand that?" Tears begin streaming down his cheeks.

Mark doesn't know how to answer. "I suppose so," he mumbles, hoping the concession will make his cousin stop crying. Antun's tears turn off like a quickly closed tap. From observing the satisfied set of Antun's mouth, Mark realizes he's unintentionally ceded an important point.

Mark and Antun barely exchange words during the two-hour flight to Istanbul. As Mark follows him out of the airport, Antun breaks the silence, saying that they need a taxi for the hotel. Mark is left guessing as to why they aren't going to an apartment or house that belonged to his uncle. He supposes that wherever Antun normally stays while in Istanbul is now off limits because of the will probate.

"It's a nice hotel near all the tourist places," is all Antun says after telling the driver where to take them. "You can use tomorrow morning to see the sights if you want. The solicitor's office is normally closed on Sundays, but he's agreed to meet with us in the afternoon."

Mark tries to pay for his room at the front desk, but Antun won't hear of it. Even though this makes him feel even more indebted, Mark gives in when Antun seems on the verge of causing a scene. They receive their room keys and agree to meet in the lobby after depositing their luggage to go out for doner kebab, a typical Turkish food. Although Mark has never eaten the dish before, he's willing to give it a try if it pleases Antun. He's tired of theatrics.

When they go out, Antun, of course, knows where to find the best kebabs. They're nothing like the more-familiar shish kebab. Thin-sliced lamb, tender and slightly charred, is served stuffed into fresh bread, along with a salad. It is all good. Afterward, they have baklava oozing with honey. Although Antun is pleasant company during the meal, Mark is relieved when his cousin doesn't suggest they do anything else together. He lets Antun pay without any argument.

One benefit of staying in a hotel is that he doesn't have to worry about Wi-Fi. Back in his room, Mark e-mails his mother right away to let her know he's in Turkey. She'll be pleasantly surprised to hear from him again this soon.

After answering a few work-related e-mails and doing a little online reading about Istanbul's major tourist sites, Mark sits on the balcony during twilight, gazing at the boats going up and down the Bosporus. The hotel is on the European side of that historical strait, and he looks for a bridge crossing to the Asian side. He spies one through the mist. It's a good distance away and would be difficult to see if not for the car lights delineating the span.

When his business is finished here, he'll leave European Turkey for the Asian side, on his way to collect his uncle's ashes from Antalya. Once that's done, he'll return to Israel with them to wind up all the details. With his obligations then over, he'll go back to California and his old, familiar life.

Mark realizes that he's thought very little about home or his job since leaving California. The time-consuming demands of travel, as well as being mired in a strange situation, have honed present realities to a sharp edge, leaving little time for dwelling on his old preoccupations. Although there are new challenges, the relief he now has from long-lived, mindless stress is a payoff he didn't expect from traveling so far from home.

The next morning, Mark breakfasts in the lobby alone. He called Antun's room before coming down but hung up when his cousin didn't answer after a decent number of rings. After quickly eating, he gets a tourist map from the front desk and sets off to visit a few of the closest sites. Because of his limited time, he decides to see only Hagia Sophia and Topkapi Palace. The Istanbul Archaeological Museum isn't on his list because the Antalya museum has a better exhibit on the very-ancient past.

Mark finds that he has no desire to linger inside Hagia Sophia. The building's minarets, multitude of domes, and glimmering mosaics are beautiful, but he finds it depressing that after being a Christian church for so many centuries, it became a mosque. Even though the site is a museum now, he can't shake the feeling of painful loss that must still reverberate through the region.

It's not that he has anything against Islam. Staring up into the main dome, his eyes rove over the Islamic elements there. But the more he learns about the past, the more history seems to be a long chronicle of one group overwhelming then replacing another group before being replaced themselves by yet another group, and this goes back to the earliest hominids.

This is a natural phenomenon, Mark understands. Still, it must be awful to be the vanquished ones—and quite fortunate to be history's winner at any given time and place. He has on the Neanderthal shirt today under a light jacket, and without noticing that he's doing so, he slips his hand inside the opening, resting on the image there as he hurries to the exit.

Outside, Mark takes a last look at the spires silhouetted against the sky. Their loveliness reignites the ache he'd felt while inside, and he throws a coin into a large fountain nearby, making a wish to never be part of a population at that moment when its time and luck run out.

The most-visited part of the Topkapi Palace, of course, is the harem, the tour guide informs them. Since Islam forbids enslaving Muslims, the majority of the harem women were Christians or Jews, mostly received as gifts from potentates and nobles. Mark finds it ironic that for many of the sultans, an enslaved non-Muslim woman provided half of his genetic makeup. After the harem tour, Mark roams through the palace complex. The place is enormous, and he has to leave before seeing it all.

Mark takes a tram partway back to the hotel and then gets off to walk the few remaining blocks. A changing light stops him on a street corner, where he sees Antun hurrying ahead, among the people who made it over. When he can finally cross, he rushes through the crowd, hoping to catch his cousin. Afternoon is almost upon them, and Antun, in typical fashion, hasn't told him what time they're to meet the solicitor.

Mark rushes up behind his cousin just as he walks under the hotel awning. Mark says his name, but Antun has on a headset of some kind. When Mark resorts to tapping his shoulder, Antun swings around as if Mark's fingers are burning him. His eyes blaze with so much alarm that Mark takes a step back.

Antun pulls off the headset. "Oh, it's you."

"Did you think someone was jumping you?"

Looking sheepish, Antun mumbles something about pickpockets.

"What time do we meet the solicitor?"

Antun glances at his watch. "Actually, we need to leave in a few minutes. Have you eaten?"

Mark stopped at a street-food cart between leaving the Hagia Sophia and finding Topkapi Palace, so he says he's not hungry. He wants to get this next hurdle over with.

"Your uncle was among my closest friends," Mr. Sadik, the solicitor, says to Mark from the end of the conference-room table. His English is good but plodding. "Sami Lahoud was a successful businessman but one with heart. You both have my utmost condolences." The older man adjusts his tie, his hand giving sharp little tugs as he turns from Mark to Antun.

Seated across from Mark, Antun inclines his head ever so slightly, his lips pursed.

"Thank you," Mark says, ending the ensuing awkward silence. The building without its workday employees is completely quiet. "We appreciate you meeting with us on a Sunday."

Mr. Sadik bows graciously toward Mark, showing his pate with its thinning hair. "It is the least I can do." He pulls an envelope out of a folder. "I believe both of you already know that the will requires Mr. Hayek to take possession of Sami's ashes in Antalya. These are the papers you'll need at the crematorium." Mr. Sadik gives the envelope to Mark. "If you have any problems there, don't hesitate to contact me immediately. My card is inside."

The solicitor takes a paper out of the folder, and his eyes flick over it for a moment before he puts it back inside. "Without the ashes, the probate will stall, and your inheritances will not be released for a long while. Is that understood, sirs?"

Mark wastes no time answering for the both of them when Antun again doesn't open his mouth. "Yes, we're clear on that… aspect of the will," he says.

But now Antun responds, trampling Mark's last words. "But not much else is understood. I, for one, have questions." Antun then starts speaking what Mark believes is Turkish. He doesn't understand the words, but Antun's voice sounds very aggrieved.

While listening, Mr. Sadik stiffens, and his untamed eyebrows lower over his eyes, giving him a hawkish appearance. He suddenly jerks up a hand. The way Mr. Sadik's palm is turned on his wrist causes Mark to think for a moment that he's going to slap Antun.

"Be quiet and listen," the solicitor says loudly in English, and Antun stops talking. "Many of these questions were to be answered later, in Israel." He shakes a forefinger at Antun. "But now that you're complaining in such strong terms, I feel justified in giving you more information today."

He gives Mark a quick look. "And this is for your ears also. Sami made two wills: one Turkish, the other Israeli. He had to. When there is immovable property in Turkey, Turkish law is applied, whereas movable assets are subject to the laws of the deceased's home country—in this case, Israel." He taps a finger on the folder. "Under Turkish law, Antun will receive the physical buildings that his father owned here in Turkey—his house and his business warehouses—but all their contents will be inventoried then sold, the proceeds to be put into a trust. All of Sami's assets in Israel are to be completely liquidated and put into the same trust."

"Everything?" Antun asks, his expression incredulous.

On some level, Mr. Sadik is obviously relishing these disclosures. He's almost smiling when his hand makes a slantwise motion. "Everything!" He looks at Mark. "Do you mind if I smoke?"

"No, go ahead."

The solicitor is reaching into his pocket when Antun reacts. "You can't be serious." He's almost spitting as he starts ranting in Turkish, his fists pounding the table.

Mr. Sadik frowns as he flicks a gold-cased lighter and lights the cigarette. Then Antun must have gone too far, because the lawyer suddenly throws the lighter on the table and the cigarette in an ashtray. Exhaling smoke, he picks up the thick folder and slams it on the table. Antun is silent.

Although Mr. Sadik's English is disintegrating, Mark can make out what he's saying well enough. "It is a shame so much faith was lost that you will receive your inheritance as an annual allowance from the trust."

Antun starts replying in Turkish, loses his voice for a moment, then begins again in English. "And I suppose you're the one controlling this trust?"

"No, not me—Nadia Hayek is named trustee in charge of dispersal." A cocky expression crosses the solicitor's face. "She will see that you receive a set allowance every year from your half."

"*Half!*" Antun screams as he jumps up, tipping his chair backward onto the carpet.

The room becomes very quiet, the three of them frozen in place. Then Antun storms out, his every footfall making the floor quiver, though he's crossing plush Turkish carpet.

Mr. Sadik and Mark stare at each other, the smoke drifting around them.

"I'm sorry, but this was going to happen sooner or later. I thought it best if I told him. Mrs. Aaron doesn't know him as well as I do." He picks up the cigarette and takes a quick puff, narrowing his eyes.

Mark stands. His ears are still full of all the yelling, and the cigarette smoke is beginning to get to him. "I should go," he says, not knowing whether he should hurry after Antun and attempt to smooth things over or if he should just go back to the hotel by himself.

As if he reads Mark's mind, Mr. Sadik says, "Don't go after him, and don't let him talk you into changing the will." He stubs out the cigarette and stands. "That won't work well for either of you; I promise."

Mark doesn't know what to say.

"I'll drive you back to your hotel if you would like."

"That's kind of you, but I'll take a taxi."

"Very well. I'll call for one to meet you out front."

While Mr. Sadik is walking him to the door, Mark unconsciously shakes his head, mulling over what has just taken place. He catches himself and glances over, but the solicitor hasn't noticed—his face is deep in thought as he opens the door. Mark understands now that Mr. Sadik was the one who told his mother's lawyer that she was receiving half, making certain that someone would show up to collect.

Stopping him at the threshold, Mr. Sadik puts a hand on Mark's arm and rivets him briefly to the spot with a wide-eyed gaze, his irises dark and mysterious. He takes away his hand, opens the door wider, and Mark steps outside. While waiting for the taxi, he stares back at the closed door. The solicitor has seared that look into his memory.

CHAPTER 13

Western Asia, Late Pleistocene

UPON HEARING A VOICE OUTSIDE the circle of stones, Leaf had jumped into action, sliding Raven quickly off the ledge. They straightened their clothing and grabbed their spears. Leaf flattened against the boulder nearest to where the voice came from and edged around it, holding his spear at the ready. He stiffened then looked back at Raven. "It's the Wanderer," he said.

She met his eyes, sharing the dismay she saw in them.

"All you can see are yourselves. I don't know how you've managed to stay alive out here," the Wanderer said when they came out from the boulders.

He had a knowing smirk on his badly bruised face. When his eyes swept over her, Raven's skin itched as though she'd been brushed by poison ivy.

"I've always wondered how good a healer you were, girl. Now I'll find out."

He took away the bloody clump of moss he held against his forearm.

"You'll find out only if she agrees to help you." Leaf looked at the angry, dripping gash on his arm suspiciously. "How did that happen?"

"The elders of the band I was staying with took a dislike to me for no good reason that I could tell. They said I had to leave today. I told them I would wait and go with a group that was traveling at the beginning of full moon, but they kicked me out anyway. I'd just left when several men from the camp caught up with me. I thought they wanted to trade, but when I put my bags down, they grabbed them. One of them cut me when I tried to get my food pouch back." He shook his head. "That's what sometimes happens when you stay with fellow tribesmen you don't know well."

He poked his long nose toward Raven. "Now are you going to help me, or shall I bleed to death at your feet?"

Raven understood it was her duty to tend him, even though she was as put off by the man as she had been when she'd last seen him. She could easily overlook his odd appearance, but something about the Wanderer gave her the same feeling she'd had after falling into a pond covered with slime. Ridding herself of the repulsive, clinging mess had been difficult.

She pursed her lips. "Hmm," she murmured, wondering if he was being truthful about how he'd received the wound. "You did the right thing by pressing moss over the cut. The bleeding has slowed, and it's trying to clot, but I need thorns for binding the edges together. Then I'll cover it with a paste." She looked at Leaf. "We should go to the river for him to bathe and wash his clothing. He smells like butchered meat. I'll find thorns there."

"I stink, do I? You could use a scrubbing yourself, little girl." He nodded at Leaf. "You as well, boy." He grinned at their obvious discomfort. "Too occupied to notice the odor, I expect."

"Your blabbing mouth is the reason that band wanted you gone," Leaf said. "You need to keep your thoughts to yourself."

The Wanderer regarded Leaf warily. "Sorry, I meant no offense."

Raven started toward the river, and the two men followed. She wanted to get his treatment over with, and then maybe, he would go on his way.

It unnerved Raven the way his stare roamed over her the whole time she was weaving the gash closed, his breath hissing through clenched teeth the only reaction to the pain. She tried to keep her stomach pulled in so that he wouldn't notice her thick waist.

"Where are the two of you going anyway?" he asked while she was applying a paste of comfrey leaves. When she didn't reply, pretending to concentrate on the comfrey, he looked at Leaf.

"We're searching for my people—the Wind tribe. Bear's band took me in after I got lost from them." His voice lost its edge. "Have you encountered them in your travels?"

"Some of that tribe was around a while back, farther along the way you seem to be traveling."

"Do you know if they're still there?"

"No, I don't, but look—we're going in the same direction. I'm trying to find a Fire Cloud band farther along the river, so maybe I could join you in your search."

Raven didn't like the Wanderer, but even with an injured arm, he could be of use, and she changed her mind about wanting him to leave. Raven glanced at Leaf's stony face, hoping he wouldn't dismiss the man out of hand.

"We need to think about it," Leaf replied.

Raven remained alert as she bathed in a bend of the river, even though she knew Leaf would stop the Wanderer from coming her way. When she finished and went back around, Leaf was attempting to show him the cat. The small animal wasn't cooperating and kept crawling back inside the bag. It seemed to dislike the man even more than it had disliked Raven at first seeing her. Upon Raven's return, Leaf let the spitting cat disappear into the bag and put the bag over his shoulder.

"Wait here," he said to the Wanderer. He motioned for Raven to follow him.

"I don't trust him," Leaf said once they were out of earshot. "Even when I'm at your side, he devours you with his eyes. We don't need him. We're doing fine by ourselves." His eyes went to her mouth. "More than fine."

His hair, damp from the river, curled around his face, softening the hard lines of his jaw. Raven sighed. She had wanted him to temper his behavior, but their amorous dallying would cease completely under the Wanderer's prying eyes. She glanced back at that disturbing man and almost snorted at the humble look he suddenly forced onto his face when he saw her watching him. "I don't want him around, either, but he is another pair of eyes, and they didn't take his spear."

"Are you saying that you'll actually feel safer with him along?"

"I know that you like to scout by yourself—and I've always worried about your safety because of it—but you know that people usually travel in larger groups."

"They did take all his food."

"He can help hunt whenever we run low. I'll start gathering greens to help feed us. Besides, if we know that he's traveling in the same direction as we are, we won't worry about him returning to Bear's band any time soon."

His eyes narrowed. He'd taken her meaning. "Very well, but just until we reach this camp he's searching for. We'll part with him there." He took her hand, sliding his palm over hers and intertwining their fingers.

She smiled at him, glad that they were in accord once more. Perhaps he would warm to the idea of traveling with more people if at the camp they encountered other, more agreeable companions going the same way.

Their pace quickened considerably as Leaf concentrated on covering ground. Although Raven knew that he was torn about leaving her alone with the Wanderer, he often scouted ahead of them. He doubled back to rejoin them whenever he located danger, letting them know they should change their route. The distant river was the reference point they used to avoid becoming lost from each other. In that manner, they traveled farther in one day than Raven had managed during the three days she'd been alone.

The Wanderer's long legs were the reason he'd reminded Raven of a stork when she'd first seem him, but he moved much more rapidly than a water bird. "I'm holding you back," she told him. "I'm sorry—it's just that you walk so fast."

"Don't worry yourself. Happens with almost everyone I travel with." He scratched his parka sleeve over his healing cut. "By the way, I wonder if you would rub some of that healing ointment you have into my arm. There's a fierce itch where you pulled those thorns out."

Raven waved her hand at the surrounding grassland. "You want me to do that here?"

"It'll only take a moment. It's very bothersome."

Raven hesitated then stopped. "Very well, I'll be quick about it." She slipped a bag from her shoulder and was about to put it on the ground when he reached out a hand.

"I'll hold the bag for you while you find your medicines." He took it from her, and Raven dug out a smaller pouch and went over to put it on a large rock. She rummaged inside until she found the ointment.

When she turned around, he was holding one of her spare leggings that had been in the bag. She watched as he brought it up to his nose and sniffed it, his mouth hanging open as if he were an animal taking in an interesting odor. She tensed, the back of her neck knotting. At that moment, a lion roared and chuffed in the distance. Raven hoped the animal was blocking their way forward, so it would prompt Leaf's quick return.

When he saw her watching, he stuffed the legging back in the bag. "I was just replacing this. It fell out. I see you found something for me."

She wanted to rake him with her fingernails as she quickly swiped the ointment over his scabs, not bothering to rub it into the skin. He would have to do that for himself. His disappointment covered his face when she pulled away abruptly and started repacking her bag.

He gave her a sly look when they were once more walking. "I have a bitter root to chew with Bear the next time I'm at his camp. I offered to take you off his hands several moons ago. He was complaining about what a difficult time he was having finding a mate for his sister-in-law. I told him I'd seen you walking around camp and that I was interested—very interested." He craned his head down to peer at her.

His face was vulturine, and she could no more turn away from him than she could from one of those hissing birds threatening to tear into her flesh. At least he was looking at just her face and not the rest of her. He would have awkward questions about timing if it dawned on him that she was pregnant.

"Bear said he'd consider my offer, but when I brought it up again, he put me off, getting all huffy when I persisted. He did find someone after all, it seems, although I can't say I agree with the choice." The Wanderer straightened back up. "But look, girl—that boy is asking too much. He can find his lost tribe by himself. You and I are from the same tribe. If Bear wasn't so stiff necked, you'd be with me now anyway."

His bold eyes watched her closely. Raven was silent, carefully considering her next words. Before she could speak, Leaf's voice came from behind them. "I heard your voices a long distance away."

The Wanderer spun around. "I don't appreciate being snuck up on, boy."

Leaf's flashing eyes said he had heard at least part of their conversation. Raven tried not to look guilty.

"What if it had been a predator instead of me behind you?" Leaf asked. "Wait and do your talking tonight after we've built a fire!"

"All right, all right. You've been clear." The Wanderer turned and started walking again but not before Raven saw his amused expression.

Raven looked pointedly at Leaf, her brow wrinkling. Surely, he didn't think she would consider running off with the Wanderer just because he was from her tribe. He ignored her, even though he took up a place close by her side, forcing the Wanderer to move over.

"I heard a lion," she said.

"They're far to the side of us—a mating couple. No threat," he said curtly.

She stole glances at him as they continued quietly over the steppes, but the scout remained distant for the rest of the day.

Unable to find a cave or overhang for the night, they had to set up camp out in the open. "Everybody can talk now," Leaf said, after they'd made a blazing fire and were eating, his words cutting through their silence.

If the Wanderer knew that Leaf was being sarcastic, he pretended not to. He began talking about things he'd seen and done on his journeys. Raven could tell that Leaf was listening, although he sat with his back to the fire, jerking around a piece of braided leather for the kitten to play with. The Wanderer's tales were interesting, but when Leaf moved a short distance away to lie on a skin along with the kitten, Raven excused herself and joined him.

"I'll take first night-watch," the Wanderer said. When she glanced back, he grinned at her in a conspiratorial way, nodding, as if they shared a secret.

She frowned and looked away, not sure what misguided notion had prompted that familiarity.

On the following day, they came upon a large, deserted encampment. A wide trail made by the one-time occupants led off into the distance. The Wanderer thought that the camp had belonged to the band he sought.

"They haven't been gone long," Leaf said, squatting to closely observe several footprints. "Two days at the most. They'll be easy to follow." He didn't look her way. His mouth was a thin line as they set out again, making obvious his disappointment that they must continue on with the Wanderer. Raven was disgruntled, as well. She'd come to believe that the added safety his presence brought wasn't worth Leaf's unhappiness and her own annoyance. They silently slogged through thick grass for the rest of the morning.

The trail led them directly to a narrow land bridge. "I told you about this place," Leaf said excitedly to Raven, finally speaking to her directly. "It's the Pass Between the Waters. My band came through here. My family was at this spot." He looked about as if he was trying to imagine them there once more.

Raven turned first one way then the other. Water filled her view on both sides, and she once more recalled flying over the area in her dream. The area looked quite different from the ground in daytime than from above at night. "Are those lakes?"

"Yes, but they're larger than any lake you've ever seen, and the water is saltier," the Wanderer said.

"Salty water... how strange." Salty was normally the way a sought-after but rarely found rock tasted when touched by the tongue to verify its character. Once crushed, the grains could be sprinkled over food to enhance its flavor.

"The creatures that lived in the shells at your feet only thrived in salty water," he said.

Raven exclaimed in delight. She'd been so amazed by the water's vastness, she hadn't noticed that the ground was covered with shells of all kinds and shapes.

"I used to live in a cave above salty waters even larger than these," Leaf said with a hushed and distant voice. Loss haunted his dark eyes and the circles below them. Raven's heart went out to him. She touched his arm gently.

The Wanderer picked out some of the smaller shells. "Everyone wants these." He held out his palm so they could see them. "They'll give me something to trade. I noticed that you have a few already," he said to Raven. "You may want to gather more."

Raven's hand went to her shell necklace. She recalled how her mother's hands had lingered on her neck when she'd given it to Raven, caressing her, straightening the leather string that held the shells. That recollection was pushed away by another memory, one closer in time, of the captive's face hovering over hers after he pulled her down onto the plants. As he'd rolled the necklace's shells between his fingers, his green eyes had become curious.

Leaf had stopped picking up shells and was watching her strangely. "Aren't you going to take some?" he asked.

Raven quickly got out a bag and began filling it. The shells might be useful as gifts for strangers encountered during their travels. When they'd gathered all they wanted, they continued over the land bridge and were soon trekking through grass again. Even though their surroundings looked the same as before the crossing, Raven felt they'd arrived in a different land.

They crested a hill during the afternoon; in the distance, smoke floated on the horizon. After climbing several more hills, they saw tents set up along the river. They'd started toward them when the Wanderer suddenly stopped in his tracks. Raven and Leaf paused, looking back at him.

He rubbed his hand over the scruffy beard covering his jaw. "Earth Mother, help me," he said. "I can't trade shells to these people. It's only a short journey for them to get all they want." He turned to Raven. "I've seen that you have a goodly amount of powdered ochre." His eyes roved over her face, looking at the markings she dabbed there daily. "Could I perhaps borrow some? I'll grind more for you when we find a source, or I'll give you something else in return."

Raven didn't want to enter any sort of agreement with the Wanderer. After all, they were parting ways soon. She almost said as such, but if he knew they wanted rid of his company, it might cause an argument that would carry over into the camp below.

She looked at Leaf, lifting her brows. He frowned and opened his mouth but then pressed his lips together as if he'd also thought better of letting the Wanderer know their plans.

"I suppose I could give you some," she said.

The Wanderer looked down the hill at the camp while Raven tried to pour ochre into a small pouch without spilling it.

"A boy lives down there that was my son for a few moons," he said. "My mate still had milk when our own child died, and I was offered an infant that nobody else wanted. The man didn't even want to trade—he just gave him to me." The Wanderer shook his head at that stupidity. "I was planning on raising him to help haul goods, but then my woman also up and died while we were with that band down there." He nodded down the hill. "I traded that baby to them for several flint-tipped spears. Strangest trade I ever made."

Raven suppressed a tremor of disgust that he would dispose of a baby so callously, but he saw the glare she gave him.

"Don't cut your eyes at me, girl. I have no teats for feeding a baby." He started down the hill. "I was going to tell you more about the boy, but I'll let you see for yourself."

Leaf was frowning, practically biting his tongue when she looked his way. He shrugged at her, and they went on.

The wooded area near the camp was so dense that no one saw them until they approached a hearth fire. The man who first noticed them whooped and pointed. Everyone around the fire turned as one, just as an alert wolf pack would. Raven was disconcerted by their hostile stares, but when the Wanderer hailed them, some of them replied and came forward, smiling. She was heartened to see that not everyone despised the man.

They made room around the fire, and the women brought them venison stew in large wooden bowls. Raven took her bowl gratefully. She'd not eaten hot food in a long while.

The Wanderer told the gathered crowd about his journey and how, after encountering Leaf and Raven, they'd decided to travel together. His eyes continuously searched the area as he spoke. "But where's the boy I left with you?" he asked.

"I just saw him," a man said, looking through the crowd. "Ah, there he is. Moth, come over here. Somebody wants to see you."

A child stepped forward hesitantly and scuffled over to stop in front of them. He almost had the manner of someone being shunned as punishment, his chin on his chest, his dark hair falling over his face. Raven hoped that his bearing indicated only that he was a shy child.

"How many turns of the seasons have you lived now, boy?" the Wanderer asked.

"Five," he replied, raising his head.

"You can thank me for them," the Wanderer said.

When Raven saw the boy's face, her breath caught, and the world shifted.

A purple splotch in the shape of a moth covered one cheek, and she realized that he was the newborn infant she'd once wanted to save. Her father hadn't left the child on the steppe—he'd given him to the Wanderer.

Raven was struggling to gather her scattered thoughts when Leaf pulled the cat out. The crowd began pressing around them. For once, the animal didn't immediately try to hide. Moth reached out, his eyes enormous with wonder. Raven held her breath, hoping the cat wouldn't scratch, but it only sniffed the proffered fingers before it noticed the others and darted back into the bag.

"I don't know why he lugs that wild creature around," the Wanderer said, his voice raised, looking around at the crowd. "It would only make a few mouthfuls if food ran short."

Leaf threw him a biting look. "Then if that comes to pass, we won't have to take the trouble of killing and skinning it."

A few people laughed nervously, but the moment passed when a curious bystander asked Leaf how he'd come about the cat. He glanced at Raven then told them a revised version that didn't mention her role. As Leaf talked, Moth slipped away.

When twilight fell, the three of them followed a woman to the area of camp used for storage and for putting up guests. When Raven saw that there were two tents, she glanced at Leaf. For the first time in several days, he smiled at her. Their guide stopped in front of the largest tent.

"We thank you," the Wanderer said. "This band has always provided adequate lodging for its visitors. I'll make sure that things are as we found them when we leave."

The woman gave a nervous titter. "Actually, this larger one is almost full of skins and other things. You'll probably want to stay in the smaller one with your mate. You're a good-sized man, if you don't mind me saying so, and there might not be room enough left for her in there."

Leaf's smile vanished as quickly as it had come. He grasped Raven's hand, scowling at the woman.

The Wanderer's big stomach shook with repressed laughter. "I dream that I will one day have so pleasing a mate."

"My mistake." The woman darted an appraising look at Leaf and Raven. "I'll leave you to rest, then," she said and went on her way.

Without looking at the Wanderer, Leaf pulled Raven into the smaller tent.

After they rearranged some skins and were resting on them, Raven told Leaf the story of how she'd attempted to rescue Moth as a baby. "All this time, I thought the child was dead. My father was overly harsh with me—I had no idea he could ever be kind-hearted." Her eyes filled, and she sniffed. "Not that I forgive him, but I do think differently of him now."

"I could never be harsh with you." Leaf gently kissed her brow before he went and secured the flap.

Safely inside a tent within a camp, Raven no longer felt cold chills of warning go down her spine whenever Leaf touched her. She set about bestowing upon him the warmth she'd partially withheld while on the steppes. The reason for her change wasn't lost on Leaf.

"I hope we'll have our own tent before long," he said the next morning when they were still lolling under the skins well after dawn.

CHAPTER 14

The Levant, Present Day

WHEN MARK ARRIVES AT THE hotel after leaving the solicitor's office, he nervously keeps an eye out for Antun. If his cousin hasn't been able to get a taxi quickly, then he'll be arriving after Mark. Waiting at the elevator bank, he keeps looking over his shoulder until he notices that people are eyeing him warily. He needs to get a grip on his paranoia.

The situation in which he finds himself is beyond anything Mark has ever experienced. He has no idea how to deal with someone who thinks part of his birthright is being snatched away—and he's sure that Antun believes Mark and his mother are doing just that. Antun has probably thought this all along but believed that nearly all the estate would come to him as Sami's only child.

Mark mentally shakes himself. As usual, he's overreacting. No matter how upset, Antun is not likely to initiate a blood feud in a hotel lobby. As the elevator goes up, he becomes aware that his fingers have unzipped his jacket pocket and are searching for sharp-edged stone. But then he remembers that he left the piece in the hotel room because he knew he would encounter security measures at the historical sites.

As soon as he gets inside the room, he takes the stone knife out of the hotel safe and feels as though he's seeing an old, reassuring friend. He hadn't meant to bring the knife along, but after they'd returned to pick up their suitcases from the apartment, Mark found that parting with it was so painful as to be impossible. Upon securing it in the bedside table drawer, he began experiencing troubling symptoms.

Although he's never had a panic attack, he's read about them—the breathing difficulty along with a racing heart and the helpless feeling of impending doom. The moment that Mark took the knife back out, all those alarming symptoms went away. Regardless of Antun's warning about Turkish prisons, there didn't seem to be any choice but to accept the risks that came with packing the piece.

Mark is becoming a wily spinner of tales as to how he acquired the knife. If he were found out while going through the various security levels at the airport, he would have said that the knife was a gift for Antun. He'd bought it from a Native American craftsman at an art show in California. He was just waiting for the right moment to give it to his cousin. Luckily, there wasn't a need to test his fable. In order to lessen his chances of getting caught, he'd put the knife in his checked luggage, where it would go through an automated scanner. When they'd collected their baggage upon landing in Istanbul, no one stepped forward to detain him.

He plans to use this same ruse if they fly to Antalya instead of driving there. Antun was unclear the evening before as to how they would proceed, first telling Mark that he was going to rent a car but then saying that the trip by car would take all day—perhaps it would be better to book flights. Mark hopes they'll fly; he can't conceive of spending an entire day cooped up with Antun, even if circumstances were different.

When Mark walks toward the bed, the telephone's message light is pulsing, and he presses the play button. Thrusting the knife into his pocket, he snatches up a pen. He begins writing as Antun's voice doles out information about the flight for which

Mark should purchase a ticket. Antun also tells him the name of the hotel where he should book a room, going on to say they'll only stay one night in Antalya before returning to Israel.

Mark's mood lifts as he uses the laptop to make reservations and give payment details. It feels good to pay his own way and not be on the receiving end of Antun's smothering hospitality for once. The flight is an early one, so he orders room service, eats, and goes straight to bed. He falls asleep easily, relieved they'll be flying to Antalya instead of driving.

But his reprieve lasts only until they land in Antalya the next morning. They no sooner collect their luggage than Antun guides him over to Antalya Airport Rent-a-Car. The agency employee shows them a European mini car that is small enough to make Mark claustrophobic from just looking inside. There are several good-size dings on the car's body, one on a door and another on the bumper.

"Piece of junk! This is unacceptable," Antun yells at the employee.

"Only car here," he responds in broken English.

The rest of the conversation is in Turkish, and after a few minutes, the employee shrugs and starts walking away.

"Okay, okay, if that's the best you can do!" Antun calls after him.

Mark opens the creaking hatch door and loads their suitcases while Antun goes to fill out paperwork.

Antun drives in his usual assertive manner, all the while muttering about the car's quality as he darts into the busy morning traffic surrounding the airport. Mark feels as though he's in an amusement park bumper car and that it's just a matter of time before they run into another vehicle.

He glances over at Antun's agitated profile. This is the first time they've been in each other's company since Antun stormed out of the lawyer's office the day before. Mark took a taxi alone to the airport upon leaving the Istanbul hotel that morning, and on the plane, he'd only glimpsed Antun, who was seated farther back. After deplaning, Mark had waited for him. Antun was polite enough, saying good morning and that they needed to pick up a rental car after collecting their baggage.

At his cousin's suggestion, they're going straight to the crematorium from the airport. Mark hopes the place will be open at this early hour, and he wonders why Antun decided to rent a car instead of using taxis since they're to be in Antalya for only one day. If everything goes smoothly, they could even fly back to Tel Aviv right away. While the car hurtles through an intersection without even pausing for the stop sign, Mark decides that he'll try to cancel his reservation at the hotel when they get there after collecting the ashes.

Because the business has just opened, Mark is expecting to see a new building when they speed into the parking lot, but the crematorium is inside an old Mediterranean-style house. Antun brakes to a squealing stop, managing to take up two spaces with the small car. After the short walk to the entrance, they have to wait until someone comes and unlocks the door. Seagulls wheel around overhead, reminding Mark that he's in a coastal city. He's enjoyed living near the water all his life, and he almost regrets that he's decided to return immediately to Israel. Antalya would be worth exploring, from what he's seen so far. He's surprised at the thought, but it doesn't matter if he's suddenly developed a taste for travel adventure. After Antun's meltdown the day before, the best thing Mark can do is complete his duties so he can return home.

Finally, the door opens, and once they're inside, a dignified elderly man assists them immediately. Mark gives him the paperwork from the solicitor's office, and the man returns after only a few minutes, carrying what looks like a large marble vase with a lid covering the opening.

Although it's nothing Mark can't handle, the urn is surprisingly heavy, and he's concerned on the way to the car that he'll somehow trip and drop it. As he settles the cool gray stone carefully among their suitcases, wrapping his jacket around it, Mark becomes fully aware that he's now responsible for the remains of another human being—even if they're only a carbonized mixture of atoms that once made up that person.

He stares into the back. The urn doesn't seem secure enough, and he begins rearranging everything so as to cushion it as much as possible. He wonders how many fender benders his cousin has been involved in since he began driving. Antun is waiting in the driver's seat, and as Mark fusses with folding his jacket around the urn, Antun cranes his head around.

"Are we ready, already?" he calls out impatiently.

Mark closes the hatchback and hurries around to get in. Antun begins backing out as Mark fastens his seatbelt.

"I'd just as soon return to Israel today." Mark holds on to the dashboard as the car swerves into the streets of Antalya once more. "I'll understand if you have other business here and need to stay. But considering how important the urn is to this..." Mark takes a quick breath. "How important it is to finalizing this situation, I'd like to fulfill my part as quickly as possible."

"I apologize for my behavior at the solicitor's office yesterday." Antun is suddenly all smiling contriteness. "I must admit, the terms of the will are surprising. And I can't lie about it—I am disappointed. Of course, none of this is your doing. I imagine that you're even more confused than I am." He sighs heavily. "Please allow me, cousin, to reveal something about myself."

Antun's voice quavers, and Mark is afraid he's in for another emotional display. "You don't have to say anything. I understand perfectly that you're upset—I guess I would be in your place."

"Thank you, brother," Antun says. "But I need for you to be my confessor today." His brimming eyes threaten to spill over.

Mark glances at the busy street, hoping Antun won't have a problem navigating with blurred vision.

"When Aliza divorced me and stole my boys away, it broke me, emotionally as well as monetarily. She moved to Switzerland with them—completely cutting ties. To relieve my heartache so I could go on with living, I turned to drugs." His voice thickens. "My father didn't understand how devastated I was. He washed his hands of my little family and thought I should do so, as well. He moved on, but I couldn't seem to."

He pauses for a long moment, but Mark can tell he has more to reveal and doesn't respond. "The thing is—I almost died from an overdose. I believe that sad episode was behind my father's decision to change the will." Antun's hand swipes away moisture from under his eyes. "But he was being unjust. I don't have anything to do with drugs anymore."

Mark is taken aback by the outright lie, and he thinks he understands why Antun's estranged wife moved out of the country, taking her children far away. Mark steeples his fingers in front of his lips. He would like to hear her side.

"That's all over with," Antun adds.

Mark can't keep incredulity off his face. Antun must think he's an idiot, a sheltered geek who can't recognize the signs of drug usage.

"Okay, I partake a little on occasion." Antun shrugs, apparently realizing that Mark has picked up on something. "Just with friends so they won't feel awkward in my company."

"Social usage."

"That's right—socially. I'm glad you understand."

Roman walls and a minaret rise in the distance. Although Antun has stopped talking, as the car enters Antalya's Old Town, Mark senses that his state of mind has changed, once more becoming lighter. The car weaves through narrow streets, and Mark is glad now that they're in a smaller model. Surprisingly, the car has a GPS. However, Antun obviously knows his way among the tortuous lanes, because he's not once glanced at the screen. His large hands clutch the steering wheel as the car judders over cobblestones, the rough ride finally loosening his tongue.

"The suspension is gone. I apologize that you have to ride in such an inferior automobile."

"It's all right."

Antun gives him a sidelong look. "I'm begging you—don't leave today. To make up for my deplorable behavior, I've planned an outing I know you'll enjoy." He motions at the view of distant mountains outside Mark's window. "Neanderthals lived all around up there. Perhaps you've heard of Karain Cave—a professor found skeletons and tools there. The cave we're going to is near Karain, but away from any crowds. You'll have it to yourself, just like the one in Lebanon."

Mark remembers Karain Cave from the e-mailed information his mother sent him the day he made up his mind to assist her in claiming the inheritance.

"What do you say, my brother? We'll go this afternoon. It's located only an hour or so from the city. That's why I rented this car. Although it's a pile of *merde*, it'll take us that far."

Mark is tempted. Besides helping his mother, he'd come to explore the places where Neanderthals lived. Although he's seen several caves, Mark would like to see more. He may never have this opportunity again. "Well, maybe. I'll consider it."

But that isn't good enough for Antun. "The Antalya Archaeological Museum is close by," he says. "They have a collection of objects from Karain Cave."

Mark had originally planned a short visit to that museum. He's weakening, and not only because of the archaeological offerings. Even if he doesn't return to Israel immediately, he'll be leaving the Levant soon enough, and he doesn't want to skulk away. He also feels he better understands Antun now. The man can't seem to help it that he's on an emotional rollercoaster, and although he's hard to stomach at times, Mark would prefer they remain amicable after everything has played out properly.

Antun rolls his eyes dramatically. "And they have a Neanderthal skull. I've been there. The exhibit is very good!"

Mark figures that if he tells him to do so, Antun will stand on his head to keep him from leaving. He shakes his head, laughing at the inane thought, and the tension within the car begins dissipating, floating out the windows. "Please. Say no more. I'll stay."

Antun laughs along with him, his mirth rumbling through the small car as they pull up at the hotel.

Like always, everyone knows Antun, so even though they've arrived at the front desk before check-in, they're allowed access to their rooms. Mark's has a balcony with a magnificent view of the Mediterranean. After settling in, he carefully places the urn on a patio table and photographs it against shining blue sea. After uploading the photo, he sends the image along with a message to both his mother and Mrs. Aaron.

Upon reflection, he also decides to send the picture to Mr. Sadik. That way, he'll know that his friend's ashes are in Mark's care. He finds the solicitor's card in the envelope and sees that there's an e-mail address as well as phone numbers at the bottom.

He's grateful to Mr. Sadik, but he struggles to put into words exactly why. After several tries, he deletes everything and sends the photograph with a single line saying that he has the urn and will be returning to Israel the next day. Mark notices that the cell number on the card is made up mostly of fives. He wonders if that number has a special meaning for the solicitor.

He takes the urn back into the room, wondering what he should do with it. The vase is too big for the safe. He secures it in the closet, looking down at it in apology for a short while before closing the door. His uncle's remains shouldn't be stuffed in among clothes and shoes, but they won't be there for long.

CHAPTER 15

Western Eurasia, Late Pleistocene

MOTH WASN'T LIVING IN THE best of circumstances. Rather than dwelling with a particular family group, he went from hearth to hearth throughout the day, performing duties and chores, eating every meal before a different fire. At night, he did stay with one particular family, but Raven didn't know if that was permanent or if he would eventually be passed along. She hadn't seen anyone treating him cruelly, although the heavy loads of water and wood he carried to some of the hearths made her gnaw her lip. She would have wished something better for him, but at least he was alive.

She took him aside one afternoon and gave him a small pouch filled with a portion of her shells. "These are yours. Don't give them to anyone else. Don't even show them to anyone. Hide them in a secret place. You may need them someday."

Moth was openmouthed, his wide eyes blinking at her.

She pinched his lips together with a light touch. "Just do as I say, little one. You will thank me when you are older and realize their worth."

He looked at her for a long moment. "I know where I can hide them," he said with a grin and ran away. Wishing she could do more for him, she followed his slight form with her eyes until he was out of sight.

During her days in the camp, Raven stayed with the women. She only saw Leaf after the shadows began to lengthen and everyone gathered at the hearths. On one afternoon, he was in particularly high spirits, joking with the others at one of the more welcoming hearths they often visited, his eyes lighthearted when he sought her out. The women had almost finished cooking, but he insisted that they go to their tent before eating.

"What is it?" Raven asked as they walked along quickly, going in the direction opposite everyone else.

"I've just heard something good. Be patient. I'll tell you when we're alone."

When they went inside, he seemed about to burst. "I talked with one of the elders. He's very old but has a long memory. His mate was a younger woman from the Wind tribe, and he went with her band when they returned to the lands of warm breezes. After she died, he came back and joined this Fire Cloud band. He told me his journey stories for both going and returning. I remember the places he described—the pass through the mountains, the high plains we'll encounter before coming to the big waters that border one side of Wind tribal lands. I'm sure I can guide us across those plains."

His enthusiasm was contagious. "What luck to have come across this elder. Has he heard news of your family?"

His face fell a little. "He lived with a different tribal band. He doesn't remember ever seeing any of them."

"I hope that we'll find them and that they are safe and healthy, Earth Mother willing."

He nodded then paused a heartbeat. "He said there aren't bands from any tribe on the high plains, other than those of the Longheads, and very few of those."

He searched her face, a little uncomfortably. "We'll have to stay with the Longheads. The captive's band isn't far from here—if what the trackers told me after they followed his brothers can be relied upon."

She started to agree that his assessment was correct but caught herself. It wasn't the time to explain that because of a dream, she knew the band's whereabouts. "Why don't we stay here for the winter?" she asked. With the need to search out the Longheads an almost certainty, misgivings assailed her. So much could go wrong, and she couldn't know for sure if they would agree to let her and Leaf stay with them. Perhaps the baby *wouldn't* be enough to persuade them to do so.

He shook his head slowly after a moment. "We'd have farther to travel when we leave in the spring. But that's not what's worrying me. What if the Wanderer goes back to Bear's band before winter? He'll tell him that he's seen us. I don't like the idea of Bear knowing where we are."

"No doubt he would tell Bear. It would help if we knew his plans before making a decision," she said. "We'll have to approach the matter cautiously, or he'll wonder why we're asking. But let's return to the hearth now before all the food is gone. We'll talk more tonight."

When Raven opened the flap, she was startled to see the Wanderer scuttling away from the tents like a long-legged spider. He'd already gone over a rise when Leaf came out. She was almost certain he'd been listening to their conversation, but Raven didn't tell Leaf what she'd seen, not wanting to spoil his happiness. A queasy feeling filled her, though, so that the food smells were bothersome when they returned to the hearth they'd left earlier.

Her appetite wasn't improved by observing the Wanderer's sullen face staring at her during the meal. She wasn't surprised when he later confronted her as she emptied bones and other food debris from a basket into the camp trash pit.

"I heard the pair of you talking," he said, his face heated like his voice. "I already thought he was a little crazy, but when I heard that he wants the both of you to winter with the Longheads, I realized that he's truly lost his mind. Hauling around small animals is one thing, but living with big ones just isn't possible. Surely you aren't in agreement with that foolishness?"

Raven walked slowly around the pit's edges, kicking dirt inside to lessen the odor. She wanted to tell him that the Longheads were no more animals than he was, but she felt a strong twinge in her belly, as if the baby was warning her that she should not.

He watched her with raised eyebrows.

"I simply want to help Leaf find his tribe and family," she said.

"You're not that bright for a healer." He narrowed his eyes. "And why is it that you don't want Bear to know where you are?"

She felt the blood drain from her face, leaving her lightheaded as she walked rapidly away from the pit. "No particular reason. It's time that I go back. Leaf is waiting for me."

"I won't turn you over to Bear," he called after her. "And I won't drag you across the world on some foolish journey. You'd best join up with me, girl!"

After a restless night, they slipped out of camp at first light. Upon hearing about her encounter with the Wanderer, Leaf had insisted they leave that next morning without telling anyone. Raven knew that was best, but she wished she could have seen Moth one last time.

Leaf believed the Wanderer wouldn't follow them because there weren't any more bands that he could trade with on their route. Unconvinced, Raven persuaded him to travel as quickly as possible toward the looming mountains. Besides wanting more distance between them and the Wanderer, the increasing chill during the nights worried her. Autumn had arrived, and she was going to have none of the dallying that had characterized their first days together. Because the elder had told Leaf about certain landmarks, they found the pass soon after entering the foothills. Although Raven could have found the gap on her own, she followed Leaf's lead.

The pass was actually a valley with a meandering river cutting through. In some places, the valley walls almost closed, becoming little more than a narrow passage; at other places, they widened, the mountains receding on either side. Because their food supply had dwindled, Leaf and Raven paused in their journey after several days to take advantage of the abundant game and fish. Raven hunted with a throwing stick, using the expertise she'd honed while thwarting Fern's scheme to starve her. She'd just brought down a rabbit on a hillside when she glimpsed Leaf below, climbing the steep riverbank with a large fish impaled on his spear. Raven smiled. They would eat well that afternoon. She collected her things, along with the rabbit, and started toward him.

He couldn't see her approaching because she was descending the slope slightly to one side, making her way through thick brush, and she stopped to watch him before he spotted her. Having reached the top of the bank, he pulled off the fish, letting his spear drop. He wore a small smile as he grasped the wriggling fish, turning it over, looking at it closely.

She knew that the pleasure he was feeling came from his anticipation of her reaction to such a fine catch. An almost painful surge of affection and desire flooded her; being with him made her happier than she'd been in a long while. She looked forward to evening in the small cave they'd found, when he would again cocoon her in his arms. But night seemed a lifetime away, and she wished, for once, to throw caution to the wind. Raven took a quick glance around the area; she could lie down for him on the soft grass beside the river or choose to feel the firmness of that nearby boulder against her back.

Her pleasant musings were cruelly interrupted when the Wanderer suddenly stalked across her view, heading toward

Leaf. With a shock, she understood that she hadn't been forceful enough in discouraging the man. So annoyed was Raven that she didn't think to owl hoot a warning until it was too late and Leaf had already turned his head with a startled jerk as the Wanderer stopped beside him.

The two men began arguing, their voices muted at first by the wind and the river, but then Leaf's voice rose. "Leave us alone," he said. "You're nothing but a leech!"

"Be careful with your words, you ungrateful whelp," the Wanderer shouted back. "Or I'll knock out all your teeth and cut out your tongue! Your woman wouldn't want you near her then." He looked in the direction she was hiding. "Where is that juicy berry, anyway?"

Raven held very still, hoping he wouldn't glimpse her among the brush. She didn't hear Leaf's next words, but the Wanderer suddenly jabbed out with his spear. Leaf jumped to one side, dropping the fish. He'd barely recovered his balance when the spear followed him, and he had to leap away once more.

Raven's dismay held her feet motionless as if they were mired in frozen mud. She watched in horror while Leaf dodged the sharp point yet again. Raven had lived with cold weather for much of her life, but the trembling that wracked her had nothing to do with the chill wind buffeting the valley. She was tired of everyone, including that loathsome man, assuming they had the right to decide her fate. Rage surged through her, thawing her feet. She dropped everything but the throwing stick and ran down the slope.

Leaf had grasped the Wanderer's spear during the last lunge and was desperately holding on with both hands. He fell backward as part of the riverbank suddenly collapsed, jerking the shaft out of his tormentor's hands.

Now empty handed, the Wanderer moved to the edge and looked downward. Raven paused behind him on the bank for only a heartbeat, taking careful aim. Her throwing stick tumbled over and over until it cracked against the back of his skull. His head lurched forward. Rubbing the area where he'd been hit, he whirled around.

The Wanderer hesitated when he saw who had hit him, surprise covering his face. Then he charged in her direction with a growl. Raven jumped back reflexively, but upon turning to retreat down the bluff, she tripped over a rock.

She struggled not to fall on her stomach and managed to land on her hands and knees. As soon as she was down, Raven snatched up handfuls of dirt and gravel. Twisting around, she threw everything up at him, but the mess only pelted his leggings harmlessly.

"I would prefer to mate you than kill you, but I'm not sure I'll be given that choice," he yelled. He bent over her, fingers swooping down like talons.

Still kneeling, she filled her fists again, crouching on the balls of her feet before springing up. Her shoulders and forearms knocked his arms aside as her hands smeared their contents over his eyes.

With an enraged shout, he took several steps back—and began to fall. He grasped at the cliff edge as he slipped down the side, one scrabbling hand finding a hold. Raven squatted and picked up the good-sized rock that had become loosened from the soil when she'd tripped over it earlier. She lifted it over her head and brought it down onto his fingers with all her strength.

He screamed as he fell, his cry echoing off the riverbanks. The sound stopped abruptly when he bounced off a boulder right before landing in the swift water.

Raven's dirt-caked fingers clasped her face in shock at what she'd done—until a wayward glee took over, and she laughed in wild relief at the tumbling arms and legs going around a bend. He would bother them no more.

She found Leaf attempting to crawl up the collapsed bank with one hand while clasping his side with the other. Raven gasped when she saw his bloody fingers.

"I need to find my spear," he said in a dazed manner. He looked at her, alarm suddenly on his face. "The Wanderer—don't let him find you."

"He's gone," she said. "The river carried him away."

"He's gone?" Leaf repeated, his expression uncomprehending.

"Yes. Now let me see your side."

"It's nothing. He only grazed me."

When she pulled up his rent tunic, she saw that the spear had slid across his lower ribs, leaving a large scratch. Heartened, she breathed out. Although it bled profusely, the wound wasn't serious.

She retrieved her bag on their way to the cave. Once inside, she cleaned her muddy fingers and bathed Leaf's scratch with cold water to stop the bleeding. As she pressed his side gently with a chamois to further staunch the flow, she explained that the Wanderer had fallen off the bluff. She wanted to describe how she'd crushed his fingers but found she couldn't form the words to do so. "I'll go down for our spears and other things," she said instead. "As well as the rabbit I caught and your fish. Some creature will find them if I don't. Where's Cat?"

"She's tethered to a rock near where I speared the fish. I don't want you going by yourself." He started to get up.

"No, stay here. You'll start bleeding again. I'll make a poultice when I come back." She gently pushed him down. "I'll be careful," she insisted.

Raven was able to find everything except for Cat. Her empty leash dangled from a rock. Raven's heart sank. She was fond of the small creature, but Leaf had a deeper bond; he was going to be upset.

"Maybe Cat will find us here," Raven said hopefully after she'd returned. "I searched everywhere." She looked at his disappointed face closely. "You have an enormous bruise on your forehead."

He raised his fingers to his head. "I hit something when I fell." He dropped his hand. "I'm going to find her."

"You need to rest," she said. "If she doesn't track us here tonight, we'll search for her in…"

A man was watching them from around the side of the cave's wide mouth. For a panicked moment, she thought the Wanderer had somehow survived his fall. But the Wanderer didn't have such pale skin—or heavy brows and thick reddish hair.

CHAPTER 16

The Levant, Present Day

THE DAY IS BEAUTIFUL, WITH a salty, refreshing breeze. Antalya, with its red-tiled roofs set against mountains on one side and the Mediterranean on the other, is incredibly scenic. Mark is upbeat as he catches a bus to the museum, relieved that Antun seems to be coming around. Accepting the inevitable has taken him a while, but Mark hopes he's put aside his bitterness over the will.

Mark goes to the prehistory hall first after he enters the large white building. He pauses in front of a display depicting prehistoric fauna and flora from the Pleistocene. The information label is in English and Turkish, but the Turkish section is lengthy, whereas the English is only a few sentences long. Mark is struggling unsuccessfully to translate the Turkish when a member of the staff approaches, asking if he can be of help.

Mark asks for a translation, and the man explains in accented English that during the Pleistocene, there was a natural dividing line of sorts within what is now Turkey. In the northernmost reaches, the animals and plants were similar to those found in Europe, whereas in all areas south, they were like those found in the Levant. Some species were found in both places, but not all. Ancient bison roamed the area around and below Istanbul, but no bison remains have been found near the Koroglu Mountains and its western fingers.

"If you lived in southern Turkey and wanted a bison steak during the Pleistocene, you had to cross the Koroglu and hunt them on flatter land," he says. "Otherwise, you could eat steak from one of the wild cows, the aurochs. They were found in the Levant as well as Europe."

The employee turns out to be a German archaeologist associated with the museum. He's full of information about prehistoric Turkey, but Mark's time is limited, so after a short discourse, he thanks him and moves on to lose himself among display cases of hand axes, spear points, bone awls, and burins. A number of Homo sapiens' skulls and skeletons are displayed along with the teeth and bones of extinct animals from the Paleolithic Age. Then he reaches a case containing a fragment of a Neanderthal child's skull.

From what Antun had said, Mark was expecting a whole skull. He's underwhelmed. Still, this is proof that they were once in the region. He leaves the prehistoric hall and quickly goes through several other levels of the museum before heading back to meet Antun for lunch.

The closer he gets to the hotel, the more Mark's mood dims. His cousin is volatile, his personality filled with peaks and valleys. There's no guarantee that the jovial Antun he left earlier will be the same Antun he'll now encounter.

But Antun's good humor is continuously on display during their seafood lunch at a beachfront restaurant. If Antun's jollity is drug-fueled, Mark can't tell; he doesn't care if it is. He's grateful the good humor has lasted this long and hopes it continues for their trip into the mountains.

Once they've been on the road for several hours, much longer than the hour Antun had mentioned, Mark starts to wonder if his cousin actually knows the way to the cave. Antun always drives without paying much attention to anything beyond the next vehicle he'll pass, but they've been going through hills for some time, and the terrain is becoming mountainous, forcing Antun to keep changing gear as they encounter curves on steep slopes. He's also turning the car onto increasingly narrower roads. The one they're bumping over now is nothing but ruts. Mark realizes that a long time has gone by since he's seen another vehicle.

Even these bad roads haven't slowed Antun very much, and when they go over a large bump, their heads bang against the low roof. The tires land hard, and the car begins pulling severely to one side.

"Dammit!" Antun stops abruptly in the middle of the road. He gets out, holding the top of his head, and starts walking around the car. Mark hears him grunting as he bends and looks underneath. Then Antun is cursing at the top of his lungs, and a continuous thumping noise begins.

Alarmed, Mark stops exploring his tingling scalp and quickly gets out. Antun is in a frenzy, kicking a tire over and over.

When he sees Mark staring at him, he stops. "Get back in," he yells. "We have to go on."

"What's wrong with it?" Mark asks once the car has been started and is veering sideways again.

Antun only shakes his head and frowns.

Mark doesn't appreciate being ignored in this manner. He starts to ask again, but Antun is struggling to keep the car on the road, and he doesn't want to distract him, so he holds his tongue.

"Don't know," Antun finally says.

All of a sudden, something darts out in front. The brakes catch with a grinding sound as a gray-striped cat crosses safely to the other side.

The car stops again, and Antun takes it out of gear. "Not good! It's bad luck for a cat to bolt across your path like that."

This superstitious proclamation from Antun, whom Mark sees as always striving to appear cosmopolitan, is almost amusing. Perhaps this tendency toward superstition is genetic, a family trait. *Antun might be related to Mark and his mother after all.* "What is a cat doing here in the middle of nowhere? I hope someone didn't abandon it."

Antun takes a deep breath. When he answers, his voice is calmer. "That was a wildcat—a European wildcat."

"Are you sure? It looked like a tabby housecat," Mark says, sticking his head out the window to stare through the dust behind them.

"It's wild, I assure you. They've been living here for tens of thousands of years."

Mark wishes the cat hadn't run off. He would have liked to take a picture. Perhaps he'll see another one. He pulls his head back in the car, expecting Antun to drive on, but he doesn't. "Where is this cave?"

Antun scans the rugged scenery around them. "Actually, we're very close."

Mark looks around at the pines and cedars blanketing the slopes but can't see anything resembling a cave.

"I wish to discuss our situation before we get there," Antun says. His eyes bore into Mark. "I've been thinking during the drive. You admitted that the will is unfair. I'm telling you now—it doesn't have to stay that way. All we have to do is agree to change it."

The words are plainly stated without any emotional undertones, but an uneasy feeling fills the pit of Mark's stomach. "I'll turn over the ashes once the will is probated," he says. "I know you'd like to have them, and it'll be easier for you to take them to Lebanon than for me or my mother."

"You know in your heart that more has to be given than ashes."

Mark sits quietly for a moment. "Look, Antun, I don't think the will can be altered so easily. Your father didn't want it changed."

"I'm talking about decency. Haven't I treated you well during your time here?"

"You've been very generous, and I appreciate it," Mark says, willing him to drive on.

"I'm now asking for the same regard. You and I both understand the sadness of being an only child—the constant loneliness. I know you're tired of hearing this, but I want to be a good brother for you. Didn't you wish for a brother when you were a child? I certainly did."

"Hmm... at times."

"I was delighted you were coming to Israel, but I had to think—how does one treat a dear brother? I pondered this for a long time." Antun holds his face in his hands for a moment, imitating someone deep in thought. "At first, I was making it too difficult. It was simply a matter of finding out what gives you pleasure. I take you to caves and suggest good museums—places I don't normally go—because that's what you enjoy. We've eaten well, stayed at nice hotels, and I make it my business to pay for everything." Antun shrugs. "Well, almost everything."

He looks sideways at Mark. "I was even willing to share a woman with you, one I usually take for myself. I know that didn't turn out well—perhaps I should have found out first—there are many nice-looking men I know who would have been happy—"

"I didn't want you to buy me anything."

"Ah yes, rich American," Antun says, rearing his head back and closing his mouth in a tight line.

Mark feels his cousin's eyes on him, impatient and demanding, and he looks away through the windshield, tapping his chin with several fingers. *What if the will could be changed?* A lesser inheritance would still help his mother, then Antun will have more resources to try to claim his children. He wonders, though, if that will be a good thing for those boys.

Mark's thoughts are a writhing mess, and he can't find a clear path among them. He would like nothing better than to get out and hike back to Antalya, even though he's hours from the coast. He has only the law-honored words and wishes of a dead man to guide him—the strong instincts a father once had regarding his son—made into a document.

"My mother and Sami were siblings. She *was* his sister. I guess that meant something to him. And I wish you wouldn't say we're rich, because we're not—"

"Excuse me. I need to call and let—uh, find out if they're still open," Antun says, taking out his phone.

Mark looks at him openmouthed, jolted by his sudden banal sidestep out of the debate. He can't believe that Antun has waited until now to make sure of the opening hours. Perhaps getting on the phone is only his ploy to end their argument because he doesn't want to hear what Mark was going to say next.

Antun mutters in Arabic over the phone for a moment. He waits for a reply, hangs up, and puts the car in gear. "It's open for visitors." The car edges up a dirt lane, going slowly at last. "She was only a half sister."

If Antun thinks this beginning jab in a new round will leave Mark gasping and stuttering, he's wrong. This is exactly what he wants to know. "How is that so?"

"Her mother, your grandmother, had a fling, a little *affaire* with an American in Beirut when she was very young. He was an aide to a diplomat. They met at the Beirut American University, where she was a nursing student. The American is your mother's real father."

"Then who is the man in the photograph my mother has of her parents?"

"A family friend whose first wife died. He didn't marry your grandmother out of friendship, though. He was given a lot of money—a dowry, even though Christian families didn't normally do that kind of thing."

"Ah, so that's what happened."

Mark detects Antun's disappointment at his matter-of-fact response.

"Uncle Sami knew this?"

"How else would I know?"

Mark is only partly aware that the car has stopped at a dead end in front of a tall cliff face. He stares blindly at the stone. What Antun has told him only validates his earlier thinking. Sami had put control of his estate into the hands of a half sister he hadn't seen in decades, a product of family disgrace, rather than give his son that authority. He must have had good reasons for doing so. Mark suspects that Sami knew he had a potentially fatal heart condition. He'd kept Antun in the dark about that as well as his decision to make a new will.

Mark turns his head, his eyes locking onto Antun's. "What you've told me doesn't change anything."

Antun utters a word Mark doesn't understand, and hits the steering wheel with a palm. "Don't you understand how weak your kinship claims are?"

Mark makes several quick calculations: "My mother and Sami shared on average twenty-five percent of their genomes. You share twelve and a half percent ancestry with my mother, and you and I have a little over six percent in common. In spite of my grandmother's indiscretion, we're all related, but—"

Even though Antun is casting him a look that could scorch stone, Mark can't help himself. "But I hate to tell you that this means we aren't brothers after all. The percentages just aren't there for it."

Antun's head moves toward Mark, his teeth bared as if he wants to bite. "I'll tell you what the lot of you are!" He pokes a finger into Mark's shoulder. "*Bâtards et prostituées. C'est quels vous êtes!*"

Everything is suddenly blown up, magnified, the way a microscope lights up the monstrous forms of those miniscule mites that live in eyelashes, exposing their repulsive intimacy, the grotesque revealed. Antun's large, reddened face is too close. The pores on his nose are enormous, his eyes dark caverns.

Mark knocks away Antun's jabbing finger, and the words burst out of him. "She had to survive in a strange land! She was vulnerable!"

The anger on his face fading into perplexity, Antun jerks back.

Mark realizes his mistake. His grandmother, not his mother, is being called a whore. In Antun's equation, Mark's mother and Mark himself, by extension, are the bastards.

Antun covers his face with his hands. Moaning deeply, he rocks back and forth. "I've done it again, haven't I?" His muffled voice leaks from between his fingers. "I have no self-control. What I said was inexcusable. Way out of bounds. It's the stress." He puts his hands together as if he's praying. "Please, please, I beg of you. What can I do to make you forgive me?"

"Find someone to take me back to the hotel. I'll pay them."

Panic flickers over Antun's face. "But we've come all this way. We only need a break from each other." He opens the car door on his side. "The caretaker will let you in. I'll take another look under the car while you're inside." He gets out.

Mark takes several deep breaths and remembers the cool quietness of the Lebanese cave. This last grapple with Antun was bloodletting. *Time to staunch the flow.* Once he's taken a quick look around and gathered his thoughts, he'll somehow find a way back to Antalya. He collects his shoulder bag from the backseat and climbs out. When the car door slams shut, the sound reverberates off the sheer rock face ahead.

Without saying another word, Antun leads the way. Mark follows carefully as they climb a rocky path that, at times, is nothing but a ledge. Antun's shoulders are stiff, and he doesn't look back to see if Mark is keeping up.

They seem to have gone halfway around the mountain before they come upon the cave entrance. It's closed, the entrance barred by a large grated door. Upon seeing them, a man sitting beside the door jumps up from a stool and opens the lock with a large key. Stepping aside for them to enter, he watches them pass, his fingers trailing through a long black beard. He slips in after them and pulls the door shut. Mark waits while the two men exchange words in Arabic.

Antun nods several times. "Okay." He turns to Mark. "This cave is government property. The caretaker's name is Abdul."

Mark looks at Abdul. "Is there an entry fee?" He's surprised by how level his voice sounds.

The man's only reply is a glance at Antun. Somewhere in the distance, a generator is humming loudly, so Abdul must not have heard clearly—or he doesn't understand English.

Before Mark can ask again, Antun says, "No, no. There isn't a fee. Follow Abdul. He'll show you to the main chamber, then he'll leave you alone. You can explore there to your heart's content. Just come outside and yell if you need me."

Abdul's narrow face, with its cold eyes, resembles a viper's. Of all the people Mark has met up with thus far on his trip, none have seemed as strange as this man. After adjusting a mujahedeen-style cap on his curly black hair, Abdul motions for Mark to follow. He strides down a side corridor, shining a flashlight ahead, with Mark following closely. Oddly, from a back pocket on his long vest, a woman's turquoise scarf trails behind like an exotic animal's tail.

Mark forgets the scarf when they enter a room filled with tables so covered with objects that he can't properly focus on any one thing. Lightbulbs dangling from the top of the cave illuminate the table's contents. His eyes roam over the clutter until they encounter enormous empty eye sockets staring back from a nearby table.

His breathing almost stops. The eye sockets are part of a skull, and from its size, the skull once belonged to a fully mature Neanderthal. He walks to the table like a fish being reeled over. As he looks down, he's bothered by the way the skull is displayed. It's sitting on top of a pile of small bronze bulls and ancient oil lamps, its lower jaw skewed underneath as if it's loose. His fingers tingle with the need to touch the skull. It should be moved to a more secure spot. This cave is like a museum, but Mark has never seen exhibits presented in this manner.

"What is this place?" he asks. When no one replies, he turns to see if the caretaker has left.

Abdul is still there, although he's not alone anymore. He's been joined by men with black masks, all of them pointing guns.

Although Mark's pulse starts racing, his feet feel stuck to the stone floor as he stares in incomprehension.

"You are our guest, Mr. Hayek," one of them says in British-accented English. "How long you remain our guest is up to you."

"Search for weapons?" someone asks, the voice guttural.

"No need. This American is only a pillow-biter."

Mark's legs finally react, the muscles all twitching at once, and he wants out of the cave. He's having difficulty thinking clearly, but it crosses his mind that people don't normally kill their guests. He thinks he sees another door farther down the room and runs for it.

"Stop, or you die," someone yells behind him, but he keeps moving until he realizes that there isn't another door, only a large indentation in the stone. He darts to the side, heading for the door he entered through.

There are curses in several languages, and just as his hand reaches the handle, he's grabbed from behind.

Mark manages to throw off the first man before the others swarm him. He fights them like a fiend, but they're too many. While he's stabbing one of them in the eye with a finger, something heavy hits him in the head from behind. His bashed visual cortex responds with a display of multicolored sparks.

Right before he loses consciousness, he hears a woman. She's wailing, an anguished sound, keening her sorrow as though grieving for someone she loves.

CHOICES THAT CUT

THE REPLACEMENT CHRONICLES
PART 3

CHAPTER 1

The Levant, Present Day

Although everything is still black, Mark becomes aware of a surrounding hollow silence broken by buzzing sounds within his head. He feels a sudden sense of urgency, and he struggles to clear his mind, but at the moment, he can't even remember where he is. And then his location bubbles up through the fog. He's in Turkey; he's come here with his cousin to collect his uncle's ashes. They did that this morning. In the afternoon, Antun drove them to what was supposed to be an archaeological site, a cave.

A feeling of cool wetness begins over his face, a gentle stroking, and his vision slowly focuses. A woman's bright-blue eyes are looking down into his. They look concerned, even though he can't see the rest of her expression because of the veil she's wearing. Her eyes are red rimmed and puffy, as if she's been crying. He remembers the wailing he heard before things went dark.

"Who...?" Mark stops when a sharp pain shoots through his head. To his dismay, the soothing wetness goes away.

"Shh," she whispers, her breath blowing out the veil. A delicate forefinger goes up in front of where her mouth would be. "We need not talk, or they punish us."

Mark is puzzled. *Who will punish us?* She stands up, her long robe-like covering swaying around her, and looks down at him on the floor. "I get you tea."

Mark watches as she slips behind a curtain that goes across the lower corner where two soaring stone walls meet, closing off a small triangular space. He sits up carefully, his head pounding. After a few moments, she returns and kneels, handing him a mug. He's only taken a few sips of the tepid liquid when she suddenly snatches the mug from him. Most of the tea spills onto his lap. Mark makes a startled sound as she jumps up, hurries behind the curtain, and yanks it closed. A key scrapes in a lock. He turns his head.

The heavy door creaks open on large hinges, and Antun walks in, his hands tied in front of him. Two black-clad men follow, one of them carrying a bucket. They all stop a short distance into the room. The man with the bucket puts it down clumsily, and water sloshes out.

"What's going on?" Mark asks Antun in alarm, his words slurring, but his cousin only shakes his head.

The man behind Antun jerks his pistol toward Mark. "Shut up. There will be no talking unless you have permission," he says with a British accent, his voice muffled slightly behind the mask covering his face. "And don't look at me."

Mark has heard that voice before. Everything comes back, then—how he'd gone over to a table full of archaeological objects to look at a Neanderthal skull and how he'd been attacked shortly afterward when he tried to leave the cave. This man is one of his attackers. His heart misses a beat when the man gestures once more with the gun, grunting his impatience. Mark quickly lowers his eyes to the tea-soaked crotch of his pants.

He doesn't know why a person covered in black like that would think he'd ever be recognized. Only the man's hands and dark eyes, typical for this part of the world, are showing. But Mark's mind is working now, and his blood freezes as he realizes that he already recognizes him, or at least his clothing is familiar. Before they'd knocked him out, they had all looked familiar from pictures he's seen on the Internet.

"My name is Hamid," Mark hears, and he has to quell the urge to look up again. "I'm in charge of your stay here. Welcome to our humble facilities." Hamid says something unintelligible, speaking to the other man with him. Footsteps approach, and a notepad and pencil are poked in front of Mark's face. Hamid's voice commands him from where the jihadist is standing: "Write down your mother's phone number and e-mail."

Feet clad in black Converse sneakers wait in front of him. Not knowing what they will do if he refuses, Mark puts the pad on his lap, steadies his shaking hand, and writes down the information. He gives the pad back to the sneakers' owner. The man makes a disgusted noise and starts shouting in Arabic.

Mark looks up at him in confusion. He's pointing to the pad that he's holding by one corner between thumb and forefinger. A damp stain soaks the back cover.

Hamid walks over. "You soiled your trousers. What cowards you Americans are behind your bluster."

A casual but hard kick lands on the side of Mark's thigh, making him wince. He rubs the spot reflexively.

"I permit you to look at me. Now stand up and listen closely."

Mark struggles to his feet and faces his captor, glaring at him, momentarily unable to control his outrage at being kicked. He swallows and tries to calm down.

"These are the rules: Keep your eyes lowered in our presence. No speaking unless told to. Knock three times on the door for going to the latrine—someone will take you." He points to a mattress shoved against the far wall. "Stay on that pallet at all other times. No strolls about the room."

His unblinking eyes pin Mark. "You share this room with another guest. That part of the rooms is hers," he says, pointing to the curtain.

Mark studies the long black drapes hung on a long metal pole, the stout ends inserted into the two walls.

"You must never speak to her. Guards are always outside the door. If they hear your voices, you will both be beaten. Do you understand?"

Mark nods, his head making rapid little jerks. He despises how frightened this man makes him feel.

"Tell me!"

"Yes, I understand."

At Mark's surly tone, the back eyes narrow, and Mark tenses for the blow that will surely come, but Hamid goes on.

"Now for the most important rule. No trying to shag the girl. Your cousin is staying in a space the size of a cupboard because he's a bit dodgy. I don't trust him in here." He gestures with the gun at Antun, who gives him a surprised glance.

"With you, I don't think there will be a problem. But in case I'm wrong, I want you to know that it isn't possible—not for you or anyone else. She's like this." He makes a fist with his free hand. "Her entry has been blocked, and if anyone forces their way in, I will find out, and there will be bloody hell to pay."

Mark looks at the tight, fleshy circle made by the curved little finger of Hamid's fist. He's not sure what he's implying about the woman's—or girl's—ability to have sex, but it sounds obscene. Mark glances over at the curtain, recalling the way she'd put her sentences together; her native language isn't English. He wonders how much *she* understands of what Hamid is saying about her.

"Now go to the pallet," Hamid says.

Walking between the tables laden with artifacts, Mark passes the Neanderthal skull. He remembers fleetingly the tingling warmth of his desire to pick up the bony remnant of an ancient life. But his inhibitions are in full force now. Stopping would be a big mistake.

Mark reaches the pallet just as the lock turns with a metallic clack that sounds like a trap closing. The thin mattress is filthy, and there aren't any sheets. The room is cool but not overly so, and he decides to lie down on top of the slightly cleaner blanket instead of using it for a cover. His headache has lessened, but a big knot on the back of his head hurts. To relieve the pressure, he turns onto his side. He's dying of thirst and remembers the bucket of water he saw after he came to, but he figures that water wasn't for drinking. They'd intended to throw it on him but then saw he was already conscious.

After a while, the naked bulbs over the tables go out. The only remaining light shines through a small window high up on the wall, but the weak glow does little to relieve the dimness. Without the distant thrum of the generator, a heavy silence fills the chamber, broken by occasional popping sounds from the cooling lightbulbs. He glances up at the irregularly shaped window. Obviously the cave is located on the side of a mountainous outcrop, or there wouldn't be any light coming in.

He stares across the gloom and sorts out his thoughts. If his captors are part of the Lions of the Levant—he's sure that they are—he's in serious trouble. Antun has some explaining to do—if they're ever left alone together. Sami was correct about his son being involved with a shady group. *Have they duped their old business partner, then, by luring Antun to the cave so they could take us prisoner?*

A cold sweat breaks out on his neck when he thinks about the hostages who've been beheaded, burned, and drowned by this terrorist group and the earlier incarnation, Daesh, "Islamic State" as it was called in the West. But Mark assumes he's been kidnapped for ransom and not to make some kind of sick statement about Americans. What other reason was there for getting his mother's contact information? Mark hopes that this imprisonment will be only a large waste of his time, a setback before he goes home to complete his work projects in a timely manner.

But these thoughts calm him very little—Hamid and some of the others are probably sadists. When he recalls that the United States government doesn't pay ransoms out of its treasury, his body stiffens on the pallet, and the lump on his scalp throbs. He can't remember if families are prohibited from paying ransoms out of their own pockets or if the government merely discourages them from meeting terrorists' demands.

But Nadia will not sit docilely by and hope for the best; his mother will fight for him. She'll find a way. He's angry that she'll have to use her inheritance to pay for his freedom as soon as she receives it, and he's ashamed that he hopes it will be enough. He runs his hands over his face; it's slick with sweat. The only other alternative to passively waiting for the situation to unwind is to somehow get free.

Mark wonders how old the "girl" is. He sits up so that he can see the curtained area. They've made a holding pen for her in the only part of the chamber where two walls meet in a right angle. Rules or not, he'll have to talk with her soon. He needs more information before he can plan an escape. If Mark can end his captivity quickly, then his mother won't have to deal with trying to free him. He'll have to exercise some patience and caution, though. Before approaching that curtain, he needs to find out how often his captors check the room.

Later, the lights blink on again, and after a short while, two men come in, accompanied by a savory smell. One carries a gun, the other a tray, which he takes over to the curtain. The black draperies part, and Mark sees the girl's hands reach out and take things from the tray. Her hands disappear, only to return after a moment and grasp the curtain's sides as if to close them, her fingers stark white against the dark cloth. The guard barks a few words of Arabic and thrusts the tray forward. Her hands hesitate, then one of them takes something more before the other

one snatches the folds shut. The guard gives a little laugh and comes over to Mark's pallet and leaves the tray on the floor.

There isn't a spoon, so Mark drinks the watery soup straight from the bowl and uses a flat piece of bread for scooping up some kind of stringy meat, probably goat, from the bottom. He's hungry, and it doesn't taste bad.

He's barely finished when the guards return with a small bucket of water, a dipper sticking out. They leave the water and take away the tray. He drinks several full dippers, his thirst finally sated. After a while, the lights go off again. Mark decides that the time has come to try out the rule for going to the bathroom. He does have to go, but it will also give him a chance to pinpoint escape routes. And in spite of everything that's happened, he still wants to take a quick look at the skull. He could be caught, but he's found a loophole in Hamid's rules that can be exploited. Mark can't knock on the door unless he crosses the chamber. The shortest route is through the tables. He can always put the skull back on the table if he hears the lock turning.

The large, vacant orbs seem to watch him in the dim light as Mark walks over, the mouth a toothy grin at his approach. He glances toward the door before he stops, wondering if a guard actually is on the other side.

His legs pressed against the table, Mark leans over to see the skull better. Based on the robust size, it would be a good bet that this individual was a male. Mark's sight has adjusted somewhat to the darkened room, although not well enough for discerning fine details. He runs his fingers over the elongated top to a bun-shaped protrusion at the back, common to Neanderthal craniums.

Mark wants to pick it up, but the way the skull's mandible is skewed gives him pause. When he carefully lifts it, a hand on either side of the cheekbones, he finds that the bottom teeth are no longer attached to the upper ones. The top part of the skull comes cleanly away from the lower jaw. He raises the face so that the teeth are at eye level. They're in good condition, large and well shaped. This man had a strong bite.

Large sections in the back, over where the neck would have been, are missing, as if someone has put the skull down too heavily, breaking off the bone. Mark carefully lowers it onto a cleared area near the table's edge.

The skull feels smooth and cool under his fingertips. High cheekbones angle to the mouth, and there's quite a large hole where the nose was. A nose and upper jaw like the ones this man had would lead the other features, creating a bit more of a snout than seen in most modern humans—*prognathism*, if he remembers the term correctly.

As Mark's fingers trace the planes and ridges, his mind forms an image of the once-living being. Drawing from various renditions he's seen, including the one printed on his T-shirt, he fills in the facial features of eyes, nose, and mouth then adds a reddish-brown beard and hair. The T-shirt image is correct that way—genome alleles associated with red hair have been sequenced for several skeletons.

He's rubbing his forefinger over the thick brow ridge, his eyes tightly shut, when the reddish hair in his mind's eye reminds him of the knife's red color. Mark's eyes fly open, and the image dissolves. *It's still in my jacket pocket!* They may search him when he knocks; he'll have to hide the knife before going on to the door.

Ever so carefully, Mark places the face back onto the bottom teeth, leaving the skull how he found it. While turning to creep away, he hears a small noise from the corner. His head swings around in time to see the curtains sway shut. Mark pauses before going on, curious to see if she'll peek out again, but the black folds remain still.

Mark turns in a circle in the middle of the room. He doesn't have a clue about where to hide the knife, until he remembers where he found it. He begins feeling along the bottom of the stone wall, searching for a crack large enough to hold it. Even though he goes around until he's under the window, he doesn't find an adequate space. Behind the pallet will be too close if they ever search the bed, but he pulls away the mattress and checks anyway.

None of the gaps are large enough where the wall and floor meet. He's about to push back the mattress when he notices small chips of stone debris scattered about. He runs his hands up the wall until more chips begin falling, and an embedded rock moves a little under his fingers. The knife's original resting spot was inside a hole made when a rock had fallen out or been pulled away, creating a pocket. He works on taking out the lump, tugging until it scrapes out.

But he isn't the first one who's had that idea. Mark now knows for certain that some other poor soul was once relegated to the same dirty pallet. Inside the hollow, his fingers encounter a folded piece of paper. When he unfolds it, he sees writing. The dim light isn't adequate for reading what's there. He'll have to wait until the generator starts again—if it ever does. He places the note back inside the gap, slipping the knife in behind it, and replaces the stone. That done, he goes to the door.

It's made of steel, this sturdy closure that's keeping him prisoner. Red tears of rust bleed from the keyhole. He knocks and waits. After a while he tries again, the rapping loud against the metal. When the door finally opens, two guards search him. Their response time tells Mark that they don't always stay at their post. To his dismay, they blindfold him. He was counting on using this bathroom trip to learn the cave layout, and now he can't even see.

A hand takes his upper arm and pulls him along. After a lot of twists and turns, he's stopped. A flashlight is thrust into his hands, and he's pushed through a door. A foul smell hits him immediately. On lowering the blindfold and turning on the flashlight, Mark sees a hole in the stone floor with a bucket of water beside it. He covers his nose with the blindfold, trying not to retch, and finishes as quickly as possible.

They return him to the chamber, and he walks to the pallet and lies down. The only thing Mark has learned is that the compound takes up a good deal of space. The tomb-like silence and darkness of the cave oppress him. He tosses fitfully on the uncomfortable mattress until finally, he sleeps.

CHAPTER 2

Western Asia, Late Pleistocene

BIRD-LIKE WARBLING FILLED THE SMALL cave. The Longheads' speech sounded as strange to Raven as when the father of her unborn baby had been taken prisoner and she'd heard that odd, singsong cadence for the first time. Upon seeing that previous captive come through the cave mouth, followed by three other Longheads, Leaf had jumped up in spite of his wounded side. His words lilted just as theirs did, and he seemed to be inviting them inside to the hearth's warmth, but the coals were almost ashes in the old fire pit where they'd started a fire earlier, making a mockery of his hospitality.

Still sitting on the cave floor, Raven quickly piled on more kindling, the talk flying back and forth over her head. She desperately hoped that Leaf could persuade the Longheads to let them stay at their cave for the winter; her baby would come during those cold months. Her choice of a stick for stoking the embers was a poor one. Spiny tips where the branches once grew poked into Raven's hand, but at that moment, she barely noticed. When Leaf suddenly reached down and pulled on her arm, she dropped the stick into the flames. "Stand up, Raven," he said, helping her up.

She was suddenly facing them all, but she had eyes only for the one. The small cave was lit well because of its large mouth, and it was as if she'd last seen him the day before, so familiar were his features—the large nose, those impossibly green eyes now contemplating her.

Memories rushed back, and she wondered if his thoughts traveled along similar paths. His scrutiny abruptly went down to her abdomen where her tunic pushed outward, and a knowing look crept over his face. She inhaled sharply. Was it possible that he'd shared her dream about an egg-laying raven? In her nervousness, Raven touched her cheeks and felt dirt crusted there, left behind when she'd fought off the Wanderer. She rubbed her face distractedly. He finally looked away and started listening to Leaf. She felt overly conspicuous afterward, as if his lingering gaze had lit her up, making her glow.

Leaf kept talking to them, pointing over and over from himself, to her, then at the Longheads. They began to look uncomfortable, all of them leaning on their spears and shifting their feet, except for the captive. He listened to Leaf gravely, his head inclined slightly. Raven couldn't detect any hostility in him at seeing a former captor.

One of the Longheads finally responded. With a palm turned outward, he made long sweeps with his arm back and forth in front of his broad chest as he talked. His face was unfriendly.

When the Longhead had finished his say, Leaf spread both hands over Raven's middle, smoothing and tightening the leather material, revealing the mound. Raven understood that he was about to use her pregnancy to persuade the Longheads to take them in. He kept a hand on her belly while he slowly held out his other hand, pointing at their old captive, all the while repeating a single word.

The other Longheads, whom Raven believed were the brothers from the long-ago bison hunt, turned their heads toward the captive. They frowned, looking somewhat appalled, then the captive was the one shifting his feet. But after a moment, he gathered himself and lifted his head high. His response to Leaf's unrelenting attention was short, a low and fast trill.

The largest of the brothers motioned for the others to follow, and they all went outside. Raven thought that Leaf had failed and that they were leaving, but then she heard their agitated voices outside the entry.

"They're discussing whether they'll take us with them or not," Leaf said. "I told them I was a hunter and tracker, and I also pointed out the rabbit that you killed. But I think the baby will be the reason they'll decide in our favor. Many of theirs die—often before they're born. When I lived with them, I saw how very protective they were of children, and they always seemed to want more."

Raven gasped. "Are you saying that they'll want me to give them mine?"

"No, Raven. All I'm saying is that they revere small children."

She frowned and looked away. He'd spoken with authority, but she interpreted the way his eyes fluttered as a lack of surety.

"I told them about the journey we're undertaking to find my tribe, and that we'll leave when spring warmth comes. If it would make you feel better, we can slip away then, just as we did from the last camp." He pressed a finger along her jaw and turned her face back. "I want the baby with us, no matter what happens."

His earnestness reassured her, and she dropped the matter.

They looked toward the cave mouth as the brothers filed back in. Raven turned back to Leaf, lowering her voice, even though she knew they couldn't understand her. "Did they say anything about how they found us?"

"I think their curiosity brought them here. They were farther up river when they heard angry voices. I told them we'd been attacked by someone and that he'd fallen in the river and was swept downstream."

The largest brother was apparently the one chosen to tell Leaf and Raven what they'd decided. He moved his hands about while he spoke, and many of his gestures were in Raven's direction. She regarded him silently, disconcerted by not knowing what he was saying about her.

With his head tilted slightly to one side, Leaf listened intently. Several times, his eyebrows flew up, and he made small snorting sounds. When the Longhead finished speaking, Leaf looked at Raven. "He says to tell you that Chukar—that's the captive's name—already has a mate. Whether or not you and I mate each other is up to us, he says. Chukar's responsibilities are with his mate, and you'll have to be satisfied with me, your brother, providing food for you when the baby comes. They want to know if you'll abide by that. They don't want us causing any problems."

The relief in Leaf's voice led Raven to believe that those types of concerns had been on his mind all along. He must have misunderstood part of what they'd said, though. No one mated their own brother or sister. "Why would they think you're my brother?"

Leaf shrugged. "I suppose to them, we look alike." He watched her from the corner of his eye. "Do you accept their demands?"

"Of course," she said, her forehead puckered. "There's no other choice if we want to stay with them."

His face went blank, and he abruptly turned back to the brothers. Raven wondered if she could have somehow been clearer.

While Leaf was speaking with them, a plaintive yowl came from outside the cave. Leaf grabbed up his bag, and after saying a few more words, he moved quickly past everyone. The Longheads looked after him in bewilderment as he went out. When Leaf began calling Cat, they all turned to Raven as if she could somehow explain his strange behavior. She kept her eyes on the cave floor, avoiding their heavy-browed regard.

Cat was out of sight inside the bag when Leaf returned. To show them what he'd been doing, he lifted her out briefly before lowering her quickly in again, not giving the animal a chance to panic. The expressions on the brothers' faces made Raven want to laugh.

Leaf began talking once more, his flustered speech full of pauses. Raven stole a glance at... Chukar. It would take a while to get used to him having a name, especially one pronounced so strangely. Just like the many times in the past when she'd been near him, his impassive expression told her nothing about his thoughts, even though he gazed directly at her. Wondering how long he'd had a mate, she sat and once more focused on stoking the fire. It was best to not even look in his direction.

The pass had narrowed, becoming little more than a ledge running beside the river. As they followed the Longheads, Raven kept looking over at Leaf, fretting that his side would start bleeding again. He'd told her that they wouldn't be traveling far, but she wished they'd remained at the comfortable little cavern until the next morning. They could have followed the brothers' tracks then and easily found their cave. She looked ahead at their broad backs, covered with fur parkas, and shivered. Leaf's wound wasn't really what was worrying her, she realized of a sudden. That was only a bad scratch. Her real concern was what their lives would be like during the coming moons. Everything was happening too quickly.

They reached the broader valley well before nightfall. Raven and Leaf had been very close to finding the Longheads' dwelling. The valley and the shape of the cave's mouth were exactly as she remembered them from her dream. When they climbed up and entered the cave, the occupants settled around the hearth didn't at first notice Raven and Leaf behind the others. They hailed the returned men noisily, then a deafening silence replaced their greetings, and all heads turned as one toward Raven and Leaf.

Their reaction reminded Raven of when she, Leaf, and the Wanderer had entered the Fire Cloud camp, and the people there had stared at them wolfishly. Her first impressions of the Longheads were even more alarming. Their faces resembled wolves to a greater extent than those of Raven's tribesmen had. The forward thrust of their noses and their receding chins gave them something of a snout, creating a strong lupine resemblance. But as Raven looked from face to face, the illusion quickly faded whenever she focused on their eyes, which were large and not at all like the sly slits of wolves.

The group was mostly made up of women and children. Only two elders sat among them, a man and a woman with short faded reddish hair. Even including the returning men, they were a small band, but Raven felt as overwhelmed as when she'd first arrived at her sister's band and seen the larger group living in that camp.

Only six children of various sizes were among the women, and Raven's eyes lit upon them in fascination. They were as light-skinned as their parents, but while the adults' faces were made up completely of large, bold features, the children's faces were more delicate. Enormous eyes stared at her from under flyaway hair. Their small tucked chins gave them a slightly petulant look. Cheered and relieved by their sweet childlike appearance, a settling occurred within her—the baby would look fine.

Finally stirring, the elderly pair stood, their brows lowered, their narrowed eyes concerned. Raven believed them to be the brothers' mother and father. The largest Longhead brother again took the lead as he had earlier, speaking with mouth and hands.

The elder man interrupted him after a while, his full-throated voice drowning out his son.

Raven realized that the matter of them staying with the Longheads was not yet settled. She moved closer to Leaf. "What is the elder saying?" she whispered.

"He says our kind are nothing but trouble, even if you are the one who mended Chukar's arm. He wants to know why they should help feed us during the winter, a time when they'll have difficulty feeding their own people. I'll have to correct him on that."

When Leaf pushed forward and began speaking, several of the children ran to their mothers and hid behind them. The women themselves stood up, gaping at him. Raven supposed she would also be astounded if one of them started speaking her language. Silence again filled the cave when Leaf finished, then one of the women came over.

She stopped directly in front of Raven. Her thick hair was blade-cut and stood out around her head in an unruly reddish-brown mass, as did all the women's hair. She began directing a high-pitched warbling at Raven, who looked nervously over at Leaf as the words trailed away.

"She thanks you for healing her mate so that he could return," he said. "She says her name is Chirrup."

Raven's thoughts were tumbling. She wondered if the woman had been Chukar's mate during the time he was captive. The way Leaf had pronounced her name made it sound like a bird's chirp. "What did you say her name is?"

"Chirrup. Their names are bird sounds—the names for bird sounds," Leaf said upon seeing her confusion.

Raven didn't hesitate. "Please tell Chirrup my name and that, as a healer, I could do no less." To her surprise, she'd pronounced the woman's name correctly without much effort. She looked closely at the shorter woman, wondering if the brother had mentioned Raven's pregnancy to the group.

After Leaf told Chirrup what Raven had said, the other women began gathering around, the children hanging onto them, their fists clenched in their mothers' furs. One of the women rubbed Raven's forehead. She looked closely at the red ochre on her fingers. Another gently pulled one of her long braids then ran her fingers down its length. They looked hesitantly in her face as if wanting to see her eyes. Theirs were all lighter than hers, a mild brown mostly, although some had greenish tones. None of them, though, had the bright-green centers of Chukar's eyes.

Even though most of the men were as tall as Raven, all the women gathered around her were shorter. Although she wasn't as painfully thin as she'd been after Fern came, Raven still felt like a tall, slender sapling standing among trees with short, sturdy trunks. Her baby would be birthed with the help of women quite different from her own tribeswomen. Raven assumed that they did assist one another through that trying time. Chirrup had no children clinging onto her clothing, Raven noticed.

There were two less brothers than in the canyon—back when she'd first seem them all—and she wondered what had happened to them or if they'd actually been part of the family group. Perhaps they were from a different band.

Although no one had formally said that Raven and Leaf were accepted into the group, Chirrup's friendly approach seemed to have indicated that they were. After a while, everyone went back to what they'd been doing before the travelers' arrival. The brothers settled beside the hearth and ate the remnants of a meal that had been prepared and eaten earlier by the others.

Leaf made a big ado of pulling from one of their bags the fish and rabbit they'd brought along. Raven helped him clean and cook them, using some fire-hardened wooden skewers that were lying about. She had just begun eating when Chirrup brought over several roasted roots and gave them to her.

Raven did her best to echo Leaf's words of thanks. Raven wished she'd thought to have him teach her their language while they were traveling, but she felt confident that she would soon learn enough to talk with them. She couldn't determine which birdcall Chukar's name imitated. It had a familiar sound when the Longheads said it but not when Leaf had pronounced it.

After they'd eaten, Raven had Leaf take off his tunic so she could check his side. The deep scratch had scabbed over without any telltale signs of infection. She noticed then that his arms were almost the same size, both muscular and brawny. For a long time, the right one had been larger than the left one from overusing it when he'd lived with his Longhead captors. While cleaning the skin around the scratch, she glanced around the cave stealthily. Everyone in the band ignored them, occupied with some chore. Only a small girl was staring their way. While Raven watched, the child's mother reached over and turned her head.

Raven put down their sleeping skins at a distance from the others so that Leaf could feed Cat without her taking fright. After feeding her dried meat, he filled a small wooden bowl with water. Raven was completely exhausted, wanting only to sleep, but she needed to better understand her present situation. "Do Chirrup and the other women know…" The words died on her tongue. She felt foolish for once again doubting Leaf. She shouldn't be treating him like a cub-killing male lion. He'd never expressed any displeasure about the baby.

He shook his head. "They'll let them believe that I'm the father."

"Why would they do that?"

He mulled over his reply for a moment. "To keep the peace. Finding a mate is difficult. The elders say that there used to be more Longheads at one time—now they're few and scattered. So they are possessive of each other, the women as well as the men."

"What if a woman's mate dies? Will another man take her to his hearth?"

"No. None of them would dare do so. It has to do with food. Everyone gets a share of group kills, but not those made by a man hunting on his own—that food is only shared with his own mate and children. Although women often share plant foods they've collected, they rarely share meat. A man's first mate would fight his taking a second woman because her offspring would have less food then."

Raven lifted her brows. "But this leaves a lone woman scraping to feed her children. The rest would let them go hungry—or starve?"

"No, no. The others would help before things went that far. Really, it's not very unlike the way we lived in the Fire Cloud tribe. The difference being that there are a lot more of us to help out when need arises, and it's much easier for us to find another mate in case of death."

Raven snorted. "Not always."

He looked at her wryly. "I guess not."

Raven wondered if Leaf had known that someone was waiting for Chukar. While Chukar was a captive, the scout was often at the pen, and they must have talked. That would explain why Leaf hadn't resisted her idea of finding the Longheads. He wasn't worried about any awkward claims on her.

"Like I said, the important thing for them is keeping the peace," Leaf said. "They are slow to anger, but once they're upset about something—" He hit his palm with a fist then lay back, his hands behind his head, watching her closely in the dim firelight, his expression inscrutable. "The brothers will tell their father about the baby, and then all the men will hold their tongues. It's best we do so, as well."

"I agree—completely," she said, crawling under the skins so he couldn't see her face anymore.

She was chilled by what he'd told her, and he had a smugness about him that she didn't care for. Right before she fell asleep, images went through her mind of being run down and caught by Longhead women who, upon grasping her with their muscular arms, choked her by wrapping her long braids tightly around her throat.

Chapter 3

The Levant, Present Day

Sometime during the night, Mark awakens, opening his eyes, and flips over on his back. He thinks at first that he's in a hotel and wonders why the room is pitch black instead of being partially illuminated by the usual irritating glows from various electronics and the ceiling fire-suppression system. Then the events of the last day flood back, and the final shreds of sweet, mindless sleep desert him. The back of his head still hurts, but he tries to ignore it.

As he looks up, the night seems to flow and eddy as though it's full of something primal. He hears breathing. The darkness over him congeals into a faint form; someone is leaning over the pallet. He tenses but realizes right away that it must be the girl. His captors would not be this quiet.

"You awake?" she whispers.

"Yes," he whispers back. "Who are you?"

"I am Larisa Koval," she says in slow schoolbook English. "Is my real name. Although here, they say I am Malak." After a small silence, she adds, "I hear them snore now, so we talk."

Her clothing rustles. When a hand pats his stomach several times, he realizes she's trying to find a place to sit. The hand quickly withdraws.

"Sorry," she whispers with a hint of mirth as he sits up and moves over so she can sit on the mattress.

He waits for a moment until she's settled. "I'm Mark Hayek. Why are you their prisoner, Larisa?"

She sighs. "It is long story. I tell you quick and short, okay? I am from Ukraine, and I think I will be model like other girls from Ukraine. This agency take many pictures, but instead of make me model, they make me slave and put my pictures in book with other slaves." She pauses for a moment. "This book is catalog so people will order, you understand? They put Malak under picture. They say this name mean *beautiful angel*." A disgusted sound escapes her. "For two years now, I am Malak. This is my sad story, you understand. Why you are here?"

He does understand, and it dismays and angers him to find out that she's been forced into the sex trade. Although she told him her story with a breezy such-is-life manner, he has picked up on an underlying desperate rage.

"What you've told me is awful." Mark hopes he's not upsetting her by his shocked tone, which is much different than her lighter one, faked though it was. He can't see her shrug, but he senses the movement.

"I make bad mistake when I let my greedy mother find this agency instead of go back to university, and now I pay. Please, tell me now about you."

He doesn't really think she's a spy for the Lions of the Levant, planted to pump him about his finances, but he senses that something is missing from her account. For one thing, she hasn't explained why she's being held at the cave. This would be an inconvenient place for clients. Mark errs on the side of caution and tells her in as few words as possible about his responsibility to collect his uncle's ashes, not mentioning the inheritance. He and his cousin thought they were going to an archaeological site when they were taken prisoners.

He decides to probe a little. "Does the Lions of the Levant, and I assume the men here are part of that group, intend to... to sell you?"

"Yes, it is Lions of Levant. They already sell me to Saudi man. I talk with him on Skype couple times."

"Does he seem all right? I mean, fairly decent?" He immediately wishes to take back his inane words. Whoever he is, the man has already proven that he's not all right and certainly not decent.

Sharp little intakes of air make her voice catch. "He is big man with cruel face."

This time, she hasn't managed to mask her hopelessness. *How strange it must be to constantly think about yourself as a kind of commodity.* Mark assumes her buyer will want his purchase delivered soon. He feels a slight twinge of loneliness even though they've only just met.

"So they'll take you to him before long?"

"I go in one more month."

Silence descends again, but Mark doesn't break it with more questions.

The mattress quivers as she fidgets. She pronounces her words carefully, as though each one has a bitter flavor. "Healing take three months. I am here only two. They put my picture in wrong picture book, you understand—book that show very young virgins…"

A man coughs outside the door, making a faint hacking sound. The mattress shakes once, and the darkness where she was sitting hollows out. She's gone. He's not clear on what she was trying to tell him there at the end, but it sounded like something appalling was done to her. He stays awake for what must be hours, hoping she'll return. Only when the room lightens a little at dawn, and he can see the closed curtains, does he sleep.

Mark's headache is gone when he awakens again, although the lump remains. He explores the tender area gently with his fingers. Repeated concussions are associated with a higher risk of developing Parkinson's disease. Many people considered

Muhammad Ali as proof of that connection, although many of Mark's colleagues at the Parkinson's Institute have opined that the notion is bunk. A sense of panic streaks through him upon thinking about the institute, and his old concerns about his work absence come rushing back. If the present situation isn't resolved quickly, they'll reassign his projects. But how foolish he is to be worrying about that at this point. If the terrorists end up killing him, then someone else will definitely take his projects.

The morning sun coming through the small window illuminates the room a fraction better than it had the afternoon before. This side of the cave faces east. He files that knowledge away for future reference.

The cave is cooler than it was the evening before, and he sits up and pulls the blanket from under him. Uncovered in the stronger light, the dark stains on the mattress stand out. Several large splotches look like dried blood. He can't tell how old the stains are, but Larisa would know if others have stayed on the pallet during her two-month imprisonment.

He remembers the note he found and hopes the bloodstains aren't from the person who wrote it. He thinks about getting it out from behind the rock but decides not to—he doesn't know when his captors will return. His stomach growls its hunger. *Surely they will bring breakfast soon.*

Deep in the cave, a generator rumbles to life, and the dangling bulbs over the tables blink on. A short while later, a key rasps in the lock, and Mark sits up.

An even leaner meal of bread and tea is on the tray this time. If these meals are any indication of how well they'll feed him, it's good he's not moving around much, or he'll quickly drop weight. After eating, Mark goes to knock on the door. He's tempted to stop by the skull again, but he's desperate to visit the restroom this time.

Everything goes as before, but when the blindfold is removed on his return, the door is already open. He enters and finds two men standing on either end of his pallet—Hamid, he guesses, along with a guard. Mark glances at the wall before he sits down on the mattress, but the loose rock hasn't been disturbed. He should have cleaned up the rock crumbles behind the bed in case they do a thorough search.

The men stand there silently. After a few minutes, Mark can't stand it anymore and looks up at the closest one. The man immediately reaches over and slaps him across the forehead before he can turn his head.

"Eyes down, faggot!" Hamid walks around to stand directly in front of Mark. "We've phoned your mother and told her that your ransom is set at two million dollars. She sounds like a sweet lady. Really wants to help her little boy."

This terrorist has talked with his mother? An indignant and illogical surge of anger blurs his thoughts for a moment. Mark gave him her number, after all. However, the feeling that she's been violated persists. He can't imagine how the conversation between the two of them must have gone. She has to be frantic by now.

"My mother doesn't have that kind of money."

"How boring. That's what everyone claims," Hamid says. "You don't understand. You'll have to beg her to come up with all of it quickly, or else—" He makes a whistling sound, and Mark sees enough through his peripheral vision to know that his hand is going across his throat. "Perhaps your memory needs jogging as to your resources. I'll send Antun by as a reminder. If that doesn't work, then there are other means that will help make you persuasive when you talk with your mother."

Hamid rocks back on his heels, his hiking boots squeaking on the stone. "There's always the old-fashioned but effective lashing to be relied upon, and I've sent for a manual on waterboarding. I didn't get it right the last time." He gives a short bark of a laugh. "Bollocksed that one up, didn't I?"

Mark reacts to the offhand menace in Hamid's voice as if the British terrorist has screamed the words into his face. His breathing quickens, and he smells the sweat lining his clothes.

"But if this drags on, I'll get another chance." Hamid crosses to the door with that chilling remark, the other man following.

After they leave, Mark lies there, rubbing his still-stinging forehead, waiting for them to send in Antun. He wants to find out exactly what his cousin has been telling them about his finances and about him personally.

Before they knocked him unconscious the day before, one of his attackers—probably Hamid—implied that Mark was gay, and now he's called him a faggot. This doesn't seem to be just casual name-calling, but how could Hamid know anything about Mark's sexual proclivities—whether he's one way or another? He couldn't—unless someone, a someone who thinks he has Mark all figured out, has already told him about Mark. The images of Yasmin and Antun arguing below the window at the house in Tel Aviv play through his mind again.

His watch, along with his pack, is gone, so he doesn't know what time the guards finally enter with a tray—some time around noon, he guesses. He wonders if it will be soup again as they go first to Larisa's curtained nook. But upon leaving the curtains, the two men leave without bringing Mark anything. Angst, fueled by his underfed stomach, racks him. He's sure they mean to starve him into submission, and he imagines himself searching out insects from around the edges of the cave walls and eating them for their protein.

Mark remembers that he should get rid of the small pieces of stone that are behind and under the mattress. After gathering them, he slips over to the far wall, where he scatters them. That takes his mind off his hunger for a few minutes.

At some point during the afternoon, the curtain folds part, and Larisa steps out, veiled and covered. He sits up to better see her. She points to herself, then to him. Next she taps her wrist, looking down at it as if checking a watch. Then she covers her eyes with both hands. After a moment, she takes down her hands, gives him a wave, and disappears behind the curtain again. She'll cross over again during the night. The thought warms him.

He settles back to continue waiting for Antun, but no one unlocks the door throughout the entire afternoon. The two guards come with a tray again shortly before the lights go out. Mark remains lying down, not eagerly sitting up this time. He doesn't want to give them the satisfaction of seeing his desperation, but when they've finished serving Larisa, they bring over soup and bread. After a few gulps, it's gone.

Mark's hearing becomes hyper-vigilant as the night unfolds, and the sweeping sound made by her floor-length covering informs him when Larisa starts across the room. He feels her settle onto the space he's left for her on the mattress.

"I bring you food," she whispers. "I know they not feed you much today."

He hears a crackling like something being unwrapped, then a tantalizing smell finds his nose. "But now you'll be hungry," he says.

"No, no. This Saudi, he not like thin women. They try to fatten me. They yell if I not eat it all. Put hand out."

He obediently sticks out his hand, and she finds it in the darkness and lowers his fingers to a plate. He feels something cold and sticky. With her still holding the plate, he leans over, greedily scooping the contents into his mouth. It tastes like couscous and chicken with a sauce covering it, leading him to believe that the cook is probably from northern Africa.

"Nothing has ever tasted so good," he says upon finishing. "Thank you."

"Take for cleaning hands," she says.

He reaches out and finds the damp cloth she holds. After he wipes off his hands and mouth, he thanks her again and passes it back.

"About this Saudi," he starts, then pauses. "And the picture book of virgins." Mark is at a loss as to how he will approach the topic. He takes a deep breath. "I don't want to pry, but I really want to know more about your situation."

"It is okay. I tell you," she replies. "Saudi man see my picture in virgin book, and he decide that I am one he will pick. They call my handler in Lions of Levant—handler realize mistake—I am not virgin, and he say tell Saudi man to pick another girl. But they say no. This Saudi, he will pay lot of money for me, this virgin he see in book. That why my handler decide to make me virgin. He take me to doctor that can make hymen restoration."

Mark wonders if he's understood her correctly. "Did you say 'hymen restoration'? Is that possible?"

"Yes, I learn word. It is hymenoplasty. Seeing blood on sheets is important, you know, so he think I am virgin."

This medical term, *hymenoplasty*, sounds like a word that someone could use in telling a bad joke. He's taken aback by the depravity of her captors. "I am so sorry," he says, the words inadequately conveying his shock.

After a short while, she says, "Saudi man think I am eighteen, but I am twenty-one. They lie again."

He doesn't want to press her, but he has to find out. "Will this be a one-time thing for him? I mean after he takes your, er—virginity, will you return to your handler?"

"No, I belong to Saudi man and will live in Dubai. He marry me—I think." Mark hears her head coverings rustle as she shakes her head. "I not sure what he mean when he say I be wife in Dubai when he stay there."

Mark doesn't know yet how he will accomplish doing so, but he badly wants to rescue her from that fate. "Do you know how much the Saudi is paying?"

"No, no one tell me."

A noise like something being dragged filters into the room from the corridor.

"Everybody not sleep. I come tomorrow night," she whispers and leaves.

He thinks she's forgotten the plate she brought the food on, but he can't find it when he gropes around the area. He's disappointed. After things quieted down, that would have given him an excuse to go over and be with her a short while longer.

He doesn't drift off right away. He mulls over everything Larisa has told him; he worries about how his mother is holding up and if she'll be able to deal with the situation well enough to put together a ransom. He wonders about what's happened to his uncle's ashes, left in the Antalya hotel room, and whether or not Mrs. Aaron in Israel will insist on having them in her hands before she releases the inheritance. Mark's savings and his retirement account can be liquidated, but it will be far from enough to pay for his and Larisa's freedom.

CHAPTER 4

Western Asia, Late Pleistocene

ALTHOUGH SHE OFTEN FORGOT TO make the proper arm movements to go along with her words, Raven managed to learn enough of the Longheads' speech to communicate with them, and she soon felt part of the group's daily patterns. Seeing men making tools and going on hunts was entirely familiar, and there wasn't anything novel about women hunting small animals and occasionally hunting larger game with the men. Raven had always foraged for plant foods with other women, and she enjoyed doing the same with the Longhead women. They didn't eat as much vegetation or as many roots as she was used to consuming, however, and were occasionally irritated by her frequent suggestions that they go out to collect those foods.

Some other things were slightly different. She'd seen her tribesmen occasionally soften skins by chewing them. Raven had rarely done so because she disliked the taste. The Longheads were constantly processing skins with their large teeth. In fact, the Longheads used their mouths as a third hand. The first time Raven saw a woman clamping a large chunk of raw meat in her mouth while one hand pulled it out taut so that the other hand could cut off a piece, she'd asked if she could help, thinking the woman needed someone to hold the meat steady while she cut through it. Raven hadn't yet picked up much language at that time, and she thought her offer wasn't understood. But the woman finally took the meat out of her mouth for a moment to say "Ot," or "No," that being the best interpretation of the word's many shades of meaning. Raven quickly realized they were more inclined to do things by themselves than share a chore.

She'd also given up working with medicinal herbs. Elder Woman was the group's healer, and her hostile glares made it clear that Raven should not treat any illnesses and injuries. To remind Raven, the woman would slap her own chest loudly, saying "Ot" if Raven so much as took out a pouch in her presence. She wondered which birdcall her name had been before she became Elder Woman—probably the warning hiss that geese made.

In some ways, and in spite of having once lived with a Long-head band, Leaf seemed to be having a harder time adjusting than Raven did. "They think I'm afraid to hunt," he told her one day after he returned with a group carrying deerskin bags full of butchered meat. "When I threw my spear at the aurochs from a distance instead of running up and stabbing it, you should have heard them guffawing about it later with that odd laugh of theirs."

Raven thought about what he'd just said. She'd repaired Chukar's arm after he'd tried to wrestle a bison's head down by its horn, resulting in injury, and all of the men at the cave, as well as some of the women, had ugly scars. "I don't think they feel as much fear as we do," she said.

"That could be true, but nonetheless, they think I'm a coward. I run faster and can keep going for a longer distance, but those things don't impress them. Only sheer brute strength wins their respect."

"Let them think you're a coward. We won't be with them forever." She wrapped her arms around him. "What would become of me if you were gored to death?"

"You always think about yourself first, don't you?" he said, but he looked pleased, and his voice held a hidden smile.

"At least they're impressed with your tool making. I've seen the way they gather round when you pick up a nodule and strike it."

"I suppose so, but it's strange. They try to copy the way I make my spear points. What they make turns out well enough, but their tools are always different somehow."

Though they weren't prone to direct staring, no one in the cave could keep his or her eyes off Raven's greatly expanding middle. Raven had already let out the sides of her tunics twice with leather insets to accommodate the growing baby. She wondered for a while if some of the Longhead women might also be pregnant; their middles were naturally large and wide, making it difficult to tell. But when she learned enough language to ask them, she found out that none of them were.

One morning, Raven and Chirrup were working together at the cave entrance to fill in holes that tended to become puddles every time it rained. As they used cobbles from the river to fill in the spaces, Raven noticed Chirrup glancing sideways at her rounded middle.

Raven straightened and patted her stomach. "It won't be long."

"May the birthing go well for you," Chirrup replied, turning her eyes away.

Raven looked more closely at the stout woman. Her words had been tinged with sadness. Chirrup squirmed, and Raven realized that her direct gaze was rude. She expected the other woman to turn away or give her the warning look that Raven was used to receiving if she wasn't keeping her eyes to herself, so she was surprised when Chirrup spoke again.

"We are unfortunate, my brother and I. Our baby came too soon. It was only four moons along." Her word usage confused

Raven. "Eoh" was the word for mate, but that wasn't what Chirrup had said. She had used "aus," the word for brother.

"Aus?"

The woman appeared baffled by Raven's confusion. "Perhaps
you did not know? Chukar has always been my brother, and
when we had the mating ceremony upon his return last spring, he
also became my mate." Chirrup peered at Raven for a moment.
"That's why they were hunting at such a distance from the cave
when he got hurt—to find bison for the ceremonial meal. They
should not have traveled that far."

"Ah, now I understand." Raven could barely keep her face
still while she digested such strangeness. A sister-brother mating
was so taboo in the Fire Cloud tribe that it would have resulted
in expulsion. Children at play that were brother and sister were
chastised immediately if seen imitating the binding ceremony.

"The rest of my brothers joined with three sisters from another band, but their group didn't have another sister for Chukar
or a brother for me."

"How unfortunate." Raven placed another cobble into the
ground without really seeing it. The world often seemed beyond
comprehension, but several things had just been made clear. If
Raven had gone with Chukar when he'd tried to make her come
with him, he probably wouldn't have taken his own sister as a
mate—then Chirrup would have been left without one. They
labored silently until the last cobbles were put down.

The insights she'd gained while helping Chirrup were revived
several days later when Raven was scouring cooking stones with
sand and Chukar suddenly sat at the nearby hearth. She was
startled to see him bared and white as moonlight, except for his
loincloth, the flames from the firelight throwing shadows over
his body. But she understood the reason for his nakedness when
Chirrup came up behind him, carrying a scraper made of bone

and a small wooden bowl filled with an unguent the Longheads used for cleaning their skin.

A tingle went through Raven's hands and arms when Chirrup began working the waxy substance into Chukar's massive shoulders and chest. She'd done something similar for him after she'd reset his shoulder, and if Raven had come to this cave with him, she would be the one working on him just then. Heat from the fire released a pungent herbal smell, and his skin glistened from the melting beeswax that was the unguent's base. The smell somehow made breathing difficult. She swallowed hard and felt that she should leave, noticing that the three of them were alone and everyone else had gone outside. Perhaps she was expected to leave and give them privacy.

Raven started to get up then changed her mind in irritation. Chukar and Chirrup had thoughtlessly disrupted what she was doing. Why should she have to go then come back later to finish? He could have waited until she'd stopped before wanting to be cleaned.

She tried to keep her eyes on her work but kept finding them wandering over to the couple, checking on the scraper's progress. She suddenly realized that her fingers were being rubbed raw by the sand because the piece of leather she'd been using had worn completely through.

Chirrup was bent over, attending his lower legs, when Chukar intercepted one of Raven's furtive looks. Only a fleeting glance passed between them, but the question in his eyes jolted her. She finally recalled the bird whose cry was his name: a type of partridge that lived on rocky hillsides made a *chukar* call. The cocks of those birds mated with only one hen. She wondered if he knew that bit of information.

She heard a small noise from behind, and a hand clamped tightly onto her shoulder. Making a startled sound, she turned her head and found Leaf standing there.

"Come see what Cat has caught for us," he said.

Raven followed him out, rubbing her shoulder where his fingers had been.

Cat, having grown considerably, was becoming independent, and she spent most days away from the cave. But she was waiting outside the cave mouth, a ground squirrel between her teeth. When Raven stopped, the small animal went to her and dropped its catch at her feet. That gesture of unexpected nurturing by a wild creature temporarily blunted the misery that had begun settling upon her.

In the darkness that night, Raven strained in spite of herself to hear the sounds coming from a particular sleeping area farther along the cave. She twisted restlessly from her side onto her back, her belly protesting at the sudden movement. It was bad enough that her eyes had strayed during the day, but her ears also insisted on betraying Leaf. Her body tensed when she realized he was awake beside her. Cat suddenly crossed over Raven's legs and fitted herself between them. She began that odd rumbling in her throat that was surprisingly comforting. Leaf's breathing soon smoothed out, becoming deep and heavy.

Raven didn't detect any difference in Leaf's behavior toward her during the following days, and when the marks faded, she forgot the way his fingers had dug into her shoulder. But one afternoon when he began enthusiastically describing the joining ceremony he'd witnessed while living with the Longheads the first time, her hand crept up to touch the area where the bruises had been.

"The rituals are different," he told her. "But the stress on duty and commitment is the same."

Raven's mind wandered, trying to imagine Chirrup and Chukar participating in a Fire Cloud ceremony. It would take a lot of rope to bind those two together. Her attention came back abruptly when Leaf said, "I think we should bring up the possibility."

She looked at him, perplexed. "You're saying we should go through *their* ceremony?"

"It wouldn't be only for you and me. It would be for them, as well—so they will be more comfortable with us, so that they won't think of us as so different, so... *other*."

She shrugged. "I suppose you could talk with the elders and find out if they'll agree to it." However, she could have told them all, including Leaf, that in many ways, everyone there at the cave was very much alike.

"I'll talk with them tonight," he said.

Leaf didn't approach the elders, though, after everyone had eaten. He huddled with the brothers near the cave entry—all except Chukar. Leaf talked in a low voice as the men listened. Raven was too far away to understand him, but she watched his hand and arm motions in the dim light. He'd completely left boyhood behind during the short while she'd known him. His voice had deepened, and his body had become more robust even as he grew taller. He had to bend down to hear their muted replies, but he still looked like a much younger man compared to the broad Longheads whose muscles lay heavily upon them like hardened, rippling lava.

CHAPTER 5

The Levant, Present Day

MARK AWAKENS WHEN THE KEY clanks and grinds into the door lock. The lights are already on. He sits up, thinking the guards are bringing breakfast, but Antun has come at last. The door slams behind him. Their inheritances are, of course, what Antun wants to talk about, although he has the humility to begin with an apology. He's sorry he's gotten them into such a mess, he declares, clapping his hands upon his chest.

"*I* was misled." He stands among the tables, some distance away, as if he's afraid Mark will jump off the pallet and try to hit him. "I told a few of my business associates I was looking for a cave, an archaeological site where old bones had been found, because my dear cousin was fond of ancient history. They knew just the place." He raises his hands in a gesture of helplessness. "And here we are, unfortunately."

"Your business associates?"

"I know, I know. When one deals with snakes, there's a risk of being bitten." He looks back at Mark and gives a shrug, the corners of his mouth turned down. "But I had no idea they could be this treacherous."

His false shame is irritating. Uncle Sami had known the truth. "You've had dealings with these guys for some time, haven't you?"

"I know they are not nice people, but they have such nice things," Antun says, indicating with a wave the tables on either side.

"Stolen things. That doesn't bother you?"

"Yes, but if it isn't me making sure these wonderful objects end up with those who have an appreciation of history and beauty, then someone else will distribute them, and they may not be as careful about their clients."

A corner of Mark's upper lip rises. It sounds like an argument used by all brokers who sell stolen artwork.

Antun frowns at him. "I've apologized. I'm sorry this has happened, but right now, we need to discuss how we'll get out of here. They'll put me to work, in a minute, with packing and pricing." He has the audacity to chuckle. "I think Hamid believes you'll somehow make a weapon from the things on the tables, and that's the real reason he wants everything boxed and removed. But I digress, cousin. You know they're asking two million each for our freedom?"

"That's a ridiculous amount!"

"I know. My father would be upset if he knew that his life's work was going to extremists, but I don't see any other way than to use our inheritances to pay them."

"But is Uncle Sami's estate worth that much—four million?"

"No. It's not."

"Then where will the rest come from?" Mark shouts. The reality that his mother will end up even worse off because of his captivity has just sunk in. She'll borrow every dime she can to save him, and it still won't be enough, not even close.

Antun gives Mark a crafty look. "There is another source we might be able to tap. The seducer of your grandmother—your American grandfather—he's a very wealthy man."

"Who exactly is he?"

"He's the venerable senator from Wisconsin, Sam Alderson."

Mark stares at him. "My mother's father is a United States senator?"

"Yes, and a typically rich one. He owns a home-improvement store chain."

"But he doesn't even know we exist," Mark says, his voice rising again. "You're asking me to beg a stranger for money?"

Antun makes an exasperated sound, and he loses all semblance of being contrite. "I'm not asking you, idiot, but Hamid will make sure that your mother does! She'll have to in order to save your life!"

The door opens, interrupting them, and four of the jihadists come in. Three carry boxes while one stands to the side, holding a pistol. Another man follows, carrying the breakfast tray.

Seeing that Hamid isn't among them, Mark decides to go on with their conversation. He doubts any of the others speak much English and doesn't care if they do. Hamid will find out what's been said, one way or the other.

He looks again at Antun. "I'm glad that you're concerned about me staying alive, but did you have to tell them about this grandfather right away? It's like you want our captors to know everything about me."

Mark lowers his voice even though Larisa can probably still hear them. "And did you know that besides fencing stolen antiques, your friends also dabble in the sex trafficking of Eastern European women?" He points to the corner. "Like the one behind that curtain."

Antun glances at the closed-off corner, his lips pursed.

"You remember—the *girl* that Hamid said should be left alone?"

Antun just rubs the stubble under his mouth as he eyes the curtain again.

"And I'm starving," Mark hisses. He indicates the tray that the guard is lowering beside the pallet. "Look at this. They're barely feeding me."

His cousin looks down with what appears to be genuine surprise at the small chunk of bread beside the mug of tea.

"I suppose you don't have that problem," Mark says. He notes Antun's damp, combed-back hair. "And I see that you, at least, are showering regularly."

Before Antun can respond, heavy boots tromp on the stone floor outside the door. Mark quails, despising himself for doing so. Hamid walks in, and Mark quickly averts his eyes. Antun goes over and picks up a box.

Hamid must have heard their agitated voices while in the corridor, and Mark expects to be lectured about breaking the rules at the least, even though Hamid wants them to talk, but he doesn't look their way. Mark watches out of the corner of his eye as Hamid calls Larisa's name and pushes through the curtains. Muted voices come from behind the folds. He picks out the word *Skype*.

Mark takes up the mug and sips tepid tea, turning his attention to the activity going on at the tables. Nothing has yet been packed from the table where the Neanderthal skull sits. A spike of anxiety jabs him. *Will they take the skull?*

Hamid comes out from behind the curtains and walks over. "Look at me."

Mark puts down the mug and stares up at him.

"Your mother has contacted the authorities. That's good of her, but she's started parroting their words, demanding 'proof of life.' I hope they won't waste our time by giving her bad advice." He pulls a piece of paper and pencil out of a pocket and hands them to Mark. "She gave me two questions for you."

Two hand-written sentences are on the page: *What did you hide in your closet for a week when you were a boy? What did you call it?*

Mark places the paper on the floor and writes "a cat." He pauses and looks down at the words, scratchy and child-like from being written over the uneven stone. Mark had found the fluffy, long-haired kitten in the middle of the street and secreted it away in his bedroom closet. He'd fed the small animal with food slipped from the kitchen, and although he tried to clean up the results of those feedings, he hadn't understood about litter boxes. His mother had smelled something while tidying his room.

"Get on with the last question," Hamid says. "Don't tell me you can't remember."

Mark quickly writes "Puff."

Hamid guffaws upon reading his answers. "What a sweet fellow you were—a little prince, or should I say princess, naming your cat Poof." He turns to the others, speaking in Arabic, and they all smirk.

Mark frowns at them. Hamid deliberately mispronounced the cat's name. His eyes narrow upon seeing that Antun also looks amused. When Antun notices Mark's glare, he turns away and starts packing again. Still chuckling under his mask, Hamid leaves with the answered questions, and Mark finishes the bread and tea.

As empty boxes are brought in and full ones go out, Mark watches from the pallet. Considering that he's now their prisoner, Antun is entirely too chummy with the other packers, constantly contributing to their conversation. Though he doesn't understand a word, Mark recognizes their friendly smiles, which signal camaraderie in any language. He wonders if Antun is still this friendly with Hamid and if he's allowed by him to continue his drug consumption.

After a time, Mark lies down, turning onto his side so he's facing away from them. He studies the wall where the knife and note are hidden, reassured by how well his dangerous secret is concealed. When the room becomes quieter, he flips over and sits up. Only Antun and one other man are at the door.

"I'm leaving now," Antun says. "They'll probably let us talk again before long." He smiles in an apologetic way, but Mark only nods. "You know that when we're ransomed, it's best that you tell whomever questions us that we met up with a business associate of mine who knew of a cave. We followed him here. That's all you need to say. I'll explain the rest... unless you *want* to be part of a long legal process."

Mark looks at him blankly. He hasn't thought about what will happen when they're freed, but he certainly doesn't want to be detained for a long period. He nods again—reluctantly. Antun pauses as though he might add something, but then with a small twitch of the shoulders, he turns and goes out.

When he hears the key turn, Mark stands so he can see the tabletops. Along with a few other items, the skull is still there. *Did Antun leave it as a peace offering?* Mark puzzles over his relief at seeing the ancient fossil. It somehow makes him feel stronger, better able to endure.

His captors bring him lunch when they come again at midday. Along with the usual soup and bread is a chunk of roasted meat, on a separate platter.

Sometime during early afternoon, a man comes for Larisa. When she's returned later, her escort comes over to the pallet and throws Mark a blindfold. The terrorist gestures with his gun, motioning for Mark to get up. He stands and covers his eyes.

When they're a good distance from the chamber, the guard stops him and gives the blindfold a tug. Mark lowers it. The small damp room he's in contains a gravity shower of sorts. An overhead platform holds several five-gallon buckets, a hose attached to the bottom of each one that ends in a hand-held showerhead. Steps lead up to the platform so water can be poured into the buckets. The floor is soaked, and Mark wonders if Larisa has just showered. The man who accompanies him steps outside. Mark sheds his clothes and puts them on a shelf that contains a damp bar of soap and towels.

The water has been heated and feels wonderful when he switches the lever. After the first bucket is emptied, he lathers up before rinsing off with the other one. He's almost finished when the door opens, and one of the men walks in.

From the mask, black eyes ogle him, flicking up and down. Mark rewards the man's blatant presumptions with a withering stare and closes off the showerhead. He walks quickly over to the shelf and, keeping his back turned, towels off before yanking his clothes on. When he's ready to go to the door, the man has moved closer and is standing right behind him.

They all look somewhat alike in their identical garb, but this isn't Hamid, because he's always talking, and his accented voice immediately gives him away. Aside from that, Hamid is taller than the rest and has a way of standing stiffly, with his chin tilted upward, staring down his mask-covered nose.

Mark hasn't yet come up with ways to distinguish most of the others. Before he puts on the blindfold, he takes a close look at the man shadowing him, and he believes him to be Abdul, the one who first led him through the cave, a turquoise scarf dangling from his pocket. If Abdul thinks Mark doesn't remember how he looked without the disguise, he's mistaken. His snake-eyed face is unforgettable.

Mark hasn't been back on the pallet for long when across the room, the curtains open. Larisa stands there, dressed like a dancer out of *The Arabian Nights*. Her frilly veils and scarves are colorful, gauzy things. She glides toward him, swathes of turquoise, purple, and pink swirling around her. He's alarmed by her lack of caution in coming over this early. The generator is still going, and the lights are blazing.

She crouches in front of him. "Your cousin—I hear his voice—in this room, maybe month ago," she whispers. Her brilliant eyes are heavily outlined with kohl, and although the rest of her face is layered with veils, they are thin enough for him to see tantalizing hints of mouth and nose. "I tell you so you not say things you not want him to know. He is friend with Lions of Levant." Before he can reply, she's already fleeing back across the room.

The curtains no sooner close than a guard opens the door. "Malak, you come," he calls out. She opens the curtains wide and swishes over. The door closes behind her.

Mark knows why she's dressed like that. How exactly they go about working with Skype within the cave, he doesn't know, but he's sure she's going for a session with her buyer. He wonders if she dances for him to exotic Middle Eastern music, all the while taking off her veils. A spark of something like jealousy flickers, but he immediately extinguishes it. She must hate the Saudi and all those before him who have possessed her, demanding she become whatever fantasized creature they want her to be.

But he's distracted; he should be thinking about what Larisa said about Antun. If he's been at the cave previously, then he knew the site wasn't an archaeological dig or a museum. He knew exactly where he was bringing Mark—to a hornet's nest of terrorists.

Mark doesn't understand how Antun could have believed that Hamid would let Mark leave after he saw the place. That would have been too risky. The terrorist must have decided from the first to grab the profitable kidnapping opportunity Antun was hand-delivering to him. He wonders why Hamid decided to take Antun hostage, as well.

And then a fanged question rises like a cobra in Mark's mind. *Is Antun truly a hostage?* Surely he is, but it's all very confusing. The one thing Mark knows for certain is that he's allowed Antun to get him into a bad situation. He should have gone back to Israel as soon as his uncle's remains were in his hands.

His agitation makes it impossible to continue sitting. He leaps up and trots over to the skull. As he did the time before, he carefully lifts off the top part and begins running his fingers along the bony bumps and indentations, his eyes closed. It takes an effort, but he clears away his thoughts, and an odd calmness comes over him. Onto the blank screen of his mind, the same brawny, skin-clothed Neanderthal reappears with his reddish hair and beard. But this time, the image isn't static.

At first he's looking off as if watching something in the distance. Then he turns his head, and Mark finds himself gazing into green eyes full of curiosity. The reality of Mark's existence is temporarily suspended; he's barely breathing, and his heart rate has plunged. Time stops for long moments until he's jarred out of his reverie by the scraping key. Gasping a quick breath, he quickly returns to himself, puts down the skull, and scurries over to the pallet.

He expects to see Larisa walk through the door, perhaps returning for something she needs. Instead, a hand slides around the doorframe and begins groping over the rock wall. Mark realizes that the hand's owner is searching for the light switch. The wiring goes up the wall from the switch plate and travels across the top of the cave, long cords dangling bulbs at intervals. While at the door earlier, Mark noticed that in some places the cord was fraying near the switch. This person could get an unexpected shock if he touches the wrong place.

With morbid fascination, Mark watches the fingers flutter around, barely missing the frayed areas before they alight on the plate. The lights go off, and he's thrown once more into gloom. A shadowy form stands in the entrance for a moment before backing out and closing the door. Mark finds this odd, because the lights are usually on until the generator stops thrumming. While he awaits Larisa's return, he lies down on his side, once more gazing at the darkened rock face where his secret cache lies. The fact that he's able to hide something from his captors comforts him, even if it gives him only a false sense of control.

CHAPTER 6

Western Asia, Late Pleistocene

For some unfathomable reason, feathers were necessary for the ceremony. Black ones were especially important, along with those from eagles. The women had set traps by carcasses to catch feeding crows and ravens, and Leaf had to lead the men in a dangerous climb up a cliff to reach an eagle's nest. He'd received several deep scratches on his arm before managing to club one of the nest's defenders out of the air.

Raven encountered her own challenge when faced with helping the women pluck the ravens. She was afraid the desecration would irrevocably damage her special relationship with the bird. Their limp bodies filled her with dismay, and she kept thinking they were calling out every time she pulled out a feather. She had made the mistake of explaining to the women in their language that her name was the word for raven, hoping they would concentrate more on crows. But that piece of information only made them determined to create a cape for her covered with raven feathers, making even more of the birds necessary.

On the day of the ceremony, everyone in the band dressed differently than usual. Crow, eagle, and raven feathers woven into their hair dangled in clusters. Faces were reddened or yellowed with ochre. Even the children wore their freshest furs and skins. Necklaces of eagle talons hung from the men's necks. The women's necklaces, as well as their bracelets, were made of shells Raven had given them.

Because she was in the cave, with no pool to show her a reflection, Raven could only imagine her appearance after the women were through with her. Her face had been completely painted with red then dotted all over with yellow. Her enormous cape reached almost to the ground, the shoulders, back, and chest black with raven feathers. So many eagle and raven pinions were braided into her hair that she was sure she looked more bird than human. Leaf's hair and face were decorated in the same manner, but his cape, which he'd made himself, was of bison hide, a gift from the band. Raven had attached several rows of shells around the neck area and down the front opening.

The ceremony was largely to do with food; there was none of the binding Raven had endured with Bear. She and Leaf sat inside the cave a short distance from the mouth, with the others standing around them. Raven began by offering Leaf a small stew she'd made from rabbit and roots. He ate it while everyone watched solemnly. After he'd finished, Raven took her turn. She ate roasted venison that Leaf had hunted and prepared.

Raven was startled when the elders began playing flutes of hollow bone while she and Leaf exchanged food. Because the group's daily lives were so similar to those of her own tribesmen, she didn't know why their ability to make music should have surprised her. Their large fingers moved nimbly over the holes, producing a sound quite different from the Fire Cloud melodies. Their tunes were not displeasing, but something about the quavering music combined with singsong chanting was unsettling. At first, only the grown-ups chanted, but then the children's voices joined in, adding long, high-pitched trills, making the cave sound as though it were filled with birdcalls. Raven could pick out the word for eat, *aulehleh*, woven over and over into their song.

The Longheads began bringing them tidbits of food they'd prepared, each person pausing to watch the gift be eaten. When

Chukar gave them each a small portion of meat, which Raven recognized as hamster, upon tasting it—she chewed his offering with the same seriousness she had given the others. But when he suddenly sang out "Aulehleh!" along with the chanters, she almost choked on the piece, keeping from coughing with great effort.

After she and Leaf had eaten the last gift, Raven waited with curiosity for the final part of the ceremony to begin. Leaf had told her that the Longheads considered the last ritual to be the most powerful one. It brought about fertility because the couple proved by their actions that their bond was deserving of children. Raven and Leaf were to feed each other in the same nurturing manner that mothers used with their babies while weaning them.

Leaf helped her get up, and Raven took a small chunk of meat from a stone platter one of the women held. The meat was straight from the fire, the juices still sizzling. She blew on the piece, holding it by her fingernails so she wouldn't burn herself, then placed it on her tongue for another moment to cool it. She chewed until the meat was completely softened, taking her time, processing it thoroughly. Then she pressed her mouth against Leaf's open lips and passed the food over. An image flashed through her mind of a fledgling raven being fed by its parent. After he swallowed, they separated, and Leaf plucked a piece from the platter and began chewing it.

When Raven had fed Leaf, the music had begun picking up pace. The sounds of flute and chanting echoed around the cave in such a dizzying manner that Raven was no longer thinking clearly. Her breathing quickened, and she felt an excitement similar to what she'd felt the time she'd taken too much salvia for a sore throat. Then Leaf put his arms around her, holding her tightly, her large stomach and full breasts against him. His mouth covered hers, and the food came over. She swallowed.

She waited for him to break off their contact. When he did not, she started to move her head away, but he didn't let her go, increasing the pressure of his mouth against hers. Raven saw that his eyes were closed under his tensed brow. She responded by closing hers and pressing firmly back with her own mouth. Her heart raced to meet the rapid rhythm of the surrounding sound, and the world shrank, becoming solely sensation. A heated thrill unlike anything she'd felt before started at her mouth and spread in a wave all the way to her feet.

Suddenly, the cave became silent, breaking the intensity. Raven reluctantly stepped away from Leaf. She knew her face had the same dazed expression that his did.

As the Longheads filed out of the cave, their gazes lingered on the pair for an uncharacteristically long while before they turned away with self-conscious jerks. If their glances indicated that they thought the couple had performed adequately, Raven couldn't tell—perhaps they were scandalized.

The only one who didn't look their way was Chukar. He was the last to leave, and he seemed preoccupied with the knife he held in front of him, pausing in the cave entry to rub a finger along one side as if testing the edge for sharpness. Sunlight struck the quartz stone the blade was made from as he went out, making it gleam red. Curiosity crossed Leaf's face, and she knew he'd also seen the knife. To distract him—and herself—she grasped his hand. Fighting to hold back the strong recollections that threatened to spoil the moment, she led Leaf farther inside, heading for the sleeping tent they'd put up against the increasingly colder nights. She wanted to be with him and him alone for a short while longer. A large fire pit had been built outside the cave earlier that morning for slow cooking a boar. The smells wafting into the cave were tantalizing, but after the ceremony, neither of them was hungry, and he followed her willingly.

CHAPTER 7

The Levant, Present Day

MARK OPENS HIS EYES, SURPRISED that he's fallen asleep in spite of all the stress. After a moment, he realizes someone is behind him, patting him along his side. That tentative touch is what awakened him. Larisa must have come back while he was sleeping. A weak glow still comes from the window; she's come over early again.

Her hands suddenly become more aggressive, running over his buttocks, kneading the flesh a little. Roused completely out of sleep, he turns over, but instead of Larisa and her veils, he sees a black-clad specter.

He yells and lashes out with a fist, aiming for where he thinks the jaw is, then he twists around and kicks with both feet. As Mark pushes himself up from the pallet, the man is rising from the floor. He's making a choking sound, his hands clasped over his neck as he flees for the door. Although Mark didn't get a good look, he's positive that his visitor was Abdul.

When the door slams shut, Mark goes over and flicks the lights back on, but he doesn't return to the pallet. He paces back and forth along the far wall, recalling all the prison-rape stories he's heard. His eyes search the room in vain for an escape.

The door and the window are the only exits. Backing away from the wall, he looks upward. The window is too small for his shoulders to fit through. Perhaps he can widen the window's sides somehow. The only way to find out is to go up there.

This wall doesn't have convenient handholds already in place like the one he climbed at the coastal cave in Lebanon, but the way up is easier than he anticipated because of the large number of natural hollows. The window is quite a bit higher than the ledge where he found the knife. This resembles free solo climbing, going up alone without gear—the kind of risky climbing undertaken by people with death wishes, Mark has always thought. He makes the mistake of looking down, and his muscles clench. Pausing, he forces himself to relax. *Think about the window, only the window, how you'll look out into freedom.*

The opening is an irregular gap made by nature, a bubble left in the wall from the time the cave was formed. He lays his forearms along the ledge, leaning over them, and moves his head forward until he can see through the piece of clear acrylic wedged into the gap. To his surprise, the ground outside isn't very far—only a short drop—but his hope evaporates when he sees how thick the wall is around the gap. Chipping out enough stone so that he can squeeze through would take forever, and even if he can find something that will serve as a tool, he would have to work hanging on the wall like a bat the whole time.

The terrain outside slants downward then abruptly disappears in the distance, indicating a steep drop-off. He's thinking about how great it would feel to be walking around freely out there, when a striped cat, identical to the one he saw from the rental car, suddenly slinks into view. "Well," he says, the word sounding loud in the box of stone framing his head.

The cat freezes and looks up, its eyes meeting Mark's for a split second before it turns and runs away. He watches the small animal until it vanishes down the slope. Mark pulls his head back. It's time to return below before he's caught. Glancing to the side as he plans his first move, he notices above the curtained area a dark vertical shadow where the two walls meet. Squinting,

Mark realizes that he's looking across at an opening between the two walls almost as long as he is tall: a fissure in the stone.

He inches sideways until he's over the curtained section. If Larisa were there at the moment, she would have gotten quite a surprise. Mark smells perfume, and although he's curious about her hidden nest, he resists looking down, remembering how he froze earlier. Although he hates the idea, Mark hopes the Saudi will keep her for a while longer. If the guards look in while returning her, they'll see he's not on the pallet.

After a few more yards, he reaches the corner and swings a leg into the opening, planting a foot solidly on rock, and pulls his body through the slit. A dark narrow passage extends in front of him. From what little he can see, it continues along the outer side of the cave for a good distance. He catches his breath for a moment then moves slowly into the darkness. The way is narrow enough that he can't get lost, but he keeps a hand on each wall to help maintain balance.

The hair on the crown of his head is ruffled slightly, and Mark starts. Ducking, he runs his fingers over his hair to make sure a spider hasn't dropped down. Nothing is there, but the sensation persists. As he moves along, the feeling becomes stronger, more like a breeze drifting over his head. That can mean only one thing. From somewhere nearby, air is being sucked through the passage, creating a draft.

Mark hears a distant murmuring that becomes steadily louder. Sifting Antun's voice out of the sound, Mark slows. His cousin must be below him in one of the cave's rooms. The room's ceiling probably has a hole or crack in it, allowing sound to escape. If the room's door is open, that could cause suction, explaining the draft. Mark is disappointed. He was hoping against hope that the passage would lead outside the cave.

"I'll wear a disguise." Antun's words are now entirely clear, and Mark comes to a standstill.

"I don't like it," Hamid replies, his distinct cadence unmistakable. "What about satellites? What if we're being watched and you're followed?"

Antun laughs. "You've seen too many American movies. But honestly, my friend, I am going a little insane here. I'm as much a prisoner as my idiot cousin."

Mark's chest tightens, and nausea flushes through his middle.

"Well, how about the rest of us? We're stuck here until his dear mother and her lawyers get off their arses. We're as much a prisoner as you are."

"I'll only be gone a few days. I'll use encryption to call in regularly."

"And if you're recognized from the telly or newspapers? You're risking our share as well as yours. Besides, I need you here to help with persuasion. I want his mother to feel his desperation when they talk."

His fingers clasping the stone on either side, Mark tries to ward off the dizziness that's hijacking his senses.

"I have to go check on Larisa out in the van. The stupid girl might pull off too many veils and prove herself unchaste."

Hearing Larisa's name steadies Mark, ending his paralysis. He has to get out of the passage. They'll be returning her soon. Moving as quietly as possible, he begins turning around. He doesn't pause when he hears chairs scraping on the cave floor below him.

"I'm sorry, mate, but I can't let you leave."

Hamid sounds emphatic, but Antun hasn't given up. "I'll bring back wine."

"Wine is haram."

"Since when did you start denying yourself? Then how about some of those lamb kabobs you like. They're not haram, are they?" Those are the last words Mark catches before their voices are no longer understandable.

He blocks out all thoughts during the climb down, but as soon as he's on the mattress, Mark begins shaking. His mouth is foul and dry with anger. He takes the dipper from the bucket, but after only a sip, throws it back in. It galls him that Antun has found his way around Mark's usual caution in dealing with the world. He's always excelled in the careful, unemotional dissection of scientific data, but that talent has obviously not carried over to analyzing a certain type of person. He's been following Antun around like a docile puppy even though his cousin was clearly not what he seemed. Antun is a sociopath, one of those charmers whom others learn to despise as it becomes clear—usually too late—that they're always deceptive.

Mark doesn't often swear. Profanity is overly dramatic, made-up words that should be bitten back, but now, he lets go. "Slimy bastard, low-bred son of a bitch," he says into the quiet air. Those overly used expletives don't even come close to describing his treacherous cousin.

He calms a bit when Larisa comes back in, chaperoned by several guards, any gauzy veils she removed earlier now securely back in place. Right away, they bring food. They leave Mark watery soup and bread—no meat on another plate this time. As soon as the corridor door closes again, Larisa looks around the curtain and waves her hand with a regal flourish. She'll feed him when she comes over.

Some hours later, Mark listens to her soft whispers as he devours the bread and stew she's brought him.

"He beg me whole time to take veils off face and hair. But Hamid, he tell me to only take veils off face, and only after he ask fifty times. If I take off too much, Hamid say Saudi man want his down payment back because I am not modest. But every time, Saudi say he not want that I wear abaya. He not even like pretty one I wear for Skype."

"Abaya?"

"These things I wear." He hears her gather up the folds of cloth and drop them heavily.

"Where did they take you to talk with him?"

"They take me outside to van. It has lot of—" She searches for the right word.

"Equipment?" Mark would like to get into that van for even a short while.

"Yes, equipment." She gives a little sigh. "You need to ask that they give you Koran."

"Why should I do that?"

"They respect anyone who learn Koran. It keep them from not getting as rough, I think."

"Do you have one?"

"Yes, in English, but I not read it much. My English is not so good."

"You just need more practice." He would like to know her definition of the word *rough*. "Larisa, has anyone else been kept in this room since you've been here? There's dried blood on this mattress."

"Yes, for maybe four days. He has bad cough. When he not eat anymore, they take him away. He speak English, but I never talk to him."

The pallet's numerous stains lead him to believe a whole series of people may have been held on it in the past, but they were probably gone before she arrived. Mark decides he can trust her. It's unlikely that Hamid has coerced Larisa into spying on him. After returning the emptied bowl, he tells her about how he climbed the wall earlier and discovered the overhead corridor. He also confides how he heard Antun and Hamid talking and that he understands without a doubt that Antun intended for him to be kidnapped.

Her voice is indignant when she responds. "I am sorry that your cousin do this to you. He is bad man."

Mark wonders if she thinks that others fool him easily. Perhaps she's pitied him from the beginning. The thought disturbs him. "The day they took me—I heard you crying?"

"You fight them so hard. I was afraid they kill you." Her fingers tap his arm several times. "So happy they did not."

She stirs on the mattress. "I have to go behind curtain. But first I ask you for favor." She continues moving restlessly, adjusting her clothing. An odor of perfume blended with her own unique smell wafts over him. He wonders how she's dressed now—if she still has on any of the colorful veils he saw earlier. Like an animal, he knows her more by smell than sight. "Something to help me," she says. "Before you go free." Her whispers have become so low and hesitant that he can barely understand her.

"I will if it's at all possible."

"I was premed at university. I want to be doctor, but I not think I am able to cut myself, even if I have scalpel."

The sound of her swallowing hard fills the space between them. He gets an uneasy feeling.

"I not want this virginity that is not real. When Saudi find out Malak is not pure, maybe he let her go."

He feels the heat of her attention. She's awaiting his reaction, but Mark is stunned into silence.

"They say you like men, but I not feel this is all true."

He finds his voice. "It's not true at all."

"Is strange request, I know—to do this with woman whose face you never seen. Please..." He feels her fingertips on his arm. "I watch when you touch skull. You think how that man looked." She runs her hand down his arm and takes his hand, placing it on her face.

Her frilly veils and head covering are gone. He begins at her forehead and slowly moves his fingers over her features. The only thing he knows for certain about her appearance is that she has blue eyes. He has to assume that she's attractive, or she wouldn't be in her present situation, but he doesn't know if touch alone can give him an accurate idea of how she looks. But as his fingers roam, a picture does form: a fine-featured young woman with smooth, luminescent skin, her blue eyes topped by eyebrows arched like wings. He imagines that her hair is blond.

He slows his fingers. "But you must know that a doctor should do this. What if there's a lot of bleeding?"

"No doctor is here. Only you."

"And what if this Saudi is so disappointed to find you de-flowered that he loses his temper and hurts you?"

"Then I hope he kill me."

"Shh," he says, pressing several fingers across her lips. "That's very brave, but you don't want to risk it. I certainly wouldn't mind doing... helping out if it would result in your freedom, but we don't know that things will end that way. Hamid may even bring a doctor in here before you go. Surely we can come up with another solution that wouldn't..."

Her chin tightens under his fingers. She moves her head back and pulls his hand away. Without thinking, he leans toward her. He only wants to console her—at least that's what he tells himself as his mouth finds hers, but the intensity of their con-tact reaches deep within, pulsing through him with a powerful and overwhelming current. He struggles to retain control, to think clearly. This instant intimacy they've fallen into is almost certainly due to the fact that they're fellow prisoners. After all, he's only known her for a few days.

And what motivation is to be found in the ardent but highly desperate way Larisa's fingers are entwined in his hair? Is there anything within her passionate response other than the desire to be rid of the unwanted virginity?

Antun's voice echoes within his head—"*Okay, okay, okay.*" Mark pictures Yasmin's pouting face, but his febrile attempt to make an analogy between the two women doesn't hold. Yasmin is free to choose the way she lives, whereas Larisa's life has been forced upon her, as bogus as her virginity.

But why argue with himself? He now realizes that she is a woman he could care for deeply. Even if she only wants to use him, and even if he never sees her again, he desires for her to remain alive. That's why he can't comply. If the Saudi doesn't kill her when he finds out she's not a virgin, then Hamid probably would.

Mark reaches up to take her hands from his hair, trying to gently detach himself. He breaks off their kiss. "We can't, Larisa," he says. She pulls away and leaves the mattress, sobbing once as she crosses the room. The sound crushes his heart, and he fears that he's offended her.

She's forgotten the bowl. He takes it over and slips it under the curtains. "Larisa?" he whispers, but if she hears him, she doesn't respond. Chilled by the cool air of the cave, he returns to the pallet and wraps himself in the blanket.

CHAPTER 8

Western Asia, Late Pleistocene

As THE WEATHER BECAME EVEN colder, more of the band's activities moved inside the cave. Some things, though, were better done outside. Raven took advantage of sunny days for air-drying and smoking meat from the kills Leaf made. He'd begun hunting alone more often, returning with deer and smaller game for her to process and preserve.

And so Raven was the only one outside, quick-smoking venison over a fire on the gray morning that a toddler slipped into a pool of cold muddy water. She'd just turned the thin strips when she heard splashing and coughing. Her head jerked toward the sound, and she saw the floundering child, a boy called Twoo. No one else was about; he'd apparently come down alone from the cave to see what she was doing.

Raven ran over and pulled Twoo out by an arm. The child was covered from head to toe with muck. To her surprise, he wasn't crying. He only made a low sniveling sound through his mud-clogged nose. His small body was shivering violently, and she led him over to the fire. After stripping the toddler of his clothes, she wet a goatskin chamois with the somewhat-cleaner water she'd been using to make the coals smoke and began quickly rubbing the mud from his head and body.

While cleaning him, she noticed how his back was almost straight with little curvature. On reflection, she realized that all the Longheads in the band were built that way. Perhaps her baby would also have that type of straightness. Twoo's lower legs were short and slightly bowed, and she couldn't help but hope that her child would not have those characteristics.

His mouth was bruised and a little bloody. Concerned, she rubbed his lips, and one of his milk teeth came out in her hand. The tooth was large for such a young child. Turning it over, she saw the back had a scooped-out appearance. She wondered if all his teeth were that way.

Twoo, sensing that he'd somehow lost her attention, gave a sharp cry. Raven let the tooth drop. She pulled off her cape and wrapped him in it. He was quite heavy, and she struggled to carry him up the incline. When she was almost to the cave, a painful spasm went through her middle, making her gasp. The pain eased after a few more steps. Twoo's mother appeared suddenly in the cave mouth, her eyes wild as they fell upon her child. She mutely held out her arms.

"He fell in a puddle," Raven said. As she passed the boy over, an even stronger spasm wracked her, and with a cry, she bent over, both hands clutching her stomach. Keeping her eyes fixed on the pebbles covering the ground, she panted, controlling the pain. When she straightened, Twoo's mother had disappeared inside with the child, but when Raven stumbled into the cave, several women were rushing her way.

She suffered for a while in silence before a particularly strong contraction wrested a scream from her, and no longer able to manage the pain, she continued crying out from time to time as the labor dragged on. "Leaf," she yelled at one point before she remembered that he'd gone on one of his solitary hunts.

Arguing voices forced their way into her flickering awareness, coming from outside the sleep-tent. Chukar was suddenly there, staring down at her. He had the same perplexed concern covering his face that he'd worn when she'd panicked after he'd pulled her down with him beside the pool. For a heartbeat, Raven almost hated him. One of the brothers came in and grasped him by an arm. Chukar shook off his hand, but after looking once more at Raven, he left. She was dimly aware that several people were in the tent and had witnessed that incident. Upon turning her head toward the silent women, she saw with relief that neither Elder Woman nor Chirrup was among them. When the next contraction tore through her, Raven muffled her mouth with a blanket.

Sometime later, Elder Woman returned and pressed her fingers impatiently across Raven's lower abdomen from one side of her pelvis to the other. "Too narrow," she said, obviously thinking that Raven was beyond hearing. But the pain had temporarily eased, and upon comprehending what Elder Woman had said, she reached for her pouch lying a short distance away. Chirrup, who had just come in, saw her struggling. She placed the bag in Raven's hands, and helped her sit up.

Pulling out a small bag, Raven asked her for a cup of water. She couldn't help how widely her pubic bones were spaced, but she could help her body fight harder to deliver the child.

The herbs she took caused the baby to finally start coming, and with the women's help, Raven got onto her hands and knees. Although she struggled not to, she was screaming her head off again as the baby left her, followed almost immediately by the afterbirth. Raven heard a wail as she eased around onto her back. Still panting from her efforts, she raised her hands toward Elder Woman, who was wiping off the squalling newborn—she felt a desperate need to see the child. Elder Woman held back, fussing at Raven to move her hands out of the way. The only thing Raven managed to determine as Elder Woman lowered the baby onto her chest was that the infant was a large, healthy-looking girl.

When the baby's mouth reached Raven's breast, she began suckling without hesitation. Raven looked down at the top of her head. It seemed rather elongated, but that was common right after birth. Her face was so tightly pressed against Raven that she couldn't tell if the child shared the Longheads' tucked-back chin. The infant's vigorous nursing caused a paralyzing feeling of contentment to settle over Raven, and she closed her eyes, losing any lingering concerns. The baby's skull would either round out within a few days, or it wouldn't.

Dirt landed close to her feet, and Raven moved a few steps farther back from the burial pit. Several men, including Leaf, were taking turns digging. The work was going slowly. They may as well have been gouging out a stone floor, so dry and rocky was the soil of the cave's innermost chamber. Only a small narrow hole was necessary, and the top layer had been soaked with water to help their efforts, but they needed to make it deep. The entire band stood nearby, waiting patiently, their faces somber in the wavering torchlight.

Wren began squirming against Raven's chest, her nudging nose and open mouth searching insistently. Raven's unlaced tunic was still open from the last feeding, and she deftly slipped the infant's head under her cape. Wren seemed to be always hungry and was growing at such a rapid pace that Raven believed her daughter would grow into an unusually large woman.

Wren-like she was not. The baby was nothing like the small, delicate bird that was her namesake. She was hardy and wriggled with such vigor at times that Raven had difficulty holding onto her—a robust display of early strength. Raven was careful to thank the Earth Mother daily for bestowing a healthy child upon her.

Twoo's mother brought her son to the pit. Although Twoo had appeared diseased over the last couple of moons, he hadn't died from a prior, long-standing illness. His breathing had suffered only since the day he fell into the icy puddle. Raven suspected that he'd sucked mud into his lungs as well as his airway passages. His skin took on a bluish cast over time, and Raven had despaired over the way his lips stretched thin as he breathed through his mouth in an attempt to bring air into his clogged chest. Raven broke Elder Woman's unspoken demand that she not interfere with healing matters, leaving a pouch of powdered thyme in front of the lean-to within the cave where she stayed with Elder Man. Raven didn't believe that Elder Woman ever used those cough-inducing herbs, because Twoo had never brought up phlegm, muddy or otherwise.

When the boy's father lowered him into the pit, Raven shivered, but her discomfort wasn't from the cold, although the chamber was freezing. Morbid thoughts had consumed her ever since the child's death, and even though there'd been no indication that the band was considering eating Twoo's flesh, she'd brought up the matter with Leaf.

He'd frowned. "No, they won't do that."

"Don't look at me that way. It's just that when I first saw you, you told me that they sometimes ate their dead."

"They aren't starving yet," Leaf said. "He'll be buried."

She hadn't been completely mollified, because even if the band wasn't exactly starving, the children's faces were clearly becoming thinner.

When Raven went forward and sprinkled red ochre over Twoo's body, she felt guilty relief upon seeing him lying peacefully there on his side, his knees drawn up almost to his chin. Raven didn't remain to watch him being covered by the loosened soil. She wanted to attend to the dampness she felt along the bottom of Wren's clothing—the dried-grass lining needed replacing.

Once inside the tent, Raven quickly cleaned Wren and changed out the lining. Upon leaving, she almost bumped into Chukar. His eyes barely grazed her before they went to the baby. Raven looked past him. Everyone was still in the inner cavern. She flipped the leather covering back from the top of Wren's head so he could see her better.

The baby looked up at him and began moving her arms. He put a finger down to her hand, nestling it in her small palm. She immediately grasped it tightly and twisted. Though he was not usually given to showing much emotion—a quality Raven had found true for the entire group, especially the men—Chukar's face relaxed. His mouth spread in the small grin that was typical of them all.

Even Elder Woman was quite taken by Wren and held her frequently, and Chirrup, always the friendliest of the women, took the baby for longer periods whenever she noticed that Raven had some task that demanded her attention. Chirrup would rock Wren in her muscular arms while making sounds that resembled the soft clucks of a broody steppe-hen.

Lately, though, Raven had detected a change among the women. They displayed an increased alertness as they looked back and forth between Raven and the baby, a kind of disquiet slowly filling their eyes.

When Wren had been born, her skin was dark, a bright brown, and her eyes were dark, as well. But her coloring had faded after several moons, and her complexion had become fairer than both Raven's and Leaf's deeper fawn tones. Her black hair had also lightened, turning dark brown with brilliant-red highlights instead of Raven's muted blue ones. The baby's eyes remained brown, but in strong sunlight and firelight, green glints slipped out of hiding and threatened to give away her secret.

Chirrup and Elder Woman, in particular, took to watching Leaf when he was around the baby. But Leaf gave nothing away. By all appearances, he was a proud father.

Wren's brow wasn't overly prominent, but there was
he back of her head that Raven couldn't find on
. She'd felt a similar bump on Twoo's head the day
᠁ᴄ d cleaned the mud from him. But it was unlikely that anyone
would discover that difference. For all the others knew, Raven
and Leaf had those bumps under their hair also. Aside from
that oddity, Wren's skull had rounded enough to be within the
normal range of skull shapes that Raven had seen on Fire Cloud
babies, remaining a bit on the long side.

Voices came from the back of the cave as the others returned
from the burial. Chukar strode over to his tent and slipped
inside. Raven sat beside the main hearth, once more nursing
Wren.

The group's two older girls saw her sitting there and ran over
to see the baby. Raven pulled the protesting infant away from
her breast and sat her up. They peered at Wren, who became big
eyed upon seeing them. Their wan faces momentarily brightening, the girls chanted a little song for the baby while she
squealed in delight. Raven couldn't see their bodies as everyone
had begun wearing their parkas and capes with the fur on the
inside to better hold in their body heat. The extra bulk made
everyone appear well fed. But the truth could be seen in the
girls' cheekbones, angling sharply to their mouths.

As winter dragged on, Raven began slipping the children
some of the dried meat stored in her and Leaf's tent. Leaf figured
out what she was doing when they began trailing after Raven
wherever she went.

"I don't like seeing them hungry, either," he said. "But if our
food is gone before spring, it will pain me even more seeing Wren
hungry because you can't make milk. They can't say I didn't warn
them. I tried to get Elder Man to tell everybody to store extra
food the way we were." Leaf snorted a laugh. "He told me that
we were able to do that because we were scrawny and ate like
birds, but they were big people and had to eat more."

Raven waved her hand toward Cat, snuggled under their bedding. "I've noticed that you're still feeding Cat even though she catches her own food now. I'm glad the others can't see you." To keep from flaunting their relative abundance, she and Leaf ate from their own supplies only in the privacy of their tent.

He looked at Raven. "The amount I give her wouldn't keep a mouse alive. You don't like Cat?"

"You know I do. But the others don't share our foolish sentiments. I see them looking at her. They know she's being fed."

Leaf made a dry sound. "They're looking her over because they think she'd make a good stew."

When Cat began staying inside the cave most days because of the frequent, heavy snow, they tried to keep her in the tent and had been successful for the most part. Cat tolerated the children's attentions, but she avoided the adults as if she knew what they were thinking when they saw her plump sides. But after she brought in a large snow rabbit as big as herself one afternoon, the band's disapproval of Cat wavered. Leaf shared her catch by cutting up the rabbit and roasting it alongside a few meaty ribs brought in from a bison yearling carcass scavenged from wolves. The band had stored the partially eaten yearling outside under the snow and had begun rationing the remnants.

Before long, all that remained of the buried bison was bones. The women wanted to eat the marrow raw after cracking them, but Raven suggested they make a soup including the bones as well as marrow. She hinted that she would add something more to the mix so that they would all have something filling as well as savory in their stomachs. They eyed her food pouch out of the corners of their eyes when she slipped in several handfuls of dried meat. Because they weren't in the habit of making large amounts of soup, Raven took charge and set up several cooking bags over the hearth.

But the soup didn't last long, and when the hungry children began moaning in their sleep, Leaf brought in part of a frozen deer carcass he'd hidden away. "I was holding it back for us," he told Raven after he'd turned it over to Elder Man. "But I wouldn't be able to swallow the meat, knowing the others are hungry." He did build a fire in their tent so they could cook and eat the deer's heart and liver away from the others.

For half a moon, the snow came down almost daily. Cold winds whistled around the cave mouth, pushing the white powder inside. Raven felt a hollow desperation as their dried meat supplies dwindled. Her weight was falling off again, and she could feel Leaf's ribs under her hands at night. The only one who didn't seem to be losing weight was Wren, whose cheeks were still chubby from her mother's milk. Raven had nightmarish dreams in which the baby's cheeks melted and she became skin and bones under her gaze.

Raven made even more soups for the band, simmering herbs from her pouch with small amounts of the remaining dried meat that had started to turn rancid. The watery concoctions contained little sustenance, but everyone seemed grateful for her efforts. The hot broth could at least warm their hands and bodies.

Then the blizzards finally stopped, and the weather broke. The days became slightly warmer, providing a taste of approaching spring. Snow began melting in front of the cave soon afterward, making it easier to get out. Leaf and a couple of the brothers braved the icy terrain and discovered a herd of fallow deer that had weathered the blizzards farther down the valley.

After a few days, when they could move around without having to struggle through snowdrifts, a hunt was planned. Even the children were to come along. They would stay at a distance behind the men along with their mothers so they could help haul the hoped-for kill.

Everyone was in a fever to get out of the cave, but on the day of the hunt, Raven decided that she would remain there with the baby. To her amazement, Wren had begun cutting a few teeth even though she was barely three moons old. She'd become more fretful by the day, making distressed cries continuously, and Raven was afraid the noise would hamper the hunt.

Raven watched everyone leave then returned inside to sit in front of the hearth. Since her and Leaf's arrival, she'd never been completely alone in the cave. The space seemed abnormally vast and empty without the others around. If it weren't for the baby, she would have felt as lonely as she had when she'd been on the steppe before Leaf had come along. She went inside the sleeping tent, where it was cozier, but the silence outside the flap still disturbed her. Usually, the muffled sounds of people talking and moving about penetrated the deerskin sides. After a short while, she went out and leaned against one side of the cave entry with Wren asleep on her shoulder, awaiting the band's return.

The treeless land sloped away in front of the cave until it flattened out, becoming part of the river's floodplain. There, a good many trees and bushes grew. A low roaring sound filled the air. The distant channel was filling with melting ice and snow, and the gray swirling water appeared angry even from a distance.

Something out of place in the landscape poked insistently at the edges of her mind, so Raven wasn't entirely blindsided when the shadows suddenly thickened into the form of a man standing within the shaded tree line. After a few heartbeats, Chukar stepped out and stood in front of the trees.

During the moons she'd lived around him, Raven had felt the touch of his eyes upon her, but she'd never turned her head quickly enough to catch him looking. At that moment, he stared directly at her and didn't turn his head in the usual Longhead way of avoiding rudeness even though he must have seen that she'd spotted him. Raven doubted that the hunt was already over. Even if the band had been lucky enough to bring an animal down so soon, the kill would still need to be butchered. He must have slipped away.

She thought he was watching for some kind of sign or signal, although she didn't know what he expected from her. Or maybe he was hoping that she would come down to him. Her heart started to pound, and she was afraid. Not of him, but of the possibilities suddenly in front of her—and their consequences.

Wren awoke, cooing in Raven's ear. She pulled the cape flap back with her free hand and lowered the baby's head to nurse. As if Raven's movements were a prompt, Chukar took several steps forward, stopping at a large rock. He leaned back against the stone, his arms crossed, the snow up to his knees, and she realized he was waiting on her to make a decision.

Raven felt she was struggling to understand a soundless language that she'd been exposed to before but still didn't completely comprehend. If she went inside the cave, would he take that as rejection and go away, or would he hurry up the incline and follow her? She thought he might do the latter, and so she stood her ground. If she were awaiting Bear's return, instead of Leaf's, her decision would have been easier, but Leaf was an entirely different story.

She didn't know what would happen if Chukar became impatient. Perhaps he would simply take matters into his own hands. She imagined him climbing up the incline and stopping in front of her. He would reach out and caress Wren's hair, then he would rest his hand on Raven's cheek for a moment and tell her that he cared for her and wanted to be with her even if it was only for a limited time. Then he would lean over and press his lips against hers.

But Raven knew that if he did climb up, none of that would come to pass. He wouldn't do those things; that wasn't the way the Longheads behaved. The band shared a particular lack of open expression, which she would miss.

She didn't doubt that the band enjoyed each other's company. Their faces took on a contented look, especially when around their children and mates or those whose companionship they were most fond of. And she'd occasionally seen them sleeping snuggled together in front of the main hearth, practically piled on top of each other. Surely, they took pleasure as well as warmth from that.

The children often pressed against the adults, looking for reassurance, and the adults in turn responded, placing their hands on the children's heads. And they were always feeding each other. The adults would pop choice bits into a mate's mouth or pass them down to the children tugging on their clothes with faces gaping like baby birds'. And yet Raven understood that despite the babe in her arms, the gap between her and Chukar would never close completely—even if one of them made a move to narrow the physical distance presently between them. She understood this, and she tried to push away the worrisome ache she always experienced when near him.

Leaf suddenly appeared, striding out of the woods farther down the valley. The difficulty of making a decision vanished like a cloud swept away by a vigorous gust. Leaf was still too far away to see her well, and Raven knew he couldn't hear her because he was close to the noisy river. She shook her head and said, "*Ot,*" her tone not quite as forbidding as the one Elder Woman always used when saying the word. She glanced at the rock to see if Chukar had heard her, but he was gone. Only the memory of his brawny form leaning there remained. Raven fidgeted with Wren's clothing while Leaf climbed the slope. "Where are the others?" she called when he got closer.

"We ran a large buck over an incline, so they'll be butchering it by now."

"You didn't stay to help?" She'd never known Leaf to shirk doing his part.

"I was worried about you here by yourself," he said, coming up beside her.

He hadn't included Wren in his concern, she noticed. "We're fine, as you can see." She pulled the baby abruptly from her breast and tilted her in Leaf's direction. Wren wriggled and cried out at the sudden deprivation.

Leaf gently rubbed a finger over the baby's small tucked chin. "I keep worrying that the Wanderer will tell Bear where to find us."

"The Wanderer drowned. And the weather has been too bad for anyone to get through the pass."

"I know, but it makes a good excuse to be alone with you, doesn't it?" Looking pointedly at her, he bent toward her over the baby, who'd calmed under his touch.

Over Leaf's shoulder, Raven saw two of the brothers burst out of the snow-laden trees. Upon seeing Leaf standing on the ledge with her, they stopped short. Right before Leaf's lips met hers, she saw them gesticulating, their movements quick and choppy. When Leaf pulled away, they were gone.

"It's been a while since we've been completely by ourselves—not since the ceremony," he said.

She smiled at him. "We should enjoy our luck now the way we did then," she said, hoisting Wren over her shoulder. She'd had enough of being outside that day, warmer weather or otherwise.

CHAPTER 9

The Levant, Present Day

Antun comes in with Hamid and a couple of guards the next morning just as Mark is finishing breakfast. He tries not to glower at Antun. If Antun realizes that Mark knows he's part of the kidnapping plot, the situation could rapidly evolve into something worse.

"Your mother is funny," Hamid says. "She threw a fit when I texted her a picture of Antun as further proof that you're alive." His voice becomes high and indignant. "*That is not my son. Do you think that I would not recognize my own son? How dare you try to replace him with that wicked imposter.*" He laughs and reaches over, giving Antun a playful but hard poke in the side. "*Wicked, wicked, wicked!*"

Antun rubs where Hamid jabbed him, throwing him a rueful look.

"Don't roll your eyes at me," Hamid says, "or I'll whip you along with your cousin." He gestures at one of the guards. "Take him out of here. He has more work to do."

Without looking at either Hamid or Mark, Antun says something in Arabic under his breath, turns on his heel, and walks stiffly toward the door, followed by the guard. Mark glances at Hamid to see if he'll respond, but the terrorist is looking at him now. He quickly casts his eyes down, but Hamid's next words prove that gesture to be futile.

"Yes, Mark, you're to be punished today. For your infractions and your mother's. That bloody woman isn't taking me seriously enough. Perhaps pictures of her bruised and beaten son will help her think more clearly."

Mark's heartbeat thumps in his ears. He'd hoped that Hamid wasn't being serious when he mentioned a whipping. Mark wonders what Hamid means by "infractions"—surely not something as petty as Mark forgetting to keep his eyes down? Perhaps he's found out that Mark has been talking to Larisa. Mark is taking in quick shallow breaths, and he knows they're watching him like foxes about to attack a terrified rabbit, but he can't stop his jagged breathing. He senses Hamid's delight, and when Mark looks up, his eyes meet the terrorist's, which are crinkled at the corners in amusement.

"Get up!" Hamid shouts, exploding Mark's nerves.

Afraid to defy him, Mark reluctantly gets to his feet, and the remaining guard blindfolds him. Once that's done, the guard grasps Mark's shoulders from behind and propels him out of the room. Sharp jabs prod him down the corridor. After a short distance, the guard turns him and pushes hard. Mark stumbles over a stone threshold. He hears creaking and scraping sounds as if people are rising from chairs. Unable to endure being blind a second longer, he snatches the cloth from his eyes.

Three masked men are in the room, and they hold long, thin rattan rods. One of them hands Hamid a rod as he enters.

He wags a finger at Mark. "You're a naughty boy. Taking off your blindfold without permission—very cheeky. Extra punishment for you." He lunges forward, and Mark reacts reflexively, taking the blow on his hands.

He gasps at the sharp pain, then he's being lashed by all of them, the canes swishing down on his body everywhere, stinging like a thousand bees. A fury like that of a cornered animal's rises through the pain. He wants to snatch one of the canes away and turn it on Hamid, but he doesn't know if the man is disciplined enough to not kill him.

Only after he's cracked across the cheek does he instinctively cross his arms over his face, letting the canes beat him everywhere else. One of the men seems to be attacking more viciously than the rest, going after his arms in an attempt to reach his eyes. Mark tries to keep his back to this man, but when he falls on his knees, the cane lashes his forehead.

Mark tries to hold on to his earlier rage so that he won't start screaming or crying, but that defiance is being beaten out of him. A moan starts low in his throat, and he grits his teeth, trying to hold it in. Then the cane strikes his forehead again, and blood trickles down his face.

Before Mark can react, Hamid yells in Arabic, and they stop. Hamid begins to rant, and Mark is relieved that he's momentarily ignored. He lowers his arms and tries to stop rasping like a spent horse.

The recipient of Hamid's wrath responds to his chastising with an angry reply. His mask-covered face is narrower than the others—the man who cut him was Abdul. Hamid shouts him down, emphasizing his words by striking the wall with his cane. Abdul stamps out of the room. Hamid's rant trails off, and Mark's clattering breath fills the silence.

Hamid steps toward Mark, who is still on his knees. "That's too bad." His voice is filled with syrupy concern. "Your favorite shirt is all stained now."

Mark winces as the rod presses into his chest where the blood from his forehead has dribbled over the Neanderthal's head. Now that the shock of the beating has lessened a bit, he's sore all over, and the skin on his bare arms and hands is burning.

"I know what we'll do," Hamid says. "Get up. You deserve a reward for taking your punishment so well. You're not a screamer like so many of them."

Mark staggers to his feet, wondering what devilish thing Hamid will torment him with next. They put the blindfold on again before marching him back down the corridor. A door opens. He knows where he is from the slight smell of perfume in the air. The hand on his shoulder guides him across the room.

"Stop here," Hamid says partway across the chamber, his fingers digging into Mark's skin. He snatches off the blindfold. "What do you see on this table?"

Mark looks down. He's being treated like a schoolboy who hasn't learned his lessons well, but he plays along with Hamid's game. "A Neanderthal skull," he says.

"Antun tells me that you like Neanderthals so much he thinks you would like to be one."

Mark keeps staring at the skull.

"A skull is part of the internal skeleton, right?"

"Well, yes."

"I'm not a magician, but I *can* turn it into an exoskeleton for you—kind of like a turtle's shell," he adds with a laugh, delighted at his cleverness. "How would you like that?"

Out of the corner of his eye, Mark sees him motion at Abdul, who's suddenly reappeared. "Put it over his head," Hamid commands him. When the other man doesn't move, he grunts. "Bloody German doesn't speak English. Probably not much German, either." Hamid gives the order again in Arabic.

Because the bottom jaw is detached and the lower part in the back is gone, the skull slips over Mark's head like a partial helmet. It's not that heavy, and the bone feels cool where it touches his face. An earthy smell fills his nostrils. As he looks around through the large eye-openings, the room becomes very quiet. The masked men stare at him, then the room erupts in hooting laughter.

Their raucous mirth is the last thing Mark comprehends with clarity. He's only partially aware that they're taking pictures with their cell phones, posing with him, their arms thrown around his shoulders as if they are all the best of friends. Their forms begin to waver and change, becoming heavy, muscular. He's peering at them as if through thick glass or a heavy fog. A dark-haired woman dressed in some sort of leather tunic appears among them. Her eyes meet his with warm familiarity before she looks away.

His gaze follows her, taking in the way her long braids fall next to her sweet, brown-complexioned face. Longing fills him, and he wants to go with her, but she vanishes. He flexes his arms, confused by the enormous, barely restrained strength he detects within them. He feels powerful enough to demolish his tormentors with only a few blows. *But what about the guns?* a voice deep within him asks.

Mark is pondering the word *gun*, trying to recall its meaning, when he realizes that he's alone, sitting on the pallet, his back slumped against the wall behind it. He reaches up and carefully pulls off the skull and places it beside him. Pain from a hundred welts immediately sweeps over his skin and through his muscles. His cut forehead is dripping new spots of blood onto the stained mattress. He takes a corner of the blanket and gently wipes his face.

But what he's just experienced when the skull was over his head was so extraordinary—and confusing—that he's able to momentarily put aside his discomfort and think about the strange episode. All his life, Mark has fallen into short dreamlike states that seem to be more than ordinary dreams. During childhood, Nadia had been concerned about these "fits" and taken him several times to see doctors. They reassured her that he was not epileptic but merely a daydreamer.

Mark isn't entirely sure that the doctors were right. There has to be something different going on with his brain chemistry or the way the neurons fire. The doctors just hadn't taken the time to make a definite diagnosis. His "daydreams" usually happen at night. None of them, though, have ever been as strong as this last one. Mark attributes its intensity to the beating. He's seen the dark-haired, brown-skinned woman before—in the same type of dreams.

Groaning, he rises to his feet, picks up the skull, and takes it over to the table. If it stays on the pallet, they may ram it over his head again to alleviate their boredom. Other pieces of bone might break off.

Within the hour, Hamid and the guards return. Even though his injuries are mostly large red welts that haven't bloomed into bruises yet, they take pictures of him without his shirt. Afterward, he's blindfolded and led outside the cave so he can talk with his mother on a cell phone. Hamid turns up the speaker-phone volume when she answers so that he can listen in. He then gives the phone to Mark after yanking down the blindfold.

She's crying because of the photos they've just sent her.

"It's all right. I'm not badly hurt," Mark says, squinting in the sunlight.

"I don't want them to hurt you anymore. I want them to stop. I've told that awful man we're collecting money as quickly as we can."

"I'm all right, really. Try to stop crying, Mother. I can barely understand you."

Hamid glares at him, clearly disappointed that Mark's not begging her to save him.

"I'm in Israel. Everyone is being very helpful." She takes a deep breath, and her voice steadies. "I don't know what I would do without Mrs. Aaron's guidance. And Mark," she says, "I know this won't make any sense, but I'm in touch with a man who is my real father. I can't wait for you to meet him. He's helping us."

Hamid snatches the phone from Mark's hand and turns off the speaker. He claps it to his ear. "The senator—how much will he contribute?" He listens for a moment before staring pointedly at Mark. "Not enough. Today's beating was only the beginning of what will happen to your son if you don't become more reasonable." He motions at the guards.

They pull up the blindfold and start leading him away. Hamid's haggling voice follows them into the cave.

That night, Larisa brings him soothing lotion for his welts. "Neanderthals—who were they?" Larisa asks, curious about the way Hamid and the others tried to humiliate him with the skull.

Mark is relieved that she's not staying away, thinking that he was somehow rejecting her by not going along with her wishes to be rid of the unnatural virginity. She says that she's heard of Neanderthals but knows very little about them. He rubs the lotion over his welts as he thinks for a moment about how he'll approach the subject. As succinctly as possible, he tells her about the many archaeological discoveries pertaining to Neanderthal skeletons and tools, and he explains a bit about the latest genetic discoveries.

"They are not here now. Maybe we war with them? Kill them?"

"That is a question no one can answer for sure." Her desire to know more about something that greatly interests him makes him happy.

"What do you think?"

"I think what happened then was similar to what happens today when two different peoples encounter each other. Sometimes they avoid each other, sometimes they fight and kill one another, and sometimes they engage in friendly trade. And whenever two different groups meet, they usually end up breeding with each other at some point. The same with Neanderthals and us. We bred with them, producing hybrid babies, so in a way, they aren't completely gone. We still have some of their genes."

He's thrown a lot of information at her, and he wonders how much she's absorbed. "I think in the end, we overran them. Neanderthals lived in small groups and probably weren't well networked. They became isolated from each other. If a band became too small, it couldn't recover by merging with another one. They were like candles burning out, one by one."

"I so sorry Hamid treat you bad with skull."

"Don't worry about that. I didn't mind wearing it—not at all." Mark clears his throat. "I'll tell you, though, what does bother me. I think I'll be ransomed shortly, and I can't stand the thought of you being left here. I'm going to ask Hamid if we can buy your freedom—for the same price the Saudi is paying."

She's quiet for a moment, and he wishes the lights were on so he can see her expression. He imagines that her face has lit up joyously with the prospect of being freed. But then she says, "If you ask him, he know then that we talk. Because it is rule, he maybe beat you again."

She has a point. Mark is so sore, he isn't sure he can stand another beating right away, but the only way to obtain her release is to bargain for it. "I'll wait a couple of days before asking."

The mattress quivers as Larisa sobs quietly. Mark is baffled; he thought she would be relieved to know that he was determined to help her. "Please don't cry. We'll work this out," he says, wincing as he draws her close with his bruised arms. Mark holds her while she clings on as if he's her last hope.

There's no telling how Hamid will react to the proposal. It may prompt him to waterboard Mark on the spot. A shiver goes down his spine. Surely the threat of torture was only a ploy to get Mark to pressure his mother.

Larisa shifts with a sigh. Her lips brush his cheek, then she slips from his arms and leaves without explaining her tears. While spreading the blanket, he feels the small depression where she sat, her warmth still there on the pallet. He lies on his side over the spot with the palm of his hand under the cheek she kissed, ignoring the stinging skin.

He sleeps poorly, awakening several times during the night. After the final bout of insomnia, he falls into an exhausted stupor and begins dreaming. He's having one of those typical anxiety dreams, and it's a double whammy. Not only is he being pursued by an unknown enemy, he's also lost something important. The quartz knife is supposed to be in his bag, but it's not. Mark pauses running in his dream, panting. Looking behind, he doesn't see his pursuer. He quickly riffles through the bag's contents once more. The knife is his only hope to protect himself, but the blade is not where it should be. He hears feet running toward him. Throwing the bag over his shoulder, he darts away again.

As he runs along, he sees an odd wall of mist ahead draped across the landscape. Mark stops directly in front of the misty veil. It's not overly thick, and he can vaguely make out someone standing on the other side. As his eyes strain to pierce the wall, he sees a hand struggling through the foggy mass. That hand is holding the knife handle, the glowing red blade pointed downward.

Without stopping to think, Mark plunges his fingers into the mist, but his hand meets strong resistance. Whatever this is, it's not simply fog. Again, the sound of running feet comes from somewhere behind him; his pursuer is gaining. Desperately, he pushes forward, his hand moving slowly toward the knife. His shoulder enters, then his head. When Mark is completely enveloped, he realizes the fog is pressing against him, trying to repel him. He's attempting to enter a place he should not go.

Staring through the veil, Mark sees that the person holding the knife has long black braids. She has a look of determination on her face, and he understands that she's trying to help him. As his hand closes around the top of the handle, he looks directly into her dark eyes. She smiles when she lets go of the knife then backs quickly away and out of the fog. He follows her lead and backs out his side, whirling to face his enemy.

Before Mark can see who's been dogging his heels, he awakens and realizes he's had yet another strange dream that included the same woman. His experiences while wearing the skull conjured her into his dreams. Morning light filters through the window, and he sits up to wait for breakfast. He can still picture her vividly, her beautiful smile displaying the charming gap between her two front teeth.

CHAPTER 10

R AVEN DIDN'T NOTICE ANY CHANGE toward her, but all the adults in the band started treating Chukar with a disdain that went much deeper than just a distant coldness. The shunning began after the hunt in the melting snow and continued without pause. Even Chirrup sat apart from him, her back stiffly turned. The hostility in the air was so thick, Raven was afraid tempers would flare like hot embers sometimes did. She was grateful that Chukar didn't stoke their ill will. Although he couldn't help but be aware of their disapproval, he refrained from confronting them, ignoring their slights.

But Raven still worried. Leaf had told her he'd seen Longheads turn on each other with the same aggressive ferocity they displayed during a hunt. Up to that point, she'd seen nothing more than the usual short-lived spats that arose from close living. The largest of the brothers sometimes argued with his mate, who was quick to retaliate with her own stinging comments. Raven noticed they only indulged in that behavior when Elder Woman and Elder Man weren't around. But when her daughter-in-law turned up one morning with a blackened eye, Elder Woman had directed a shrill rant at her oldest son.

That particular brother was the only one who approached Leaf in height. It amused Raven to see the enormous man defer to his mother with bent head, not meeting her eyes. He finally fled the cave and didn't return until late in the day. Besides that episode, the only other indication of a tendency toward physical violence was the occasional slapping of a child who was deemed out of hand. Hopefully, the band would relent before Chukar reached his breaking point and reacted poorly to their animosity.

When Chukar began spending time with Leaf, Raven knew their treatment affected him more than he let on. If he'd ever felt any ill will about the way Leaf had almost speared him at Bear's command during his capture, he'd put it aside. Whenever Leaf made tools, Chukar joined him, working nearby on his own things. Occasionally, they discussed the pieces emerging from the rock cores, passing them back and forth.

They seemed to enjoy each other's company, but Raven didn't know what to make of their unlikely friendship. On the one hand, she felt an odd, almost perverse pleasure at seeing the baby's real father and stepfather side by side in amiable companionship. But on the other, she was suspicious of their reasons for pursuing each other's company and felt bad about not accepting their friendship as genuine. She saw their amity as only temporary, a way to convince the others that all was well. Her suspicions proved wrong when the band suddenly ended its shunning, and the two men still sought out each other.

With spring's arrival, the weather warmed considerably. Raven and Leaf began making plans to continue their search for Leaf's tribe. Wren, born almost five moons before, was thriving. Raven believed she was ready to withstand a long trip. The longer they waited, the harder she would be to carry. Raven had never seen an infant grow so quickly. She suspected that Longhead babies developed more rapidly than Fire Cloud infants, but because there weren't any babies in the band, she had nothing to base that on.

Cat had not been seen for almost a full moon. "She's turned all animal and forgotten about us," Leaf said. But Cat did reap-

pear one afternoon, not far from the cave. She came up out
of a dry ravine near where Raven was gathering early-growth
dandelions and watercress for eating later that day.

Cat rubbed against her legs, and Raven sat down to stroke
her and to rest. She looked into Cat's green eyes. "Where have
you been all this time?"

Wren, tucked in a sling across her mother's chest, awoke at
hearing her voice. Raven kissed her forehead before easing the
sleepy girl down to sit on her lap. Wren settled back, staring
at Cat. After a moment, she brought her hands together and
squealed. Cat started but didn't run away; she merely sniffed
Wren's feet. Leaf had been busy stretching hides on frames when
they'd left the cave. Raven regretted that she hadn't asked him to
come along; he would be disappointed he'd missed seeing Cat.

The small animal walked back and forth under Raven's
hands with her tail up, making her rumbling sounds. The stripes
on her sides looked stretched, causing her stomach to seem abnormally large. When Raven gently ran her hands underneath,
she realized that Cat was carrying kittens. How quickly the small
animals matured.

Raven was rummaging inside her bag to find Cat a bit of
dried meat when she hissed. The fur rose around her face and
down her back. Raven looked up to see what had alarmed Cat,
and her heart tightened into a little knot. On the opposite side
of the ravine, a group of men approached, carrying spears. Cat
darted away, heading for the woods. The identity of the large,
black-bearded man leading them was impossible to mistake.
Bear had found her somehow. Raven's mouth went dry with bitterness. She had done her best to be rid of him, overcoming her
fears for herself and her future child to flee over the steppes,
and it hadn't been good enough. She'd soon be right back where
she'd started.

Paralyzed by her dismay, Raven stared at them. She picked
out the trackers who had followed the brothers to make sure

they'd left the steppes. Their presence explained how Bear knew where to find the Longheads but not how he'd known she was with them. The only way he could have known that she was alive and where she'd gone was if the Wanderer had told him.

The group stopped, and Bear called to her across the ravine. "You have a tendency to take up with all kinds of animals, don't you?"

Raven remembered how she'd always hated his cynical familiarity. "It was a motherless kitten that I've been taking care of," she called back, straining to keep her voice calm.

"Better that than trying to heal lions, I suppose. Speaking of healing, you're looking healthy for a dead woman whose bones were scattered over the steppes. And it's ironic, don't you think, that a man who was supposed to have died told me where I'd find you?"

Raven's relief at hearing that she hadn't caused the Wanderer's death was fleeting, a quickly snuffed flame. Perhaps if she'd used her spear on him rather than her throwing stick, he wouldn't have recovered.

"Bring that baby over here," Bear called. "I want to see it. Is it a boy or a girl?"

"A girl." Raven thought she detected disappointment on his face. "I suppose you've come for us."

"I certainly didn't walk all this way just to look at you over a cut in the earth, so you may as well cross over." Bear's voice bristled with menace, hinting of punishment soon to be meted. She wondered what he had planned for her, and if his ill will was meant for her alone.

Raven didn't believe that Bear wanted a fight with the Longheads. He'd avoided conflict with them in the past. Collecting her and the baby was his priority, but she still wanted to keep him away from the band. Somehow, though, she must let Leaf know right away that she'd been taken. He would follow her—he always did. Somewhere on the trail, she would break free from Bear and rejoin him.

Hugging Wren tightly against her shoulder, she struggled to her feet. "I need to get my things from the cave before we start out." She pointed slightly away from where the men stood. "It's in that direction. I'll cross the ravine farther down, where it's not as deep. It would be best if you waited for me here."

The cave was actually on her side of the ravine. She suspected that the trackers hadn't followed the brothers all the way to their dwelling. They probably didn't know the cave's exact location. If allowed to go alone, Raven could warn the band that Bear's men were in the area, and she and Leaf could at least decide on what signals they would use when he followed her. She hoped Leaf wouldn't get the band involved by insisting on hiding her at the cave.

Raven feared that Bear would react negatively to her suggestion that she should go to the cave alone, but he ignored her, glaring over his shoulder at the men. "Why aren't any of you watching behind us? That's where anybody that's seen us will come from."

The men in the rear looked at each other then shuffled around so they were facing the opposite direction.

Bear nodded at her over the gap. "You're being oddly agreeable. Why is that? Have you tired of your young stag?"

"Leaf is dead," Raven answered. She slipped her unlaced tunic down so the restless baby could nurse. "He died from a spear wound the Wanderer gave him. The Longheads found me soon afterward." Raven tried to muster heartfelt emotion into her voice. "I miss living with my tribe."

He stood there for a few heartbeats, gawking at the nursing little one.

She scooped up her bag and started walking along the edge of the ravine. "I'll return quickly."

"Stop!" he shouted. "Do you think I'd let you go back there by yourself?"

Raven turned toward him slowly, not surprised that he hadn't fallen for her ploy. It had been a weak plan. She'd lead Bear's group in the wrong direction for as long as she could get away with that ruse, but the band still needed to be warned. "I'll let them know we're coming." She took in a quick breath and hooted loudly.

Wren, startled by the sound, flailed. She pulled away from Raven's breast and let out a sharp cry.

Bear jabbed his spear in Raven's direction. "Be quiet, woman! We're not going to those animals' lair! You'll have to make do with whatever we have. Now come on over. If you leave that bag of poisons, you can cross here with the girl—it's not so steep as that."

Raven put down the bag and began putting Wren into the sling. As she desperately pinched her over and over, she hoped that Leaf would hear the baby's screams. Raven's eyes stung from what she was doing to her precious child. "Forgive me, little one," she whispered, the words drowned by Wren's distraught howls.

After walking to the downward-leading path, Raven stopped. "I have things in there that I need for the baby," she shouted over the wails. "I can't leave it." She hoped to keep him away as long as possible. As she returned for the bag, a layer of sweat began shimmying to the surface of her skin, making her cape uncomfortably hot.

Bear paced the edge of the ravine. "You're as stubborn as ever!" He threw down his pack. "I'm going over to get them," he told the others. "Keep a close watch on the rear."

Raven's throat tightened as Bear started down the ravine. Her earlier confidence that she would be able to escape him while on the trail was already vanishing. She was a butterfly, fluttering futilely in a web, while the spider crawled closer. The urge to flee was overwhelming, but the only place she could go was to the cave. Even if she did risk the band's safety by running there to plead for help, she wouldn't be rescued—not even for the baby's sake. Upon seeing that Bear had so many men with him, Elder Man and Elder Woman would think it best that she take the baby and go with him, sparing them a confrontation—and they would be right.

Raven glanced at Wren, who had settled into the sling but was still only halfway to calm. The baby's skin had browned again, now that she was out of the cave daily and in the sun. She looked enough like Bear to fool him into believing he was her father, so at least that wouldn't be a problem. A rustling sound started in the woods behind Raven. Someone was moving around in the brush at the edge. Surely Leaf would remain prudently hidden and not confront Bear. That brave but rash undertaking would be hopeless. He'd be captured, too—or killed.

But as Bear, using his spear for support, climbed over the edge of the ravine—Chukar, not Leaf, was suddenly at her side. Raven's heart sank when she saw that he didn't have *his* spear. He must have been some distance from it when he'd heard Wren's cries.

Bear stopped short upon seeing his one-time captive. For several heartbeats, the two men glared at each other, their mutual animosity overflowing the distance between them. "Move away from her," Bear said. Remembering that Chukar couldn't understand, he looked at Raven. "Do you speak their gabble now? Tell him to leave."

"He wants me and the baby to go with him," Raven said to Chukar. "It's best that I do what he says."

Chukar kept his eyes on Bear. "You do not wish to go?"

"I will go," she said, unsuccessfully keeping a sob out of her voice.

"Bring me my daughter, Raven," Bear snarled. "I don't want my blood-child near that beast."

Chukar held his head alertly, narrowing his eyes, his face becoming so wolfish that Raven thought he'd somehow taken meaning from Bear's words. He turned to her, his raised brows more of a demand than a question.

Raven's hands flew around wildly as she explained. In spite of the circumstances, talking with him felt good. They hadn't spoken to each other even once since she'd arrived at their cave.

Upon hearing that Bear thought Wren was his child, Chukar made a sound that Raven took for derision. "Let me take her," he said, pulling Wren out of her sling.

Before Raven could protest or ask him what he intended to do, the baby sat balanced in Chukar's large palm. Her lingering whimpers stopped. She turned her head toward him, cooing and laughing. Raven stared. That was the first time Chukar had held the baby, and although Wren's features were much finer, Raven saw the resemblance at once in her tucked-away chin, in her brow ridges, and in her reddish-brown hair glinting in the sun.

Chukar placed his free hand on top of Wren's head, then with a deliberate gesture, he clapped that hand onto his chest, all the while looking at Bear. The look on Chukar's face was easily understood: pride mixed with challenge. He repeated the gesture with only one finger, touching the baby's head with it before insistently tapping his chest with the same finger.

Understanding swept Bear's face; his eyes bugged out, and his jaw dropped. Raven glanced at the men waiting across the ravine. They were rooted where they stood. The lookouts had given up pretending to watch behind them.

Now that the truth had finally broken loose like a fox leaping jubilantly away from a snare it had chewed through, Raven felt reckless with giddy exhilaration. "Yes, Bear," she said in a voice barely loud enough for his ears. "All of your efforts came to nothing."

His face darkening a vile purple, Bear charged with a roar. Chukar threw Wren in Raven's direction. She caught the baby by an arm, and Wren cried out in protest over being treated so roughly. Chukar jumped in front of Raven. She hunkered behind him, holding Wren tightly against her chest, not knowing if she, Chukar, or the baby was Bear's intended target. Perhaps they all were.

Because Chukar's broad back blocked her view, Raven couldn't see where the spear went. She saw Chukar shift slightly and stiffen. Then the shaft flew away off to the side. A loud thump followed as the bodies of the two men collided. Raven moved away from their struggle.

Bear grabbed Chukar around the neck with both hands but wasn't able to hold on when his opponent grasped both his wrists, pulling his fingers down. Chukar kicked at Bear's legs, trying to knock his feet out from under him, but Bear pressed against him tighter so that he couldn't use his feet. They grappled, neither of them giving ground. Then Chukar pushed away from his attacker, creating a space between them.

Raven was about to run into the trees, when Leaf suddenly came out of them, darting forward, his spear held high. Just as he reached the two men, something glinted red as Chukar lunged at Bear, his hand slashing in an arc, upward toward Bear's head.

Their struggle ended abruptly. Bear lay on his stomach near the edge of the ravine, the shaft of Leaf's spear sprouting from his back. After a few convulsive twitches, he became still.

Raven felt everyone else's shock as well as her own stunned uneasiness at seeing a spear protruding from a man instead of a bison or aurochs. All was quiet as everyone stood frozen, watching Bear as if expecting him to rise up and pull out the spear.

She felt that a long time had passed, although it was only a short while before the raven began calling from a tree, making the excited jabber that ravens used for alerting predators to a nearby carcass.

Then movement returned on both sides of the ravine. As several spears flew over the gap, Raven turned and dashed for the woods. The shafts bounced harmlessly around her as she entered the brush-filled glade. She crashed through the undergrowth, Leaf and Chukar right behind her as the three of them fled for the cave. When she glanced back, Raven saw Chukar running with a hand spread over his chest.

By the time they burst, panting, through the mouth of the cave, Wren was shrieking once again. Raven hadn't been able to put her into the sling while fleeing, and her face bore several scratches from the brush. Upon hearing Wren, everyone inside hurried forward. Raven tried to calm her daughter, holding the baby close under her cape so that the others could hear Chukar as he explained what had happened. Beneath the warm dark fur, Wren's cries became muted sobs mixed with hiccups.

Raven was relieved when Chukar left out how Bear had charged them after he realized that Chukar was Wren's father. Chukar simply said that Bear had charged them while they stood there. He'd fought him until Leaf arrived.

Raven looked at the way Chukar held himself. The way he pressed his arms over his chest, hunching forward a little, worried her. She glanced at Elder Woman, who'd not yet noticed something was wrong with her son.

When Chukar ended his narrative with Leaf's arrival at the ravine, Leaf took over, telling them how he'd speared Bear when he saw the two men apparently fighting to the death. He paused, the expression on his face changing several times. "That man is probably dead," he finally said. "But the other men with him may have followed us."

Upon hearing those ominous words, the brothers and Elder Man walked quickly to the cave mouth and looked down the slope. Leaf followed them. Raven, along with some of the other women, pressed behind the men, trying to see out.

Chirrup's sharp cry brought them all back inside. She was holding up Chukar's rent tunic while he talked to her in a hushed voice, trying to brush her hands away. He gave up when his mother came forward and looked closely at the leaking wound in his chest.

Elder Woman sucked in her breath. "Go to your tent," she said. "I'll get my bag."

Without protest, Chukar started walking farther back into the cave. Raven looked after him in frustration, seeing how he was still bent over. Asking Elder Woman if she could take a look would be futile.

As night fell, several fires were started at the base of the cave so that anyone attempting the climb up would be immediately visible. Several in the band had argued against the fires, saying it would lead the enemy to the cave. Elder Man pointed out that they already knew the cave's location if they'd followed the fleeing trio. A full moon would rise later that night, but without the fires, they would only have their ears to rely upon until then. Everyone except for the children would take turns watching from the cave mouth, he told them. He and Elder Woman would decide what else would be done to keep the band safe.

During her turn on the ledge, along with Leaf, Raven paced back and forth, keeping her eyes focused down the incline. Her arms were distressingly empty. "Elder Woman was almost fighting me to take her," she said. "I finally gave Wren over when I saw that our arguing was making her fret. The poor child has had an awful enough day already. But I don't trust Elder Woman. I think she'll tell us to leave as soon as we've finished our watch."

Raven glanced at Leaf. "What will we do if she won't give Wren back?"

"How will she feed her? There's no milk in those withered dugs," Leaf said. "Elder Woman will give her back. She's being a grandmother, wanting to hold—"

Raven turned to see why he'd gone silent. Elder Woman was coming out onto the ledge, the baby asleep on her shoulder. She handed Wren over to Raven, who felt immediate relief at having the familiar weight in her arms once more.

Elder Woman told them that the band was abandoning the cave in the morning. "We're traveling on to the Great High Plain to find a different place."

"May we come with you a short way?" Leaf asked. "We were going to leave before long in that direction to search for my tribe."

Elder Woman frowned, distaste on her face. "Follow in our trail," she finally said. "But we do not want to see you." She abruptly turned and left.

Shaken by the turn of events, Raven hadn't thought to ask after Chukar until Elder Woman had gone. She took up the watch again, her eyes vigilantly roaming as far as the light would allow. But there was nothing to see, and when the full moon rose, all remained tranquil for the remainder of the night.

CHAPTER 11

The Levant, Present Day

MARK'S HOPE THAT HAMID WOULD forget about water-boarding is dashed when Hamid enters while the guards are bringing lunch.

"That's your last meal for a while," he says. "So enjoy it. The manual has come! It says that victims may possibly choke on their vomit, so I'll wait until tonight. Your stomach should be empty by then."

Hamid chuckles. "Oh, but what a face you're pulling. I don't really need to do this. Things are moving along nicely for your ransom, but I need the practice," he says. "I'll be careful not to kill you. I have to keep you alive for the exchange. So cheer up." He starts back across the room, followed by the others. "Enjoy your meal."

Mark looks at the greasy goat meat lying on flat bread. His appetite is gone, but he forces himself to eat it all.

He knows very little about waterboarding. He's heard that victims feel as though they're drowning, but he's not sure how it's done. If only he knew what to expect, he could prepare his mind and body to endure. He's scouring his memory for scraps of details when the guards return. One of them comes over and throws some clothes at Mark then pantomimes that Mark should take off the clothes he's wearing and put on the others. The man has the decency to turn his back while Mark changes. Over his shoulder, he explains in French that it's washday. Most of Mark's captors seem to have lived in Europe.

"*Merci beaucoup*," Mark says when he hands over his smelly clothes. The man's eyes meet Mark's for a moment, and his head mask dips in acknowledgement before he walks across the room. The other guard has already collected Larisa's clothes, but the men don't leave right away.

"You come out," one of them says to the tightly pulled curtains. When she doesn't open them, the guard repeats himself, and she peeks around the edge of the cloth. "Come," the guard says, motioning with his hand.

Larisa's veiled face turns his way once before they lead her away. Mark watches the heavy door swing shut. Perhaps they're taking her for a Skype session with the Saudi, but he doubts that because she isn't wearing any of her colorful scarves and veils. Perhaps they want her to help wash clothes.

The afternoon drags by. After a long while, which Mark estimates to be about two hours, the door opens again. Before it even closes behind her, Larisa's draped form scurries over to the curtains. She doesn't look his way, much less give him one of her jaunty waves. Disquiet fills him.

He tries bringing his attention back to how he will survive the coming torture, but he keeps remembering the way Larisa looked crossing the room with her head bowed over sagging shoulders.

Her distress radiates through the curtains as the afternoon fades and the window darkens, but he doesn't dare go to check on her. They might come get him at any moment. The guards bring her food, then to Mark's surprise, they bring the tray over for Mark and collect the old one. He leaves the soup and bread uneaten, and he doesn't drink any water from the fresh bucket they also brought. Hamid must have forgotten to tell the cook about the planned waterboarding. The lights go out shortly.

No one comes for Mark as the night wears on. Though thankful for the reprieve, he still worries about Larisa. Although it's too early for her to come over, he strains to hear the hem of her abaya sweep across the floor—to no avail. When he can't wait any longer, he risks slipping across the room. If they do come for him and find him over there, it will only give them another excuse for waterboarding him.

"Larisa," he whispers. "May I enter?" He hears a murmur from the other side and, taking that as assent, eases through the curtains. There's a flare of light, and he sees her sitting on her bed, lighting a long red taper with a match. The wick catches, and she blows out the match and puts the candle into a jar to hold it. Her face and hair are uncovered. She's just as he thought she would be—blond and luminous—stunning, even though her eyes are puffy from crying.

Larisa is looking at him oddly, and he realizes that his clothing is causing her reaction. The clothes the guard tossed him earlier included a long shaggy vest along with baggy tie-string pants and a long-sleeved shirt.

"I steal candle and matches today from room where they take me," she says.

He barely hears her as he tries to stop staring. Her blue eyes, nose, and fair hair and skin are Nordic, but the full mouth and classically shaped face make her somehow seem Southern European. She watches him approach and doesn't shrink from his dazzled appraisal. Mark moves her tray of uneaten food so he can sit beside her. As he lowers himself, he can't shake the feeling that he's accidentally walked in on her before she's dressed. She still has on the abaya, but without the veil and the hijab, she seems unclothed.

His tongue finally starts working. "Why did they come get you?"

Her breath catches, and she looks away. "They take me to be with Hamid and your cousin."

Mark grasps immediately what's happened, and tension ripples over his scalp. "What did they... did they...?"

"The Saudi find me still virgin," she says.

Mark figures that Hamid is using Larisa to entice Antun into remaining at the cave. Hamid has given him access to her—a limited sort of usage, but a violation nonetheless. His cousin is dealing with someone even more manipulative than him.

Antun—my evil twin. "I want to kill him," Mark hisses. He despises how much he physically resembles his cousin. Larisa cannot have helped but notice the similarity. He worries that from now on, she'll think of Antun every time she sees him.

Her face is blank and still, but her eyelids flutter, and she won't look at him. "It was both. I make bargain. I tell Hamid that I hear him talk about waterboarding, and I feel sorry for that man—you. I make bargain with them."

"What kind of bargain?" he asks sharply, suspecting what her reply will be.

"They no waterboard you, I no fight them. Antun not want me to fight. He want to be—" She looks to the side, biting off the words. "Lover boy."

Mark snorts. He supposes that Hamid stayed with them to make sure she remained "intact"—but at some point decided he would join in the fun.

His jaw grinds, and his breathing is ragged with useless rage as he stares at her. He wants to grab her by the hand and pull her down the corridor to the shower and scrub down every inch of her. Then he wants to bring her back to her bed and cover their tracks with his own—go wherever they have been. Even if he can't obliterate them from her mind, Mark would like to lay down another, kinder memory along her synapses. But he can't do any of that; they'll be all over him before he even gets her into the shower.

She sits slumped with her head lowered, the abaya puddled around her, and he feels beastly about the pressure building in his groin. Another sexual encounter is the last thing she will want at the moment.

"But in his own way, I think Antun try and help you," she says.

Mark refuses to accept this. She's reached a point of distanced pragmatism about everything that happens to her in order to protect her sanity, but Antun's greed is what got Mark into this mess, and it's his greed that is now further harming Larisa. And he doubts that her treatment was a one-time thing. Of course Antun will want her again. Mark will watch her cross the room over and over...

He reaches out and turns her head toward him. "Fight them next time. They won't dare mark you, and they're not going to kill me if they do waterboard me. Maybe they'll leave you alone if you resist them. I appreciate what you did, but never again."

At first, she offers him only a shrug, a small spasm of sadness.

"Tell me that you'll fight them!"

She nods and lowers her eyes. "I will."

Mark realizes she doesn't mean it and takes away his hand. Then an even more worrisome thought occurs. The other men might start protesting their exclusion once they catch on to what's happening. He looks with unseeing eyes at the wall behind her. "We have to get out of here."

His vision suddenly focuses as he realizes that the cave ceiling is slightly lower at this end of the room and that the wall slants backward somewhat as it angles up. Gouges are everywhere in the stone where lumps have fallen out over time. The candlelight dances over the wall as if blown by a draft, and he remembers the breeze that played over his hair in the overhead corridor.

My head—not my lower body! That means the airflow was probably coming from somewhere above him and not from the room below, as he thought. He springs to his feet, walks across the bed, and touches the wall.

"I'm going to climb up and take another look at the passage I told you about," he says. "Hold the candle higher so I can see better."

She stands up slowly, raising the candle carefully so the flame won't go out.

"When I get back, hold it up for me again, so I can see while coming down. I won't be gone long." He scans the pitted surface for his first move.

Mark climbs up easily, barely feeling the pain where his bruises rub against the stone. When he reaches a height that he thinks is at the same level as the fissure, he reaches for the corner, and his fingers slip into empty space. Lowering his hand, he finds the ledge within and pulls himself onto it.

He looks down at Larisa, who's still standing with the candle held high. Her hair, a color of blond usually only seen in very young children, is a halo around her head and shoulders. When she told him her captors had renamed her Malak, he'd thought it an ugly-sounding name, but if Malak means *beautiful angel*, then the name is very apt. He waves at her and slowly turns into the corridor.

In complete darkness, Mark places each footstep with care. He looks up often, searching for any hint of an opening. After a while, a slight breeze whispers over his hair, but this time, he doesn't hear anyone talking in the room below. Around a slight curve in the wall, the breeze gets stronger, and then he sees moonlight filtering through an irregularly shaped hole in the wall, a little higher than eye level. This gap is similar to the one that makes the window back in the chamber, only larger.

Mark jumps up and supports himself with his forearms to look outside. Close beneath the opening, a mound of rocks and soil tapers sharply down to the ground. A few scraggly pines with twisted limbs cling to the incline a few feet away. He heaves his body up, feet scrabbling for leverage on the wall, and thrusts forward. His head brushes the top, releasing a shower of grit and dust. Suddenly, he's outside. He grips one of the low-hanging limbs from the nearest tree to break his slide.

Holding on with one hand, Mark swipes rock debris off his face with the other. When he opens his eyes, a full moon is hanging low in the sky in front of him, making the rocky landscape both beautiful and forbidding. A trail weaves around the mountain, leading, he guesses, to the cave's front entrance. The sound of water rushing over rocks rises from the drop farther down. If he wants, he could easily scoot down and find that noisy stream. He can follow it as he flees, and eventually, he'll encounter a village or city on its banks.

The night feels old. He pictures Larisa, standing there as he last saw her, hair falling back from her face as she looks up, waiting patiently for his call to raise the candle. He can't go on now and leave her; they'll move her somewhere else before he can come back with help. Mark sits there a few minutes longer, considering his options then crawls up and pulls himself back into the mountain's unfriendly womb.

A growing excitement speeds Mark through the passage. After descending, he sits with Larisa on the mattress and tells her what he's found. He quickly explains the escape plan he came up with while he was outside.

She hears him out wordlessly. Her earlier dejection vanishes; the wild hope shining in her eyes isn't just a reflection of the candlelight. "We will do this," she says when he's finished. Her abaya flies around them, making the flame sputter while she gives him a quick hug. "Together, we will leave here."

Larisa sits back, and they're both smiling quietly. Her sudden shyness matches his as, for the first time, they truly study each other up close.

He could bask forever in her attention, but he breaks the silence. "We need to go right away. Do you have anything that we can pack a few things into?"

She thinks for a second before her face brightens. "I make bags out of abayas!"

"Great," he says. "I'm going to the pallet for a moment. Be right back." Mark feels his way over, helped a bit by the moonlight leaking through the window. He glances upward at the acrylic pane. They're lucky that the moon is out tonight. He kneels on the mattress and pulls away the loose stone.

Mark puts the knife into one of the vest pockets instead of packing it in the bag. A strong feeling of confidence surges through him when he rests his hand over the bulge. Then he puts the letter he found on his first day of captivity into a different pocket along with the bread from his uneaten meal. Hopefully, he'll get a chance to read the letter soon. After he yanks the blanket off the mattress, he goes to the table and wraps the skull, carefully padding the lower jaw with a corner of the material.

When he returns and goes behind the curtain, Larisa is pulling an abaya over her head. He watches her wide-eyed. Underneath, she's wearing jeans and a shirt. Mark feels embarrassed. He'd mistakenly thought that women wore that type clothing over underwear as if it were a gown. Jeans are much better than the abaya. The clinging material would have hampered her legs and arms.

Without her usual covering, she looks taller and more modern, her slim but shapely form suddenly part of the hip western world. She notices his scrutiny of her body without flinching, but he feels he's being invasive.

Larisa sits down and folds the hem of an abaya up to the armholes. Using safety pins, she starts pinning together the sides at intervals. When it's finished, Larisa hands him the hobo-style bag. "Maybe it not fall apart too quickly," she says.

He puts the bundled skull into it. "It's good enough for now." She quickly fashions another bag for herself.

Before they start out, Mark makes two trips up the wall, each time with one of the bags over his back, the sleeves tied around his neck. He wants them both unencumbered when Larisa climbs after him. Once that's finished, there's nothing more to be done in preparation for their escape. Mark has memorized the way up, but she'll need to see where to put her hands and feet. He explains how her hands will use the places where she sees his feet as fingerholds. The route he'll take has lots of places for footholds. The mattress will catch her if she falls. She nods, her eyes large and unblinking.

"We'll be up there before you know it." He sticks the candle into an opening over his head, careful to leave it slanted upward a little so the melting wax won't put out the flame. He bends to give her a reassuring kiss. A small shiver of pleasure runs over him at actually being able to see her mouth before his lips brush her warm ones.

Mark begins climbing, with Larisa following a few moments later. He goes slowly so that he can carefully position the candle as they go higher. When they are a little more than halfway up, he hears her breathing shallowly under him. "Almost there— you're doing fine, Larisa," he whispers in encouragement.

Finally, he reaches the corner and swings himself inside. When he's firmly within and she's edged over and trying to come around the side, he reaches for her arm, grasps it tightly, and gives her a quick, hard pull. He's not going to chance her falling now. She collides with him, and they both go down inside the corridor, a tangle of arms and legs.

She's shaking all over. Mark sits up and takes her face between his hands. He's giddy that they've surmounted their first major hurdle. Drawing out the syllables of her name, he says, "La-ri-sa, you did it!" He gives her quick little kisses that land on her eyes and nose.

Larisa catches his mood, giving a breathless laugh. "Yes, because you are with me."

He reaches around the edge for the candle. They take turns holding it while they put the abaya bags on their backs. When that's done, he blows out the flame. He doesn't want to risk anyone glimpsing the light through a crack in the ceiling of the rooms they'll pass over.

Like his first time through the passage, Mark hears voices soon after they start out. He pauses, wondering if they should return and wait until everyone is sleeping. He decides to keep moving. They need to start out early in order to distance themselves as far as possible from the cave by morning. He presses on very slowly so as to not make any noise. He almost whispers back to Larisa that she should be very quiet but decides not to. He barely hears her behind him.

Once more, Antun and Hamid's liquid murmuring solidifies into words. "I don't see you praying five times a day," Antun is saying. "Your move."

"So, I've lapsed. It's understandable under the circumstances. But I'm telling you, Christianity is going to be entirely replaced by Islam in this part of the world. You'll have to convert sooner or later." A small silence ensues, then Hamid asks, "Did you mean to sacrifice that pawn?"

A rattling sound comes from below. "Of course—pawn in the game, my friend," Antun says. "You forget. I live in Israel."

"And you think Israel will survive? You might be an old man by the time it happens, but you *will* live under Sharia Law." Hamid's voice is sarcastic. "Your move, my friend."

"In the unlikely event that the LL eventually controls every country in the Levant, I'll simply move to Europe."

Mark is far enough past them now that he can't make out exactly what Hamid says between bouts of derisive laughter over the future of Europe, but he's stopped listening anyway.

The two of them probably play chess often, continuously advancing their arguments along with their pieces, each man always trying to outdo the other, pursuing their one-upmanship in everyday life as well as on the board. Hamid and Antun have jointly maneuvered him so far in their kidnapping game—without much opposition—but Mark is now moving as a knight would, instead of a pawn. He's leaping over them while taking their queen.

The moon is fairly high when Mark oozes out onto the jumbled heap of rocks and soil. The shadows are still deeper and longer than he would like, but that will improve as they go along. Larisa holds the bags up for him to haul outside. Once that's done, she jumps up and hangs on the ledge by her forearms so he can pull her through the gap. They ease down the heap, being careful not to cause a rockslide.

Larisa pauses at the bottom. She takes deep breaths while looking up at the moon, almost gasping. Mark finds it touching, this reaction to her first moments of freedom. Although he's impatient to start out, he waits until she looks over, then he leads them to the path.

After they've gone only a short way, a faint sound of coughing comes from farther down. Mark takes Larisa's arm, dismayed. He pulls her behind nearby bushes. After a few minutes, he smells cigarette smoke, although he can't see anyone. They hunker down for long minutes, but the smell still persists.

When Mark thinks the best part of an hour has been wasted, he can stand it no longer. He places his bag gently on the ground beside Larisa and motions that she should wait while he investigates. He's fed up with these thugs stealing his time while they go about their callous abuse of everyone in their path. Some of the fury he felt when he found out Larisa had bargained herself away returns, and something inside him shifts.

He moves along the path, bent over, slipping behind boulders for cover as he goes. The smell of burning tobacco is growing stronger, but Mark still can't see anyone. He can't hear anyone, either, because of the noisy stream. He searches in vain for the red tip of a cigarette. *Maybe the smoker has left.* But when he goes around another boulder, his heart squeezes his lungs. A man is standing right in front of him, his back turned.

His foot skids on the ground before he can freeze. The man turns sideways, and Mark finally sees the glow from the cigarette in his hand. Although not a single conscious thought goes through his mind about what he will do next, his body leaps into motion.

He only becomes aware that something has happened when the man smoking the cigarette is on the ground, writhing on his stomach and making a desperate hacking noise. Mark stares down at him while he arches his back and struggles onto his knees. He flops back down again, flailing as though he's trying to swim through the soil. A few moments later, his arms slow, fluttering to a stop.

Mark is holding something so tightly in his fist that his arm muscles are about to spasm. It's the knife. He raises it so that the tip points skyward toward the moonlight. Warm dark liquid trickles down his hand and drips off his wrist. This knife has just cut someone's throat, his brain belatedly tells him. *No. I've cut someone's throat.* That hand around the shaft is most certainly his, but he can't even remember reaching for it.

He lowers the knife and looks down at the man whom he supposes is now dead. Mark's breathing is steady, and he's surprised by his lack of remorse. He doesn't even know which man this is. He's possibly killed one of the guys who brought him food every day. But he doesn't care, or it could be that what he's done hasn't registered yet—but he's wasting time, having one of those tangled conversations with himself when he needs to get moving.

Mark wipes his hands and the blade over weedy groundcover then puts the knife into his vest pocket. He decides to move the body from the path before he returns to Larisa so it won't be found right away and she won't have to see it. He's not sure how she'll react to what he's done. Mark grasps the legs and begins pulling backward toward the rocks he was hiding behind earlier. After he's moved only a few feet, he hears Antun calling from a short distance down the path.

"German boy, Hamid wants you! I know your English lessons aren't going well, but that's no reason to sulk out here all night." He says something in Arabic as a flashlight sweeps the slope, then he reverts to English once more. "There's fresh tea made. Come back inside."

Startled by Antun's arrival and the knowledge that the face bumping over the ground is Abdul's, Mark stops and drops the legs. They land with a thud, sending pebbles noisily skidding down the slope. He curses himself for not easing the legs down.

The beam comes around quickly. Mark is blinded by the glare. He can't see Antun, but he can sense his cousin's surprise as he hurries closer.

"Mark? How did you get...?" Antun begins, just as he stumbles over the dead man's legs. The light shoots wildly over the rocks before he catches himself and points the flashlight onto the body. "What have you done?"

Again, the light strikes Mark's face. When he doesn't answer, Antun turns the light downward again. He nudges Abdul's sides with his feet to turn him over. When that doesn't work, he bends, grasping an arm, and flips the body onto its back.

Abdul wasn't wearing his long mask when he'd led Mark inside the cave to be captured, and he doesn't have it on now. The still-bleeding gash across his throat is in full view. Mark steps back reflexively, a low sound escaping him. The flashlight jerks back up momentarily then once more onto Abdul as Antun bends over for a closer look.

Mark steps past him so that he's poised to run down the slope. If he bolts, they'll come after him, and in the confusion, Larisa can slip away. But it will be difficult for her to find her way alone through Turkey if Mark is caught or eludes their captors but can't manage to find her. And where will she go? Most likely, without the advantage of a head start, they'll both soon be recaptured. Mark turns back around. He knows what he must do.

But taking out a stranger is different to killing a blood relative. He reluctantly slips his hand in his pocket, and his fingers find the handle.

Antun whirls to face him.

"Get that light out of my eyes," Mark says.

"You've freed us!" Antun exclaims and moves toward Mark, closing the gap between them. "I should have known my smart brother would come up with a way." He stops in front of Mark. "How did you get out without anyone seeing you?"

He finally turns the light from Mark's face, plying the beam around the area. Mark's fingers press hard into the knife handle, but he doesn't pull it out. Abdul's rifle, leaning against a nearby boulder, is lit up for only a moment before Antun whips the light back into Mark's eyes.

Mark's heart twitches with disgust. Because of his hesitancy to act, Antun has located Abdul's gun. He looks at Antun bitterly. His cousin now considers Mark to be dispensable, an unwanted echo of himself. "I could ask the same thing," he says. "What are you doing out here? Was Abdul guarding you?" Mark is going to have to do something before Antun makes a dash for the rifle, but the glare is again pinning him like a spotlight. He puts his empty hand in front of his eyes. "The light, Antun," he says, but the beam remains focused.

"Yes, he was—"

Mark can almost hear his mind working, trying to come up with a way to explain why Hamid would have sent a supposed prisoner out of the cave to find his own guard.

"Well, you know how these fellows kind of know me already. He was guarding me, and—but that's not important now. We're free! I'll get Abdul's rifle, and we can get out—"

The beam suddenly swings downward as a loud thwack echoes among the rocks. Antun falls to his knees, dropping the flashlight. It skitters down the slope.

While Mark struggles to see through the red dots over his vision caused by the light, he hears a woman's small scream. Then the same thwacking repeats, as if someone is trying to crack open a coconut.

His vision clears enough that he can see Antun lying facedown. Larisa is beside him, bashing the back of his head over and over with a rock. She stops at last and looks up. Her unfocused eyes are enormous in the moonlight, her face contorted. She's still beautiful, wildly so.

"Malak," he says under his breath. The beautiful angel is also an avenging one.

Larisa drops the rock and rises. She staggers, and he reaches for her, supporting her while she bends over, gagging.

"It's okay," he says. "We're free now—that's all that matters."

She straightens so suddenly that his hands are almost wrenched away. "I am slave no more," she says, her voice trembling violently along with her body.

Mark gathers her in his arms, and he wants to shake along with her, but he represses the sensation. After a moment, she calms a little. Her wavering voice sounds loud in his ear. "I do it so you not kill your own cousin."

"I appreciate that," he says. How strange and absurd their conversation would sound if anyone could hear them. He begins to laugh quietly; the almost silent exhalations are mirthless. She leans her head back to look at him, then she begins laughing also, though it sounds as if she's crying.

He realizes they're both in shock, but they must leave if they want to remain free. With an effort, he gets hold of himself. "Go bring the bags while I get the flashlight." He releases her, and they both spring into action.

Mark finds another flashlight latched onto Abdul's belt as well as a wallet in his jacket. He forces himself over to Antun's body. He's reluctant to touch him, but he wants his wallet, as well—and his cell phone. He remembers the phone's passcode was the last four digits of the number Antun used for Wi-Fi at the apartment. Mark concentrates on not looking any higher than the body's shoulders as he checks both jacket and pants until he finds them.

Within minutes, Mark and Larisa are going around the side of the mountain. Mark is looking for a path that branches away toward the ravine so they can find the stream to follow. When Mark finally spots a worn trail, the cave mouth is uncomfortably close by, but no one comes out.

Aided by the flashlights, they travel a lot faster than they could have by moonlight with only the candle. By dawn, the stream is considerably broader, fed along the way by rivulets until it's almost the size of a small creek. Mark pauses on a bridge over the quickly flowing water at the edge of a village, scanning the streets for dogs. Barking had erupted throughout the last hamlet while they were rushing through the streets.

At the moment, the wary, suspicious side of his nature is paralyzing him. He's trying to decide if they should ask for help within the village, or if he should call one of the lawyers involved with the inheritance. He remembers both their numbers, but he's hesitant about turning on Antun's phone in case it could be tracked.

Smoke rises from the chimneys and vents of the small houses. The village looks poor. He worries that instead of helping them, someone there will capture them for profit. The LL's tendrils reach everywhere, and the residents may be affiliated with the terrorist group. Mark is still surveying the area when a man comes out of a small store, carrying a cardboard box. He fills the box with things he pulls out of the covered back of a truck then goes back inside.

Mark looks over at Larisa resting on her bag. Her face is filled with exhaustion, purple shadows smudging the skin under her eyes. She's not had much exercise during her captivity and is unprepared for this kind of exertion.

"Follow me," he says. "We're going to catch a ride."

CHAPTER 12

Western Asia, Late Pleistocene

RAVEN AND LEAF STOOD ON the ledge the next morning, watching the band leave. "I want to see if his body is still by the ravine," Leaf said. "I'll only be gone a short while."

She thought about how the raven had announced Bear's fall for all of the Earth Mother's children to hear. There probably weren't any large predators close to the cave, but lacking their competitive presence, even a small one like a badger might be tempted to feed. "The men probably did something with his body, but if they didn't, do you want to see him like that?" she asked. "And what if they made camp near the ravine when night fell?"

"I need to know for sure that he's dead. As for the others, most of them have never known a time without Bear telling them what to do. They're on their way back to their families."

"Surely he didn't live."

"We thought the Wanderer was dead, and he wasn't. Besides, I want to try and catch a last glimpse of Cat."

Raven tapped her tongue nervously against the gap between her teeth as she watched Leaf disappear into the woods. She'd told him while they packed their things the night before that Cat was carrying kittens. They'd agreed that it would be impossible to take her with them. Besides, Cat no longer needed their help to survive; she was a good hunter and could take care of herself. Raven hoped Leaf wouldn't take long searching for Cat after he left the ravine. They would fall too far behind.

She thought about how the band had simply walked away without saying any farewells, not acknowledging them standing on the ledge, even when Wren babbled and waved her arms to get their attention. Only Chukar had glanced up at them. Although he'd seemed fine, striding along with the others, she wished again that she'd had a chance to examine his wound.

Holding Wren, Raven sat among their packs. She kept thinking that she heard voices in the empty cave behind her. Perhaps the spirits of previous dwellers were already moving back in. She got up rapidly when Leaf finally came out of the woods below, eager to leave.

"Bear was gone," he said when he reached her. "I saw blood on both sides of the ravine." He hesitated for a moment, his face troubled. "I followed drag marks for a distance on the far side, and then I couldn't tell for sure because of all the footprints, but he could have started walking. The drag marks suddenly stopped."

Damp morning air slipped under her cape, chilling her. Surely the raven hadn't lied. "That still doesn't mean he's not dead. Perhaps they left his body somewhere—or they tried carrying him." She couldn't think how that might have been done, given his size.

He shook his head. "I don't know. I couldn't take the time to follow any farther." Leaf started picking up bags. "The band will cover ground quickly, and their presence won't protect us if we don't leave now." He sighed. "I didn't see Cat anywhere, but she'll be fine." After fastening everything securely on their backs with leather straps, Raven put Wren in her sling, and they went down the incline and started out, following in the others' footsteps.

They'd completely traversed the pass by midmorning, leaving behind the mountains, as well as the river. Leaf, always silent when traveling, was even more withdrawn as they trailed after the band across the flattening land. Raven's thoughts went to the night before at the cave. He'd been sitting on their sleeping pallet, staring blankly at the side of the tent after they'd returned from their watch. His body began shaking from head to toe, and Raven recalled how he'd trembled the first day she'd seen him, when he'd stood up to Bear. He barely glanced over when she sat beside him. To still the hand nearest hers, Raven covered his fingers with her own.

"He didn't even see me coming," he said.

"Chukar cut his throat a heartbeat before you got there. I saw him do it."

His eyes remained unfocused, as if he hadn't heard her. "Bear took me in after I escaped the Longheads, and for that kindness, I killed him while helping one of *them*." He spat out the word.

"Didn't you hear me? He would probably have died from the wound Chukar gave him."

"That doesn't change what I did."

"You were still a boy when Bear came upon you. Did he really treat you any differently than the Longheads? He wasn't being kind—always sending you out to scout by yourself as if it were unimportant whether you returned or not." When he didn't reply, sadness settled over Raven. "Would you rather that I'd gone with him back to the Fire Cloud tribe?"

He straightened, giving a final shudder. "No, never," he said, unclenching his muscles. "I would spear him again if it came to that." He took a deep breath. "Besides, Chukar's company is more agreeable than Bear's ever was."

She'd looked at him closely and seen only sincerity in his eyes.

Raven was happy that Leaf had returned so readily to the easy confidence she'd always admired. But watching his somber face as they hurried along, she knew he wouldn't put the matter behind him for a long while to come. Neither would she.

Because Leaf had told her that the band would travel quickly, Raven was prepared to exert herself, but by midday, they were moderating their pace to keep from catching up. The pace was even slower the following day. That night, she and Leaf made camp close enough to see the band's fire, risking Elder Woman's wrath—she would see their fire.

"We've been driven to the edge of the herd by the lead mare," Raven told Leaf. "She wishes to punish us."

"It's difficult to blame her," he replied.

Raven fell silent. Ultimately, she was the reason the band was moving away from a place that met their needs well. But she didn't know what she could have done differently. Raven put her hand down to the sleeping baby on her lap and smoothed her hair as she stared at the red glow in the distance. The slowdown was a bad sign, and she worried that Chukar's wound had given him a fever or that another of the Longheads had fallen ill. But that was wasted sentiment—they didn't care anymore whether she was concerned about them or not. "We've become like the Wanderer," she said. "We're lingering where we aren't wanted."

On the third morning, they were still waiting well after dawn for the day's journey to begin when the brothers began howling. Raven's back stiffened at the sound, and she looked at Leaf as nearby wolves joined in. Wren made a fretful noise from the sling. The mournful cries from wolves and humans blended into an eerie song, filling the early-morning air. As soon as the brothers fell silent, their lupine supporters also quieted.

"They want us to come over," Leaf said.

Raven rubbed tightness from her shoulder. "Why don't they just make owl hoots?"

"Because they're not Fire Cloud," Leaf said.

They were completely ignored as they entered the dismantled camp and approached Elder Woman. Chirrup stood facing away from them. Even the children averted their eyes.

"He wants to see the baby." Without looking at them, Elder Woman motioned with her head toward an overhang.

Raven looked at Leaf. "Go ahead," he said.

She bent over upon reaching the opening, holding Wren close as she went under the lip. The overhang was quite a bit larger inside than she would have imagined. She was able to stand upright and walk over to where he lay on a pallet near a small fire.

Chukar's eyes were closed as she sat beside him, his chest rising and falling rapidly. A poultice covered his wound, but bloody fluid dripped down his abdomen, where the muscles were taut from his labored breath. When she looked again at his face, his eyes were open. They were deep-green pools of pain.

His face became blurry as Raven's eyes flooded with tears. She dashed the dampness away and took Wren out of the sling, sitting her beside him. He placed his hand on top of the baby's head. Wren's hands went up and found his fingers. She began feeling them, making a low cooing sound.

Just as Leaf had done several days before, Raven shivered with the effort of controlling her grief. She could not lose herself the way she had after Willow's death, or Wren would suffer. Raven forced herself to become still and leaned over so that her forehead lightly touched his chest beside the wound. She could feel his heart beating rapidly under his hot skin, driven by the pain. She felt his hand gently smooth her hair, pause for a moment, then begin again.

That gesture of consolation made her throat almost close. She hadn't understood him, after all—she had failed to understand any of them. Like their anger, their affections had a stronger expression, becoming something much deeper.

"Raven," he said shortly. "Sit up. I wish to give this back to you." He rummaged at his side then held out the knife. "It is yours again."

The handle that she'd glimpsed at the ravine had been removed. When he placed the blade in her hand, Raven took it reluctantly, dreading to see the dull stain of dried blood covering the edge. But the quartz sparkled in the firelight. It looked exactly as it had when she'd given it to him the spring before.

After removing a back pouch and putting the knife inside, Raven brought out a packet of powdered willow bark. She mixed some of the powder with water in a wooden bowl. "This will ease the pain," she told him.

He took the bowl. "Your medicine always helped." Chukar drank the potion in one gulp, just as he had while being held captive. He closed his eyes again, and she sat there beside him, nursing the baby. When his breathing slowed, she put the packet beside his head under a flap of the skin he lay upon. Raven hoped that he would find it before Elder Woman did.

But she needn't have worried about that. She'd no sooner come out of the shelter than the band stirred as one and began striding away from the camp.

Raven and Leaf stood, waiting for them to pass out of sight. After a while, Leaf glanced down at the ground then up at Raven. "Do you want to go in again before we leave?" he asked.

Raven looked across the plain. The band had gone over the horizon. She couldn't see them anymore. She shook her head.

They followed the trail for the rest of that day, then another one, scrambling to keep up. "I can't tend the baby properly," Raven told Leaf that second night. Grasping Wren under the armpits, Raven held her out. Wren's lower body dangled under the hitched-up tunic. "She'd learned to make water this way, but after a day in soaked moss, she's forgotten how. And we're walking so quickly, I haven't been able to feed her often enough."

Leaf watched as the baby began kicking impatiently. "I suppose it's time that we went our own way, then."

The next morning, they'd gone only a short distance before Leaf turned away from the trail. When she realized what he was doing, Raven came to a standstill, looking at the bent grass leading off into the distance. Leaf stood a short way down, waiting for her. She tore her eyes away and hurried to him.

CHAPTER 13

The Levant, Present Day

THE TRUCK IS ONE OF those white refrigerated ones, with a plastic flap instead of a door covering the back. A scuffed place high on the cab shows were the cooling unit used to be. After crawling over a raised wooden tailgate, Mark and Larisa find themselves among freshly harvested fruit and vegetables, loose dirt still clinging to some of the roots. They hide the best they can among the piles and baskets. Only a short while passes before footsteps come toward the truck and the door slams. The engine starts, and the truck jerks forward.

When they've gone a few miles, Mark crawls over vegetables to the tailgate and moves the plastic flap aside. The rising sun is on the left of the highway; they're going south. He looks out for a few more minutes then goes back to Larisa. If he wants to reach Mr. Sadik in Istanbul, the truck is heading in the wrong direction, but Mark isn't sure they should go to Istanbul.

Hamid will figure that he'll return there. Besides haranguing his mother for quick payment, the jihadist has probably been hassling both lawyers, as well—he would have made it his business to find out from Antun where their offices are located. He'll move quickly with his search for Larisa and Mark; his particular LL group stands to lose a lot of money if they get away. Spotters may already be in place, watching Mr. Sadik's office. It's time to get out of Turkey—the sooner the better.

Mark remains on edge as the truck lumbers along. The driver will stop again for delivery, and when he does, they'll have to jump out the back quickly to avoid a confrontation.

Remembering the wallets, he pulls them from a vest pocket. He swipes off crumbs from the bread he was saving and opens Abdul's tattered wallet. He finds a small amount of Turkish lira inside. It doesn't contain any identification that would leave a trail, so Mark tosses it over the tailgate.

Antun's leather wallet is large, made like a folder with several pockets. Larisa watches Mark open it. To Mark's surprise, it contains not only credit cards and a good deal of money in different currencies, but Antun's Israeli and Turkish passports, as well. Mark now has more hope for their escape than he had at any time since they've fled. He waves the passports at her and smiles. This is the only time he's ever been glad that he and Antun looked alike.

She takes the Israeli one from him and turns to the photograph page. When a shadow crosses her features, he's afraid she's noting the resemblance. Her face hardens, and her chin goes up defiantly. "There is only you now," she says, confirming his fears.

When Larisa returns the passport, she leans forward and gives him a quick kiss, and his worries about the similarity vanishes. She understands better than anyone that he and Antun were nothing alike. He returns her kiss with a longer one, then they're clinging to each other. But as his mouth probes hers, his earlier happiness upon finding the passports fades. He can pass as Antun, but Larisa doesn't have any documentation.

They drink the last of the water Larisa brought along in a large plastic bottle and eat the bread he has and other things she packed, resisting the temptation presented by the small amount of figs in a basket nearby. They're not that clean, and a ride is really all they need from the truck's owner.

Whenever they pass through a town, Mark and Larisa move close to the plastic in preparation for jumping over the tailgate if they need to. So far, the truck is only stopping for stop signs and the occasional stoplight. After the first town, Larisa gets an abaya from her bag and struggles into it. Then she covers her head with a hijab, letting it extend out in front like a small, shielding visor. Anyone who looks directly at her face will immediately realize that she's not Middle Eastern, so Mark understands what she's doing, but he's still upset to see her covered again.

After a long while, the driver begins encountering more stoplights. Mark peeks around the flap. They're entering a city. Mark utters an exclamation of amazement when they pass a sign advertising the Ramada Plaza Hotel of Antalya. He's back where his misadventures began. The Ramada isn't far from the hotel where he left his uncle's ashes. Mark wonders if they're still there.

He looks over at Larisa. "I know this city. The next time the driver stops for a light, we're getting out."

The back end of the truck bobs when they go over the tailgate. In case the driver noticed the movement, Mark quickly guides Larisa in the opposite direction.

They're exposed walking the streets. Antalya is large enough to hide in, but Mark wants them out of Turkey entirely. In order to accomplish that, he'll have to use a phone. They find a phone booth quickly, but neither can figure out how to pay for usage. Rather than waste more time, Mark pulls out Antun's phone. They stand in the shadow of a palm tree while Mark turns it on and keys in the passcode. Luckily, it's the same one Antun mentioned in Tel-Aviv.

Solicitor Aaron's voice crackles her astonishment when he tells her where he is. She's confused because the caller ID displayed Antun's name, and she wants to know if he's with Mark. He tells her that they planned their escape together, but he's not sure if Antun ever left the cave. "I need to turn off this phone soon—they may trace it," he says. "I want to leave the country, but I need a passport."

"Go to Istanbul," she says. "Sadik will help you."

"I'm afraid to do that. They'll have him watched."

"You could contact the authorities."

He gives the beard along his jawline rapid little tugs with his free hand. "I don't know if they can be trusted. I'd like to fly to Israel."

Silence at the other end.

"Solicitor Aaron?"

"I'm here. I can't give you a name, but I'll give you a phone number. Do you have any money for a cab?"

"Yes."

"Good. We need to set up a pass phrase that my contact will ask for when you arrive. A piece of information your mother can tell us so you won't have to say it over your phone."

Mark thinks for a few seconds. "Ask her what kind of flowers are on her living room coffee table and their color. And, Mrs. Aaron, don't let her talk to Hamid. He'll only try and pump her for information. Is she still in Israel?"

"Yes, I'll get in touch with her right away. Here's the contact's number. Wait fifteen minutes before calling."

As they walk, Mark repeats the number every few minutes so he won't forget it. As soon as he figures fifteen minutes have gone by, he dials. A man answers, gives Mark an address, and abruptly ends the call.

Larisa watches him silently while he says the address several times to memorize it, her expression tight and closed like a rosebud kept in dim light. When she sees him look at her quizzically, she rearranges her expression, but her tremulous smile reveals her thoughts. Her doubt hurts a little.

"The passport will be for you," he tells her and has the pleasure of watching her face open to him as the words sink in. "I would never leave you here on your own, Larisa."

"I know," she says, but he's not sure if she really does.

They need a taxi. He stops a woman and asks where he can find one. Her eyes are fearful as she replies in broken English and points down the street. Mark realizes that she must think he's with the Lions of the Levant. His Levantine ancestry shows in his face and hair, and he's dressed in a style favored by some jihadists. And the cut on his forehead and bruise on his cheek make him look like a brawler. She walks away quickly after he thanks her. Mark runs his fingers over his jaw. The beard is suddenly itchy. After this is over, he intends to shave it off. Mark glances down at his clothes. He misses his Neanderthal shirt, but at least he's blending into the local population.

Their contact is a brusque man who doesn't give his name when Mark tells him his. "And the pass phrase?" he asks.

"Blue roses on the coffee table."

"Thank you, sir. Please come in."

His English is only slightly accented, and Mark isn't sure about his nationality. He's probably Israeli. Mark just hopes that the man has access to authentic passport blanks and printing equipment. The man's expression doesn't change when Mark explains that the passport is for Larisa.

"What country?" he asks.

"The United States," Mark replies.

The forger takes a closer look at Mark then at Larisa, his eyes going down the long gown as if her history is plainly written there for him to read, a page out of an old, familiar story. Mark keeps his face neutral and slips an arm around her shoulders.

The man's eyes turn away. "Let's get started, shall we?"

He writes down the information that they give him. Then he takes Larisa's picture without the hijab and abaya. When that's done, he goes on his computer. After a few minutes, he suggests that she keep Larisa as her first name but take the surname of Smith. "Your Ukrainian surname, Koval, has the same meaning as Smith in the English-speaking world. They're both derived from *blacksmith*. And importantly, I don't see a problem associated with any Larisa Smiths."

After giving Mark a wry smile, she agrees, and he shows them to a small room where they can wait while he works. Mark wonders if he should ask for a second passport for himself. But if he's been told that Mark would ask for one passport, then asking for another will cause problems.

They don't sit there long before the passport is ready.

"To which country will you travel in the near future?" he asks Larisa. He's frowning at her like it's a test and she may give the wrong answer.

She looks at Mark.

"Israel," Mark says. "Today."

The forger rewards him with a small upturn of his mouth that shows his small teeth. "Good. Wait at least one hour before using the passport. The phone number you called no longer exists, and this office will be closed for some time in the future. Please get rid of your phone as soon as possible. I've called a cab. Turn right after leaving the building. It will pick you up on the corner."

"I'd like to ask you something before we go," Mark says. He pats the bag he's been about to throw over his shoulder. "We have some items that we want to ship or mail back to the states. Is there some sort of mailing service here that does that?"

"Clothing?"

"Yes, clothing." Mark can tell by his expression that he knows they won't be mailing just clothing.

"There's a place called Send My Suitcase located at Migros Mall. Customs leaves them alone. You can buy a suitcase at the mall. But don't travel without checking any suitcase, or you'll be stopped and questioned at every airport."

"I understand. Thank you." Mark reaches for Antun's wallet. "What do we owe?"

His hands flutter in refusal. "No, no—it will be taken care of. Good luck."

The woman's response earlier to Mark's appearance while he was asking directions wasn't lost on Larisa. She points at his vest after they're seated in the cab. "We need better clothes."

Mark looks down. Spots of dried blood edge the vest pocket where the knife is. "You're right, and I need a watch, as well. We'll do some quick shopping."

The Migros Mall is a large building complex. Mark pauses when they enter. "We've come forward in time now." She appears mystified. He waves a hand toward the stores. "Everything is modern."

A nearby shop has rolling suitcases among the items displayed in front. Mark goes in and buys three, two small ones for him and Larisa and a slightly larger one for mailing. He doesn't want to pack them with so many people around, but he wants to get rid of the odd-looking abaya-bags, so after buying the suitcases, he takes them to a deserted park on one side of the mall. First, Mark moves everything from his vest pockets to his pants pockets before tossing the bloodstained vest into a trashcan. Next, he opens the bags and lays out their contents on a bench. He throws the flashlights as well as the bags in the can. Then he unwraps the blanket from the skull and puts the knife with it before swaddling both objects in several abayas then again in the blanket. When they're secured, he places the bundle inside the largest suitcase. Larisa has been watching closely as he does all these things. Mark is thankful she's not asking questions, because he's not sure what he would tell her.

He chews the inside of his cheek, trying to decide what to do about the phone. Taxis are already waiting in front of the mall, so he won't need to call one when they finish shopping. He pokes the phone deep within a paper bag of remnants from someone's meal and puts the bag back into the trash can.

"Larisa, you want to match your passport picture as much as possible," he tells her.

She's come out the department store bathroom, wearing her new jeans and blouse but with a hijab covering her hair and swathed around her neck.

She reluctantly takes off the hijab. "You are right, I know, but I feel wrong without it. Like I am naked. I wear it for so long."

He recalls how he felt when he first saw her without the full garb back at the cave, and he understands how she feels. Still, he's surprised she doesn't despise the hijab. Her long hair falling freely, she's so pretty in her new clothes. With her stylish pocketbook dangling from one shoulder, she could be the model her mother had hoped she would be. Their new clothes have put them firmly back into the worldly, secular culture of the twenty-first century. Before leaving the store, they stuff their old clothing in the two smaller suitcases.

The Send My Suitcase business is located on the mall's second level. Mark is nervous when they enter, not knowing what will be required. The whole process turns out to be well streamlined for the customer, however, and is soon over with. Antun's passport and credit card are all the identification Mark needs. The only hiccup occurs when an employee asks him to come over to a counter, calling him "Mr. Lahoud," and he fails to respond until the man calls him again.

The only way to reach Tel-Aviv from Antalya is through the country's capital of Ankara, so Mark and Larissa buy tickets including the connecting flight. He's frustrated by having to fly north before flying south to Israel, but the flight is short.

The connection between Ankara and Tel-Aviv doesn't leave for some time, so they eat hamburgers at a food court. Mark eats two; the familiar fast food is entirely satisfying. After they finish, it's only a matter of finding the boarding area and waiting for the flight. While they sit there, Mark writes down Mrs. Aaron's number on a clothing receipt with a pen he finds in his seat. "If we somehow get separated from each other, call this number for help," he tells Larisa, although he's not sure how Mrs. Aaron will react to such a call. Without saying a word, Larisa puts the receipt in her purse.

The plane is late. Mark is fidgeting impatiently in his seat when he senses that he's being watched. He vaguely noticed a dark, bearded man entering the area a few moments before, dressed casually with a sweater draped over his shoulders in the European manner. Mark looks down to where the man is seated. His body stiffens on meeting the man's hostile stare—those eyes are all too familiar. Mark tears his gaze away, fighting the panic he feels. Even if Hamid has found them, it doesn't make sense that he would try to recapture them in such a public place. *It's just a man*, he tells himself, *another man with black eyes*.

He turns to Larisa. "Someone is staring at us. Tell me if he looks familiar. He's sitting four or five seats down from me," he says in a low voice, motioning slightly with his head.

She senses his nervousness, and her face is frightened as she bends forward a little and looks past him. "I not see him."

When Mark glances over, the man has left. He stands, scanning the concourse in both directions, but he can't spot him in the crowd. "I thought it was Hamid. It's probably my imagination. I've never seen his face to recognize him. That's why I wanted you to take a look."

She turns her head away sharply. "I never see his face, either. His black mask stay on him—always."

Stabs of regret go through Mark that by involving Larisa in his paranoia, he's made her remember her ordeal.

The flight to Tel Aviv is without incident. They both sleep, but shortly before landing, Mark jerks awake, his heart beating wildly. The seatbelt sign has dinged on. A flight attendant is coming down the aisle, checking for compliance. He stops her and asks for writing paper.

Mark gently shakes Larisa. She raises her seat, her impossibly long lashes, several shades darker than her hair, blinking her sleep away. "We should go through passport control separately." He keeps his voice low. "If all goes well, we'll meet up again at the luggage carousel."

His gaze holds her weary eyes, willing her to listen closely. "If you don't make it through, then I'll be able to do something about it. But if I get stopped—" He hopes what he says next won't throw her into a panic. "Then I want you to fly to California and wait for me there." He leaves out the worst scenario. If they're both detained, he doesn't know what he'll do.

She's fully awake now. His heart sinks at her bewilderment. She gulps several times. "How—"

"Hear me out. We haven't had a chance to think this over. I'm afraid we'll end up in a media-circus nightmare if we're not careful. Our story and especially what you've been through will be in the press all over the planet. I know you're strong, but you need more time. And there will be all kinds of law enforcement debriefings—you have to leave Israel as soon as possible."

He looks away for a moment, taking a deep breath before continuing. "Larisa, no one can ever know about what happened to Antun—or the other man. No one. Ever."

Her face is drawn as she concentrates on his words.

"It's best if only one of us has to face the authorities, and that should be me. But if you're stopped, don't talk to them until you hear from me. Understand?"

She nods.

The stewardess gives him a notepad. "I need that back when you're finished," she says, smiling.

He thanks her, and when she walks away, he takes out his pen and turns back to Larisa. "You already have Mrs. Aaron's number. Only call her if you have an emergency and have to contact me." He writes frantically on the notepad. "Here is my condominium address in California." He rips off the page and gives it to her.

She stares down at the words.

"You'll find the key in a box on the wall beside the front door. You'll press in a number code, and the box will open. I'll write the code."

The pilot's voice comes over the intercom; the airplane is well into its descent. Under the entry code, he quickly sketches off a picture of a box with numbers on it and imitates pressing in the code. "It opens, you take the key out, unlock the door, and go inside." He tears off the page and gives it to her. "The mortgage is paid up for several months. No one will bother you. Now give me your purse."

She looks puzzled, but the expression passes quickly.

He opens Antun's wallet, pulls out most of the money, and stuffs it into a side pocket within the bag. He snatches up the pad again. "Use the shekels to buy an airplane ticket to San Jose, California." He draws a ticket and writes "Mineta San Jose

Airport, California" on it. "When you arrive, take a taxi to the condominium—just show the address to the driver. You'll have enough dollars left over for buying food until I come."

Last of all, he gives her the paperwork she'll need when the suitcase they'd mailed arrives in California. "You'll need these papers when they deliver the suitcase to my condominium. The two things I put in there are very important to me, and I'll explain why when I see you again."

The plane has landed and is taxiing toward a gate. He hopes he's not forgetting anything important. "I want you to leave the plane first. I hope I'll see you at the carousel. If not, I'll see you in California. I won't call before I arrive at the condominium. I don't know who'll be listening."

She sits there, still clutching the papers, as the plane stops and everybody starts pulling their carry-ons from the bins.

He kisses her crinkled forehead. "Put everything in your new purse. Larisa—" He takes a breath that rushes out with his next words. "I love you."

His revelation jars her into action. "I *adore* you," she says. Her lips press firmly against his before she stuffs everything inside the bag and climbs over him to the aisle.

When he returns the notepad at the exit, the flight attendant's eyes tease him. "I think she'll want to see you again."

Mark tries to smile. "I hope so."

He waits, watching nervously from farther back in the queue, but Larisa is only at the counter for a minute before she's waved on. Mark heaves a sigh of relief. When a large family peels off the line and goes forward, suddenly no one is left in front. Sweat breaks out on his neck as he watches all of them pass quickly through.

He greets the official in English. After a nod, the man looks closely at Mark then at the passport and then at the computer. His face is impassive as he studies the screen, but then he motions to another official standing nearby. "Will you please step aside, Mr. Lahoud? We need to check a few things."

Mark reluctantly moves away so the next traveler can approach the counter. Larisa is on her own now, and he should be worried about her, but he's not. It's an absurd notion, but he feels that the skull and knife are like amulets or talismans and that being the owner of those objects somehow protects him and Larisa. She'll find her way to California, and he'll soon join her there.

Mark refuses to talk, only telling the officials to call his lawyer. Eventually, they do. Mrs. Aaron's face is a study in contrasts, going from relief to puzzled annoyance when she arrives and sees Mark instead of Antun. The first thing she does is request to speak with her client alone.

"Why do you have Antun's passport?" she asks.

Mark concentrates on keeping his face calm. "He had two passports, a Turkish one and an Israeli one. We located them at the cave where we were held but did not find mine. He was to use the Turkish one when we escaped, but then he lost his nerve at the last minute."

"But why didn't you use your new passport? I flagged Antun's in case he did come back to Israel."

"A pickpocket took it." The lies are piling up quickly. He must be careful to remember them accurately.

"You'll have to cancel it sometime soon and apply for another one," she says.

After long conversations with various officials, she manages to extricate Mark from customs in only a few hours. His reunion with his mother is an emotional one. They're making the kind of scene he's always detested, but that doesn't seem to matter now. He cries along with her in front of Mrs. Aaron.

"I have Sami's ashes," Nadia tells him after they've calmed a little. "The manager at the hotel where you left the urn saw a news bulletin about your kidnapping. The ashes were mentioned, and he contacted the proper authorities. Your story is everywhere in the news—on television, in the papers." She gives a little shudder as she lightly touches the crusted cut on his face. "I saw that in the photos they sent me—"

"I want to show you something," Mrs. Aaron interrupts. She takes out her phone and, after a moment, turns it around so he can see the screen. "This went viral."

The tweet reads: *LL torture victims are now being turned into #NeanderthalZombies.* The picture shows Mark with the Neanderthal skull over his head. A man in a black mask has his arm flung companionably around Mark's shoulders.

This is yet more of the usual maligning of Neanderthals, but he remembers the fugue he fell into that day. The tweet may contain some truth.

He realizes that he's avoided the letter ever since he found it in the cave, and he makes himself read it that night when he's finally alone. It begins, "Dear Mom and Dad," and as Mark suspected, the poor guy, a captured reporter, was waterboarded by Hamid and became deathly ill because of the water he'd inhaled. The next morning, Mark turns the note over to Mrs. Aaron so she can notify the parents. Within a few days, Mrs. Aaron tells Mark that the kidnappers broke off contact with the reporter's family two months before.

For a long time afterward, Hamid's words occasionally run through his mind like a repetitive, unwanted tune: *Bollocksed that one up, didn't I?* Mark worries that he hasn't seen the last of Hamid. The Lions of the Levant is known for their revenge tactics. They're almost as persistent as the Mafia.

CHAPTER 14

Western Asia, Late Pleistocene

THE LONG DAYS OF WALKING blended together, one day much like another as summer found them. Wren's skin turned as brown as Raven's under the strengthening sun. When they reached the coast, Raven marveled at the rolling waves. The water was salty, like that at the Pass Between the Waters.

"These are the *big waters*—the sea," Leaf told her, waving his arms at the horizon. "I lived near here with my family."

They began following the shoreline, eating fish caught with nets that Leaf made, as well as shellfish taken during low tides. Then one day, when they rounded a curve, they saw people fishing farther down. Their large nets flashed in the sun as they cast them. Raven waited with Wren, hiding among rocks while Leaf went to investigate. After a short while, she heard voices and laughter approaching, so she went out and met them. The fishermen all had wind tattoos on their brown chests.

At that time, part of the Wind tribe dwelled in a series of caves along the coast. The only family member that Leaf found living among them was an older sister. None of the original group he'd left with as a boy had ever returned. His sister had children, and Leaf was grateful when she insisted that he and Raven live in the same cave with her family. He wanted Wren and any future children he and Raven might have to be part of a larger family group.

Raven found the Wind tribe an easy people to live with. For one thing, their language was almost the same as the one spoken by the Fire Cloud tribe, and she could fully interact with them. They were friendlier than the Longheads or, for that matter, the people of the Fire Cloud tribe. Sometimes, though, she missed her old tribe when she returned from foraging and smelled the hearth fires below the caves before getting close enough to see them. That sentimentality didn't keep her from joining the Wind tribe when Leaf asked her to. She often looked at the wind symbols on her wrist, tattooed there during the ceremony, admiring the flowing lines.

The family groups from the various caves went out almost daily to fish. They traded with a Wind-tribe band that lived a short way inland, swapping fish for game. On a particular day when her family was fishing for trade, Raven returned alone to their cave after leaving Wren in the care of Leaf's nieces. Since the toddler had begun walking at ten moons, she'd proven to be fearless and had to be constantly watched so she wouldn't get into trouble.

Raven was looking for a spare net they needed. After finding it, she paused. A crab pinch was festering on her wrist. Treating it with an unguent from her pouch would take only a moment. When her fingers ran over something sharp inside the bag, she snatched her hand out again. While sucking on her cut finger, Raven peered into the bag's depths, pushing things aside until she saw the quartz knife hiding in the bottom. She reached for it.

Since they'd found Leaf's tribe, Raven had been happy— happier than at any other time in her life. But upon seeing the knife's glimmering red sides, such a sting of melancholy went through her at remembering Chukar and his people that she almost dropped it. As the sorrow she'd successfully tamped down threatened to erupt, Raven decided not to keep the knife. That left her with the question of what should be done with it. She couldn't just throw such a beautiful object into the sea.

As she applied the unguent, Raven remembered an odd little hole she'd seen in the wall up from the storage ledge. She would put it in there and cover it with sand from the beach at a later time. As she climbed, Raven grasped the handholds firmly and made sure her feet were settled inside the notches before going higher. Leaf would be upset if he saw her. She was four moons along with her pregnancy, and he would think she was being foolish, risking herself and their baby because of a knife.

Upon reaching the ledge, Raven piled up the skins stored there. She then stood on them, easily reaching the hole. After placing the knife inside, she sat for a while on top of the skins, looking at the cave from that unusual perspective. But her mind kept going to the hole, and she glanced back up at it. Perhaps someone else would climb the ledge one day and, out of curiosity, reach inside the small hollow.

Chukar had retouched the cutting side, making the edge even sharper, so that lucky person would find the knife ready for immediate use. Or perhaps the discoverer would only admire its beauty and put it aside after showing it to friends and family. She wondered if she were hiding the knife too well, and if it would ever again see the light of day. But tribes seemed to be like the sea; they came in waves, tribe replacing tribe. Surely, at some point in time, someone from one of those tribal waves would enter the cave and find her father's knife.

CHAPTER 15

California, Present Day

Two weeks later, Mark sits nervously in a taxi as it approaches his condominium complex. He's been allowed a week at home so he can take care of his affairs before going on to Washington, DC, for more debriefing.

He'll stay with his grandfather while in the capital. He's already met the senator, who flew to Israel to be with his daughter and grandson. Senator Alderson is a likable man, but the fact that he's a senator has helped keep the media flames roaring. In contrast to Mark, he seems to enjoy their joint press briefings, even as the news of his early affair with Mark's grandmother fills the airwaves. There are benefits, though, to having a senator as a grandfather. A government airplane slipped Mark out of Israel without the media noticing.

He takes out his new phone and looks again at the most recent message from Mrs. Aaron. It shows a photograph of Mark with the senator. "Neanderthal zombie safe in Israel with grandfather," the caption reads. Mark wonders if this offends the senator then decides it probably doesn't.

Once at his condominium, Mark taps in the code with fumbling fingers. When the box opens, the key is gone. Instant relief washes over him. His hand trembles as he presses the doorbell. After a moment, the door opens, and with a small cry, Larisa flies into his arms, her joyful exuberance making him stagger. They hold each other tightly, and he's melting into her, the sensation so intensely pleasurable that it's almost painful.

As the months go by, he tries to determine if he was correct to protect Larisa from scrutiny of any kind. She's been having a difficult time adjusting to her freedom. After he arrived, she stopped leaving the condominium at all for a while, but now she's venturing out more and has just enrolled in English classes. Her speech has greatly improved under his tutelage, but the Cyrillic alphabet is quite different from the English one. She needs professional help in order to develop proficiency in reading and writing. Luckily, he found a language school that didn't ask too many questions on the application form.

Thanks to all the black-market services for illegal immigrants in California, he easily obtained a driver's license for her, and he's teaching her how to drive. Getting a social security card is something he'll tackle soon, then they'll get married.

His mother is delighted. She really wants him to marry Larisa, and she's doing her best not to be intrusive by asking probing questions about her future daughter-in-law's background. Mark has told her that Larisa is shy and doesn't like talking about a somewhat-difficult and sad past. Nadia respects his request. She doesn't want to scare Larisa away; this may be her last chance for grandchildren.

Larisa plans to attend an area university when she's ready. She doesn't really have to do anything. Mark's mother has insisted on giving him half of her inheritance, though her gift is to be doled out in annual payments so that it won't trigger enormous taxes. He and his mother will also inherit the rest of Sami's estate if Antun doesn't turn up. Money is no longer one of their problems, so he tells Larisa not to worry about school or finding a job if she would rather not, but she says that she still wants to be a doctor.

Mark is thinking they should have at least one child, although not for a while. They're lucky that Larisa didn't become pregnant right away, because being careful was the last thing on their minds once they took care of her virginity. He'd wanted to find a discreet doctor to remove the false hymen, but she disagreed. "I need for *you* to undo what they did to me. Only you," she told him. He was relieved that there wasn't much bleeding.

Mark wants them to travel eventually, but he's aware that she's still fragile. She spends time on the condominium patio in order to increase her vitamin D intake to help alleviate any deficiency caused by living for two years veiled and enclosed. When Mark suggests they buy swimsuits and go to the beach to boost her absorption, his proposal is met with such vehement opposition that he realizes how desperately she wants to hide. If she changes her mind, Mark will take time off from the Institute and make it into a vacation. He's lost his compulsive work habits and even gets home every day at a decent time.

She orders new clothes over the Internet to wear for English classes. They're loose, baggy outfits. On class days, black-framed glasses cover her bright-blue eyes, although she doesn't need them, and her shoulder-length hair is pulled back severely and bound at the nape. But she can't change her bone structure or those sensual, curving lips, shaped like those in paintings by Italian masters. She's failing in her attempts to mute her beauty, but he doesn't tell her that, because he's afraid she might start wearing a veil again.

He sometimes fears that by trying to prevent her from becoming a titillating sideshow for the world, he's enabled something unhealthy. "I love the genuine you—all the genetic traits you were born with," he tells her.

"When people look at me, I feel disgust for myself and for them—especially men," she replies. "If I see even a hint of lust on their faces, I feel nauseated."

He feels his face fall.

"But not you," Larisa says quickly. "I am not all sick. I need for you to want me. You are *my* choice, *my* desire." She reaches out and gently runs her hand over his clean-shaven face as she says this. Both she and his mother like his new beardless look.

From time to time, Larisa will withdraw even from him for a day or two. During the evenings of those days, he spends more time with the stray tabby he's adopted, letting it stay on his lap for hours. Hearing the cat purr massages his aching heart. His emotions were hibernating during his other relationships. Now that they've become fully awake, they're a little raw. He manages, though, to put aside his feelings. He has an infinite patience with Larisa. Besides, Mark grasps that he's not completely recovered, either.

He often goes into his study and takes the skull and knife out of a locked drawer. He touches them and mulls over the events that led to their acquisition. For the life of him, he can't understand why he thinks these two disparate objects somehow belong together. Even more worrisome, he's starting to believe that all the events that happened since Uncle Sami's death created a path, as if by design, leading him to *both* of these ancient relics. If this is true, then as soon as he found the knife, he was fated to end up in a cave full of terrorists just because the skull was there. But that can't be so. Science has taught him that the universe doesn't work that way.

He's explained to Larisa how he came about the knife. She knows how he got the skull. He tells her about the strange emotions, thoughts, desires, and dreams they provoke. She listens to him, when he carries on this way, with a deep patience of her own.

ACKNOWLEDGMENTS

I would like to give special thanks to:

Family and friends for their interest in this ongoing project.

Flint, who by his very existence gave me an idea for a character.

Floyd, who helps me to get out of the starting gate when working on a project and is always supportive of my efforts.

Valerie who has a good eye for searching out pesky errors.

Alison, whose suggestions, corrections and insights were succinct and highly helpful.

The talented editors and proofreaders at Red Adept Editing (www.redadeptediting.com).

My husband Cleon who has encouraged me every step of the way in this writing journey.

All my early readers whose contributions were invaluable.

I am also grateful to the members of the Prehistoric Writers and Readers Facebook site who so willingly share their research and knowledge.

ABOUT THE AUTHOR

Harper Swan lives in Tallahassee, Florida with her husband and two sweet but very spoiled cats. Her interests include history from all eras, archaeology and genetics. She especially enjoys researching ancient history and reading about archaeological finds from Paleolithic sites. As well as writing stories with plots based in more recent times, Harper is also following a longtime dream of writing books that include the distant past, her inspiration drawn from Jean Auel.

Harper is the author of *The Replacement Chronicles*, a three-part series. The series titles in order are *Raven's Choice, Journeys of Choice* and *Choices that Cut*.

The series is now available as an omnibus issue containing all three parts going by the title, *The Replacement Chronicles*. This novel is available in both paperback and e-book. *Raven's Choice* is also published as a standalone e-book and is free on iBooks and Amazon for as long as the latter allows it to be so. *Journeys of Choice* and *Choices That Cut* are both contained in an e-book entitled *Journeys of Choice*.

If you enjoy her writing, Harper is presently giving away *Gas Heat*—a story of family angst that takes places in the Deep South—to anyone who would like to subscribe to her mailing list. Just use the link below.

http://eepurl.com/b3MpEv

59220361R00246

Made in the USA
Middletown, DE
20 December 2017